GREAT WHITE GORILLA

lilian fish

For Mom and Dad

And for the Ape who I followed into the jungle, who taught me everything—
I am eternally grateful to you.

LISTEN ALONG

Check out this playlist, specially curated to correspond to each chapter of *Great White Gorilla*, excluding the Prologue.

Slug Trip

There was a young boy on the big move West with his family. They had packed up everything necessary, and said goodbye to the relatives, the neighbors, the friends and the congregation. The boy's older siblings were emotional— angry to leave behind friends, sports teams and first crushes— but he was the youngest, so he didn't have a care in the world.

They endured long travel days and camped roadside in the evenings. The boy chased his older siblings across sprawling, gusty prairies and into shaded woods. He placed his mind's full will into his body to follow them, to keep pace with their long-legged strides and matured agility. On one of those chases, in a hopeful attempt to become second-to-last, he slipped on a rock and scraped his knee. He cried when he saw the blood emerging, but he was more curious than afraid. He watched the liquid begin to thicken and change from crimson to burgundy to brown. He wondered how his body knows what to do on its own.

The children continued on the trail, which came to an abrupt end at a very mossy creek. The moss was thick and gave the creek a welcoming, fluffy quality, as if one could bounce around from rock to rock. The older kids began daring each other to jump into the creek first. The little boy overheard the challenge and did not hesitate; he jumped with a bold running start. He was lucky to have missed the unforgiving rocks hidden under the mossy cover, but he wasn't so lucky to be the first to touch the water. The fresh snowmelt stung his skin and took his breath away. He squealed and desperately climbed the green bank as the siblings laughed.

A little moss slug, a slimy, unassuming agent of fate, nestled comfortably in a fold of the boy's cut knee. No one noticed it. It wasn't until he sat at the campsite picnic table and his mother went to clean his wound that the ugly little creature was wiped off. He picked the slug out of the dirt, balanced it on his pointer finger and held it up close to his face to get a better look. It was an objectively unappealing creature: slimy, of course, a dirty-looking yellow-green color, and shaped kind of like a turd. But up close, the boy thought it almost looked a certain kind of beautiful. As he fixated on the texture of the slug's keel, his sight grew ever sharper; the creature was becoming shinier, bumpier, and more beautiful every second. The aperture of his pupils widened to shift focus to the world behind the slug. A gust of wind rattled every tree branch in the campground; the canopy of green leaves shook like frantic fans in a stadium. The whole world became a colorful kaleidoscope then, the sky's blue almost blinding through the strobing shades of green. The boy saw every tree and every creature and every human then, all of everything all at once, and he decided that just like this slug, it was all terribly ugly, and equally beautiful when you looked at it all at once, or if you put your eye up real close to it.

The parents didn't know what was happening to the boy. They thought maybe he had eaten a poisonous mushroom or berry, and forced him to purge, but it didn't help. They fretted but the child was calm. He had sweaty temples and a rapid heartbeat, but his face held a pristine euphoria. He sat up all night, silently smiling with enormous eyes that he couldn't take off of the trees and the sky. Though he was young, he woke up the next day and knew. It was the slug, the slug from the mossy emerald bank. He searched the campsite for it, attempted to return to the creek to find a new one, but there was no time. They left right after breakfast. They were anxious to start their new lives in the West.

The family began a new life in their new home, and like his siblings, the boy went to school each day, and played outside until the sun went down. He went through the phases of obsession that all boys do, with dinosaurs and baseball cards, with video games and pretty girls. He became a young man. He played on the basketball team and had high marks in math. His first heartbreak came at sixteen. They sat on the porch swing and he listened to the girl admit that she liked another boy. He watched her walk away, and his head hung down. He lay on the front lawn, feeling sorry for himself, and stared at the sky. An autumn wind rolled through and shook leaves off the trees, and a whiff of euphoria ran down his spine and raised the hair on his arms and neck. For the first time in years he remembered the slug, and the experience stirred in him.

His curiosity about what had happened wouldn't leave his mind. When he left home a year later, he chose to pursue answers through a scientific education. He undertook years of study to learn the laws of nature, the strides and limits of human understanding, and how to practice the scientific method. He read books about slugs and gastropods and mollusks, moving his way up and down the Tree of Life; he read about mosses, creek ecology, hydrology, and the food web. He sat in libraries on weekday mornings and cafés on Saturday nights, reading all the related books and studies he could find. He went into the woods and observed slugs living their unfathomably slow existence and rapid lives. He married briefly, but a discontented wife, who became reasonably tired of coming second to a slug, departed.

He lived in a tiny, unkempt field station and had a revolving door of young scientists as roommates. Most would enjoy three weeks to three months of field study, and then return to their lives. He obsessively pursued his theory that the slugs, in their mucousy protective slime, were emitting a trail of subtle poison everywhere they went; a poison, he believed, that had a critical effect on the local ecosystem. The insects and small mammals that ate the slugs had developed a cumulative tolerance to this toxin, which, the man believed, was protecting them from the harmful effects of Bisphenol A, an endocrine-disrupting compound that humans have been using to produce consumer products for over a century. The upstream plastics factory had caused hormonal havoc for several species in the ecosystem, including infertility, sexual deformities, and impaired development— but not for the predators of the slugs.

For nearly fifty years this man dutifully observed the slugs and their ecosystem counterparts, and recorded his findings with meticulous precision. He went into debt purchasing chemistry sets and equipment on his own. He didn't trust the local university, convinced they would take a hush payment from the plastic manufacturers or politicize the data. One evening in his early seventies, while walking home from the creek in a cold autumn storm, the man was paralyzed with stroke and fell to the ground. After a long night of exposure in the wind, bitter cold and rain, he died amongst his slugs on the forest floor. He was a grotesque sight by the time he was discovered, by a group of children playing through the woods– darting along the creek, slipping on moss and getting their own scraped knees. His work was never published, and as of now, no young scientist has attempted to pick up where he left off. He had no children, his family was ashamed of him, his friends had all but forgotten about him, and he was right about the university.

All of that being said, as far as scientists go, he is one of the lucky ones. The subject he chose to fixate on did have greater ecological and perhaps even global significance, even if he had not finished proving it in his lifetime. He worked outdoors on his own terms, which many natural scientists would prefer to an office or a sterile laboratory. And most importantly, he worked so diligently and persistently because his work evolved from fascination, to purpose, to an earnest sense of utility and urgency.

Perhaps the most challenging moment any aspiring scientist will face is the one thing this man had figured out young: choosing a subject of study. There are elephants, amoebas, swarms of krill one billion strong; carnivorous mushrooms, fifty-foot cacti, immortal jellyfish, poisonous flowers; food systems, root systems, weather patterns, and the position of Earth in the greater Cosmos. What to choose? What to make of it? What to make of your seven or so decades observing this all transpire?

A scientist's pursuit of truth is very much like one's romantic quest for a soulmate, and it is perhaps why many scientists wind up alone. Not unlike our quest for love, we often stumble upon our subject of study in an unexpected place and time, but once we encounter it, we are emboldened by a renewed sense of certainty.

The author of this study has spent many years asking herself this question until she suddenly realized she had already been studying her subject of fascination for many years. And like our man and his slugs, my relationship with my subject of study has evolved from fascination and a hint of fear, to purpose, to an earnest sense of utility and urgency.

-Nina Distrella

PART ONE

SUMMER

1
Villain

"I just don't think I am enough for you."

A little voice in my head goes, *I called this!* and she's right, we did call this. I cross my arms, cross my legs, and brace myself. *Don't you DARE cry in front of him.*

"You're just so passionate– you're so dedicated to your work and your causes and I… I just don't have that. I mean I have things I care about, sure… but I don't have the same drive to dedicate my whole life to it.

"It's like how you say I've been spoiled by growing up here. Maybe you're right. I can't relate to half the things you talk about, all these systems and *isms* and invisible forces that need to be undone and dismantled, and replaced with something else. It's like I understand there are many injustices in the world, and suffering and all that, but I don't *feel it* inside. When I try to, it just feels like I'm forcing it– like I'm putting a giant rock onto my own shoulders just to feel something heavy. It's not like we can do much about all these things, so why focus all our energy on it?" Tyler shrugs and cracks a little smile in the corner of his mouth, as if he believes he has said something comforting. "I don't know Nina, maybe you would be happier with someone more from your own background–" His eyes widen in the classic male realization that he has just dropped a match on a thick fuse.

"From my *background?* Are you serious?"

"Okay that didn't come out right, I—"

"From my background. Got it. So not only are you so coddled that you can't relate to the struggles of other people, you don't even want to *be bothered* with it. Not even by your *white trash* girlfriend, is that it? You'd rather float around in your grandfather's swimming pool."

"Okay easy– I didn't say that. That's not fair. It's not like I have never tried, or struggled…"

"That's true, I've watched you try. You've been trying. I wouldn't be with you if I didn't see that. What has changed?"

"You see the way things are going in the world. And it's only going to get worse, maybe sooner than we think. And I'm afraid, Moon. I'm afraid of not being able to live my life the way I want to."

"You don't get to call me Moon anymore. And do you think anyone wants to? You think anyone—"

"Let me finish. You know how I feel. I belong outdoors. It is who I am. I can't be confined behind a computer, working for some government agency or climate justice nonprofit, I just can't. I'm like that plant in your room– you dug it up and brought it inside because you loved it, but it's dying in there, Nina. I am that plant. I can't live an indoor life. It's not living. The best I can do is to go out and enjoy what's left of nature before it's gone. I want to witness what's left of it…"

"Well, that sounds *lovely!* Why didn't I think of that?" I clap my hands together and sway to the side in phony appreciation. My insides are flaming, bubbling lava, but I attempt to tone down my rage, and I speak slowly.

"Playing outside is not an *identity*, Tyler. It is not a cause, and it is not a vocation. You're not unique or noble in your desire to be in nature. It is no more than a thin veneer over your desire to live entirely for yourself. Do you know who recreation is for? For people like you, the *leisure class*, who have nothing to worry about and no one who counts on you. People– *real people*– have to work to meet their needs. Do you think the guy who's cementing a sidewalk on a July afternoon sighs and thinks to himself, 'Ah yes, this is who I am'?"

"You're wrong." Tyler squares his shoulders and looks into my eyes. I kind of like this rare sight of him, standing up for himself. I'm a little turned on, if I'm being honest. Too bad.

"It's not about living for myself. Being out in nature is what we're all supposed to be doing. Recreation is healthy, *essential*. And it's not all fun and games, either. You learn real skills. And you learn to struggle out there– but you also get a sense of what is worth struggling for. People don't get enough of it, and I think it's wrong. I can't help the work-obsessed society that we were born into. But it's not what I want. I–"

"It doesn't matter. The world you desire is gone; extinct. We've paved it over. It's not what I want either, or what any of us wants. I suppose a phony version of it is available to a select few people… people like you. But you've never understood that your world– your crunchy granola, beach yoga membership, six-thousand-dollar-mountain-bike existence simply isn't available to me. I don't have a trust fund, or an inheritance, or jack shit to count on but my next check."

"But if I have the opportunity to pursue the life I want, I should have the right to do it… shouldn't I?" I heard Tyler through his words: *You're holding me back. You and your needs, your whining about food and rent, are holding me back from enjoying my life.*

"So thirty summers of family vacations, backpacking through southeast Asia, playing in national parks while your grandparents paid your bills… that wasn't enough for you. All that talk about saving the planet, about climate action– that's someone else's problem. So while everyone else works tirelessly toward saving our asses, or simply surviving, you're just going to wander off into the wilderness because you can afford to?"

Tyler looks down at the sidewalk. "Yes. But–"

"Great! You should start now." I about-face and attempt to march away with dignity.

"I'll always love you Nina. That's not what this is about."

"Save it for someone who cares." The words fall out behind me as I walk away, the severity cut short by the embarrassing squeaking of my non-slip work shoes.

Despite the grimacing pout on my face as I stomp down the sidewalk, I'm not really that upset. My ego's bruised, but my heart is fine. That thing can really take a pummeling. I'm mostly angry at his reasons for going, not the going itself. I like Tyler, but I don't *need* Tyler, especially not right now. He's a nice guy, handsome, sure; a solid lover and very intelligent. But he's right about himself. He's been more of a distraction than anything else, always trying to take me away for the weekend to his friends' many lake houses and ski chalets, or inviting me to concerts I can't afford, or convincing me to spend weekday evenings playing volleyball instead of picking up extra shifts. I have more important things to do in life than to sit in a kayak on some pristine alpine lake. I have rent to pay, a student debt tunnel to dig my way out of, and most importantly, a film to write.

For the record, I am not one of those "writer" types. I will admit that I'm smart enough to get by, but I bullshitted my way through my education and I have zero desire to prove to the world that I am interesting. I am writing this story because I *have to*. One morning a few months ago the idea entered my brain, settled in on the couch and refused to leave. It's been tormenting me ever since, peeking into my thoughts and quoting itself in my conversations, forcing itself into existence by using my body as a host.

The idea came to me just before the heat of summer set in. I live in a tiny flat in the foothills outside of Mount Mirage, a seaside town considered one of California's best-kept secrets. (I think that's just what people say when a place is so expensive it's exclusionary to most of the world.) But if I've learned one thing from moving from place to place, it's to settle for a lousier, smaller, more expensive dwelling if you can manage to live near the rich people. The tap water tastes better, the power never goes out for long and the streets are almost eerily quiet because the kids don't play outside.

My current home consists of four broke, post-college girls packed into a flattened cube on the skirts of a mountain range. Half the place is built into the hillside, and the other half sits on precariously old stilts. It's a musty old place, but our view is unmatchable: down the hill a sprawling palm-speckled city reaches out to teal ocean. We have a wobbly balcony attached to the back end of our kitchen that bathes the place in late afternoon light. In the late summer we live in darkness, covering the glass doors and windows to prevent the stifling sun from roasting us and our houseplants.

It was early spring, but nearing the threshold of hot. Unusually heavy rains appeared for a few days and the humid air filled every room. It was a stark departure from a decade-long drought, so we basked in it and let our sheets get damp. For about a week the house became a freshly used shower stall.

The morning when the idea came along, my eyes flung open hours earlier than usual, right at the first signs of light. I had dreamt up a character, not exactly imaginative in her look: a buxom blonde in the classic American style. Wide hips, big hair, tiny waist, bulbous eyes and red lips. She worked as a dancer in a desert biker town, but underneath the sheen of baby oil and bright lights she had all the intellectual makings of a genius. Behind closed doors she was an avid reader and thinker, talented in both mathematical reasoning and literary theory. Had she picked up a paintbrush or sat at a piano, she could have been a marvel; but she preferred adrenalizing video games, gluttonous fast food, and reckless deathwish benders on the Vegas Strip.

The entirety of this woman's identity was built around an all-American sense of cynicism. Her hypersexualized beauty and lust for life were distractions from an inner bitterness toward the things out of her control, until she became motivated to act on a personal vendetta. This head-turning, cheap-beer-drinking, beautifully crass woman used her brilliant mind– and her endurance for flashing computer screens– to hack the servers of major student loan and medical debt companies and erase their accounting records. My mind's eye fondly gazed at her sitting before a giant makeshift control center of her own creation, casually tapping away while sipping a can of Four Loko in her underwear.

When I opened my eyes, I was devastated by the recognition that this woman was not real. I gripped my damp sheets; my heart was racing and a lump in my throat told me I was welcome to cry if I felt like it, which

I did not. I quickly stood and left my room to shake myself out of the feeling. I stepped onto the wobbly square balcony. There was a thick ring of marine fog around the foothills, dissolving into flying whisps just above our altitude. It was so thick I was unable to see the balcony beneath me, and my periphery was surrounded in complete white. I wondered for a moment if I had died– if that big California earthquake had finally come while I was sleeping– and the whole bungalow was being transported to some heavenly place along with me. Or perhaps I was having some profound revelatory moment; a visit from something divine. (I guess you could call me a sucker for that kind of stuff. At least I used to be. But sometimes I still get caught up in illogical spiritual whimsy. When you grow up believing in Santa Claus and god and ghosts and fortune-tellers, you have a permanent space in your mind for things that don't make any sense. You foolishly trust that you're more special and cared for by the Universe than you really are, even despite knowing better.) As a north wind began to whip up the surface layers of cloud, I could begin to faintly see the sky above, and it overruled my decision not to cry. It was my first time shedding tears in years, and I haven't since.

The combined experiences of the dream and the balcony were enough to stick to my mind for several days. I felt a tremendous sense of triumph for this woman, almost as though I wished to be her. I understood she was getting some sort of revenge; that she had some stake in the rigged game of the capitalist American economic system and was settling the score. After a few days I saw her as part of some bigger score-settling, a heist of a grander scale– and that's when it came to me.

I've been working on the story ever since, talking to myself while I walk down the street, writing little notes on receipt paper at the bar where I work, keeping a notebook under my pillow so I don't miss a scrap of dialogue that pops into my head. This story– a film, like I said, because I can't expect any sizable audience to pick up a book– is a tale of retribution and victory for the ladies of America. One for the girls, as the saying goes. It goes like this: an old heiress, who is dismayed by her colonial-era wealth, decides to spend it all on ruining the lives of a group of diabolically rich and powerful men. She gathers a cadre of scrappy women from all walks of marginalized American life, and they use their skills to destroy these evil billionaires' empires. My dream-blonde is a valuable member of the team, perfect for the "wild card" trope.

Tyler doesn't understand my obsession with this story, though he has tried to be supportive. *Had* tried. He was raised by a tough single mother in coastal California with a pair of lesbian parakeets, so he considers himself a male feminist. But his version of supporting gender equality involves having no opinions whatsoever, making him a great listener but virtually useless for discussions or debates. And I *need* to discuss and debate, as I have gone from attending Tea Party rallies to attending tree-saving protests in the last few years and I'm still figuring a lot of things out.

Which brings me back to how I ended up in Mount Mirage. Frankly, it was no more than a roll of the dice. The Mount Mirage Zoo's human resources department happens to be run by a delightfully ancient woman who keeps paper records and doesn't use her email account, making her organization the sole zoo in the country I am not blacklisted from.

Let me start at the beginning. I was shoveling huge mounds of elephant shit into a wheelbarrow— which was not an unusual day for me. My internship at the Animal Paradise Zoo in suburban-hell Ohio consisted mostly of shit-related activities, which I actually didn't mind so much, because I was thrilled to be in the company of its source. Rose, Dorothy, Blanche, and Sylvia are elderly as far as zoo elephants go, and they have spent the entirety of their captivity-shortened lives in this lousy one-tenth acre exhibit, complete with fake baobab trees, old car tires for entertainment, and a depressingly gray swimming hole. Their trunks hung droopily while I questioned them about how many years I'd have to work at this place for free before I'd get hired for real. They scoffed and kept eating their lunch.

I was instructed to make the exhibit extra-spotless for the evening's special event, for which I merited an invitation to bus tables. The party was truly a celebration for me, as it marked the permanent departure of Dolphin Trainer Barbie, my arch nemesis and world's most excruciating human being. I was even willing to wear the caterer's dehumanizing butler outfit, complete with bowtie and vest, without complaint. That's true elation.

Barbie tapped the microphone with a hot pink polished finger. *I wonder if anyone has ever told her how bad nail polish is for the marine environment.*

"Excuse me– thank you everyone *so, so much* for joining us for this very special evening," she smiled with blinding pearly whites.

I bet those whitening chemicals aren't great for the ocean either.

"It is certainly bittersweet to be leaving Animal Paradise. I will of course miss my dolphins, who are my dearest friends and the most dedicated entertainers I have ever met. But tonight, my husband Brad and I embark on a *new* adventure: to sail the globe, to inspire the next generation of marine mammal trainers, and to promote my amazing new book, *Gossiping with Dolphins: A Mer-girl's Journey!"* The room's phony praise drowned out my deliberate slamming of dishes and cutlery. "But if I may get serious for a moment… I'd just like to share that I truly believe God has put me here for this purpose. I hope you will be inspired by my story to ask Him to speak to you in the same way– that you may find your own path into the Light."

As she winked flirtatiously at the ceiling, I turned to one of the caterers. "Hey, could you please stab me in the eye with this dirty fork?" He cupped his mouth to prevent an audible burst of laughter.

"I hope you'll all purchase a copy of the book tonight and contribute to our boat fund. And prints of Brad's award-winning wildlife photography are for sale in the gift shop. And don't forget to follow our adventure on Youtube, Facebook, Instagram, and on our blog!"

Poor Brad. He's going to be stuck with this monster on a boat, taking orders and faking smiles for the rest of his sorry life.

"Now let us enjoy this beautiful surf-'n'-turf feast! God bless!"

As the zoo lawn erupted with another round of unwarranted applause, I found myself slipping behind the fake rocks, around the zebras, and to the large metal gate behind the elephants' dusty prison. I stared at them through the bars, standing motionlessly, trunks still drooping. I pulled some stolen watermelon from a bucket and they took the slices greedily. "The only joy you have is food." I rested my head against the cold bars. "Surf-n-turf and bacon-wrapped shrimp at a zoo event, unbelievable," I mumbled. "No fucking respect." Another uproar of applause, and something snapped.

Just one code; six buttons.

Six little beeps, and one long, low, loud tone, drowned out by the band.

The massive gate slowly swung open, but I didn't see it. I was already walking away.

The zoo worked hard to keep the incident hushed. The charge was led by Dolphin Trainer Bozo, who was worried the story would shadow her book tour. But a few guests (or perhaps fellow resentful interns wearing bowties) leaked videos of it online. "Escaped Elephants Trash Zoo Garden Party" had nearly two million hits on Youtube by the time they took it down. Luckily for me, Dean was high up in the local police department, a combat veteran and a well-respected member of the community. He sat at the head of the kitchen table with a stack of papers and a cold cup of coffee, staring at me like a parent about to give a stern lecture.

"So."

"...So."

"You will not be doing any jail time. But you will be making financial restitution for the damages of the incident." He didn't wait for me to ask. "Fifteen thousand."

"*WHAT*? Dean, you know I'm in debt for more than three times that amount! How am I supposed to—"

Dean raised a hand to silence my hysteria. "I have already given them twelve K, but you'll have to pay the rest."

"Great, that's my entire savings. My grad school fund..."

"Nina, how about a little gratitude? I just spent three days on the phone to save your ass *and* I bailed you out."

"You're right, I'm sorry." I curled up into his lap like a cat that's just been fed and wrapped my arms behind his neck. "I am very grateful. You've saved me, once again." I rested my head on his shoulder and breathed in the scent of his neck. "You're my hero," I whispered with sincerity.

Dean looked down and let a sigh escape his massive body. He was still built like an American soldier, but one who had come home from war and gone back to American food. "I was going to take you to the lake this weekend. I was going to propose. That money was meant for our wedding."

I knew that was coming. Dean had already attempted two very romantic and creative proposals that had gone awry, and each time I could feel him becoming more anxious to get the ring on my finger. "I just don't understand what you were thinking. I know you really hate that obnoxious dolphin chick, but you love those elephants."

I slid into a neighboring chair and laced my fingers in my lap. "I stand by what I did. In the holding cell I thought about it. My sweet girls, when they blew past that gate, and trampled the buffet tables and the band equipment, they were truly living for the first and only time. And when I saw the video of it I knew, and I was happy."

Dean put his head into his calloused hands. Good god, do I miss those hands. "Someone could have been seriously hurt. Those elephants could have been euthanized."

"I know." My face hardened for a moment at the thought, but a grin returned to my lips. "I stand by what I did."

After Dean and I split I didn't go home to my parents, because at that point in time I hadn't spoken to my father in six months and it felt imposing to suddenly ask for their hospitality. It wasn't a sudden argument or event that began the silence; we had just been speaking less and less for years, until the last trickles of the hose finally stopped. Nothing to talk about, I suppose. We are worlds apart. He fixes fishing boats for a living, and I'm a fishes' rights activist.

Instead of going home, I stayed with an old friend in New York for a few months. I kept busy doing odd-jobs delivering food, waiting tables, and walking dogs while I looked online for wildlife conservation jobs. It felt good to be out there and moving around in the world, no longer confined to the monotony of the midwestern suburbs and impending housewifedom. But I was getting no nibbles from job applications, and my housing situation was becoming increasingly delicate. Living with said friend came with certain requirements that I wasn't particularly up to fulfilling. I stretched the parameters of my job search, and came across a minimum-wage gig as a camp counselor at the Mount Mirage Zoo. A Google Images search of the city brought up vivid panoramas of palm trees, blue ocean, margaritas, and happy surfers. But how could I justify doing a teenager's job in the twilight of my twenties? Never underestimate the power of the inner lawyer. "*I will teach the next generation about wildlife conservation!*" I packed up my car once again and drove cross-country shortly after.

I lost that job in three weeks. It wasn't that bad of a gig; tiring, certainly, to rein in the kids and get them to pay attention. But it turns out six-year-olds aren't emotionally ready to learn about their animal friends being annihilated by climate change and habitat destruction. The firing was a little embarrassing, but overall I'm happy with how things turned out.

To pay the rent while I figure out my next move, which hopefully will be pitching my blockbuster hit to thirsty film executives, I am working in Palmetto, Mount Mirage's even richer and fancier neighbor. I pour booze into sparkly glasses for old rich people… *very* old, *very* rich, *very* white Baby Boomers. So there is no resentment at all. Who, me? *No no no*, everything is fine!

That's an easy sell, right? A 29-year-old, freshly single, broke, working in food service and writing a screenplay is textbook "not-fine". But this is how all good movies start. Do you think J.K. Rowling would have escaped into the world of wizards and magical trains if she had a hot boyfriend and a fat bank account? Didn't think so. You can't become a winner without first being a thoroughbred loser. So technically I'm right on track.

I cross the bridge into Palmetto Cove, shoes still squeaking, wondering how long Tyler watched me go before he turned and went on to his unhindered single life. I didn't dare look back. I usually enjoy this commute;

Palmetto is a remarkably beautiful place on its surface. This tiny seaside village looks quaint and rustic, but it's fake– it's Boomer Disneyland. These mom-and-pop-looking shops host pet masseurs and thousand-dollar ugly shoes. There are mega-mansions hidden behind the town's dense greenery that are home to the shadowy bosses of pop stars and presidents: the elites who *really* run the world, shape the culture, and decide what our society should care about. They own TV networks and oil companies, and are the people responsible for Tyler's fair judgment of the world only getting worse. Palmetto sits just far enough from the city so these monsters can go about their business of despoiling the planet at a safe and undisturbed distance from the great unwashed.

I get to Vero's early so I have some time to write before my shift starts. I say hello to Richard, a friendly regular who has lingered at the bar through the transition from lunch to dinner. He nurses his martini and watches me as I work. I like Richard; he's a successful journalist with a worldly air about him. He recently gave me a signed copy of one of his books– haven't read it yet, though. Too busy working on my own artistic creation.

I go through all the motions of setting up the bar: wiping everything down, cutting fruit and herb garnishes, stocking the fridges with wine bottles and fancy mixers in vintage glass bottles. After it's fully prepped for the happy hour crowd I sit in the corner with my notebook and reread my notes. The female characters are gold, but the assemblage of villains I have come up with are too cheesy, too basic for evil capitalist billionaires. I want them to feel complex and real; I want the audience to hate them as much as they hate a Bezos or a Zuckerburg.

I flip through a copy of the *Palmetto Press* for inspiration. The cover features a typical headline for the conservative paper: "String of Main Street Robberies Committed by Illegal Immigrant– Local Media Silent". I roll my eyes and flip ahead to my favorite section, the obituaries. Before you call me morbid, I'll just tell you honestly that despite my unfettered cynicism toward almost everything, I'm a mushy, gushy, pathetic romantic inside. And you should hear about some of these dead peoples' lives.

It's like those intolerably sappy movies they make every Christmastime. These dead old people have won the human existence lottery, if you ask me. Either that or their surviving family members are lying through their teeth. Listen to this one:

Marybeth Sucre was born on her family's farm in Idaho in 1946, where she spent her days playing in the woods with her siblings and helping her parents care for the farm's animals. After marrying her high school sweetheart Tom Carpenter, Tom joined the Navy and they were stationed in Mount Mirage. Tom and his brothers built the seaside home in which generations of the Carpenter family have built their lives. Tom and Marybeth were hopelessly in love for their 52 years of marriage, and Tom took her for a milkshake date every Friday evening up until his passing in 2016. While raising her family, Marybeth was deeply involved in her community: volunteering at the animal shelter, teaching a sewing class at the rec center, and singing in the church choir. Once her children were grown, Marybeth worked as a teacher at Mount Mirage Junior High for 20 years. She won Teacher of the Year three times!

Before leaving behind her six children and fourteen beautiful grandchildren, Marybeth spent her retirement traveling the world, always bringing home gifts and interesting stories for the family. She and Tom loved hosting holiday gatherings and the annual family camping trip in Yosemite National Park.

A celebration of Marybeth's life will be held at H. Caulfield Memorial Church this Sunday. In lieu of flowers, the family asks you to consider a donation to the Mount Mirage Animal Shelter in Marybeth's name.

"What an absolute BITCH."

I can't help but be a little bitter. Can you blame me? Back in the '60s Marybeth and Tom probably built their house for a few thousand bucks. That same house in Mount Mirage sells today for $1.6 million, and hasn't had an upgrade since 1982. *Bitch.*

Give me a break– anger consoles my envy, for I know that I will never be Marybeth, Toms no longer exist, and neither does the world their generation got to build their lives in… for a few thousand bucks, on cheap coastal land… available, cheap, BEACHFRONT land. *Maybe sea level rise will suck that house right into the Pacific in my lifetime.* I smile, tickled at the thought.

What feels like a lifetime time ago, I used to dream big: about a life of freedom, achievement, grandeur of experience and traveling the world, and I feared nothing more than Marybeth's life. Maybe that's why I left Dean. That's definitely why I left Dean. Isn't that a kick? After all that, I was the one who left *him*. I bet you thought it was the other way around. But the way I see it, I did the man a favor. He was a simple, wholesome guy who wanted a simple, wholesome life– which scared the daylights out of me. Maybe he was a Tom Carpenter– maybe one of the last ones. I look him up on my phone.

His profile photo shows his wedding-banded left hand over the bump of a pregnant woman with expensive-looking highlights. Married with his first kid on the way. *Christ, that was fast.* Oh well, no turning back now.

I flip the paper to the op-ed section. There's a photo of a slick-looking middle aged man atop a letter titled, "CEO of Kantian Consulting Co. 'Most Hated Man in Mirage County' as Power Plant Battle Drags On." The editorial carries on with the usual, the endless tug-of-war of grassroots environmental groups against The Man, the powers that be– the villains.

Giles Pion, former Board President of Kantian Consulting, was named CEO two years ago to continue the campaign to transition the Invisible Hand Power Plant to nuclear energy. He is confronting a diverse coalition of local groups that are committed to stopping the project.

The fate of Invisible Hand has been a topic of contentious debate for decades. It was one of the first power plants in the state, built at the crest of World War I when fuel prices soared, making hydroelectric generation an obvious choice. The Mirage River Dam system was built in the 1930s to support Invisible Hand as the region's population boomed with Midwestern Dust Bowl refugees. It was considered a tremendous feat in American engineering and provided electricity to over a million homes. The dam system was dismantled by environmentalists in the 1970s, with the help of the newly-passed Endangered Species Act— but without the dams, Invisible Hand would no longer be able to reliably meet the region's growing demand for electricity. The '70s energy crisis left people panicked about the local energy supply, so the power plant opted for coal and natural gas, which it has been running on ever since. But as California inches closer to the deadline to meet its greenhouse gas reduction goals, Kantian is making the case for nuclear power.

Various special interest groups, led by the Mount Mirage Earth Defenders, are vehemently fighting this effort. They are pushing for a rapid transition to solar and wind energy instead, paired with large-scale energy storage in the form of lithium-ion battery farms.

'We know what needs to be done to protect our future,' says Piper Hammick, Campaign Director at MMED. 'Not only do we need renewable energy as soon as possible to save the planet, but we also need to acknowledge the injustice that Invisible Hand has inflicted upon Indigenous Californians and the damage it has done to their ancestral lands. We must atone for past and present oppression by using less energy across the board— from the individual to the farmer to the large corporation. We will not let Kantian Consulting, which is ruled by a boardroom of old white men in suits, decide what is best for this community.'

Pion appears to be undeterred, despite the bombardment of negative press and protests outside his private residence, stating that with support from local politician and gubernatorial-hopeful Roger Wilkes, permits could be approved as soon as spring 2020.

I stare at this grinning, slimy creature, and suddenly it dawns on me that it would be much more satisfying for the characters in my movie to obliterate a single man— a man so terrible that he embodies the white capitalist patriarchy itself. As I start scribbling out a new paragraph, Richard interrupts.

"Stuck on a scene? I love a good case of writer's block. It's kind of like a long dry spell… miserable during its time, but makes the breakthrough that much more sweet. What are you stuck on?"

"My male lead," I hesitantly explain. I'm not sure what Richard would think of my story. He certainly seems progressive, but he is also a full-time resident of Palmetto with white hair. "I want him to be strong, stoic, *masculine*." I carefully emit the word "toxic" for fear of losing him.

"Hmm… Well, sometimes the best characters are drawn up from our own lives and experiences. You should do some good old-fashioned people-watching. There's a place–"

Richard's phone rings. "Excuse me Sweet, I need to take this." He pulls down his readers to see who is calling. "Arnold! I thought you were coming for lunch. Caught up with work, yes– I know it well." He swirls his lukewarm martini. "Well those beautiful Klipspringer's steaks aren't going to eat themselves, are they? Yes, I'll see you there in an hour-ish." He gives me a guilty look. "I really have cut down since you shared that article with me about the Amazonian farmers. I just can't resist a steak on a guy's night out."

"I'll make you a deal." I bite my pen. "I won't pester you about eating meat again, but you have to promise to read my screenplay when it's done."

"Now that, Miss Nina, is an excellent deal. Done!" He downs the last sip of the martini, and I shudder at memories of drinking warm vodka in college. "You ought to come out on the town one of these nights. The Cove has some beautiful and sultry little spots. Jack Bunsby plays ethereal jazz piano at the Seashell Lounge on Wednesday nights. And their old fashioned's may be the best on the West Coast. No offense, of course."

"None taken." I sigh as I fondly consider how many rich suckers have spent $26 a pop on my poorly-mixed cocktails.

~

I walk the cobblestone path to Klipspringer's Steakhouse. Palmetto Cove is coated in golden lamp light, but I don't have time to be enchanted by it. My mission is singular and I must focus. Richard was right; I can't think of a better place to find what I'm looking for. My regulars at Vero's bar speak of this place often, as though their patronage there is a stamp of being a member of some exclusive club. Klipspringer's is the watering hole for a specific breed of Palmetto's elite: oil execs, hedge fund managers, war profiteers, one-percenters with hobby ranches… and that is exactly why I'm walking through the door.

It's Saturday night and the place is packed. It is not what I expect— no crystal or elegant sconces. It's dark and proverbially greasy. Brass railings and forest green velvet, waiters with slicked back hair. I'm relieved to see a single open seat at the bar; I hastily grab it and order. The bartender, a red-haired woman in her late forties with a belly squeezed in half by her apron, does not seem to approve of my presence. Maybe she thinks I am a prostitute making a lazy effort, with my simple sleeveless top, jeans, and dirty shoes. But something in her contemptuous glance holds a layer of satisfaction, as if to say, "At least I'm not reduced to doin' *that* to make my living." *Fair enough, lady.*

I glance around with a tiny notepad in my lap and try to conceal my disgust with the characters in the restaurant. Old droopy men with white hair and dark shirts gnaw on bloody-rare USDA Prime steaks. Their botoxed and shellacked arm candies sit daftly at their sides, getting jolly on hundred-dollar bottles of wine.

So this is what living the American dream looks like, eh? All I scribble into my little notebook is, "*Fuckers.*"

The wine I order is smooth— and six bucks more than the same exact glass at Vero's. I could have mentioned that I tend bar for an industry discount, but I don't want to give away any details about myself. This is a research excursion so I'll chalk it up to a business expense. I sip slowly to give myself plenty of time, and I glance down the bar. I spot one of my favorite patrons from work, a dopey-faced, doe-eyed man— Richard's friend Arnold—sitting at the other end. Our sights briefly cross; I feel obligated to get up and say hello. I'm kind of relieved to have a way into conversation with someone, so it seems like I have a reason for being here. He looks surprised as I approach with a friendly smile. He is sitting with a man in a black Palmetto Motor Club t-shirt.

"Well hello, Miss Nina! Funny seeing you here." I smile and wait through an uncomfortable but short pause. "Why don't you join us? I'm sure these folks will slide down a seat." I stuff my notebook into my bag and grab my glass.

As I settle onto the warm barstool I hear, "And who is this sweet little cannoli?"

"Excuse me?"

Arnold's friend points to the tiny Italian flag tattoo on my ankle. I blush with embarrassment at the obvious barcode of my social class. "I'm Nina: future film producer and tattoo removal survivor." I extend my hand confidently. "And you are?"

"I'm Cam, as in camshaft." He waits for me to ask what that is, but I don't.

"Pleasure to meet you, Mr. Shaft."

They keep telling me how "bold" I am for showing up to a place like this. It's insulting, but I get it. I'm the hired help in a town full of pot-bellied kings. But hesitation to trespass into their world hadn't even crossed my mind.

When I was twenty-one, I had my ultimate, greatest-ever childhood pipe dream come true. I boarded a tiny sailboat and spent several months exploring and studying the Great Barrier Reef. Tropical waters, pods of dolphins, diving with an underwater notepad in a globally-significant ecosystem… the ultimate dream. And you know what? Turns out the damned thing is on its way out. Every professor and documentary said the same thing: It's bleaching; it's dying. It's overfished and polluted, and won't be able to keep up with changing temperatures. And I got a front row seat.

I don't know if you've ever had the chance to achieve your life's wildest dream and then watch it shatter before your eyes, but I highly recommend it. You're untouchable after that. Nothing can shock you anymore. Nothing can scare you or hurt you. I returned to America feeling like I had already seen it all. Two rich dudes in a sleazy steakhouse don't scare me.

When I got home to finish college, I had a hell of a time testing my limits. In my brokest period of life– or maybe second-brokest– I entertained myself by marching right into designer boutiques and trying on gowns and diamonds; I toured and sampled exclusive day-spas posing as the maid of honor for an upscale bride, and snuck into the VIP sections of concerts, all just for the thrill of feeling like someone I was not. I would sit in fancy lounges and make up characters for myself with glamorous or mysterious lives. I started doing it everywhere I went, sort of addicted to the anonymity of being a good liar. My own audacity glazed over my ability to feel hesitation, shame, embarrassment, or really anything at all.

I sit languidly at the Klipspringer's marble bartop and carry myself impressively in the conversation– not just nodding my head and laughing at jokes. I am *in it*. This is not an easy thing to do around wealthy older white guys, because they are both highly educated and remorselessly vulgar. They bounce between discussing haughty intellectual topics and spewing bigoted, offensive garbage all in rapid succession, always with the utmost confidence and authority, even when they know they're talking directly out of their ass. Wit and pace are critical. If you don't keep up, you can put your foot in your mouth, or worse, show offense to something. Then your respect is gone, just like that. And you don't get it back easily, if at all. In this moment I am grateful for spending half my childhood hanging around fishermen and boat mechanics at Dad's old garage. Here it's the exact same game, just with some more sophisticated vocabulary thrown in with the vulgarity and racist jokes.

While I'm wielding rapidfire manspeak I'm simultaneously at bat, swinging hard at any condescending flattery or suggestive remarks, coming solely from Arnold's friend Cam. Arnold is more of a Southern gentleman with a New Orleans accent. He would happily listen to someone else ask an inappropriate question, and wait for the response with childish hope in his eyes, but he is not the kind of man to ask them himself. I am just defensive enough to maintain some semblance of honor, but not enough to change the course of the conversation. I know how this game works. They like a little resistance. You make it too easy, or seem too eager or interested, and you're worthless. Contrawise, if you cross the line into combative or self-righteous territory, you're a snowflake or a mad dyke. (Their words, not mine.) It's a fine tightrope to walk, and I am being deliberately slow with my drink so I can keep my head in the game. These rich guys have no reservations about boozing you up. Money's no object, and neither is time.

I reach forward to grab my second glass of wine and Cam comments on my unshaven underarms. I was curious if and when someone would say something. I intentionally wore a sleeveless shirt to challenge myself to confidently own my new "liberated look", as my adopted hippie grandma Paula calls it. Plus I knew it would make people in this particular environment especially uncomfortable, and for some reason that thought brings me a bright, citrusy kind of joy.

"It's intentional," I respond, "to scare away weak men."

His silent reaction– a smirk and a lifted eyebrow– tells me that he likes this answer. "I bet your boyfriend likes it. I can just picture him: man-bun, distressed seventy-dollar t-shirt from Urban Outfitters that says *Save Earth*, or *Namaste Bitches*."

"Wow, you think that little of me, huh?" I touch my wine glass to my lips. "My boyfriend's dead, actually." As Cam's face begins to change to offer token sympathy I add, "Well, at least to me." I break my own rule and take a big sip.

"Dark," he smiles. "I knew I liked you." Before I can change the subject, he bears down.

"Let me guess– he left you, out of some fear of commitment, or because he gave you some lecture about monogamy being a social construct to justify cheating on you, or as a means to ask you to 'open up' your relationship while he travels around in a van?"

"I mean, some of that is true–"

"You don't even have to tell me, I know it. I see it all the time." He is indignant; his brow is full of rolling folds. A lecture is imminent.

"Here's the funny thing– and you're just young enough to learn this lesson before it's too late. I've been in this town a long time, and I see this happen over and over again. This inexhaustible conveyor belt of young, college-educated, 'wild and free' women, falling for these faux-virtuous, neolib 'male-feminist' weasels, or these trust-fund-hippie surfer bros. They all reach their thirties the same way: heartbroken, bitter and lonely, because you simply can't rely on a man like that. Or they realize they're wearing the pants in their relationship and they can no longer bring themselves to fuck a neutered wimp. And *bam!*– They're suddenly 35 and alone, desperate, and they come sprinting after guys like me– the stable ones with real jobs, with security and common sense and retirement accounts. And then they can't accept us as we are, as real men, and they start to lecture us about their feminism and their ideals. And then they either realize they've been sold a lie, or they dig their heels in deeper, dye their hair blue and start their cat collection."

Sheesh. Sounds like someone's a little bitter himself.

"Well– *thank goodness* we met then! Please, won't you enlighten me so I can be spared from such a horrendous fate?"

Cam is a fascinating ball of arrogance and entitled rage. His brassy hair is slicked back behind his ears and it stays solidly in place as he gestures and shakes his head in time with his remarks. His skin is youthful for a man in his forties, but it could just be the steakhouse lighting, and his very expensive-looking spray-tan. I bet he spends five grand on it a year. Easily.

I'm not sure exactly what he does, because he's mentioned doing an impossible number of things: starting companies, building and racing cars, inventing new technologies... *You think you're James Bond or something?* But one thing is clear to me: he's got that lunatic problemsolver mind, the likes of engineers and inventors, paired with an inexhaustible drive to get what he wants. He's the kind of man that can either save the world or destroy it.

"You've obviously got a brain... why the hell are you working at a restaurant?"

"Because we live in an unjust, brutal society ruled by petty tyrants. And I'm too smart to take out another lifetime's worth of loans to go to graduate school."

"Nice try. That social-justice-warrior-victim shit doesn't fly around here. First off, you absolutely don't need graduate school. It's a scam meant to make people useless academics who contribute nothing to society but bad ideas. What did you study in your undergrad?"

"Coral reefs. I helped with some research on the Great Barrier Reef, and I thought that was going somewhere, but I checked out before I lost all will to live. It's just too depressing."

"A fascinating subject, I love the ocean too. I had a great view of it in my old office at Invisible Hand."

This is not registering in my brain. He said it so casually, so... *proudly*. How on Earth could someone with internet access be comfortable admitting their involvement with that power plant? I don't verbalize my disgust, because I don't want to set him off, but he catches an involuntary wince. "Don't worry Mr. Shaft, I'm not going to throw my drink on you– but I may picture it in my mind, just to make myself feel better." I wink and smile in an attempt to diffuse the tension.

"Let me ask you something, Miss Distrella. How did you get here tonight?"

"I drove, at least most of the way. I walked the last quarter mile so I didn't have to pay for parking."

"Thought so. And when you turn on the lights in your home, how does that work? Or did you dress by candlelight this evening? Wait wait, let me picture that a moment..." I give him a shove powerful enough to make him grip the bar.

"Alright, I get it. I still have to rely on the energy status quo. But the system..."

"See, this is what pisses me off. You so-called 'eco warriors' bark your demands, but you're oblivious to how the world you live in works. You demand zero emissions immediately, but you refuse nuclear energy. You want less oil spills, but you protest the pipelines that would move that oil more safely." He explains that after consulting for an oil pipeline he received death threats from activists and had to hire private security. Friends and relatives stopped talking to him, including his girlfriend at the time.

"She was hot, but I knew it wouldn't last— I could sense she was a typical Lib pretty quickly, once she started talking about all that green white-guilt nonsense. Pipelines are by far the safest way to move oil and gas," he grumbles. His voice is braided with defensive hostility; he speaks a little louder with each breath. "I put tireless years of work into making that plant safer *and* more environmentally friendly, but what have I gotten? They want to sabotage this project but they still want to charge their fucking EVs. You know what those electric vehicle chargers downtown are running on, while Mount Mirage Earth Defenders whine and cry about nuclear? COAL! Natural gas and fucking COAL!"

I only knew that because I read that article in the *Palmetto Press* the other day, but I'm obviously not about to say that. I quickly cut off my involuntary reaction to his mention of the Earth Defenders, the organization I've been interning for for the last year and a half, and where I hope to soon get a paid job.

"But Shaftie, doesn't it seem like the paradigm is inevitably shifting away from fossil fuels? Is there any real justification for our inaction to convert our energy system to renewable sources?" He smiles at me with patronizing condescension, ready to lecture me once again, and my blood pressure rises.

Arnold turns in after a while, bored with our segmented banter about energy subsidies, the "feminization of society", whatever the hell that nonsense is, and the impact of offshore wind farms on marine mammals. Cam and I end up being some of the last patrons in the place. His attitude is dripping in what I can only describe as classic right-wing anger: his comments are peppered with racist, misogynistic, homophobic, xenophobic, and anti-Californian notions. It's alarming to witness, and yet, in this period of artistic research, the conversation is an absolute goldmine. So I stay and listen with dutiful concentration, only wishing I could pull out my notebook so I don't miss any of the disturbing gems flying from his mouth. I am mortified by his unflinchingly offensive sense of humor, but the chuckles and approving nods he receives from surrounding patrons remind me where I am.

I am in Hell.

It's near midnight; time to go. The town is dead. Palmetto and Mount Mirage both practice Boomer hours and shut down early, even on a Saturday night. "Would you like a ride to your fossil-fuel-burning car?" I nod and climb into his comically oversized white pickup truck and we roll down the block.

"Do a lot of hauling, do you?"

"Excuse me?"

"This thing could surely transport a lot of hay bales, timber, mounds of dirt? Livestock perhaps?" I smirk at his recently manicured fingernails.

"I wouldn't let any of that shit anywhere near this truck."

Didn't have to tell me that.

We argue-talk until a quarter past one. He walks around the front of the white beast to open the passenger door.

I make a snap decision: *I should keep this going.* The Universe has *finally* done me a solid: a more perfectly terrible person couldn't have possibly fallen into my lap. *He is my villain.*

He opens the door for me with a sarcastic gentleman's bow; I jump down to the unforgiving pavement and curtsy, fanning out an imaginary skirt with my middle fingers. As I reach for my keys, I turn and kiss him. And I make it a good one.

Mr. Shaft

I can't believe I kissed a girl with hippie pits.	1:46 AM
I can't believe I kissed a capitalist.	1:49 AM
Goodnight, Miss Distrella.	1:49 AM
Goodnight, Mister Shaft.	1:50 AM

STUDY: ETHOLOGY OF THE
GREAT WHITE GORILLA

INTRODUCTION

"Great white gorilla" is the common name given to the dominant adult male individuals of the white western gorilla, *Gorilla-industria violentus.* Much like the silverbacks of the African gorillas, great white gorillas are physically and socially distinct from other white gorilla males and wield power over their family groups, referred to as troops. White western gorillas have a patriarchal and tribal social system in which the great white gorillas assume leadership roles, determine and enforce the social hierarchy, and wage wars with other troops to gain territory and take control of natural resources.

This subspecies of gorilla has its evolutionary origins in the colder, higher latitudes of the northern hemisphere, which has given it its lighter fur and pink skin, but it is now found throughout diverse ecosystems all over the world. Over generations of territorial expansion and warfare, other subspecies have become incorporated into white gorilla troops, some willingly and some by force. Because of this, there is contentious debate in the scientific community over whether or not all western gorillas are members of the same subspecies, regardless of phenotypic presentation of fur, but that is not relevant to this study nor the issue it intends to address. For the practical purposes of this study, the white western gorilla will be referred to here as a single species.

NECESSITY OF STUDY

The issue of the great white gorilla begins and ends with a fundamental quandary of all species' survival: food. The geographical ubiquity and population success of *Gorilla-industria violentus* is due in no small part to its unprecedented ability to extract food and other natural resources from any ecosystem it inhabits. As a troop drains resources from a place, they migrate elsewhere and encounter other troops. There has been continuous inter-troop hostility as well as interspecies warfare as the white western gorillas, always led by the ruthless and violent great whites, continue the destruction of their biological competitors to expand their reign across the world.

The great white gorilla has climbed to the top of the food chain and has not had any natural predators for hundreds of years. Any species' population is typically kept in check by either the success of its predators or the limitations of its food supply. When any species becomes "too successful" in proliferation, it will eventually burn out its food source and the population diminishes– or in extreme cases, disappears altogether. This great balancing scale of nature happens on all dimensions throughout the global biosphere.

If the demise of these creatures was simply a function of nature's equilibrium, it would not be up to humankind to lean on the scale. But it is not just the continuation of one species that hangs in the balance.

Since the great white gorillas have claimed territory worldwide, it is not just a single ecosystem that will be thrown out of balance by its self-destruction, but the entire global biosphere. The disturbance of such an event will create a ripple effect throughout all life on the planet, and it has already begun. It is estimated that biodiversity is being lost between 1,000 and 10,000 times the normal rate. The impact of the white western gorillas has been so devastating, some scientists believe we have entered the sixth mass extinction event in Earth's 4.5 billion-year history, in which thousands of beloved species will be lost.

One theory, as proposed by Dr. Gretchen Rumbelow from the University of Antimann, states that as the scarcity of food rises, all gorilla species will engage in troop warfare, decimating natural resources and causing a chain reaction of extinctions. As the leaders and most aggressive individuals in any troop of white gorillas, the great white gorillas are considered the primary drivers of such a collapse.

OBJECTIVE

Ethology is the study of animal behavior. The purpose of this study is to observe and analyze the behaviors, habits, communications, and social structures of great white gorillas to determine the best methods for ecological intervention. Through careful, consistent observation and the recording of habits and behavior, a new depth of understanding may be gained of this formidable and infamous creature.

2
Wing Woman

"You look great!"

Camilla pushes an unruly strand of hair out of my face. "It is so *his* loss."

"Thanks, but you really don't need to say that. I'm fine." I stare at Camilla, who is surveying my hair and makeup, pleased with her work. "I'm honestly just upset that I don't have anyone to take me into the backcountry anymore. Tyler was my ticket into the wilderness."

The thought gives me a little jolt of sad-panic that makes me start to sweat. It's true; Tyler is the one with the four-wheel drive and the state park passes, the recreation maps and field guides, the tents and sleeping pads, the kayaks and camp stove, and the friends with the cabins and lake houses…"Oh god…" I start doing that move where you flap your arms like a flightless bird to air out your underarms. "All that gear… it's so *expensive…*"

"Let's not focus on that right now– put your arms down. We'll find you a brand new guy to take you camping, and hiking, and all that other nature shit you like to do. Tylers are a dime a dozen in Mount Mirage. Just look around." Camilla sweeps out her arm, gesturing across the brewery, and she has a point. From behind, half the guys in the room could be Tyler. Flannel shirts on tall, narrow frames, caps and beanies with snowboarding and surf logos, twelve-dollar pints of craft India pale ales in hand. As they talk and gulp they glance up at the bar's row of TVs.

Camilla is from the city and, as she puts it, "doesn't do nature." Her idea of getting earthy is wine tasting at a manicured vineyard in the valley. She trades in her tips at Vero's for lip filler treatments and is on a rigorous hunt for a Palmetto husband. We aren't friends. But she happened to be working the night Tyler dumped me and has latched herself onto the righteous cause of finding me a rebound man "to shove into his face." So here we are. To her credit, she's an ideal wing woman: busty and outgoing, but so vapid and obnoxious that her subject looks to the person beside her for relief.

She picked out my outfit: a tight-fitting white tee and a burgundy plaid miniskirt. "I love this. I feel like it fits your personality... It has an innocence to it, a 'nice girl nextdoor' vibe. But the skirt is Catholic school-ish, therefore has slutty implications. Love it. You have to wear it."

Camilla knows absolutely nothing about my personality. But Tyler has a thing for this skirt, and looking in the mirror I was starting to get into the "shove-it-in-his-face" spirit. One Saturday night about a year back I was standing in front of my closet in this skirt, getting ready for a date. While I was debating a sweater or a coat, Tyler snuck up behind me. He held my hands to my sides, kissed the back of my neck and walked me into the closet, pressing his body against my back. The surprise of it overwhelmed my senses, especially since Tyler was doing it. The guy is excessively respectful, nearly to a point of nauseation. "May I kiss you?" "Is this okay?" "You know how much I respect you, right?" In the dark cover of my hanging clothes, he let some hesitant, fearful part of himself go. We didn't end up going out that night.

"Alright. I'll wear it. I feel good about it." I find the less I care, the more easily I am talked into doing things.

Camilla pushes her way to the front of the bar. "Do you guys have any non-beer things? Like cider or something? Nina, what do you want?"

"I'll take a pint of the Eco ale, thanks." One buck per pint sold goes to the Earth Defenders. I take a couple hefty sips and casually glance around the room at the sea of Tylers. The environmentally-responsibly-brewed ale warms my empty stomach and I feel confident in my outfit, ready to catch a rebound– a distraction from my distraction. But that moment is short-lived. *"Oh, for Christ's SAKE–"*

I flip around and desperately tug on Camilla's shirt. The *actual* Tyler has just walked through the door. If I'm wrong and there is a god, he hates me. "He's here he's here– *what do I do?*" Before she can answer, an instinct takes over and I charge through the crowd, stopping in front of a 6'3" bearded man in a dirty Invisible Hand Power Plant t-shirt.

"Excuse me, uh, Sir... may I buy you a beer in exchange for a huge favor?" The man is amused; I waste no time. "My ex just walked in and it would mean the world to me if we could pretend to aggressively flirt right now." The man's laugh is deep and booming; I have picked the perfect candidate.

"It'd be my pleasure. Where is this fool?"

"Was at the door, last time I checked. Tall-ish guy, faded green hat. Please be subtle if you're going to look." I smile charmingly and reach up to touch his shoulder, initiating our scene.

"Yeah, I see him. His loss, honestly. You're adorable." He winks at me. His breath is bad but he's got an honest sort of charm about him. I like those working-man types. He smells sweaty. "Let's do this."

He leans down, puts his pointer finger under my chin and tilts it up toward him. He gazes into my eyes with a big smile. *My god, his breath is bad.*

"I look like I am saying sweet things to you," he says softly, and after one more heavy sip I return a dreamy gaze into his eyes. "In a moment, you're going to toss your head back at something that I am saying now that is making you laugh. And you'll give me a playful little shove."

"You are too much!" I throw my head back and laugh sincerely, because what we're doing is fantastically funny to me, and I push his muscled chest. I lean in and softly repeat his technique. "Okay it's my turn. I'm saying some funny banter but then something kind of sensual; and now I'm going to poke you and you're going to laugh!"

Poke, booming laugh. Booming only in his natural tone– not forced in volume. He's a real professional.

"Do you think he's noticed us yet? You're taller."

"He's been slowly heading over to the bar, he's probably seen me but not you. Let's get that beer, then he'll definitely see us."

Camilla caught onto my antics and opted to sit at the bar, sipping her lavender cider with amusement, while I made a giant ass out of myself. I ended up spending thirty-six bucks that I don't have on pretentious beer and a sour empty-stomach buzz. And you guessed it: I ended up tasting that gas station hot dog breath. Kissing the power plant guy... kissing the henchman of the enemy. Shameless, absolutely shameless. But I must admit he was nice, and his laugh delighted me. His beard felt alright too.

And Tyler, who was comfortably nestled in a large cluster of friends and enthralled by the soccer game playing on the patio TV, was blissfully unaware of my presence at the brewery. And that is the real kicker: that my life will change radically without him in it, suddenly full of voids to be filled, but his life will stay exactly the same. He'll have the same friends, enjoy the same activities and the same places, and venture into the wilderness just as often– probably more often, since he has one less weight dragging him down. Me. I get it now. This is the difference between us. Who's *really* not enough for whom?

I spotted him walking out the door of the brewery, laughing and being slapped on the back. He looked happy. It certainly wasn't the first time he made me feel no larger than an earthworm, but good Christ let it be the last.

Power Plant Guy

babe u r 2 cute... come ovre tonite??? :)   10:12 PM

3
Flat

It's Monday night and I'm back to work at Vero's. Richard is perched in his favorite seat, drinking with Cam's friend Arnold. The dining room is quiet and I stand by the well with my notebook, reviewing the four pages of feverish notes I took after my recon mission at Klipspringer's. It's mostly unanswered questions and unfinished quotes. Cam left me a voicemail yesterday morning to inquire about my plans for the week, but I haven't returned his call.

I drove home Saturday night with a jolt of victorious energy, certain that my screenplay is about to get a whole lot more interesting. But something about our interaction left a strange impression on me– a vexation in my stomach that I haven't been able to shake. The only thing I can compare it to is a middle school crush on a boy you outwardly hate: an unsettling cocktail of butterflies, curiosity, and terror.

I want to ask Arnold about Cam, but not in front of Richard. Richard has been here since noon so he's on borrowed time. Arnold throws back two screwdrivers in quick succession and orders a vodka and club soda, which tips me off that this is his last round. As I fix his drink I listen to their discussion about a machine that does the casing in a hot dog factory. *Gnarly.*

"If you get a single tear in the material the whole line goes off," Arnold says.

Richard notices me tuning in from my periphery as I polish a glass and pretend to stare at the TV. "You'll have to forgive him, Nina," he cuts Arnold off mid-sentence and winks at me through his wire-framed bifocals. "Arnold's from a land where hot dogs are still a proud delicacy. Despite the obvious conclusions you'd draw from hearing him speak, the technologies in his factory are exemplary in industrial food manufacturing. What is it Arnie, three hundred thousand dogs an hour?"

I've heard Richard speak down to Arnold in this way more than once. As I always try to do at work, I evaluate the situation economically before I respond.

Risking my tip with Richard may be balanced by a boosted tip from Arnold. Worth it.

"Oh Richard, I'm certain you've partaken in an all-American hot dog at Dodger's game. Just because it's $9.50 doesn't mean it's made from a less gruesome cocktail of animal parts." I wink back, and then shift my eyes toward Arnold's. "Is this that out of touch 'coastal elitism' everyone keeps talking about?" His eyes light up and a half-suppressed chuckle leaves his belly. I give him a reassuring grin as Richard spears the olive in his martini with a toothpick.

"Rich 'r poor, everyone loves a hot dog on a summer day." Oh, my sweet Arnold. Never deterred, never bitter. "You know, they use my machines for the vegetarian franks too."

"That makes sense. Same shape, different stuffing." We exchange smiles. Maybe this crazy world is going to be okay after all.

One more martini sip and Richard pays his tab. "See you soon," I wave as he turns to go. Still got a twenty-five percent tip. He's my most frequent regular. I wonder if he comes just to see me. Perhaps he sees a bit of himself in this scrappy young writer.

My opportunity has arrived. "So Arnold... Cam and I talked at Klipspringer's until closing on Saturday. Is he..." I pause to think of exactly what I want to say. *Dangerous* is the word I want to use, but that would be foolish to ask someone he considers a friend.

Arnold comes to my rescue. "I gotta tell ya, I talked to him yesterday and he is *smitten* with you. His words. I don't know what you two talked about the other night, but he is very taken by you."

I blush and look down to hide a devious grin. "He's a very interesting man. How long have you known him?"

"An' smart as all hell. Coupl'a years now."

I hear him relaxing into his accent now that Richard has gone. It reminds me of an ex of mine– a real bastard, but had an accent that would make any girl's skirt flutter.

"He called me yesterday. He's asked me to spend more time with him. I'm just wondering what I'd be getting myself into. He seems like a real... character."

"Character, yep– that he is. He's one of them 'larger than life' sort of folks. People either love him or hate him– he forces you to draw that line. I've gone out with him many times, and I must say... sometimes he can be quite... *confrontational*. Especially with females. It can be hard to watch, embarrassing even. 'Specially around here. Folks don't really have a tolerance for that sort of behavior aroun' here."

I nod and wipe some old foam from the beer tap. I imagine Cam talking the way he did at Klipspringer's in any other place in Mount Mirage, or anywhere on Earth for that matter. It would be both embarrassing and dangerous.

"Please don't mention that to him, he's a good friend. I like him a lot– he's a hilarious and loyal guy. Tremendously loyal guy."

"I understand. Can I get you another drink?"

"Just the check, thanks. My driver's almost here."

Thirty-three percent.

Tyler

Hey Nina, how are you doing?   6:24 PM

    6:58 PM
Call me back if you can, I have some news

    9:24 PM
Ok I'll just tell you– I got a summer fellowship in Alaska, I leave in a few days. I was hoping we could talk before I go...

Tuesday, July 1

> I understand if you need space. I just thought you'd think the project I'll be working on is really interesting. And I'll be stationed out in the wilderness! I think you'd be proud of me…

12:24 AM

> Good luck and good riddance. I've already sent word to the bears to eat your snacks and piss in all your socks.

2:08 AM

He calls another time and I swiftly hit the red button. God damn, I wish I still lived in the days when you could slam a phone down on a receiver and make that piercing "click" on the other end of the line.

~

I didn't sleep all night. A cruel, insecure brain was projecting a series of short films on the back of my eyelids. Titles included, *Tyler Traverses Iconic Wilderness While Nina Spills Full Bottle of Cabernet in the Wine Fridge– Rich Boy Enjoys Organic Brews While Fool in Slut Skirt Maxes Out Credit Card* – and the Academy's frontrunner: *Tyler Falls in Love with Gorgeous Environmental Scientist, Nina Dies Alone: An Endless Loop.*

I am haunted by relentless images of Tyler camping beside babbling brooks and strumming his guitar beside campfires; sharing beautiful moments with other people, other women…

A voice appears out of the ether of my gray matter. "Why do you think you need a *man* to take you into the wilderness, anyway?" Felicia growls.

"'Cause she *does,*" retorts Debbie in her Southern Belle drawl. "Ever hear of mountain *lines,* an' cougars? Heavy things to lift? Scary *huntuhs–* with GUNS?"

These two bickering alpha-bitches have been residing in my head for as long as I can remember, each with their own radically different ideas about how women– or rather, me specifically– should behave. Felicia is an indomitable third-wave feminist with tats on her stunningly developed biceps and a unilateral wardrobe of activist slogan t-shirts. Debbie is a cautious and moralistic debutant with big hair and infallibly elegant taste. They don't get along.

"I say you march your ass to the outdoor store right now, buy some camping gear and go out there yourself. Who's stopping you, other than your patriarchal conditioning that you must be escorted everywhere by someone with a prick?"

"What about her finances? Surely you have more responsible things to spend your money on… like a haircut, or some half-decent undergarments, perhaps?" Debbie shakes her head in quiet disappointment at the period-stained panties I am slipping on. "Then again, spending time in the outdoors may help your courting prospects. I imagine many a handsome *may-an* is out there, and Lord knows you don't have any time to waste! In just'a few months you'll be turning thirt–"

"Don't you *dare*!" Felicia looks ready to put Debbie into a headlock. "This is about you, and your empowerment to enjoy nature on your own terms– *on your own*!"

I turn on some music to drown them out, quickly dress in my 'less-than-half-decent' thrift store clothes, and head to the outdoor store. The decision has been made. I've got the next two nights off from Vero's and the Earth Defenders newsletter isn't due until Friday.

I sit outside the store in my car and jot down a list of the absolute essentials, because I know the guys in there are going to insist that another five hundred bucks worth of gear is also essential.

-TENT -SLEEPING BAG -SLEEPING PAD
-CAMP STOVE -PROPANE -FIRE STARTER
-HEADLAMP/ LANTERN -COOLER -??

At the cashier I look away and shut my eyes tightly, the same way one does right before getting blood drawn. I don't want to know; just put it on my tab. I'll pay it off when my film hits the box office, or when some distant relative calls and says they've hit the Pick-Six lotto.

I load up my car with the backpack Tyler's mother gave me last Christmas, the cooler stuffed with the contents of my fridge, and my new gear. I drive out of town to Cliffside Highway 84 out of Mount Mirage, toward the mountains.

I put on a CD– yes, a CD; the compact disc is not yet extinct, though mostly scratched– in my 21-year old RAV4. *The Very Best of Yes.* I crank it up and roll down the windows. *Yes, YES, I am doing it!*

I searched online this morning and found a first-come, first-served campsite about 30 miles away. I figure it's early enough to claim a decent spot and still have time for a hike. I only get through four songs on the windy road up the pass before I drive over a pile of landslide rubble with one fatefully sharp stone.

I make it to a dusty pull-off, adrenaline pumping and tears welling up in my eyes. I force them back in– I can almost taste the salt in my mouth– and try to calm myself down. I let the stereo play "Owner of a Lonely Heart," which is irritatingly upbeat and I sit there, afraid to look at my phone to see that I have no reception. My phone buzzes; guess I can call myself lucky. It's my boss.

I don't answer. There's only one reason why he's calling me, and if I ask him for help, I'm working tonight. Who else can I call? I scroll through my contacts list:

"Haven't spoken to her since college–

"Lives on the other side of the country–

"Tyler's friend–

"'Katie from Bathroom'? I don't even know who the hell they are–

"Dad–

"Tyler's friend–

"Dean, HAH! –

"Tyler's friend–

"Tyler's weird aunt–

"Tyler's friend–

"*Crap.*"

I heave a defeated sigh. It's clear what I have to do.

I swallow my stomach and dial. He answers.

"Miss Distrella."

"Mister Shaft."

"I was hoping you'd return my call today. How are you spending this lovely morning?"

"Funny you should ask... I find myself in a bit of a pickle."

"Damsel in distress, eh?" I can feel him beaming through the phone. "Perhaps I can be of assistance?"

Should I just hang up? Perhaps I can fashion my car into some kind of permanent outpost and sell hand-carved rocks to tourists from the side of the highway.

"...My tire is flat. I'm on Cliffside 84, about ten miles out of town."

"I'll be there in twenty minutes."

The giant white pickup appears behind me precisely eighteen minutes later.

I have taken out the jack to give the impression of effort. I attempted to watch a "Change a Tire" Youtube video, but it wouldn't load. I know my Dad has taught me the steps, but my brain has deleted the file to make room for other things, like the theme song from *Full House*.

He pulls some tools out of his truck, takes off my tire and starts flicking pieces of gravel out of it with a sharp metal pick. After no sign of the hole he pulls an electric pump out of nowhere and starts filling it with air to expose the leak. "These are round patches– they're better than the strip ones." He has both kinds. As he goes through the process of patching the tire he explains each step in a condescending play to make me feel included. I'm in my hiking clothes, so I at least look the part. After he mounts the repaired tire we start screwing the five nuts on. I'm trying not to make eye contact.

"Nice lez outfit. Going to a pussy march somewhere?"

"Going to a witch coven in the mountains, actually. I offered to bring a right-wing chauvinist to burn at the stake, and you've fallen right into my trap."

"I'm not surprised this tire punctured, it's completely bald. You need to replace this ASAP."

"Oh yeah, I'll get right on that. Let me just go prune my money tree..."

"I know a guy in town who may have a used one, cheap. Now get into the car and hit the brakes." I do it. "Thought so. Your rear light isn't the right one. I'll order you the right one."

I feel a lump in my stomach. *Why is he doing this?*

"Why are you doing this?"

"Because you called me. Nice to have men in the world, isn't it?"

I roll my eyes.

"And honestly, it is *insanely* easy for me to do this. And I like you, Nina."

4
Meat Loaf

VILLAIN NOTES

Observations, Notions, Ideas

IDENTITY: White, Western, cis, straight, able-bodied, middle-aged, wealthy, American, Christian?, Gen X, male. (Assuming Christian— find out.)

PHYSICAL DESCRIPTION: Tall, attractive, groomed, well-dressed. Physically powerful but slightly overweight around the middle.

PERSONALITY PROFILE:

-AMBITIOUS.

Driven by bitter resentment and anger, sourced from the outrageous delusion that he is undervalued and vilified by a society that views him as "inherently oppressive and irredeemable simply by virtue of immutable characteristics".

Furious to be stuck in Mount Mirage. Hates California in general.

Seeking to regain power from a life-shattering "Betrayal", which has stripped him of much of his wealth and social standing. Primary goal is to retake his company, which was lost in a hostile takeover. He has been following the company for several years, working toward an opportunity to recapture it.

Considers himself an underdog despite immense inherited (and therefore undeserved) power, through his status on the American social hierarchy as a cis straight white man, born to upper class parents.

-SHALLOW.

Spray tanned, manicured, dyes his hair. Very concerned with appearance, cleanliness, orderliness, fitness, aesthetics. Socially pressured to keep up with other elites in Palmetto/Mirage society. Enjoys and appreciates quality and excellence, almost obsessively.

-BIGOT.

Perceives his way of thinking and doing as superior; credits capitalism and Western culture as the primary source of liberty, prosperity, and innovation in human history. Believes Western thought and civilization have been proven superior by history and fears the growing presence of other cultures in the West.

Sees globalist politics and multiculturalism as weaknesses that erode, fracture, and decay communities rather than strengthen society.

Perceives himself as justified in his privilege; as embodying the so-called "virtue" of masculinity, intelligence, individuality, self-reliance, and strength of character.

Perceives everyone beneath him on the hierarchies of status and power as weak, flawed, broken, and deserving of their place in society. Believes in the "virtues" of free markets and meritocracy, but is concerned that they are being actively dismantled in the west by "falsely moralistic identity politics."

-SEXIST.

Narrow and regressive views of sexual identity and gender roles. Obsessed with "biology"; believes men and women are fundamentally different, down to their DNA, and it is the natural order for the world to be ruled by men simply by virtue of women having to bear and rear children.

Particularly resentful of feminism, which he views as a toxic movement that has been a net failure for both men and women, and provides women with "endless opportunities to weaponize their own frailty against men for crass personal gain."

Often jokes bitterly about feminists, calling them "feminazis." Also hates male feminists, queer women, trans women, ugly women, powerful women, rich women, rich mothers, overbearing mothers...

Believes "feminists don't want genuine equality", but instead want to "cherry-pick the benefits of both manhood and womanhood for themselves."

Especially resentful of any of the above in academia or the corporate media.

Blames social decay, crime, and the mental health crisis on feminism and something he calls the "fatherlessness epidemic." Believes the "divorce-custody industrial complex" is rigged against men to steal their wealth and separate fathers from their children.

Believes that the fight against the patriarchy is actually a projection; that we actually live under a "passive-aggressive tyrannical matriarchy made up of miserable upper class liberal white women, and whomever they feel like using as props to their performative empathy".

Disgusted by men who aren't "manly" enough by his standards. Believes American society is becoming "feminized" and therefore "weaker, less rational, more dependent on the state, and increasingly dysfunctional". Goes back and forth between hating and pitying young men who are being raised by "bitter misandrist women."

Resents the young generation as a whole, which he perceives as embodying "feminized fragility", self-victimhood, false moral posturing and hypocritical mindless consumerism, "as they tout their 'save the planet' platitudes".

-INTELLECTUAL.
Since childhood, intelligence has been funneled into rage by boredom. Frustrated by his spoiled and self-righteous peers; disillusioned by the surrounding community of ultra-rich people who have no desires, no drive, no needs unmet.

Extremely well-read. Can quote whole paragraphs of the U.S. Constitution and historical political speeches. Describes complex physics concepts in great detail, as they relate to mechanics or his work in fossil fuels. History buff, of course.

-FATHERLESS.
Born in 1970. Grew up in southern California, born to rich parents: a self-made father, and an "old money" mother. Parents divorced when he was in elementary school. His mother moved to her parents' estate in Palmetto. He stayed behind with his father for one year; a retired airman and commercial pilot— so he was often left home alone. Relishes those memories: raided his father's closet and wore

his military and pilot uniforms, read his books, looked through his boxes of memories from the war. After that year with his father, was placed in a Palmetto boarding school and got into trouble often. Only saw his father once since.

Left home as a teen and supported himself by working at an auto shop, Black Knuckle Motors, where he discovered his adoration for the combustion engine.

Often references a man named George Peterson or "Big G," his boss at Black Knuckle. Big G was his first (and perhaps only) male role model; someone he deeply admires.

Spent his late teens and early twenties immersed in southern California's motorhead culture in the early 1990s. Loves other car people, bikers, "tough guys", men who speak the language of motors and machines.

Joined a car club and went from drag racing down LA back streets and running from police to working on elite cars and racing on the Irwindale — eventually went to college and became an engineer. Worked in the oil and gas industry until he founded his own company, Kantian Consulting Co.

Lifelong desire to prove himself.

-MOTHERLESS.

Deep issues with his mother, who he describes as neurotic, manipulative, and self-pitying. She was bitter at his father for leaving, and indulgently disparaged him to her son. He felt his mother's resentment toward his physical resemblance to his father; she was dismissive and emotionally neglectful. She spent his childhood at resorts and country clubs between terrible bouts of manic depression, in which she would not leave her bed— a condition he believes to be fake, "like most mental health diagnoses". She has never held a job; lives off of family inheritance and alimony. He sees his mother as embodying the essence of the overprivileged, self-aggrandizing female victim.

-BOOTSTRAPPER.
Lack of familial support system made him develop a strong, obsessive work ethic. His fierce independence compounds his indignation at both his own community— the wealthy do-nothings of the world— as well as the "self-victimizing" poor who rely on the welfare system, who he perceives as "leeches of society". Believes "faux-compassionate" elites are the ones keeping the poor down by providing entitlements to them, rendering them "useless, corruptible, and without purpose."

-LOST.
Not properly socialized; raised by nannies and groundskeepers, was often disciplined in school after outbursts of frustration and anger. No intimate long-term friends; a long string of short-term relationships that ended poorly, a few romantic betrayals, but hesitant to discuss.

One half-sister who he never liked, as she is one of the jobless self-victimizing elites he always despised.

A sensitive man hidden under a hardened exterior. Ego bruises easily.

-ALIENATED.
Misguided charisma and unbridled sense of humor toward the offensive; masculine "garage humor," in which everyone is fair game for teasing and witty insults, which is unacceptable in current West Coast culture. His refusal to self-police his language has caused him

to alienate himself in many ways, which only feeds his indignation and frustration with the world.

-LOYAL.
Seems to be obsessed with the idea of serving those who he deems worthy of his loyalty. Even if the energy is misguided, it seems that he finds satisfaction in life from being of service— which, again, explains anger and bitterness in a world that does not recognize his service to it.

A QUESTION:
Are the garages of this country filled with angry men like this, who hover around combustion engines— smoking metal heaps of hundreds of parts, tremendous, dangerous, stinky, oily, biting machines of velocity— and curse a world that has suddenly rejected them?

Have we accidentally backed them into a corner to a point where it unifies them and justifies their rage?

A NOTE:
Subject has been inspiring hours of research, questioning, and evaluation of my own beliefs and convictions. He is challenging me. It has been keeping me awake at night. In some strange way, it is making me feel alive.

Yet I still know he is dangerous, not only for my reputation in this small town, but maybe in all senses of the word. Don't forget to keep your walls UP. Don't get too personal and don't share too much.

~

Got off track last night. I arrived home from Cam's garage around three in the morning. I snuck into my place with slow, painfully delicate movements to avoid explaining to my roommates where I had been so late in a town that shuts down at 9:15. I felt my way to the bedroom; the summer swelter nearly knocked me backward when I opened the cube's groaning door. The cracked hopper window had done nothing to cool my tiny bedroom, but it's either be kept awake by the formation of my own sweat, or by my nostrils' complaints about the smell of my roommate's litter box. I closed the door behind me, swept half of an unruly pile of clothes and papers off my bed, stripped down, and lay quietly on top of the rest.

My mind was racing back over Cam's every word, his bed and his precious objects, what he was wearing, the desirous looks he had given me. I was too tired to write it all down, but my mind insistently pored over it all one more time, to lock in the memory until tomorrow. We didn't sleep together, if that's what you're assuming. But it did get... personal.

Starting at the beginning. Since the night at Klipspringer's, Cam has become a nebulous presence, always hovering near the top of my text messages and recent calls. We have seen each other on multiple occasions, and each time I rush home to my laptop and try to write down everything I can remember. The strangest and most confounding part of all this is how often we talk on the phone. He calls me almost every day... *just to talk*.

Let me explain something. Nobody calls anybody "just to talk" anymore, except maybe your mom. Especially not men you meet in bars. After sensing his romantic interest in me, and Arnold's confirmation, I have attempted the allure of aloofness: I keep busy at work when he stops by to see me, and I respond sparingly to his insane meme text messages. (In case this online trend goes out of fashion, though I can't imagine it will, I'll explain: a meme is just a picture with words on it that circles its way around the internet. Pretty momentous, isn't it? The Boomers invented the World Wide Web and the birth control pill, and we invented a picture with words on it. That, and eating Tide Pods.) I received a barrage of three or four horrible memes in a row the other day. One of them was just a smiling '50s-looking guy in a suit that said, "*Of course I am a feminist—These gals need strong male leadership!*" I am secure enough to admit that I laughed aloud at the sick irony. The only thing I could think to respond was, "I see your copy of *Misogynist Quarterly* came in the mail?"

But the phone calls. I don't know why but I can't help but answer them. I even get excited when I see the name I've fondly given him, "Mr. Shaft," appear on my vibrating screen; a little rush of adrenaline and curiosity. He often opens with some angry anecdote about a negative social interaction, which leads to a philosophical or political rant of some kind, and as I listen carefully, the image of my villain gains another layer. I have also learned that when he speaks, it's best not to interrupt him, or to disagree, or share some relevant statistic that cuts his argument, or to point out a contradiction. He has very little tolerance for dissidence or interruption; he's even hung up on me once or twice. So I listen attentively and giggle at his jokes, suppressing my desire to correct him or chide him when he crosses the line from cynical to hateful, all in the name of literary research. It's really no different than working in food service: degrade me, mock me, horrify me, as long as you give me my twenty percent.

He's come into Vero's a few times now and I'm worried my coworkers are starting to notice. One night he showed up for a drink before an '80s tribute rock concert in magenta zebra-striped velvet pants and a black leather jacket.

"You look…"

"Bitchin'? Choice? Like I *kickstart your heaaaart?*"

Oh boy, here comes the air-guitar.

"I was going to say 'ridiculous'. But I respect your moxie, Mr. Shaft."

"For the tenth time it's Benzin, not Shaft– though if I ever get into porn–"

"Oh, based on that outfit I assumed you already had."

"You're just jealous that you didn't live during the greatest musical decade of all time."

"Maybe a little. But I was fortunate to have spent my childhood listening to all the hits without having to endure a single day of the Reagan presidency."

"Don't get me started on our last decent president– aside from our current one, of course– I will lecture you into a hole. Come here, can you fix my collar?"

As I came around from behind the bar and folded over the softened cow skin I recognized the blatancy of what I was doing, and why he had asked me to do it. I scurried back behind the bar and buried my head in cocktail orders.

On Thursday evening he came by unannounced and sat in the seat right next to my roommates. *DEAR GOD.*

They struck up a conversation and my skin began to crawl down my shirt and toward my shoes as he made them blush and giggle. But I knew Cam couldn't help himself. It only took a few more moments until he made one bad joke, and the girls darkened and proceeded to shun his presence entirely.

"Typical." He shrugged. "I have your new rear bulb. And I found a tire for you too, you just have to go by my friend's shop to pick it up." He went to, he claims, "five auto shops" to find it.

So I had to meet him yesterday to get said bulb. He gave me an address in that part of town with all the seedy old warehouses and garages that are all slowly morphing into hipster watering holes. The Bushwick of Mount Mirage, if you will.

He has a double garage slot with a dwelling on one side and a car lift on the other. The place is out of a movie. It is his soul thrown at the walls, every single crevice bursting with him. A shiny black muscle car hangs securely from the ceiling on a mechanized lift. (I have no clue what year it's from, or what it's called, but it looks fast— and expensive.) World War II and Vietnam War relics, model planes, a Harley something-something motorcycle (again, lost on me), an enormous safe with George Washington's face on it. He turned the spoked bank-vault handle and opened it— a rack of guns, boxes of bullets, cash, photos, a dog collar and leash, a shoebox sealed with a die-cut sticker of a slice of cherry pie. He pulls out a stack of papers, addressed to Michael Bauer. *Cam's father.* He closes the door.

"Did you know that George Washington was one of the oldest signers of the Declaration of Independence? He was 44; the same age I was when I got my first multi-million dollar contract with Kantian. Most of the Founding Fathers were in their twenties and thirties, believe it or not. We always think of them as these crusty old men, but they were young and passionate thinkers– full of life, eager to build something."

There's an entire wall of VHS tapes, cassette tapes, and CDs, including many live recordings of concerts from the '80s and '90s: a micro museum of twentieth-century entertainment. A bed with black sheets, a projector screen on the wall and one of those clear plastic sets of drawers from every freshman dorm, full of balled bright white socks and neatly folded black boxers. A crowded clothing rack forms a sort of door to his "bedroom," full of uniforms, costumes, and jackets. He caught me staring at it. "I never throw out my Halloween costumes."

The far corner is occupied by a shrine to a dalmatian named Troy. Photos of him with the classic dopey dog-smile and several photos of him taking a shit. "He died about six years ago." Cam appeared behind me and stared at the shrine, touched the old metal tag hanging from the top of it. "Had to move out of my place after he died. I just couldn't go back to it empty."

We replaced the bulb. I tried to participate as much as I could, but it was a one-man job, other than testing the light at the end. Upon glancing at the interior of my car, Cam shook his head at me. "Nina, this is *gross*. Completely unacceptable. We're going to clean this right now. Didn't you say you and your boyfriend just broke up?"

"Yeah, so what?"

"So no respectable man would let his girl drive around with a car this dirty."

"Well, he wasn't exactly a *man*, by your standards anyway."

"I'd bet my life he either drives a Prius or a Subaru."

I chose not to respond.

"Ah, you see? You don't need a boyfriend, you need a *man*friend. I'll be your manfriend."

Going to pretend I didn't hear that. "I've just been on a budget..."

"Baby, we need to clean this car."

"*Do not* call me baby."

He laughed. "I knew you'd say that."

51

We took the car to be washed at one of those self-serve places around the corner. I was not prepared, in a sundress and old canvas shoes that could have used a bath too. He went for it without speaking; I stood aside and watched. He worked meticulously, washing and drying every crevice like he worked there for tips. I was lost in thought watching him. I kept picturing my brother George washing the caravan of cars in the driveway when my sisters and I were teenagers. *What is this? What are we doing? What am I doing?*

Back at the garage we dumped everything out of the car. He vacuumed out the stratified layers of sand, dirt, french fries and dog hair (I sometimes walk dogs for a few extra bucks on the side), and I hastily disposed of the old protest signs in the trunk, placing them face-down into the dumpster so he wouldn't see the Earth Defenders' slogans. He wiped dust and cobwebs off the dash and scrubbed coffee grime out of the cup holders. I did not realize how bad the car really was, especially once I saw it clean. I guess I've never paid attention to it. When I lived at home, Dad and George cleaned the cars on Sunday mornings. I'll admit I was quite embarrassed— and I don't embarrass easily anymore.

"Please don't judge me," I tried to laugh it off and appear unaffected. The car looked incredible when we were done, like it had shed ten years of age. "Thank you," I said, eyes cast down. He leaned across the center console and gave me a modest kiss.

It was a hot afternoon, the sun bright and angry in the sky. The job made us both glisten with sweat. "Listen, I have to run an errand for a friend. But would you like to meet me back here later? I want to show you my meatloaf tape."

"*Excuse me?*" He was tickled by my wincing face, a misunderstanding that 'meatloaf' was some sort of gross euphemism.

"The musician, snowflake— Meat Loaf. I have a videotape of *Bat Out of Hell* live from his 1992 tour. I know how much you like him."

He was a good listener. I had that album playing in the background when I answered one of his phone calls. "I just think he's so cute: he's got the badass album cover with the motorcycle and hellish gargoyle and everything... but what a softie. Those ballads are poetry, pure poetry."

"Don't go ruining Meat Loaf for me, please. Did you know he doesn't believe in climate change? I heard him on Billy Darling's show. Says that all you young people are brainwashed."

"*What?* Now who's ruining Meat Loaf for whom?"

"It's a timeless conundrum. Should we, or must we, separate the art from the artist. You would be shocked and disturbed if you knew the kind of deviant behavior that goes on in elite circles. But if a celebrity makes one comment out of line with the Far-Left's political agenda- *Poof!* Canceled, exiled..."

I placed the back of my hand to my forehead. "Those poor celebrities, the little dears! Exiled to the depths of Palmetto's lush gardens with their millions of dollars!"

"Point taken, Miss. Amen. Meet me back here at 8."

We separated for dinner. He had a bacon-wrapped steak at Klipspringer's, I had a strong cup of black coffee and a slice of vegan banana pie at Mallory Café, my typical writing place. It's my favorite spot to work in town: the wi-fi is decent and it's the only place where a cup of coffee costs less than four bucks. (The vegan pie is eight a slice, but it's worth it.) Mallory sits in the heart of downtown on the corner of Cicero and Main; I sit by a big window beside the sidewalk. The foot traffic and noise that spills into the place reminds me of home, of wandering around the boatyard next to Dad's shop in New York, and it settles me.

Before spending time with Cam, I could come here and focus on my work for hours. But this time, I couldn't help but be distracted by the other patrons. Mallory serves organic vegetarian food, which means Cam and his type of person would never step foot inside. I looked around at the sorts of people this establishment attracts: rich hippies fresh off of a full day of surfing with crusty golden skin and greasy blonde hair, old ladies in pastel Lucille Bluth blazers complaining loudly about the quality of the salmon salad they ordered. Thirty-something tech yuppies speaking in gentle whispers to their unruly children, who are flinging tofu nuggets across the table, while their doodle dog in a "SUPPORT PLANNED PARENTHOOD" bandana paces under the table, sniffing the nuggets and choosing not to eat them. A pale woman with half of her head shaved openly breastfeeding her four-year-old boy while she watches videos on her phone.

I tried to gather my thoughts about Cam, about his George Washington safe and the VHS tapes and the wartime collectibles. The dog shrine was surprising. I would have assumed Cam was one of those people who wouldn't go near an animal for fear of getting fur on his designer jacket.

The costumes, that was a strange one. The Halloween excuse is clearly bull. Could it be a fetish thing? My junior year of college, upon moving all my belongings into an apartment down in Sand Dollar, I discovered a forgotten drawer of BDSM fetish costumes in what was to be my closet. A black pleather jumpsuit, a riding crop, a red and white plastic nurse suit with red rubber gloves. My new roommate, a very respectable-looking pediatrician who was working to set up a charitable clinic in the city, claimed "Oh, it must have been left behind by my last roommate– but if you want to keep them, I bet you're the right size… Why don't you try them on?" A housing arrangement that lasted less than 48 hours. Lesson learned: a building with a gym and an indoor pool always has a hidden price.

I sipped coffee and pored over my notes from the day before. *An idea! What if my blonde heroine runs into the villain at some point in the second act, and they sort of hit it off, and she doesn't realize who he is until Act III when they're taking him down? What if they have a sort of spark, a little crush on each other that makes the story a bit more interesting?* I took some furious notes, deep in the world of my story, until a gentle touch to my shoulder made me jump out of my seat. I covered the notebook with the urgency of a preteen hiding her diary from her mom.

"I didn't mean to frighten you! Did I interrupt a flow state? You had the most wily little smile going."

"Oh, hi Paula– no, nothing's flowing, whatever that means. Just brainstorming an idea for something. How are you?"

I met Paula a couple years ago at Mallory Café. I was asking the guy behind the counter if the coconut pie was vegan, and she tapped my shoulder as I started off with my plate. I turned abruptly, my expensive slice of pie flopping over onto its side. I had seen her face before, but up close it was weather-aged and beautiful, framed by curly, graying chocolate hair. Her lips were dry but kind; they formed a smile, amused by my jumpiness.

"*Whoops*– didn't mean to startle you. I just think I know you… Did you attend the City Council meeting about the proposed composting program?"

I lit up instantly. "Yes, that was me! I shared a comment about setting up compost collection bins at the farmer's market."

"It was a great idea, and you were so passionate in your little speech. Thank you for doing that."

I blushed. I knew exactly who she was, and in my world, she is a legend. She sells homemade goods and produce from her garden at the farmer's market and writes editorials for the paper about standing up against consumerism. "I still can't believe the measure didn't pass. I was the one who had written the original proposal."

"I was disappointed, but not entirely surprised. Paula, right? You're everywhere! You do great work. I reference your low-waste website all the time. The household cleaner recipes are great."

"Thank you, I'm glad you find it useful. Would you like to join me? I only have a half hour but I'd love to hear about what you are working on."

This first chat with Paula was the first organically friendly conversation I had had with a woman in longer than I could remember. The only women I'd interacted with since moving to Mount Mirage were from work– like Camilla, and you saw how that worked out. (In my experience, most of the friends you make while working in the service industry are a bad influence.)

At the start of my relationship with Tyler I spent many evenings with his friends and their girlfriends. The boys knew each other from elementary school; men have an uncanny and enviable ability to maintain lifelong friend groups. They would turn 'the game' on the TV, or set themselves up with some intense empire-building board game, and we girls would be left to ourselves. The girlfriends were beautiful with shiny hair and manicured nails; they wore expensive workout clothes and drank white wine. In conversation they would go frighteningly intimate right away, discussing issues in their relationships while their partners were mere feet away, and recounting intense childhood traumas. They would give long hugs and take turns telling one another how strong, brave, and capable the other was. I would swing between trying too hard and not trying at all, always unsure of myself, always keenly aware that I was not one of them, and always distracted by the question of what exactly it was that made me different from them.

For a while I was obsessed with the idea of it, being part of a tight-knit friend group like the cast of *Friends,* bursting into the coffee shop with some drama– participating, belonging, being known. But I have never come close. Pathetic as it sounds, I feel closer to the characters on the early-2000s shows I binge on repeat than to most real human beings.

But speaking to Paula was like a breath of fresh air. She was old enough to be my grandmother, but had the youthful air of someone who loves her life. As we spoke I took out a notebook to scribble down the names of books she recommended to read, people to follow online, documentaries to watch. Our passion for simplicity in lifestyle as a means of social rebellion created a sense of understanding between us, a commonality based in ethics and virtue. The only difference was that she was really living it, and I was only a poser. The afternoon disappeared in our conversation. She missed her appointment but she laughed it off.

"Paula, can I just say how fun this has been? The only other people I know who care about this stuff are strangers on the internet. It can be isolating."

"I'm glad you mentioned that. Next week I am hosting a dinner at my place with some like-minded women; it's a new tradition I'm trying out. I would love for you to join us."

"That would be so amazing, thank you! I'm happy to bring something or help you set up– just name the place and I'll be there."

We gathered around a large redwood table on a shaded stone patio behind Paula's garden. About fifteen women showed up with dishes meant to impress: sushi made with brined watermelon and papaya instead of fish, barbecue pulled-jackfruit sliders, a cashew cheese plate, beautiful cakes, cookies, chocolate truffles. I loaded up my plate like I was next in line for the electric chair.

We discussed the food we were eating, the agriculture industry in Mirage County, the politics of food and its impact on the environment. I sat next to an entrepreneur starting a shoe company with leather made out of pineapple skins. On my other side was Piper Hammick, Campaign Director at the Mount Mirage Earth Defenders.

Paula tapped her glass and stood. "Everyone, thank you so much for being here tonight. Hearing your stories has been a delight, and the food you all brought was remarkable. Please be sure to bring the leftovers home with you.

"This is the first dinner I've hosted exclusively with women in the environmental conservation space. No matter your reasons for being here, we all know the social challenges that can come with a more conscious lifestyle. But together we can do more than enjoy the comforts of food and companionship… we also have the opportunity to work together to create positive change in our community."

We started meeting once a month, then twice a month. We had thrilling discussions and exchanged useful information. Word spread and more women joined. Then there were dinners out, film screenings, and birthday parties. We formed a local action committee. We asked restaurants to add plant-based options to their menus. We wrote letters of protest to the City Council. We attended climate marches and guest lectures at Mirage University.

It's not that I liked all those women. Many of them were rich entitled Mount Mirage housewives, and only some were vegan. I had nothing in common with most of them, but this one thing brought us together. It made us sisters, this unifying choice that isolated us from the rest of the world; this commonality of compassion; this consciousness about the connection of our choices to the greater world around us. After years of building walls around myself, I felt at home with them.

But group dinners cost money. Time costs money. I need time to write, and I need cash to pay my bills. I slowly stopped responding to email threads and RSVPS for gatherings. At first they sent a few concerned emails and a few who were closer would stop by Vero's while I was working. But pretty quickly they stopped coming and stopped asking. They probably think I've rejected them. And I can't explain myself. I don't know how to describe what I am doing without sounding crazy.

Now that I've met Cam and have really dug into my movie, I have needed space from sisterhood. I realized it the other night: it's not just about Cam. It's about getting inside the heads of all these men whose time is up; who are whining and railing against being given a taste of their own medicine. I need to immerse myself in this world in a pure form: no distractions, no alternative modes of thought or being for a while.

"I won't keep you– get back into your flow! Maybe I'll see you at Friday's dinner? It's been a while."

"Yes, I know. Just been really busy. But I'll come Friday– unless I am still working on the Earth Defenders newsletter." *Shit, I forgot about that.*

"I hope you applied for that job, by the way."

"What job?" My ears got instantly hot. *Job? Money? Pay for hours worked? Job??*

"I thought Piper would have called you. The Earth Defenders are looking for an oceans correspondent, someone to report on events and issues with our local fishery, and the marine environment as a whole. They posted the job on Facebook last week. Sounds right up your alley…"

OF COURSE they didn't tell me about it! Damn me for not being on Facebook! The opportunities I must miss! The events and groups! The cute puppy videos!

"Wow– thank you *so much* for telling me! I didn't know. I am going to apply right now."

"Excellent! See you Friday."

Since the internet was invented you've never seen a person so focused. I filled out the tedious online application with all the information in my resume, and then after meticulously updating it, which I do exhaustively for every single job I apply for, I uploaded my resume. The next page asked for three references. One, Paula; two, one of my roommates, who I will pay to lie and say she was a former manager; and three? Can't tell my boss at Vero's I am job hunting. I can safely say no former zoo colleague will sing my praises. And Cam can't know that I'm involved with the Earth

Defenders, which is leading the charge against his former company, which he is on a mission to retake.

Tension over the power plant has really been heating up now that Kantian has officially filed a permit to convert the facility to nuclear power. "You want zero carbon emissions, we're trying to give you people zero *fucking* carbon emissions!"

In Cam's rants he still speaks as if he is CEO of the company. In my dedication to villain espionage I have foregone the MMED meetings and confined my contribution to the newsletter, which I still haven't started, but will need to spend extra time on so I can land this job. The third reference spot remained empty. Could Camilla pretend to be my boss at Vero's? She would almost certainly screw it up somehow. I futilely scrolled through my phone's contact list.

"Oh for Christ's *SAKE*."

I let the phone ring once before I hung up. Screw it. I don't need his help. He's probably been eaten by a grizzly somewhere in the tundra by now...

Yeah, *right*. Tyler lives a charmed life. I'm sure he's journaling in some candlelit yurt beside the Yukon River.

I found a website where you can register a fake phone number through an email address. I'll put on a phony accent or some deep voice and be my own damn reference.

I gave the full application a once-over, closed my eyes and said a prayer to no one—

Please-please-please— let this be the one. I have so much to give. Please just let me give my efforts to something worthwhile. Please. I tingled all over at the sharp little *click* sound as I pressed the submit button.

I can't even tell you how many 'submit' buttons I have clicked in the last... *Jesus*... I guess it's about eight years now since graduation. Hundreds. Thousands, maybe. I have been rejected by every discipline in the natural sciences, and for hundreds of roles within: lab assistant, research assistant, curator, campaign coordinator, outreach, marketing, education. I've always fallen back on the work I truthfully prefer, animal care, but at a steep cost. The most you'll find for such work is a buck or two above minimum wage, and the lowest is no pay at all, and you have to buy your own muck boots. I've worked at zoos, aquariums, farms, and pet shelters– while also working as a waitress, clerk, delivery driver, dog walker, and bartender. No one ever hesitates to take advantage of a young person's passion. But I like the work. It's stinky, hard on the body; lots of lifting and raking, scooping, chopping and sweating– but it's got its rewards. So I've always taken those animal jobs, knowing they'd go nowhere. Trouble is I never stay in a place long enough to move up. I get frustrated with management, or can't survive the pay any longer... or I let 28 tons of elephant on the loose out of pure spite. I guess I deserve everything I get. (Still don't regret it, though.)

I rejoined Cam back at his garage around 8:40. He looked pissed. "In war, if you're late, you're dead. Or worse, you've left your brothers to die." I couldn't help but find this funny, a war ethics lecture from a guy with manicured fingernails.

"I didn't realize those army uniforms you have are real." I gave him a phony salute. "Thank you for your service to our nation."

Dean *hated* guys like Cam, grown men who buy surplus gear, "play army," and act like they have any clue what real combat is like. "These guys watch *Saving Private Ryan* and play *Call of Duty* and suddenly they think they've seen a war." Few things got under Dean's skin, but that sure did. He'd spit on the ground. "Fucking *pussies*."

Cam did not correct my derisive gratitude. "Not all war is fought on battlefields, my dear. Shall we Meat Loaf?"

The bed in his garage had transformed into a couch. *Thank god.* Watching a film at night, alone, on his turf– I didn't think this through. *Expectations; expectations are afoot.* Knowing what I know about Cam so far, he will not take any kind of rejection well. Do I have enough material to construct a compellingly despicable villain? Not quite yet...

Crap.

I should have had booze for dinner, not coffee. "Make yourself at home," he said. As if he read my thoughts, he handed me a can, but to my dismay, it was sparkling water. I have managed in such circumstances before, for various expediences and necessities, but the secret to success is always alcohol. Alcohol loosens the body and dulls the brain. By my third or fourth drink, Deb and Felicia both recline on lounge chairs and say, "Let him go for it, who cares? We're all gonna die someday anyway."

The projector screen came down, the sweet Meat Loaf ballads began, and the conversation started flowing. He ranted, he cracked jokes; I listened, I laughed. We sang aloud and bobbed our heads and smiled at each other with the comradery of loving the same artist. I can't describe exactly how it happened, but over the course of *Bat Out of Hell* we became two girls at a sleepover, jumping on the couch cushions, using random objects as our microphones as we sang our guts out, nothing held back.

We were red-faced, uninhibited, sober, *happy*. Mister Masculinity had let his guard down, and it had happened completely organically. I didn't drug him or blackmail him, or hold my body hostage. We just... *bonded*.

This '80s karaoke bash distracted me from my predicament until the video ended, and the familiar sound of the VHS tape auto-rewinding settled us back onto the couch. And then we talked. And talked and talked and giggled and talked. It was pillow talk without the sex. It was a goddamn *slumber party*. It was past midnight.

I reached out and ran my hand over his stiff hair. I let my voice soften. "I wish you were always like this. Isn't it tiring to be so angry all of the time?"

"It's not me." He sat up, and I feared I just ruined the whole moment. "It's this fucking place. Not so much the place itself, but the people here. Now that you've been talking to me, you don't realize it but you're already waking up– you will start seeing it, and you won't be able to unsee it, and it will make you crazy too. Just you wait and see. They'll drive you crazy and you'll start fantasizing about where on this planet you can go to escape these insufferable people. Trust me."

I chuckled knowingly. "I already feel that way, but not about rich Californians per se, but human beings in general. Since I was a child I've fantasized about living under the sea, or in a jungle, like Tarzan, with a troop of go–"

"Do you mind if I set up the bed? I'm going to stay here tonight, I have an early meeting downtown tomorrow."

Here we go. My predicament had returned. But it was late, and it seemed quite simple just to leave at this point, without the risk of rejection.

"It's so late Cam, I'll just let you get to bed…"

"No, you can't!" There was a fleck of desperation in his voice. "I have Pink Floyd, *The Wall!* 1982! Just stay for the first few songs."

"…Alright…"

We were sitting up in his bed, still dead sober, listening to *The Wall.* "You seem tense," he said.

"Hah, do I? I guess a couch is one thing– but I haven't sat in a man's bed in a while." He scooted behind me and started rubbing my shoulders. "Wow, you are a wreck back here." His motions were painful bliss on my many knots and frozen muscles.

"A decade in manual labor will do that to a lady."

After a few delightful minutes, he paused. "Can… I have a turn?"

Oh boy, here we go. Why did I let him do that? I placed a quick bet in my head on whether he was going to be subtle or simply pull himself out of his pants.

"Actually, can you lay right here, facing me?"

"Uh, sure…"

He lay beside me and pulled me to him, not to kiss, but to wrap my arms around him, then his arms around me, and then he grabbed my leg and draped it over his waist, so we were woven tightly together. Despite my stiff uncertainty, his body relaxed; I half-worried he had fallen instantly asleep. And then he let out one big satisfied sigh, a sigh so grand and full of relief that I could almost swear I saw little ghosts fly out from his body as from the windows of a haunted house. And then he was out, snoring peacefully– and I just lay there, my neck cramping, wondering how I find myself in these situations.

MAMMALOGY LENDS INSIGHT TO GREAT WHITE GORILLA BEHAVIOR

Like our own species, the Western white gorilla is a mammal, which gives us some context into its behavior and social characteristics. Mammals share a few key traits, including an endothermic metabolism, meaning they must generate their own internal heat. This requires them to ingest large amounts of food at relatively frequent intervals. All mammals also have hair or fur. (Even dolphins and whales have some whiskers during the early stages of life.)

Though Australia hosts five outlier species of egg-laying monotremes, such as the platypus, the other 5,000-plus species of mammals are viviparous, giving birth to live young. Embryos grow and develop inside the wombs of females, nourished by placental tissue. There are several benefits to this method of reproduction as compared to egg-laying: carriage of offspring in the uterus means they are kept warm, protected, and portable. These are mechanisms for extensive parental care, which vastly improves an offspring's ability to survive. Mammalian females give birth to relatively few progeny, therefore the reproductive stakes are high. Intense emotional wiring to nurture and protect their young ensures the survival of the species. (Consider the ocean sunfish, by contrast, which may lay up to 300 million eggs over a single spawning season, and therefore can reproduce successfully without any parental effort.)

The word 'mammal' relates to the most essential and unique common feature all female members of this group share: the mammary gland. Once offspring are delivered and separated from the placenta, mothers must nourish their young with milk from their mammary glands, a particularly extensive and sophisticated form of parental care. There are many neural and hormonal mechanisms in place to foster mother-infant bonding, which have developed in complexity in the higher mammals, particularly in the large-brained and highly sensitive Great Apes. This wires mammals to seek social belonging and physical intimacy throughout their life cycle.

Despite the ubiquitous mammalian need for intimacy, affection, and social bonding, previous studies of great white gorillas have cited an absence of– or even a distaste for– this need. Some scientists have argued that a rejection of intimacy altogether is a prerequisite of white gorillas reaching alpha status.

Observations of the current subject of this study are defying previous understandings of this animal and its needs. It appears that GWGs may outwardly reject shows of intimacy to appear more formidable and to avoid vulnerability in front of other males, but they are not an exception to mammalian wiring. It is therefore necessary to increase the sample size and study additional individuals, particularly in this context, to test this hypothesis.

THE AGE OF THE MAMMALS

In terms of Big Time, we currently reside in the Cenozoic Era, which from its Greek roots means "the era of new animals." This era is commonly referred to as the Age of the Mammals, as mammals are the largest living animals, dominating many ecosystems as apex predators and filling a wide variety of biological niches. Mammals first appeared in the fossil record around 200 million years ago, but the Age of the Mammals didn't begin for another 135 million years. Early mammals were kept small and meager by the global dominance of the terrestrial dinosaurs.

An infamous asteroid, about seven miles wide, crashed into the Earth off the coast of Mexico 65 million years ago. The impact sent unfathomable volumes of debris into the air, created tidal waves that washed over the Americas, and created a massive cloud of soot and dust. Without sunlight, ancient plants perished, sending a shockwave of starvation throughout the global ecosystem.

More than half of all plant and animal species on Earth were wiped out from this chain of events. Large animals like the dinosaurs required too many calories and could not survive. The small and scrappy mammals were able to squeeze through this bottleneck and made it out the other side with fewer predators and more ecological space to fill. They could grow in size, variety, and inhabit new territories. An ecological tragedy for the dinosaurs created the conditions for mammalian flourishing.

It is a comforting feature of life on Earth, this resilience; this cosmic creativity consistently inspired by the transformation of living beings into forms that can sustain and perpetuate themselves through existential change and billions of years. The demise of the dinosaurs and the consequential rise of the mammals is not a unique circumstance. Their story contains the underpinnings of every living organism's story. Conditions change, a species fails to adapt; an ecological hole appears, and a different species fills it. Entropy does not form a line, but a web, as complex as the Universe itself. It waits for no one. And all must abide by the same set of rules and limitations. No exceptions.

Some scientists believe that the mass extinction event being triggered by the ecological domination of great white gorillas is ushering in the end of the Age of Mammals. Approximately 1 in 5 of all known mammal species are believed to be threatened or extinct. The primates, excluding humans, are among the most threatened.

It is possible that we are living through the final chapter of our own reign.

5
Behind the Rock

Six months ago

"It's just a little further, you're going to love it."

I followed him down, down into a rust-colored canyon laced with rambling weeds. They stretched high into the air, with thick red stems. The leaves looked like hands with fat pointed fingers, their veins and venules thin and red as blood. When they caught the sunlight they illuminated from stewed spinach to Saint Patrick's green.

"You know what? I'm not going any further. I'm still mad at you." I parked myself on a rock shaded by the green hands and crossed my arms.

"I know you are Moonie, but I said I was sorry. Besides, I don't think you're really that mad, or else you wouldn't have come this far."

"You locked me out of my own apartment, I don't have anywhere else to go."

He held my hand to escort me off my rock and down a steep narrow crevice.

"Don't you feel better now that you're out in the fresh air, away from your desk?"

"No Tyler, I don't. The emails are still coming. I didn't plug the leak by walking away."

After we emerged onto a sandy path, he stopped abruptly; I ran face-first into his backpack. He turned to face me. His eyes matched the cliffs– earthen, shades of stone and mud, and little specks of green things growing around the edges. He took my hands in his; they were stained with dirt from coming down the cliffs. The sight and feel of them excited me; I quickly caught myself and looked up to glare at him.

"Nina, I know it's hard to walk away from it. I know your work is important to you, and that right now it feels like every moment away from your computer is a lost opportunity to get published. But you need this."

I narrowed my glare. "What I *need* is to get more proposals sent out to editors. What I *need* is to be able to eat next month."

"You are a remarkably smart and ambitious person, you are going to figure something out. And if you don't, I will feed you– you know I make a killer eggplant sandwich. Now grab my arm as you step down, this way–"

We emerged from the walls of the canyon and paused beside a stream bed. Reeds hid it but I could hear it, smell it. To my left I heard a rustling sound; a coyote and her pups ambled out of the reeds. She grabbed one by the scruff of its neck and carried it as two more followed behind her. Tyler removed his backpack and looked back at me. "Pretty nice, huh?"

I was still bitter, but couldn't deny the obvious beauty, enhanced by its separation and secrecy. Camus Preserve is my favorite place in all of Mount Mirage, but I'd never been this deep inside it before. The preserve isn't far, just into the foothills outside of town, but nobody goes there. It's actually a difficult place to find: you have to park on a little patch of dirt on the side of the road, run across the highway, and trace a narrow path through the treeline before you hit the trail. The first time Tyler took me there, I thought he might be trying to murder me. The only other human being I've ever seen at Camus was a man who looked like Tyler forty years from now: part scientist, part mountain troll, part wizard.

He pulled me into his chest and took an animated deep breath. "Smell that fresh air. The only thing that matters is this." He touched my head.

"Don't! Your hands are dirty."

"Fine..." he reached down and took my ass into his hands.

"*Don't!*" I squirmed under his touch but I didn't push away. We both started to giggle like children and suddenly, like waking up from an immersive dream, I finally became present. He noticed the change and touched my cheek, and after a moment's stare from those earthy eyes, we kissed. His mouth was cold and tasted like the fresh air we breathed. Our movements were gentle and had a touch of innocence, like two high school lovers. We started to stroke each other and buttons started coming undone. My bare body stretched over a round, warm rock, arms wrapped over its smooth surface, cooing sweetly as he took me.

I glanced around the canyon; the wind tickled the reeds and a flight of swallows caught a riptide of air and swooped upward into the late afternoon sun. I closed my eyes. *We're just a pair of animals clinging to each other in the wilderness. Nothing has changed since the beginning of time and we have never left it; we are still a part of all of it. Everything else is secondary, manmade, illusory.*

I reached behind me to pull his head down closer to mine. His body bent over me and I twisted around to meet his lips.

~

I stood pantsless in a patch of sand next to the creek and swore when the warm urine stream slowed and diverted onto my leg. "*Shit.* I'm the worst at this. TYLER! *Don't look at me!*"

Tyler chuckled and watched me from his spot a few yards away. He went over to his backpack and pulled out a towel, hand sanitizer, a metal bottle of water, two apples, and a bar of my favorite vegan dark chocolate.

"Look at you, Eagle Scout. Always so prepared."

We sat together on a rock with our bare feet in the cold water. The stone beneath us still held some warmth from the afternoon. We passed one of the apples back and forth one bite at a time.

"Do you feel it now?"

"Feel what?"

"Better."

"Yes, yes, I guess I do. Thank you. I know I fought you hard."

"You always do. I respect the dedication to your work, I really do. I wish I had something I cared about so much."

I remember when I met Tyler. It was my third month in Mount Mirage, and I hadn't spoken to a soul outside of work. I was still dealing with the shock of getting there, stunned that I had the gumption to leave a man who was willing to marry me despite knowing me, and amazed that of all the places in the world I could have ended up, that I had landed here. I would take day-long walks, down the foothills, down the gentle slope of Main Street all the way to the ocean. A paved path runs along the beach, connecting joggers and bicycles to Palmetto to the south, and to the north the path ends at the cliffs that isolate Camus Preserve from the city world.

I walked the beachside esplanade to Palmetto many times, and my journey usually ended with staring resentfully at elegantly-dressed people eating beachside brunch at the Waterfront Hotel. One morning, upon reaching the end of Main Street, I finally opted for a right turn on the path instead of my usual left.

The northward esplanade winds past the sprawl of Mount Mirage's golden beaches, past the snack shacks, the volleyball courts, and surfer's point, and then climbs up onto a bluff. The path ends at a small park that's usually full of neohippies tightroping between two palm trees or dancing erratically in silent disco headphones, even on weekdays. If you climb over the fence that guards the cliff's unsteady edge, you'll find a rickety wooden ladder that lowers its carriers back onto one last spit of beach, protected by cliffs on both sides. On the north side sits the boundary of Camus Preserve, which connects the Mirage mountains to the Pacific without human interference. Coastal access to Camus is protected by jutting rocks and cliffs that can only be passed during a spring tide, and only for a few hours. A memorial plaque is bolted to one of the rocks to commemorate a few of the fools who dared to defy the ocean's very strict rule.

The ladder did not look inviting, but the relief of the cold wet sand on my feet was worth the adrenaline of climbing down. I started tiptoeing along the shoreline's tide pools; the touch of the waves and the slimy rocks chilled my whole body. It was a relief to suddenly feel isolated from Mount Mirage and the human world, and something in me exhaled. I impulsively shed my clothes and ran to the ocean. The cold brine was like an elixir; I licked the salt off my lips greedily and dove under a curling wave. I grabbed a rock on the seafloor and clung to it as long as I could bear the lack of oxygen. When I shot to the surface, half-drunk with brain freeze, I was surprised to see a figure crouched at the base of the cliff. He looked tall despite his posture, and he was obviously young, but something about him seemed somewhat out of place in this time. I emerged from the water, curious as to what he was so intent on observing that he didn't notice a naked woman swimming right behind him. I donned my sandy clothes and crept up cautiously behind him, worried I might scare away some creature that was garnering his undivided attention. To my disappointment, his gaze was intent on a wall of saturated green algae that covered a patch of the cliff.

As I got closer, still unconvinced that this man was this fixated on a clump of green slime, a gas bladder from a piece of kelp popped under my foot. The sound caused Tyler to lose his balance and fall forward, his forehead slamming into the slimy cliff before his hands could rise to catch him. Laughter erupted from my nostrils; I quickly covered my mouth with my wet hand.

He turned to face me, and I was correct– this man was strangely incongruent in his age. The skin around his eyes was thick and wrinkled from many sunlit days, and it gave his face a gentle old-worldliness, and he was dressed like an old man on a nature hike– but something about him actually seemed much younger than he was. The wrinkles deepened as he smiled sheepishly at me.

"I'm so sorry, I didn't mean to scare you. I just wanted to see what you were looking at."

"It's alright." Tyler rubbed the sandstone sheddings off his forehead. "Take a look."

Out of seemingly nowhere, water was steadily trickling down the cliff, along the deep grooves of the sandstone. When it reached the slime patch, the trails of water converged and absorbed into it, making the green blob swollen and shiny. As I moved closer I could hear a faint dripping, like the last quiet movements after a rainstorm. The algae grew in fine hairlike fibers, and as the water weighed it down, the lower hairs clumped and hung off the edge like the ends of a wet hillbilly beard. Each clump redirected the stream and had a perfect little trail of water dripping from it. They formed a line of dots in the sand. Tyler's hand was cupped under one of the streams.

"The water seeping through this sandstone is coming from the Camus watershed. It's exciting to see it this time of year, as it's usually dry by now. See, the mountains slow the air flow that comes off the ocean and forces it upward, and if it is cold enough up there, the clouds will condense into rain. And then it runs all the way from the mountains down here to the ocean–"

"Do I look like an idiot? I know how the water cycle works, pal."

"Okay sorry, I was just saying–" he saw my scowl and found it amusing. "No, you don't look like an idiot. Sorry. Last summer I worked as a naturalist tour guide– I still get into that mode sometimes." A wave rushed up and lapped at our feet. "We should get up the ladder, the tide's coming in. I'm Tyler, by the way. We could go for a walk up there, if you wanted to?"

We walked along the bluff and I eagerly questioned Tyler about his many seasonal jobs: ski instructor in Colorado, naturalist and kayak guide at a dude ranch in Montana, park ranger at Yosemite. "Did you have to wear the Smokey the Bear uniform? With the hat and everything?"

"Yes, I did…"

"*Hah*! I think I am going to need to see a photo of that. You know, I'm a sucker for a man in uniform–" I teased, half-honest, half-flirting. I was fascinated by Tyler's life. He had done it all, traveled all over and done every wilderness sport: whitewater rafting, rock climbing, ocean kayaking, things I hadn't even heard of.

"*Waterfall ice climbing*? You're out of your mind! You must be bored to death here in Mount Mirage, where all we have is surfing and hiking and–"

"Yeah I grew up here, but I came back for my Master's degree. I'll be graduating from MMU next year. I thought it would help me break out of seasonal work and find a more solid career path, but it's kind of been a nightmare. All the subject matter is just so… depressing."

"Tell me about it, I barely finished college for that exact reason. I studied coral reefs. It was devastating."

"I've taken classes about all different types of ecosystems, and professors say none of them are doing well. No one with an understanding of the data is hopeful for the future. And they talk about all the attempts being made to correct it, or slow it down, or prepare, but it seems both exhausting and futile. And then you see what the politicians are doing and it's like, how are we going to get anything done at all? I don't know; our professors talk about the younger generations like we'll be some miracle saviors of mankind and the planet. But that feels like a lot to ask."

We settled on a spot for a break, and he laid his flannel shirt over a patch of grass for us to sit on. "You know, these grasses are almost all invasive. European settlers brought them for ranching herds of cattle. I've read that the Mount Mirage Earth Defenders are partnering with MMU's environmental department to restore native plantlife, but the removal of invasive species is both incredibly difficult and sometimes ethically contested. But I think it's– oh no, am I doing it again?"

"Nah, I'll give you a pass this time. I didn't know about that."

We both pulled the same brand of crackers from our bags. "You shop at the co-op! I'm pretty sure they're the only place in town that sells these."

"They're also one of the only places in town that have bulk bins." Our eyes met in shared admiration. Two plastic-free dorks had found each other.

"Want to trade?"

Tyler had everything-seasoned crackers, I had multigrain.

"Why would you want to trade? You have everything!"

"Yes, but I always buy these. When you have everything all of the time, it starts to taste like nothing."

We traded boxes and I scooched over to him. "Veggie cream cheese?"

"Don't tell me you're a vegetarian too?"

"It's kind of new," I admitted. "I've been working on it for a while. It all started with a certain... *kangaroo* incident."

"Well now you've got me hooked. I'm gonna need to hear this story." He twisted open a bottle of green apple kombucha and offered me a pour into my empty water bottle. "Here's to the water cycle, to new friends, and to living in the generation that will either fix the entire world or witness the end of it!"

"Cheers!"

As the bottle left Tyler's lips, the same impulse that sent me into the ocean took over and I brought my lips to his. We giggled and stared out at the ocean for a moment, then back at each other, both tickled by the awareness that we had felt the same thing.

6
Things We Hate

$$\bar{v} = \frac{\Delta d}{\Delta t}$$

In the classical sense, Cam and I are nemeses, standard as they come. The things we care about are mutually-exclusive, and oppose each other unequivocally. I care about living things, he cares about machines. I care about slowing the world down, he cares about velocity.

"Velocity is the state of gaining the most distance toward something in the smallest amount of time. Or, distance *from* something. Even better.

"Velocity, in a nutshell, is efficiency. And efficiency is among the highest of human virtues."

Easy does it, Henry Ford. I have trained myself not to roll my eyes when he goes on his rants, and instead, to simply listen. Or I'll ask thoughtful questions, panning for gold nuggets I can use in my writing.

"Is it, though? Surely quality matters more than speed?"

"I said *among* for a reason. Try to think outside the production line, my pretty little Marxist."

Can he hear my thoughts?

"I'm not a Marx–"

His hand goes up to stifle my interruption. "Consider this. It is efficiency that allowed humans to have their first surplus of food. That was the foremost fundamental change in human existence. It created time beyond survival. And then with that time, we could become even more efficient. Which gave us even more time. You see? And then suddenly we are careening to the top of the food chain, able to create weapons, medicine, the arts, toilets, chocolate, and all the other things we have come to require, enjoy, and take for granted." He did a little reverent flourish with his hand to emphasize the word. "*Efficiency.*"

"Wait, I thought we were talking about velocity?"

He gave me a look as if to say, *Try to keep up.* "Velocity is a product of efficiency. Efficiency is a product of velocity."

"Are you sure you're not just talking about how much you enjoy driving fast in your car?"

In the things we care about, we are nemeses, plain and simple. But it turns out Cam and I have uncanny commonalities in the things we hate. We hate organized religion. We hate meeting new people. We hate professional sports. We hate glitter. We hate people who like any of those things. We hate rich people (he the liberal ones, I the conservative ones). We hate people in general.

I didn't realize it at first, but Cam had warned me: "*Now that you've been talking to me, you will start seeing it, and you won't be able to unsee it, and it will make you crazy too. Just you wait and see.*"

I didn't have to wait very long. It was everywhere, waiting to be noticed, and Cam had busted it wide open. I moved to Mount Mirage because I was enchanted by images of palm trees and waves. I didn't consider that I was supposed to be choosing a place to make a life for myself, to build a community, to find love. I'm 0 for 3. I can admit that I carry a certain resentment on my shoulders, living in a place like this. But now I can call it out by name.

Cam uses the terms *affluenza* and *affluent adolescence.* Upon careful inspection, it turns out there are no adults in Mount Mirage. At least not in the previously understood sense, involving things like responsibility, self-restraint and general togetherness in appearance and behavior. Everyone has fake jobs, poser identities and manufactured spiritualities. I can't even tell you how many aspiring "coaches" I know, with glowing self-aggrandizements on their personal websites– most of whom have the inner lives of a neurotic, quaking chihuahua. Life coaches, nutrition coaches, skin coaches, sex coaches, social media coaches, spiritual guidance counselors. Main Street is full of yogalates studios and craft microbreweries that are full on weekday afternoons. Shops sell potted succulents and dream catchers made by a white woman who lives in a gated estate for sixty bucks a pop. You can't walk four blocks without seeing a street vendor selling healing crystals or jewelry crafted out of beach trash. And good luck finding a spot down at the park out of earshot of a drum circle or musical protest.

Everyone is dressed in phony workwear. Faux-farmers, faux-laborers, faux-mechanics, wearing fashionably pre-distressed overalls, jumpsuits, and of course, the egregious summertime knit beanies, all of whom have never done a day of honest work in their sunkissed lives. They're taking some time off to "train for the marathon", or teaching meditation on Youtube, or writing screenplays. (I know, but at least I have a job.) Their designer-bred "rescue" dogs have five-figure pet food promotion deals on Instagram. There are grown men here who have made a non-sport called "ultimate frisbee" their entire personality, and they work at startups that make apps to help other app-makers build other apps. And they're making more money than you. A lot more.

And the toys. The TOYS. Prepubescent children race down Main on $4,000 electric bikes and electric skateboards, fast enough to keep up with cars. But what's worse is that the toys are mostly enjoyed by adults. Grown men in pastel Bermuda shorts and baseball caps, dressed like little boys with beards and smartphones, zipping down sidewalks on what I can only describe as 21st-century unicycles from a nightclub in Hell. These motorized one-wheelers not only flash multi-colored lights, but conveniently include a high-quality bluetooth speaker, so you can assault the senses of the unsuspecting public more completely. There's a trio of guys who have become famous in town for rigging those electric one-wheels to beach chairs and cruising down Main on their asses.

I think of Tyler and his garage full of toys at his grandparents' house. Surfboards, wakeboards, paddleboards, skis, snowboards, skateboards, city bike, mountain bike, backpacking gear, car-camping gear, dive gear, climbing gear. At first it was a dream come true– an opportunity to spend more time outdoors and experience hobbies I had never tried. But more and more I could see that I was not a mainstay of his experience, I was an accessory; a cumbersome extra piece of gear. If I could not keep up with those hobbies, I would be placed after them. In Tyler's world, play comes first. Everything else comes second.

And Mount Mirage *is* Tyler's world. I am treading water in a sea of Tylers.

Palmetto is no different; perhaps even worse, where the affluence is even more perverse and the people in even greater denial of their own irony. Cam sees himself as a stark outsider of his community, his culture, even his own affluence, but only in his mind is he truly a rebel. He would chew me out for saying it, but he is absolutely, without a doubt, one of them.

It's not his fault; it's been baked into him since birth. We're all born into our little places in the world: our families, our communities, our castes; and no matter how hard we try to move on and transcend, or reinvent ourselves, we still have the remnants of our past tucked away in our psyche.

Mr. Shaft

Sunset walk at the cliffs tonight?	4:29 PM
Would love to. Let's meet there at 7:30. Dinner after?	4:35 PM
Ohh yes, do you know what tonight is?	4:36 PM
?	4:36 PM
It's TOFU NIGHT!!!	4:37 PM
.....	4:37 PM

I am running late.

I was fussing over the details of the house, tucking things away, making sure the dishes were done. I wanted the place to be spotless if for some reason he comes here later. The house is an artistic version of my happy place: tons of natural light and open space, bright green house plants against white walls. Shelves stuffed with books and records serve as the decor. The scent of nag champa hangs earthy in the air; a backyard garden is equipped with summer's burst of tomatoes, herbs, melons, and abundant fruit trees. A hammock and swing are supported by tall shady trees, and tall fences ensure enough privacy for sunbathing in one's birthday suit, if one desires it. And a little scruffy dog with a mustache named Wilbur sits by the door to walk down the cliffs to a quiet surf beach.

When I am house-sitting at a place like this, I don't leave. I pack in all the food and paper I'll need, and the only trips into the outside world are for dog walks and work. The isolation recharges me. I cook, I stretch, I write. I smoke joints and practice giving speeches about the opportunities to innovate in light of the climate crisis. "It is humanity's ultimate challenge, the opportunity to mobilize against its own demise!" I declare to a snoring Wilbur.

When I get into my creative mode, I can get a little messy. Dishes may stack up. Clothes may be strewn around the bedroom. Most people live beyond this level of disarray, but I refuse to let Cam see any of it. He has been passive-aggressively ranting about the stereotypical flaws of my generation and my gender, and I have accepted all of it as a challenge to prove him wrong. Yes, I am the exception. I may be broke, but I work hard, and I have my shit together. (Or at least, I will happily pretend to, to spite him.)

But I fussed so much about the house that I forgot about myself. I pull up to the cliffs with a wet head of hair at five minutes to eight.

He glances at his watch. "Sunset is in six minutes you know." His face is stern. So much for looking like I have it together.

"I'm sorry– I don't even have an excuse."

We stroll through a patch of woods that protects the sea from view. The air is perfectly cool and the air smells piney, dusty. He says something offensive, I punch his arm; he pulls me to him and wraps his arm around me as we walk. We are acting like a couple; it brings me to realize we are in a place where it is all too possible that I will see someone I know. Tyler's friends come out here often to drink and strum guitars. How would I introduce Cam? What would I say?

'This is my friend'*?*

'This is the man I am using to write a villain because I lack creativity and I'm the right combination of delusional and pompous to think I can write a movie'?

I just have to accept that at some point I will have to take ownership of what I'm doing in the face of a stunned or disapproving acquaintance. Hopefully that time is not tonight.

"So I did some budgeting today. According to my estimates, I have made about $13,000 so far this year."

"Wow. It is extremely impressive that you can survive on that little in Mount Mirage."

"I know. When I finally calculated the total, I had a moment of shame, but then it was replaced with pride. I survived on that *and* my student debt went down." By like $260 bucks. Still, it's something.

"You have the makings of a CEO," he smiles.

"See? If I didn't run away from Dean, I would have never uncovered my incredible earning potential and began my journey toward girlbossdom."

"Tell me about Dean, I'm very curious. Knowing what I know about you, I can't envision you as an Ohio bride."

I try to give Cam the short version of the Dean story, but it bleeds into a story of all my exes, the string of losers, cheaters, and monsters, and how it made me realize that putting a relationship first is one of the dumbest things a girl can possibly do.

"At the end of the day, I think it came down to respect. All of my relationships ended, in part, because I was with guys who I couldn't bring myself to respect."

"Do you think that was on purpose?"

An interesting question. I stop and glance out at the cliffs, hopeful for dolphins or whales. Nothing.

"You know what? Maybe. Maybe I always knew that my own dreams, my own aspirations for career and creativity were more important, and it was easier to choose relationships that I couldn't take seriously. Maybe I was just bored, and looking for amusement, or a distraction."

"Or maybe you just didn't want to get hurt. Maybe you still don't and you're telling yourself what you need to hear now so you don't have to regret your poor decisions."

"Ouch. But yeah, maybe." Why deny what could obviously be true?

"I don't think you should cut yourself off from love in the name of career or 'creativity', I think you'll come to regret it. But if you want to find someone you respect, perhaps you should start with yourself."

"You don't think I have self-respect?"

"I mean… I've seen the interior of your car."

"Yeah, but that's not– I mean, men and women see their cars differently…"

"Oh that's funny, I thought you feminists believe that men and women are the same?"

"You know, I suppose you're right. If I had any self-respect at all, I wouldn't be seen with the likes of you!"

We engage in more flirtatious shoving. I quickly turn around, self-conscious that my joke is true. A jogger passes by in all her color-coordinated Lily Lime glory; a man in a backwards hat walks a pair of French bulldogs wearing mini Hawaiian shirts; a woman with a greasy bob follows her little boy, six or seven years old, skipping in a striped t-shirt, fairy wings and a tutu.

Uh oh.

"Gee, I wonder who bought that tutu for him. Mom, or Dad?"

"Maybe they bought it for themself with their allowance."

"*Their* allowance? How many people are you talking about here? I see one sad, confused little boy."

"Don't–"

"I will bet you your entire year's earnings that Dad is either long-gone or Mom is actively trying to get rid of him. But one thing is for sure: that tutu is Mom's idea. Mommy wants a little girl, or Mommy wants to be the center of attention with her friends, or Mommy wants likes on Instagram. That woman is sick. And that kid is going to be fucked up for life. Mark my words."

Cam continues for a while about his own mother, and how much terrible behavior she was able to get away with without the presence of a father in their home. Since I've heard this story before, it gives me a moment to gather my thoughts. Many conclusions have been drawn here. *How to respond, how to respond…*

It is true that I've been seeing an inordinate number of little boys in similar fairy-esque costumes or clothing in recent years, mostly online, but certainly more than average in Mount Mirage. I rarely see the reverse, at least for the little ones. It's the teenaged girls who dress like boys, in baggy t-shirts and jeans, terrible haircuts and flattening sports bras. But as I understand it, these are just symptoms of the gender binary breaking down. These are the times. I've seen videos about it online. It's one of the last frontiers of civil rights. Break down the gender binary, abolish the patriarchy, beat the system. Down with the old, uprising of the new; some better system; a system in which people can find respect, and freedom; a system in which the planet is cherished, not abused, and… whoops. Back to the matter at hand. *How to respond?*

"It is interesting to me, when you speak about this single-parent syndrome, and complain about how everyone is so messed up from it… don't you see that you're commenting on your own situation?"

"That's why I'm not racist. I–"

I slap my hand against my forehead.

"*What?* What does that have to do with–"

"Well if you'd let me *finish*. I'm not racist because I hate everyone equally– including myself."

I smile and wrap my arm around his back and squeeze my side into him. I whine, "No no no, you can't hate the world *and* yourself! It's too much, I won't have it. Not on tofu day."

"Tofu *night.*" He points over the cliff at the last arc of sun dipping down below the ocean. We watch it in comfortable silence. I hope for the green flash, but no such luck.

"What does that mean, by the way?"

"It means that you're taking me to dinner, and you're going to try tofu."

"Good luck with that."

We go to a nearby seaside restaurant that happens to serve an excellent tofu dish on Tuesdays. We order and Cam winces at my choice. "And two bourbons, on the rocks, please. Do you have those big giant single ice cubes? I like those."

"You trying to get me drunk?"

"If that's what it takes to get you to try tofu, absolutely."

The glasses arrive and I take a pleasing little sip. Nothing tastier than something you don't have to pay for yourself.

"Cam, what were your dreams when you were little?"

He doesn't hesitate to respond. "To go fast. And to be in command… of something that went fast."

"That sounds about right." *Velocity.*

He begins to ask me about my childhood dreams but I have already begun talking. "Mine's to raise a bear cub. And then be best friends with said bear."

"Would you let him hibernate?"

"Sure, if he wanted to."

"Would you sleep outside with him?"

"Of course. In spoon formation, ideally."

"Big spoon or little spoon?"

"Switch off."

"Would you paint his nails?"

"Fuck no! I don't even paint my own nails."

"That may change someday."

"Not while I'm making $12,642 in six months! HA!" I burst out laughing, the bourbon distracting me from how many hours of my life I've traded in for that amount of cash. "I can't believe I live in Mount Mirage on that. I don't know how I pull it off."

"Not by spending money on car washes, I guess. Or razors."

Our dishes arrive. His looks grotesque to me; mine looks grotesque to him. We both take sips from our glasses.

I cut a little square of tofu and drop it onto his plate. He holds it up on the fork and examines it, sniffs it. He takes a bite and holds the morsel in his mouth while he speaks like an ashamed dog holding onto a muddy sock. A young kid appears to fill our water glasses. *Oh no.*

"Hey kid, you ever had tofu?"

"No sir, I don't think I have."

"It's so good here!" I smile hugely at the bus boy, a sixteen-year-old surfer with stringy blonde hair. "The marinade they use, it's fantastic. It's why we came tonight. Tell the chef that."

"Oh… cool. I will have to try it sometime." He tries to inch away from the table, but neither of us will have it.

"Would you like to try some?"

"Oh no, hah, that's okay…"

"Do you know how they make tofu?"

"Don't you *dare* make the joke I think you're about to make!"

We look back from each other's glance and see that the kid has disappeared.

7
Billy's Darling

July 4, 2008

I handed the lady at the ticket window a week's worth of my McDonald's wages. Through the slot she passed me a ticket to the amusement park and a red white and blue wristband.

It was rumored that after the "Go America Go!" rally, Billy and some of the other high-profile speakers would be available for a meet-and-greet. Youth at such events are always pushed to the front of the line by an approving audience of elders.

My sisters and I marched through the park in our Sunday Best toward the concert arena, past the cotton candy stands and hour-long rollercoaster lines. Life was good. I had just graduated high school, bought my first car with my McMoney, and as of Sunday's Confirmation ceremony, my Friday evenings would no longer be spent in the youth room at church. And today, on the 232nd birthday of our fine nation, I just might meet Billy Darling.

I'm not quite sure when Billy Darling became a fixture of Dad's garage. It seemed like he was always there, just another worker chatting in the background, his radio antics making the men laugh and shake their heads. Then he got a TV program, and he followed us home to the living room. Matching a face to his voice made him all the more real to us— an uncle echoing the same grievances and cracking the same jokes, but with more charisma and authority, with a patriotic newscaster's stage surrounding him. Billy became the voice of reason in our house. His show became a ritual that had us spending one hour each weeknight holding plates and silverware and staring wide-eyed at the television. In a confusing and immoral world, Billy Darling was our ray of light, shining on us the truth, bravely spoken to power.

He looked directly into the camera, into our eyes, and spoke with urgency to the fears that weighed on our hearts and minds: *America is not what it used to be.* Something has been dissolved into the fabric of our culture, something insidious and corrosive; it's hollowing out our communities, our energy, our national spirit, and has been for a long time. Something is making American life harder; chipping away at our savings, making the food lousier, the weekends shorter; leaving our homes in disrepair and check-engine lights on. He assured us it was no fault of our own, nor was it a natural force of progress. It was being planned, and carefully orchestrated. People were responsible, and cheerful to see us suffer, cackling openly and loudly at us from high perches.

Mom and I especially loved him. We would listen to his show while we prepared dinner and rush over from the kitchen to the living room to see the charts and graphs he displayed on screen, receipts lending credibility to his complex theories. "Don't take my word for it," he'd always say. "Go look this up. Do your own research. I wish it weren't true, and this blatant— but they really do hate you that much."

Billy Darling was doing his homework. Billy had answers. He knew who the shadowy figures were, and the tools they were using to harm us: the hardworking people, the families, the small business owners like Dad, the nice folks caught in the middle; the "normal".

"When did being normal become such a crime in this country?" he said. "And what's giving all these whiny weirdos and academic quacks the gumption to make so much noise all of a sudden?"

They were being egged on, given a platform, and pushed into the spotlight to cause chaos, Billy said. "When chaos strikes a society, people demand order. They'll crawl on their knees and beg for it. And that's exactly what these people are trying to do: bring you to your knees, so they can take over and control you. They don't just want your guns, either. They want your minds. They want your free speech. They want your children. They want your *souls*. And they are orchestrating the circumstances to make it look like *your* idea! They think you're that stupid!"

His rage would steadily bubble up as his narrative developed, until he was standing in front of his desk and shouting at the camera. But once he reached the peak of his red-faced sermon, he would pause, calmly sit atop his desk and lace his fingers in his lap, so he could speak to us earnestly about what we could do to save our country.

Dead-eyed government bureaucrats and slimy politicians are merely the henchmen of a handful of very powerful elites who make the decisions and pull the strings, he said. They mostly come from Hollywood and the universities, and they worship Marx, Lenin, and Satan. I nodded along, increasingly terrified, titillated, fascinated, furious.

Billy Darling started a *Go America Go!* club, and a week after I mailed in my membership application, I received a letter with two iron-on patches and a pocket Constitution.

You are a true Patriot, NINA. You are part of an ever-growing army of Americans faithful to God, country, and gentility. Carry this pocket Constitution everywhere you go as a reminder of your dedication to truth and liberty.

Refer 5 friends and family members to join the Gold Star Patriot Circle!

I kept the little book in my backpack and ironed the "Billy's Darlings" patch onto the upper arm of my favorite denim jacket. It was like the second coming of Christ when I heard that a "*Go America Go!*" rally would be taking place in the next town over.

Rows of blinking colored bulbs lined walkways to beckon visitors into gift shops and toward boardwalk games. They lit and busied our path to the rally. We fell into step with a pair of retired couples who held up matching wristbands and nodded with approval. "Love the patch on your jacket!" the one man said. "See you in there!"

A pavilion outside the arena was filled with tables: people selling Billy Darling's books and merchandise, a group of men wearing powdered wigs and colonial attire wielding clipboards, a face painter giving both children and adults glittery stars and stripes on their cheeks.

Denise bought two of Billy's books, one to read and one for Mom's upcoming birthday. One of the colonial men waved us down. "Look at you— just *look at you!* Young patriots! What brings you lovely young ladies here this afternoon?" He put his arm around my shoulder and gave me a sideways squeeze; I blushed.

"We're here to see Billy's speech," I smiled, "and we kind of hope to meet him."

"As you should! I am sure he would love to meet a couple of Tea Party teenyboppers!" His breath was old burnt coffee. It made the collar of my jacket feel damp against my neck. I smiled and giggled politely, even though I had no clue what the hell a teenybopper was.

"See that guy in the yellow shirt over there? With the lanyard around his neck? Go tell him you want to meet Billy. But first, will you sign this petition to abolish property taxes?" After we added our names, the man winked at us and gave us a gentle push in the direction of the lanyard man. Soon we were given lanyards of our own, and with our hearts fluttering we found our place in the crowd before the stage.

We said the Pledge of Allegiance. A raptor handler sent a bald eagle into the air to circle the venue while a woman sang the National Anthem. It returned to his leathered arm and received a fish; the crowd went nuts. An opening band played a cover of "Proud to be an American" while a junior gymnastics team did a floor routine in silver and red leotards. The crowd sang along.

The mayor walked to the podium and gave an impassioned opening speech about the duties of American citizenship. A retired judge and political commentator told scathing jokes about the Democratic presidential candidates and the glaring hypocrisies of progressive elites. "Every single one of these politicians who talk about gun control live in gated communities and have private security on their payroll. And the Greenies, you don't need me to tell you, they're the worst. How do you think they're getting to all these international environmental summits? A raft of carrier pigeons and hemp rope?" The audience roared and loosened with laughter, ripened and ready for the main event. "And now, the man of the hour– Mister Billy Darling!"

Billy took the stage in a cobalt blue suit with a deep crimson necktie. He was a fairly short man with slender limbs and a tenderly protruding belly. He took the roaring, jubilant energy of the audience and immediately snuffed it with the solemn raise of his right hand, like a pinch to the wick of a candle.

"Americans. Patriots. Friends. Before we begin, let us look back up to that beautiful flag and say the Pledge one more time, slowly, with careful contemplation of each word– and when we conclude, let us bow our heads in a moment of silent prayer."

He held us all in his hands, and stroked our emotions uniformly. We were an orchestra of a single instrument; he moved us along each note with his words. He spoke to us as a father would: he loved us, he was worried for us; he would do whatever it took to protect us. He wanted the best for us, now and especially in the future.

"We must never forget that this country stands apart in the history of the world. The philosophical and cultural roots of Western civilization grew elsewhere, in the academies of Greece and the basilicas of Rome, but *here,* in *the United States of America,* is where they blossomed. This is where the ideas of liberty, human dignity, and unfettered prosperity were truly cultivated, put to the test, and gloriously triumphed.

"It is hard for us to imagine, isn't it? A world without free men. But it was the norm, for thousands of years and billions of human lives. Arbitrary persecution. Petty tyranny. Enslavement, oppression, brutality, and ruthless conquest. That is the reality of human history. And then a group of men sat in a room in Philadelphia, and they discussed and argued and pondered, and they decided that Man could do better– could flourish– if only he were free."

Billy paused for a moment and smiled to himself, as if he had been in that room in Independence Hall in 1776 and recalled something clever someone had said.

"Let us not forget that these men viewed freedom solely inside the context of their mortal humanity: the freedom they sought was from the rule of other men, but never from the rule of God. Our nation's Founders, intellectual and ahead of their time as they were, stood humbly before their Creator to design a new form of earthly rule. An America without God is no longer America. Never forget that.

"No matter what they tell you, no matter how much they try to get you to hate this country, to hate your heritage or to hate yourself, don't forget that. Don't forget that greater perspective. We haven't always gotten it right. Our government has only grown since its founding, as all governments do– to the detriment of who they are meant to serve. They've betrayed us, made fools out of us. But a nation is not made up of its government; it's made up of The People. Individuals, families, and communities built this country, from the first gatherings of pioneers in a sod schoolhouse to the audacious men who built New York City's skyline. The American people know the value of being free, the 'benign influence of good laws under a free government,' as Washington understood. The globalists can mock 'American exceptionalism' all they want; we know what makes us exceptional. We understand that this is a sacred responsibility that will always be questioned and attacked until the end of time. We must never relent, or apologize for who we are. The fight to preserve what we have must always, *always* continue."

The twins and I looked for another yellow-shirt and showed her our lanyards. We were ushered past the carnival of patriotism to a fenced area behind the stage, within earshot of the log flume. While we waited we could hear the shocked guffaws of the riders hitting the water.

Billy appeared with the mayor and the judge, and a few other nicely-dressed people. They shook hands and posed in front of a "Go America Go!" backdrop. When our turn finally came, I had sweated through my denim jacket. He placed his hands squarely on my shoulders and looked into my eyes. "You, my dear, are our future. Finish school. Find a good husband. Have many beautiful children. And raise them proudly, with our sacred values." He kissed my forehead and signed my pocket Constitution. I cried through my smile.

8
The Slide

2009

My slide into the abyss was subtle. I was too young and uninformed to recognize it while it was happening, and even if I had noticed it, I had zero skills or knowledge to stop it. It began in high school, as more of a "family problem" than a "me problem", with my parents arguing over bills and expenses. Easy to shrug off and ignore. The infamous 2008 financial crash coincided with my senior year, so it went right over my head, right under my graduation gown. I was too busy with college applications, scholarship essays, and stalking Henry Ribbit on Myspace to see what was happening to my family or my country. The safety net around me was dissolving, but I didn't see that I needed one. I was clueless about the fact that I was freefalling– it just felt like there was wind in my hair.

It shifted into second gear the day I moved into my freshman dorm.

I'll call it scarcity because I'm not comfortable calling it "poverty." Poverty clearly isn't the right word. To use it seems perverse and unearned. It just doesn't seem to be the right appraisal for a young American white girl. Who would believe it?

The "p" word is reserved for the people on the news, living in rusty tin huts in far away places. I was more like a circus animal suddenly released into the wild. There were resources around me, but I had never used my teeth or claws before. I was helpless, useless. All I knew was how to be polite, a good student, a hard worker.

Attending college was a mandate, not an option. Every adult in my life made that abundantly clear. "You're a smart girl." Smart girls don't waste their potential. Smart girls dream big. Smart girls can be anything they want to be. Smart girls go to college and learn how to become scientists, CEOs, and future First Female Presidents.

Smart girls with no money go to college and learn how to become hustlers. I didn't realize this would be my path until I was on it.

It's not the tuition that gets you in the beginning; most of that is deferred until you graduate in the form of predatory loans. It's everything else that slowly wears you down, raindrops that eventually form a stream that sweeps mud over the sidewalk. Rent, groceries, commute, car trouble, medical bill, holiday, snowstorm. The first year on campus was fine, while housing, food, and school were all lumped together. The price tag is tremendous, but at least you don't see it coming in. The first year is an illusion, that creepy amusement park from *Pinocchio*. It's the second year when you're on your own. The Pied Piper shows up with a stack of textbooks and says, "$249.99–*each*."

My pride kept me quiet about it. The last thing I wanted to be was the girl at school who was always saying no to plans because she's broke– or worse, a burden to my parents, who were being eaten alive with the guilt of their quiet struggle. I became a master of the magic act of invisibility: a creature with no needs whatsoever, financial, emotional or otherwise. If anything I tried to offer support, over the phone with my fretting mother, or to buy some groceries when I came home for the weekend, or to slip a little cash somewhere in the house so it would look like they had just misplaced it.

In my dorm I kept a lean fridge, and lucky for me, a little hunger made my body stand out as something special. I got asked out a lot, always said yes, and always picked a place with food for our first date. I bragged about it to my girlfriends, about the free food, like I was some wiseguy grifter. But my dates were usually nice once they opened up, and the guilt would get to me. I was grateful for the distraction, for the conversation and the free food, so I would try to do something to make it fair: laugh at their jokes, let them talk about sports and why they hate their stepdads. I'd go out of my way to look beautiful, and if the combination of atmosphere and alcohol was right, passively receive their end-of-the-evening advances. The drinks helped, and they were never afraid to spend money on that. The alcohol would wash over my senses and numb them. All they really had to do was ask, and I wouldn't say no. We'd stand in my doorway, he'd kiss my neck or touch me over my clothes, and I'd stare blankly at the stars.

After that first delusional year, I rarely had one job. There were always at least two or three moving parts in the mix: waitressing, hostessing, clerking, babysitting, dog walking, crap-shoveling at a nearby horse farm. When tips at the pizza place were lousy, I took more dog walking shifts. When spring break ended and the kids went back to school, I picked up more hours at the restaurant. School fell into the background and became the same white noise as high school. Lecture halls and the library became places to sleep between shifts. Doing the bare minimum to ace the test but gain zero knowledge was a necessity masked as a point of pride, "scamming the system" as I called it. Through the fog of grind and exhaustion, I forgot how badly I had wanted to learn, that I was working to pay for the education I was wasting.

One afternoon sophomore year I darted across campus to meet with my "career mentor". I was irritated to be inconvenienced by this mandatory meeting; it was cutting into my driver's seat naptime before work. The program was meant to help students choose the right classes for their career aspirations. I tore through a maze of a building, past dozens of cramped professor offices bursting with papers and books, to get to Dr. Ambrose's door. He was a chubby elderly man in a Hawaiian shirt and a baseball cap. Nonchalant grayish eyes looked at me through old-man glasses. He looked like he was already long-retired.

"So, Miss Dirstela. What steps are you taking toward the career you want to pursue in the natural sciences?"

"It's Distrella." I cleared a painful lump in my throat. I had no answer to his question. After an uncomfortable pause, I attempted to swallow my instinct to be defensive, and attempted sincerity instead. "I honestly haven't given it much thought. Haven't had the time. Lately I've been focused on getting through the next few hours as they come up.

"I thought I wanted to work with animals, you know, study them in the wild or observe their behaviors in captivity. But now I'm not sure that has any value."

"What do you mean?" He leaned forward. Something about that really got his attention.

"What's the value in studying a species that is going extinct?"

He leaned back in his ergonomic desk chair. The gray eyes stared past me at an illustrated guide to Florida Keys fish hanging on the back of his door.

"A pessimist. Go on."

"Not a pessimist, just a realist, Sir. I'm a smart girl and I went to a decent school in a decent suburb. I'm nineteen years old and I just learned about climate change for the first time *this year*. The severity of the global environmental crisis has been completely hidden from my view, for *nineteen years*.

"It appears that no one knows how bad it is, the path that we are on, except the scientists. No one is listening to the scientists– I don't know if it's because they're not yelling loud enough or because they were dorks in high school, or if people just don't want to hear what they have to say. But by the time people finally figure out what is happening, we're going to be powerless to stop it."

"And what are you going to do about that?"

It was my turn to pause and stare past him. My view wasn't as colorful as his; just a bulletin board covered in double-spaced papers and red chicken scratch.

"What can I do? Like I said, I'm just trying to get by right now. I'm treading water. My dreams seem useless. Why go through all this trouble of becoming a scientist, collecting information for years, even *decades*, and no one believes you? Or worse, what if they believe you, but they just don't care?"

He crossed his arms over his round belly. A few gray chest hairs poked out from on top of the Hawaiian shirt. "Maybe you're not meant to be a scientist then. It's good that you are asking yourself these questions now rather than later. But let me tell you something about being a scientist.

"A scientist's job is to observe the world and collect information. Uncorrupted, a scientist's only agenda is to seek to understand nature's rules, phenomena, and patterns. There is nothing more useful on this planet than having complete and reliable data. How can we expect to respond to urgencies, correct mistakes or prevent disasters, without having the information to understand what is happening and the rules of the game we are playing?"

"Yes, but what purpose does that information serve if we don't use it? How do we convince people of the urgency, convince them to act?"

"That is a science all itself. And it's a territory that most scientists won't touch. ...Same with physics. Won't go near the stuff."

"Yeah well I don't blame them. Seems like an insurmountable task to me. Why do you think I've chosen to study animals? Their world makes much more sense than the human world."

"You forget, my dear, that human beings are animals. If you're feeling conflicted about your path, perhaps take a class next semester that explores a new topic. I suggest a psychology course."

He handed me a "Careers in the Natural Sciences" pamphlet as I rose to go. I left in a hurry so I wouldn't be late for work.

On the way out, as I came around one of the office maze's many corners, a poster caught my eye. It was the color of the photo they put on the ceiling at the dentist's office: the bright azurean turquoise of shallow tropical water.

The poster was mixed in with a bulletin board full of study abroad flyers. Bright and saturated photos of ancient architecture, dishes of food, and racially diverse groupings of students with perfect teeth. "Discover China!" "Explore South America!" The turquoise poster, which hosted a photo of a small cruise ship, advertised a semester of adventure and leisure on the Mediterranean Sea. "Live and study aboard our 600-foot luxury vessel while exploring the many cultures, flavors, and natural wonders of the Mediterranean. The world is your classroom!"

I scoffed. *Way to kick me when I'm down, Universe.* I muttered in my best infomercial voice:

"Dear rich parents: Are you wishing you could further indulge your spoiled child while they work on their degree in 'General Studies', all while wrecking the environment on an international scale? Look no further! The world is your nanny service!"

As I turned to go, even more defeated, my eyes caught a small flier barely hanging on for dear life on the bottom of the board. It was the only one printed on a regular sheet of paper, in plain old black ink.

MARINE SCIENCE INTERN NEEDED
ASSIST RESEARCH PROJECT
GREAT BARRIER REEF ECOSYSTEM
MUST BE CERTIFIED DIVER, LIVE ABOARD SAILBOAT.

In the bottom corner was an email address to learn more and apply.

One word, as childish as it may be, appeared in my head and stayed there.

Adventure.

I needed that. I needed an adventure. All thoughts of climate catastrophe, spoiled brats on a cruise ship, and everything else I was worried about in that office two minutes ago were gone; all my brain could process was, *adventure.* I snatched the paper off the board and power-walked to my car.

~

The next morning I was at the study abroad office when it opened. "Is there anyone I can speak to now, briefly?"

"We usually don't take appointments until 10:30."

"It's kind of urgent. I really just need five minutes of someone's time."

The girl at the reception desk, who looked like this job was her resting spot between classes, pointed me down the hallway.

"Biscuit can help you."

Biscuit was cozy in her cubicle, slurping down a quart of Dunkin Donut's cookie-dough flavored iced coffee and scrolling through a Tumblr page titled, "Poshest Puppies of Paris". For a moment I had completely forgotten my mission and solely wanted to ask if her name was really Biscuit.

"Hi, are you– Biscuit? I need to pick up some forms to complete an internship application."

She looked up at me and didn't take the straw out of her mouth. There was something strangely, cartoonishly seductive about her. Under two hours' worth of makeup, her face was round and beautiful. She didn't need the feathery fake lashes and the stenciled eyebrows; she could have spent those two hours doing anything else– perhaps exercising. But the art on her face was done so perfectly that it transformed her; she almost looked like a comic book character come to life. I respected the artistry despite its absurdity, especially considering the time of day and her placement in this back-corner office in a crappy state university. No wonder she needed a 32-ounce cup of caffeinated sugar.

Her plum-colored lips left her drink. Without speaking, she jutted out her hand; I almost jumped at the threatening sight of her sharpened inch-long fingernails, glossy and bone white. I passed her the application I had filled out.

"Do you plan to get credit toward your degree for this internship?"

"Yes. The natural sciences program has a 'professional development' requirement that needs to include an internship or personal research project."

She licked her finger, again while making eye contact, pulled a pink form from a stack and handed it to me. "And financially? Have you talked to your parents about paying for this?"

"No need to discuss with them. I have a scholarship grant that covers tuition, and I'll be living aboard a ship. They provide meals and pay a living stipend of a hundred bucks a month. I just need to save up for a flight and enough money to put my stuff in storage."

Another lick, another form. This one was green.

"Living *aboard*? Like, what kind of ship? Have you thought about this?"

"Not really. I can't explain it, but there is something in my gut telling me I *need* to be on that boat in January, Biscuit."

"I don't have a form to prepare you for that. You know there's study abroad programs on cruise ships and in, like, cool cities, right? Like you can tour Europe between classes and have laundry service and shit."

Adventure.

"I know this will probably sound like nonsense, but that sounds like a nightmare to me."

She let out one brisk chuckle. "Alright. I like it." She pulled a stack of cat-shaped sticky notes out of her desk. "Take one of these and write this down."

I reached for a pen from her desk organizer; an orange one with a boa feather sat closest. She quickly said, "Not that one."

She gave me a list of offices I needed to go to to get more forms to fill out. I skipped every class that day and called out of work sick so I could get it all done in one shot.

I was on a flight to Australia two months later, puking my lungs out into an air sickness bag while a middle-aged stranger patted my back and said, "There there, dear."

9
Captain Don

I can pretty cleanly divide my life into two distinct parts: before Captain Don, and after Captain Don. The pre-Don era was a simpler time, but becomes harder to understand as time passes, the same way a dream is as vivid as real life until you open your eyes. My pre-Don existence was theoretical; watched on television and read about in magazines; dreamt about, pondered, fretted over, and assumed. Life seemed to become Real the moment I stepped on the plane to Australia. The first flight I had ever taken and I went about as far as one can go.

I was in giddy disbelief of my situation, that I had really done it: filled out all the paperwork, saved up the cash, got a passport– which arrived an agonizing six days before departure. My stomach bubbled with the acids of anxious suspense. While other girls dreamt of becoming movie stars, ballerinas, or brides, I dreamt of exploring coral reefs. I religiously watched a junior science TV program called *Wonders of Water*. In one episode a scientist couple was studying the reefs of the South Pacific. They flew over the reef in a tiny makeshift plane to map them from above. (The film was made in a time before the skies were filled with the irritating buzz of drones.) They dove the same reef for several weeks, hoping to capture the corals' elusive spawning event on film. In their regular visits the woman befriended a tiny blue damselfish, who appeared from behind a massive brain coral to visit her.

I can talk a big game about why I chose my field of study, and why I chose that internship: how I wanted to help with important research, or advance my education, or save the ecosystem– but truthfully, all I *really* cared about, all I *really* wanted, was to make friends with a fish. That was pre-Don me.

~

2010

I raised my hand to my brow to block the glaring sun and I searched the dock, hopeful to spot a vessel with the university's logo, or someone holding a sign with my name. I knew the boat had sails, and that was all. I silently scolded myself for not asking more questions about what to expect. I exchanged emails with a rep from the Australian university about academic logistics, but the only contact I had with the boat captain was a single email with no capital letters:

> *tidda marina, cairns*
> *duffel only. limited space*
> *mask fins snorkel. zinc stick. paper. pen*
> *metal water bottle. seasickness meds.*
> *read up on parts of sailboat and knots.*
> *welcome aboard.*
> *-cptn don*

I opened my backpack and pulled out a printed copy of the email, hoping there was a clue I had missed. Nothing. The dock was a bustling place, with fisherman shouting obscenities to one another, boys carrying wire crab pots and plastic tubs. A couple of pretty crew girls in pressed white polos and khaki shorts wheeled provisions toward a sparkly yacht. I backed myself into a guardrail to avoid getting in everyone's way.

As I looked up from my paper to make sure I was at least at Tidda Marina, I was startled by the massive shadow of the man standing before me.

When I was a girl I went through a phase of fascination with the Wild West. On Sunday mornings after church, we had this tradition: Mom and the twins would run errands, and I would insist on being dropped off at home to be with Dad and George. By that time they would be finished with the morning's yard work and were parked in front of the TV with bagels, watching old westerns. It became our special thing, and over time and puberty, as Dad and I became worlds apart, it became the lone place we could return to find each other– until around 2016, when we started arguing about how racist and sexist those films were. Then it became another landmine to avoid mentioning.

As I got a little older and started going out on Uncle Mick's boat with Dad and George, my obsession with cowboys and pioneers transformed into an obsession with pirates. Different backdrop but same draw: wildness, danger, freedom, adventure. I must have worn the same pirate costume for six Halloweens in a row.

At the intimidating first sight of Captain Don, the little girl inside me twinkled with delighted awe and a breathless hint of fear. I could not have created a better alloy of the cowboy and the pirate inside of the best drawing room of my imagination. The man had stepped out of a time machine: you could have told me he was a privateer, a Union soldier, a Viking, a member of the Lewis and Clark expedition, and I would have believed any of it. A stained and torn shirt opened across his broad, tanned chest, a sun-worn cap shaded his eyes, and a dented, ancient silver coin dangled from a chain around his neck. His beard was lightened by the sun, strands of white, blonde, and penny-red. It was thick enough for a family of small crustaceans to be living inside of it comfortably. It hid most of his face, excepting his eyes; surrounded by sea turtle's skin, his eyes matched the shallow seas that surrounded us. But the most powerful sensory clue was his scent, a musky cocktail of diesel, salt, male body odor, and zinc oxide.

"Intern." His voice boomed over the busy marina, and matched his leathery face and body. "Nina."

It took me a moment to snap out of my awed stupor. "Intern," I repeated. "Nina."

The enduring silence of his stare forced more words out of me. "You must be Captain Don?"

He grunted in the affirmative and looked down at my small duffel bag. "Light packer." His brief approving glance made me glow, like a pat on the back from a stoic father. "Pick that up and let's get to it."

I followed him down a ramp, past a variety of charming and historical-looking sailboats. I got excited. I had never sailed before, but had long-missed the days of cruising around Raritan Bay with Dad, George and Uncle Mick. All three of them teared up a little the day Uncle Mick had to sell the boat.

We stopped in front of a shiny white and navy schooner named *In A Minute*. She was sleek and clean, with her mainsail neatly stored under a navy cover. "Huh," I sighed. It was a gorgeous boat, but I was expecting a vessel that matched its captain; something a little more… piratey. Don reached down toward a gray post on the dock and unplugged a yellow cord. The cord veered right, to the vessel next to *In a Minute*.

"Ah, yes– that makes much more sense."

A lifesaver ring was lashed to the stern pulpit; it was dented and looked like it would not be saving any lives. The transom read *Siren's Revenge* in old-English calligraphy. The letters were crackled and three-dimensional as their vinyl edges curled off the ship's steel hull. A large Indonesian batik tapestry of stained cream and dark shades of blue was draped from high on the backstay. It outstretched like giant hugging arms around the pulpit, giving it the look of a field soldier's makeshift tent.

The wooden fixtures were faded and old, but showed signs of recent sanding. The various metal furnishings looked the same: old, but recently polished and cleared of rust. Various tools and instruments were secured to the rigging and the coach roof: buoys, pennants in the scuba colors of red and white, and alpha blue; dive tanks, nets, a kayak, a small silver UFO-shaped grill. The canvas mainsail cover was frayed and washed out with sun, but still gave the appearance of neatness, order and effort. *Effort*; there was evidence of effort everywhere: effort to repair and restore– to maintain the function and dignity of an old vessel that was at the age when a ship continually attempts to sink itself.

The captain led me belowdecks to a cabin with a tiny galley, two tiny bunks, and two tiny doors– one, I would learn, to the head, and the other to Don's quarters. The salon held an oblong wooden table with a booth seat on one side. The cabin walls held shelves stuffed to the absolute brim with books, organized by subject. A tiny chart table in the corner was covered with papers; nautical charts and anatomical drawings of corals hung from the walls. An antique sextant was displayed elegantly on its own little shelf. We were both surprised to see a young woman sitting there, head buried in a book titled *Polynesian Geomorphology*.

"Alice." Don's voice startled her so the book flew out of her hands. His surprise to see her aboard made me wonder if he had intentionally left the ship's name and description out of our correspondence. Alice stood at attention; I thought she might salute him.

"Apologies, Captain— I know it's bad etiquette to come aboard without permission," Alice explained, "but I called the Marine Science office to get a name and description of the vessel." Her voice was soothing, songlike. Her accent was an Aussie's, but refined in such a way that suggested she spent some time in England as a child. Her hair was neatly braided behind her head, exposing a face ripened and freckled from sunshine. Her mouth was a pale raspberry, a question always resting in its corner. Her eyes, hazel and large for a small face, gave her a vibrant and perpetually curious quality. I am describing Alice in poetic terms because she was worthy of such a description. Alice was intrinsically balanced: soft, delicate in her presence and demeanor but with a counterweight of relentless intellectual curiosity and enthusiasm for the natural world. Her fear of everything didn't stop her, but instead propelled her into an unquenchable thirst of knowledge about her fears.

Don didn't waste energy on words, knowing his silence would force us to acknowledge each other. "Hi, Alice. I'm Nina."

"Very nice to meet you."

"Choose bunks, settle in. Briefing in the cockpit in a half hour." Don disappeared above. I chose the bottom bunk while Alice returned to her textbook. Neither she nor I were the type of person to start a conversation. I decided it was important that we got along, since it looked like we may be the only ones.

"I don't know why, but I thought this would be a bigger operation." I forced a chuckle, nervous as I was. "Do you think it's just going to be us?"

"Yes, I think so. Don't think this vessel could even fit another person." Alice placed a fully-marked notepad in the book and began rifling through her bag. "I'm glad of it. We'll get lots of hands-on research experience and log plenty of dives. I'm just so happy to be getting back to sea. I've missed this life." She took a deep inhale through the nose, and glanced around adoringly. The smell belowdecks made me wince.

"What took you away from it? School?"

"I spent most of my childhood on the water, with my dad." Alice kneaded a t-shirt into a ball. I quickly understood how she and I were the same sort: drawn-in observers, not particularly interested in sharing, but incapable of withholding our thoughts when asked. We became instant friends, pushed together by our shared love of corals, our seasick bellies and tight living quarters, and our reverent fear of Captain Don.

It wasn't that he was cruel, or domineering, or even disrespectful. He was just in his own world, a general too consumed with his mission to bond with the infantry. In the first week I tried to open him up a bit. It had been several days, and he had said exactly eleven words outside of orders and lessons. I was counting. "So, *el Capitán*, I've noticed that you have two lady interns… attractive to boot." I winked at Alice. "Was that just a merry accident? You're not one of those creepy professors who tries to take young girls 'under your wing', are you?"

I smiled, hopeful, curious as to how he would respond to such a poke. He didn't look up from his work.

"I did not know what you looked like, but I did intentionally choose two women." Before I could crack a joke in response, he continued. "This is a small vessel. I didn't do a whole lot of advertising. I only got a few worthy applications. Once I had chosen one female candidate, it was imperative to choose another. It was always going to be two men, or two women. There would be no productivity otherwise. And I'm not a professor." It was clear to me that Alice was the undeniable first choice, and I was the compatible counterpart.

Don's briefing on our first night was the most he spoke in the three weeks the three of us spent together. "Welcome aboard the *Siren's Revenge*. This vessel is old, modest, and rigorously cared for. We may be a small crew, but we will operate like members of the Queen's Navy: with discipline, dedication, and precision. While I am certain the world out *there* has changed dramatically," he gestured vaguely toward land, "*here*, it has not."

His words titillated Alice and I. We were like school children being loaded into the family van, headed for Disney World. Our faces held wonder and fierce concentration; we would take every word seriously and enjoy the work. *Adventure.*

It only took a day or so to realize that this was no Peter Pan ride. This was work; relentless, grueling, physical work. I began with a serious learning curve to overcome. Uncle Mick's boat was a powerboat, and even if it wasn't, I never participated in anything but hanging over the side, looking for fish to make friends with. Alice was already an expert sailor and diver. Her father was a novelist who said he couldn't write on land. He used to tell her that the rocking of the waves mixed up just the right cocktail of genius and courage in his brain, just enough so he could get the words right. On their family sailboat he would get so caught up with his writing that he named Alice captain. By twelve she was a better sailor than him, burying her head in manuals, sailing magazines, and nautical charts. When he committed suicide shortly after her fourteenth birthday, Alice's mother promptly sold the boat. They moved inland to take a job with a mining company and to hide from their memories.

While her mother was at work, Alice started taking the Queensland Railway to the coast and paced around the marina, talking to anyone who noticed her, hoping to find an opportunity to get back to sea. The young fishermen took a liking to her, though perturbed by her bookishness, and she became their proverbial little sister. Her heart was claimed as the territory of Burt Lowell, an expert tugboat crewman and leader of a pack of boorish fishermen who haunted the Tidda Marina's bars. Burt was 30 and Alice was 22. He had proposed but she declined, saying she didn't want to be engaged until she was ready to plan the wedding, and that she didn't want to be married until after graduation.

"What I didn't clarify with him is the *kind* of graduation I meant," she said, half grinning and half guilty. "I plan to stick right through for my PhD. But he's not going to like that…"

"Do you think he will wait that long?"

"I mean, he sees how it is out there. The fishery, I mean. When I can show him the results of this research and how important it is, I think he'll come around. I just need to humor him for now."

Our days were intense, every minute of daylight utilized for chores and research tasks. We sailed along a circuit of reef sites that Don had charted out based on the locations of collapsed fish populations and bleaching events. "Once corals bleach, they are not actually dead– *yet*. There is a chance they can come back, dependent on how bad the damage is, both on the corals and on the ecosystem as a whole. Our job is to prove that protecting these areas can help bring them back to life." He warned us to brace ourselves. "You've probably seen a documentary or two by now, but the devastation is harder on the spirit when you see it in person. Do what you need to do to keep things in perspective. I recommend the book in the salon, '*Geologic Time*.'"

As much as I adored the idea of myself as a disciplined and competent deckhand, I faltered often and struggled to work the long hours. A constant dosage of seasickness medication kept both Alice and me in a drowsy stupor. Alice found no relief from the pills and stopped taking them. "If I'm going to hurl anyway, I might as well be alert."

I felt a constant, desperate urge to complain, but began forcing myself to swallow it down. One silent look of disappointment from Don was all it took. The man never stopped working. He was awake before us each morning, and even when I'd wake in the night to use the head he'd be up on deck or reading at the chart table, or there'd be a glow of light from beneath his cabin door.

Instead of a reprimand or a lecture, Don would respond to us by rattling off some profound one-liner, something that could have been a quote from a philosopher or a Founding Father, while staring off into the distance from behind the helm, or without looking up from his work. Then he would return to his stony silence, leaving Alice and I to quietly ponder the meaning of his words until it felt safe to chatter and sing again.

We spent five or six days at a time out on the reefs, and anchored beside little coastal islands for supplies and rest. Alice restlessly searched for an internet connection so she could chat with Burt. I had no one I wanted to call; I was relieved to be unreachable. Things at home weren't going so hot. Dad sold his shop to pay off some bills and was working for a landscaper. He was embracing the 'work more, feel less' philosophy, and I worried he was turning into the horse from *Animal Farm*. Mom was still grief-stricken from George's death and had become sleeplessly nocturnal. My sisters chose colleges out of family earshot. There was nothing I could do to improve the situation, and the powerlessness of being around them was unbearable.

Adventure meant leaving all that behind. I was connected to nothing, nothing but that boat, which bobbed on the blank slate of the sea. I passed my evenings with the *Geologic Time* book, flipping to random pages and pondering concepts so big they crowded out all other thoughts and emotions. A part of me wished to remain trapped in this routine forever, as some sort of compromised paradisiacal purgatory: flipping banana flapjacks in the galley before sunrise; polishing the deck's brass furnishings and filling dive tanks; dipping below the azure with a deep exhale, feeling the sea's pressure like a full body hug. I had gone diving once before this adventure, in a Pennsylvania rock quarry to prepare for a vacation that I never took. The water was freezing and we had to wear hoods, boots, and thick gloves. A spring algae bloom reduced the visibility to no more than an arm's length. The irritatingly enthusiastic instructor bragged of a sunken car hiding in the quarry, for those skilled enough to find it through the thick green muck. I wonder if he has ever seen a coral reef before. Poor bastard. Perhaps it would shatter his little world if he did.

The reefs were both what I'd hoped for and feared. Don had warned us fairly. *Wonders of Water* had shown glittering reds and pinks and yellows, and huge silvery schools of fish swirling above like shattered disco balls. We saw little patches of healthy reef, not as vivid in color as the touched-up films, but with living corals and a sprightly community of creatures living amongst them. It made my heart sing to finally be there, to be *in it*, in their world. I would squeeze my legs together with my flippers and swim like a mermaid, singing silent songs in my head. I would descend to the ocean floor with my tank and just kneel there, breathing slow bubbly breaths, waiting to see who would swim by, or pop out of some crevice. But the vast majority of our work took place in bleach zones– underwater graveyards of bluish white, with staggerings of small fish grazing on overgrowths of brown and red algae. Don was relentlessly hopeful that this study would help prove that his marine preserves could save both the reefs and the local fisheries. "The idea is to show that protections benefit everyone, not just the wild for its own sake. A healthy reef provides economic value in ways we don't consider or quantify, but someday we will. It's a fairly new field of study."

We measured every detail possible of each reef site: water temperature, salinity, turbidity, oxygen levels, pH; depth and type of reef; size and frequency of hard coral species and soft coral species, and what percentage was alive and healthy, bleached, or fully dead; size and frequency of key fish species, size of their schools, proportion of juveniles to adults.

Don coached us to be meticulous in our measurements and to record everything carefully. He spoke about the scientific method the way Billy Darling spoke about freedom.

"Careful, earnest inquiry." "Empirical, steady observation." "Objective reasoning without agenda." "Evidence is everything."

I adjusted to the constant motion of the *Siren's Revenge* after about a week, but Alice did not. She only became sicker, struggling to keep up with the days' work and having to skip dives. On the twentieth day we were back at Tidda, exchanging emails and promising to keep in touch.

"I can't believe you're leaving," I whined as she brushed a tear from my cheek. "Who am I going to talk to now?"

"I'm sure you'll open Captain Don up–" We snickered and shared a playful eye roll. "Burt thinks it's for the best. Guess I've lost my sea legs…"

With those parting words, I heard something fragile and glassy inside Alice shattering. She stepped off the gently rocking vessel, loose in its suspension over the infinitely restless ocean, and planted her feet onto the dry, unforgiving cement. Burt was waiting for her on the dock with his arms crossed over his chest. He was a handsome young man, tall and with a large square forehead, a beer gut resting above his belt. He embraced Alice and scooped up her belongings. They disappeared behind the rows of masts and burly fishing vessels.

∾

Something sunk in me, watching Alice go. I couldn't describe it at the time, but I think it was grief. I was uncomfortably certain I would never see her again. Don appeared on deck with splicing supplies in hand and a coil of rope hanging off his shoulder. He paused and looked out at the marina, dirty cap in hand. "Congratulations, you two, and may God have mercy on your souls." He sat and began his work.

"*What?*"

"That girl is pregnant."

My stomach dropped. "How do you– you don't know what you're talking about. I think you're being kind of dramatic, making a lot of assumptions…"

Don shook his head. He sat with his frayed ropes; the metal fid bounced up and down in the corner of his mouth as he spoke, like John Wayne with a cigarette. It bugged me.

"Amazing– you spent twenty days with her, talking day and night, and yet you looked right past her. That girl grew up sailing; that wasn't sea sickness. It was morning sickness."

Hm. I considered his theory. It was solid. "Even still, she's in school. She said herself she wasn't ready for marriage and family. She probably won't keep it."

"Again, right past her. Alice bowed her head in silent prayer before every meal and before we raised the main. She will keep the child. At least, she won't abort it."

He gestured to me to get a move on some preparation to leave the marina. I refused to move, my body unable to respond while I processed Alice's situation. "But she is so smart! She can't just waste her potential like that!" I shuddered at the mention of *wasted potential*– the horrifying prospect every teacher, coach, and mother warns smart girls about.

"So only dumb women should raise kids, is that it?" He chuckled at my offended grimace. "Why couldn't she channel all that intellectual curiosity into being a mother? Children are fascinating creatures– wild little primates that parents transform into miniature humans, with language and table manners. It's only a few years before they're in school and then she can return to her academic pursuits, if she wants. It goes fast."

"That's not how it works and you know it. It's going to ruin her life!" My mind pored over our conversations, the stories she had told me about Burt. "And now she's stuck with Burt, forever! And he's toxic, a drunk! I'll bet he's abusive to her!"

"That is a hefty accusation for someone you've never met."

"You haven't met him either, and yet you feel the need to defend him? I can tell just by looking at him– he's one of those roughneck types, dominant and unreasonable, all muscle and emotion and no brains."

Don kept to his work, sighing a groan of impatience. "I've seen more of Burt than you. Tidda is the *Siren's* home. I can tell you grew up in a city. Out in the working country, there's a different breed of people– a different kind of man. People are just rougher, because they have to be. Rougher forms of living– stockmen, miners, fishermen, those types. You get hardened from it, by what you see and the work you've got to do. Generally speaking, there are two kinds. One's like growing a shell of armor– it protects you and fits over your skin, it's malleable so it can take a beating and still be repaired. And the metal still conducts warmth. The other kind is like being coated in stone– it's heavy, inflexible, cold. And it's impenetrable only to a certain point, and then it crumbles.

"So much of a man's fortune out here is a product of luck: money can be great at the mine or on the construction site, *if* you don't get injured or killed on the job. It can be a smooth go at sea, or you can get huge squalls, cyclones; swell that lifts you up to terrifying heights and holds you there just long enough to contemplate every sin you've ever committed; storms that can test a man's very soul. Some can handle it, some can't.

The ones who start to break, they cope in different ways: drugs, the drink, gambling, brothels and affairs.

"I've seen bad men at this marina. Burt's not one of them. He drinks too much, but that's because he can. He makes good money and the work is tough out there, so he blows off steam with his men. But having a kid, getting married, these things usually force a man to grow up."

"Well, I hope you're right. Maybe it will all work out for them. Maybe we are misunderstanding the whole situation. I mean, it's her choice either way."

"What is her choice?"

"Whether or not she decides to keep the child."

"You mean, whether or not she kills her child."

"Are you really going there right now?"

"I'm just speaking objectively."

"She would not be 'killing a *child*'– don't villainize it."

"But you just used the word 'child' before, did you not? You can use terms like 'fetus' or 'embryo', 'terminate' or 'abort' if that makes you feel better about it, but objectively speaking, ending a life is killing, and a fetus is a child."

"It's a ball of cells."

"Aren't we all?"

"What are you doing? Why are you picking this fight right now?"

"I'm not picking a fight. We are just having a discussion. If you have a stance, you should be able to rationally defend it. Now, if your assertion is that Alice's embryo is a ball of cells lacking in the complexity to be considered a human being, at what date will the cells become human and worthy of the same moral consideration?"

"I... I don't know. I've never thought about it. Maybe when it has a heartbeat?"

"That's about five weeks. So Alice is probably past that point now."

"Or– maybe when it has a brain?"

"I believe the brain starts developing around week three, and then the first electrical impulses begin around week five or six. So she's about there."

"Okay well, you know what? If it's killing, at least it's justified. It's her body. You can shoot someone who invades your home, can't you? Why wouldn't you be able to kill someone inside your own body?"

"So a tiny, helpless child is equivalent to a home invader? Guilty of a crime punishable by death? How'd it get there in the first place? By its own choice, or–"

I went from indignant to weepy. "But... Don't you understand? It's going to *RUIN HER LIFE*!"

Despite my growing upset, Don spoke in his usual aloof, objective tone. "We all make choices. And we must live with the consequences of those choices, regardless of whether or not we knew better, or should have known better."

My tender weeping became buckety sobbing. When I used to cry like that, it would really pour: fluids, noises, involuntary heaving breaths. It startled him. He finally stirred and looked up at me, and touched my arm distantly. "Look, I'm sorry. I know that as a man, I can't know what that feels like.

"On the one hand, I'm the first to say that life is sacred, and that our moral judgment is the primary thing that separates us from other animals. But I also understand that from a biological standpoint, females are the fundamental gatekeepers of life.

"In nature, the males are decorated and gifted with songs, dances, colors, and calls because the females choose whose genes get to carry on. If a lioness has a cub that doesn't seem viable, she eats it."

My sobs were stunned into silence. *What did you just say?*

"It's more common in the animal kingdom than you would think. There are many forms of it, perpetrated by the males too, who are trying to stifle future competition. But at least they engage in a fully acknowledged version of it: they are dealing in the violence by their own hand. It's not some medicalized, intellectualized, distant 'ball of cells'; it's their flesh and blood right in front of them. That's an important difference.

"But outside of animalistic brutality, the point is that females have an indisputable responsibility. You choose the direction of the species. And the males' reciprocal responsibility is to protect females from unworthy males. Before modern birth control, for all of human history, that choice had to be made at the outset: choosing a mate was inextricable from reproduction. We think we've progressed beyond that, but try as we might, we can't rewrite the laws of nature.

"I believe Alice loves Burt but objectively speaking, she has settled for less than she deserves. No matter what her father was going through when he chose to take his life, he was still selfish and a coward, for failing to see through his duty as a father.

"But bottom line, there is a human life inside her now, and if she chooses to kill it, it could protect her from ending up with Burt— or it could drive her more deeply into his arms. She might use her loyalty to Burt to protect her from being haunted by that decision for the rest of her life."

"She could have the baby and leave him."

Don stood, casting a shadow over the companionway. "Babies need fathers. Was your dad around when you were growing up?"

"Yes…"

"Imagine for a moment that he wasn't. Imagine what that would have been like."

My veins flooded with anguish, confusion, and weary concession. "For Christ's sake— you barely speak for three weeks and then you talk like you know everything."

Don sat and continued his splicing, unfazed. "I like to listen. It doesn't take long to get a sense of who a person is, if you just let them speak. If you can stay silent, and let a person talk long enough, they will tell you exactly who they are. Scientifically speaking—"

"Can you shut the *fuck up* with all your science talk?" I snapped, unable to control myself, even for this frighteningly robust and calm bear of a man, who was still in charge, was still the captain. "Not everything is science and mathematics. These are people's lives, their feelings…"

He looked amused. "Everything *is* science and mathematics, if you reduce it down enough— or zoom out enough, depending on how you view things. The emotions you are feeling right now are a product of various chemical reactions, neurotransmitters being fired off in your brain, in reaction to stimuli being picked up by sound wave vibrations in your ear drums, and neurons processing colors, shapes, light, and motion in your visual cortex."

He looked up and could see that I was on the verge of pushing him overboard.

"It's comforting, if you consider it carefully. It makes life simpler. We are animals, no different than any others living on Earth, susceptible to the same processes and followers of the same laws. Humans just have the simultaneous blessing and burden of an enormously powerful brain. Most of human existence is just trying to figure out how to cope with being this complicated."

Have you ever been in an argument with someone who is perfectly calm? You're red-faced, heart racing, and they can't even be bothered to take a break from splicing their stupid little rope. He was making me look like a fool; there was nothing else I could say or do. I got up and started preparing the sails to get the hell out of this marina, to get back to the bottom of the sea where the world made sense.

Don and I spent another month aboard the *Siren's Revenge*. As time went on, we took fewer days off, pushing to record enough data from all the reef sites to make Don's case. He had been working with the university for the last several years to set up these small marine preserves along the reef, and was attempting to prove that rotating a series of protected areas over extended periods could renew the health of the reef and restock the fisheries without devastating the regional economy. The funding was running out and he was under pressure to produce some kind of encouraging results. In this long stretch of just the two of us, I finally got Don to speak– at least, to answer my many questions.

"So you view science as sort of your religion, huh?"

Don's glance did not shift from the horizon. He gripped the helm with both hands. "Absolutely not. Religion implies faith: believing in something despite logic, because it's what you have been told is true, or what you *hope* to be true, or what makes you feel good. I have no faith.

Science should never contain faith. Unquestioned scientific dogma is even more dangerous than fundamentalist religious doctrine.

"But I suppose you could say that I view the *scientific method* in a similar light to how people view religion. The process of objective questioning, observation, and repetition is our best shot at identifying Nature's laws and Man' s limits inside them."

He sounded like Professor Ambrose, my so-called mentor back at school. But Don's words entered me differently than from some old pot-bellied guy in an office chair. From a man like Don, every word was buttressed with articulate conviction.

"The scientific method is humanity's process for improving the human experience; a means of seeking truth and order in a chaotic world. A way for us to remain peaceful amongst the madness. It is the wise who are peaceful. It is the ignorant who are agitated."

"What? I would call it the exact opposite. The more I learn about the world, the more upset I get. Ignorance is bliss."

"Perspective, kid. Perspective. Go back to the *Geologic Time* book," Don grunted and pointed to the companionway.

I stared at the colorful timescale inside the book's cover. The foreboding Hadean Eon sat at the bottom of the scale, shaded in a deep purple, beginning at 4.6 billion years. *Billion.* A thousand millions. 4,600 million years. I recalled an episode of Billy Darling's show when he talked about big government spending. He showed a graphic of what a billion dollars actually looks like in cash, with a football field covered in dollar bills a foot thick. Over four football fields worth of years.

There was a little star at the 3.7 billion-year mark with a handwritten notation: *Earliest evidence of life on Earth.* I traced my finger up the scale, past another several billion years, stacks of bills in football fields, and the next star read, *Earliest evidence of multicellular life,* around 600 million years. *Earliest evidence of vertebrates* at 450 million. *First mammals* around 200 million. And then, at the very top, almost to the present day, was a final star, *First Homo sapiens* around 300,000 years.

Three hundred thousand. Chump change. Barely enough to buy a decent house in this economy. All of human existence, everything and everyone that led to the Pyramids and the Inquisition and the Boston Tea Party, the invention of soap and plastic, the gun and the printing press, the lives of Jesus and Da Vinci, Magellan and Walt Disney, the Incas and the Mongols, the Mormons and the Beatles, all confined in that little fingernail of time. And it's even smaller than that, because we don't even know what the hell happened before humans started writing things down. I felt a little sick in my stomach, sick from the smell emanating from the head, or the rocking of the sea, or from staring at the little words, loaded with meaning. I quickly flipped to the "Dating Methods" section, hopeful I could find some hole in their calculations that would make me feel differently.

One afternoon we stopped back at Tidda to drop off a huge haul of plastic and trash that we had scooped out of an eddy. It took us a full day and we still couldn't collect it all; it spread over the water like a seep of oil, with smaller and smaller pieces swirling around the periphery. I pulled a familiar piece of plastic from my net and examined it. It was an unmistakable chunk of Mister Bucket– a hit toy from the early '90s that had been the centerpiece of one of my Christmas mornings. Several dead fish and a cormorant were mangled and choked in a mass of netting, polymer rope, and fishing line. It was the first time I saw Don show any emotion. He cussed and growled with a serrated knife hanging from the corner of his mouth.

After unloading all the trash I felt filthier than I'd felt the whole trip, and that is saying a lot. I was worn out in about four different ways and wondering what the hell I had gotten myself into. I thought of those colorful laminated study abroad posters, and all those rich kids who were spending their spring semester "tasting the flavors of the Far East" or whatever. And from those options I grabbed the one slice of plain printer paper, in Times New Roman size 12? *For Christ's sake,* I thought, *I make terrible decisions.*

I stood open-mouthed on the dock, watching a uniformed crew polish a heaven-white yacht with a jacuzzi sitting above its stern. My stomach ached with longing.

"Why would you want that?" Don's booming growl made me jump. "What do you think your life would look like? What kind of people do you think you'd be spending your time with?"

"You know, people aren't inherently evil if they have nice things. People have a right to do what they want with their money. And the government—"

Don grinned. "I know, I heard you talking to Alice about Billy Darling. So you're a Tea-Partier, huh? Traditional-minded, frugal, anti-government. Have you thought all that through?"

"What do you mean?"

"Well, if you're going to take on a belief system, especially at your age, you should make sure you genuinely understand it, and embody it in the way you live. Do you feel as though you do?"

No one had ever asked me these questions. I had nothing to say. "I know my principles," I attempted to anchor myself. "The American system works because it is built on liberal principles, and freedom may be harsh at times, but it is the only way. I wouldn't expect a man who abandoned his country to understand."

Don liked that. A rare smile appeared across his zinc-stained face. "Ah yes, the Land of the Free, of mass incarceration and the Patriot Act and school shooter drills. Perhaps I don't understand. But there is an important responsibility that comes with freedom, as we know it. Understanding the difference between *can* and *should* makes all the difference."

He glanced up at my perplexed scowl. "For example, if we were truly free, we would be welcome to fish this reef to oblivion; to blow it up and catch rare tropical fish to sell to aquarium collectors. If I'm free to do what I please, I can dump our trash over the side of the boat with reckless abandon; dump my fuel tank right over a sea turtle taking a nap for a good laugh. Why not?"

"Because *can* doesn't mean *should*, I get it. But in that case, I'd also be free to stop you. With my all-American GUNS!"

"If you're talking about those new sailor biceps, I've got myself a challenge!" I giggled and flexed, grateful for relief from all this political talk. And he was right; my body had become strong from the long days of hard work. I felt good in my skin, for once.

"Look here kid, I can tell you've got passion. And I can tell that you care very much about being a good person. I imagine you've excelled at pleasing authority your whole life, which I'm sure has reaped many benefits. Good daughter, good student, good citizen. But you're far from home, out here on the ocean, and all of that has been left behind for now. Perhaps it is a good time to consider how much of all that is really you, and how much of it is your desire to be liked, or praised; how much you simply want to be considered a good girl."

"What's wrong with being good? Of course I want to be good, and to attract a good guy. A man with principles; a *real* man." I shuddered as the word left my lips, thinking of Burt, and where Alice may be at that moment.

Don pointed back to the yacht. "And do you think that's what a real man is? Real men don't need to prove themselves in showy or useless ways. Buying a ridiculous bloated yacht, shooting an elephant, bullying someone weak. Real women laugh at a man like that."

I sighed and glanced back toward the yacht one more time as we boarded the *Siren's Revenge*, which needed a serious scrub-down after the day's work. "Can't I just have my fantasy about a life of luxury? Is it so wrong, even if I know it'll never happen?"

"You can do whatever you want. But keep this in mind: we move toward what we *aim* toward. And with your potential, the worst thing you could do is settle for what glitters over what is real." Don sighed and looked aloft, as if remembering a woman who had done just that. "You have all the makings of a real woman. You're by all means still a girl, and you will be for a while yet. And if life gets hard for you, you may even fall behind. But catching back up will make you all the realer.

"And when you become a real woman, you'll realize how comically impossible it will be for you to settle for anything less than a real man."

"And what, by your noble standards, is a real man?" I was frustrated and defensive, but I knew that a real man was standing before me. I was curious how he would describe himself.

"A man reveals himself in his most routine and mundane actions. How he prioritizes his time. How he keeps his living space. What he feeds himself. His ability to resist the male temptations of laziness, fleeting pleasure, and greed. His ability to lead others, to discern which people he wants around him. His ability to say no, to stand up for himself and others; to think logically; to persist, or pause; to be patient. His sense of duty, in stewardship over himself, his family, his village, and creation. His commitment to his purpose. The sacrifices he chooses. You'll know a real man when you see one. You won't be able to miss him."

On our final night, we anchored at a barely-inhabited spit of an island that he called "Bubba's". There were several scrappy fishing vessels anchored in a row parallel to the shore. Only a small handful of yellowy lights shone from the island. We walked up to an open-air bar called the Jolly Roger. He bought me a beer and ordered a black coffee for himself.

"Oi, if it isn't *mista* save-the-sea-*tah-tles*!" A huge hand slapping Don's back seemed to shake the whole establishment. We were suddenly surrounded by a huddle of burly leathery Dons. Their voices boomed with drunk laughter, playfully picking at Don's chosen profession and lofty ideals, but they embraced him and me, and I knew instantly that these were his brothers.

I had never seen Captain Don drink, or smoke, or look at a phone, or make a lewd comment about a beautiful woman. His only vice seemed to be his cups of black coffee, taken at ritualistic intervals throughout the day. When the man wasn't working he always had a book or chart in hand, and always looked deep in thought while engaged in his duties. He did pull-ups on the rigging and operated his life and ship with disciplined precision. He was like a brawny monk, silent and frustratingly calm. But these rowdy, goofy men ignited Don. They pulled him out of himself, perhaps returning him to some previous state from his youth, before he became this rugged philosopher who took the world so seriously. I even heard him laugh, a whole-hearted, from deep within his body sort of laugh, and it sent a shiver of joy down my spine.

Don's friends were poor fishermen, merry with reunion and alcohol, but told heartbreaking stories of divorces, bankruptcies, and suicides.

These men were from small towns where fishing was everything. The fishery began to descend when they were boys, and work became scarce in town. They watched their fathers attempt to transition to tourism to stay afloat, which unfortunately coincided with the industrialization of the upland farms. The farms, enchanted by the ag revolution that was thriving in the United States, began using gratuitous amounts of chemical fertilizers to increase their crop yields. The Queensland wet season washed those fertilizers down the watershed and into the ocean, feeding superblooms of algae. The algae blooms suffocated the fish and scared off the tourists. Their adolescence was spent watching this devastation take the life out of their town, their community, and their beloved ocean.

Many dropped out of school and left for the riches of the inland mines, but these men stayed home and clung to the only life they knew, hopeful to carry their grandfathers' and fathers' fishing tradition forward. Each year would come a glimmer of hope: rumors of a good catch, forecasts of favorable conditions. But each year got harder. The stakes became higher. Competition was fierce and families who'd been friends for generations started to turn on each other. Men desperate to feed their families betrayed their own principles and took jobs on large commercial fleets with low pay and grueling stretches at sea. These friends of Don's were the stubborn few holdouts, relentlessly hopeful, and relentlessly intoxicated.

They got Don to drink a beer, and then another, and he began to open up, and smile, and even join their raucous laughter. I snuck away from the Jolly Roger, feeling unsettled to be there, as if I was invading a moment of the other sex's intimacy; a reverse of the teenaged boy who's found a hole in the girls' locker room wall. But Don was right– all it took was listening quietly for a short while and you could learn so much. I learned that Don loved these men; loved their wives and children, and their sisters, and their parents. I learned that Don had no family of his own, but that these men had become his family– and everything he did, he did for them.

I sat on deck with the *Geologic Time* book open before me. I gazed down at the billions of years of life on Earth, and then turned my gaze up at the infinity of stars above. My heart could not grasp how simultaneously small and essential I was; that I was a piece of all of this, and that a universe of neurons and compounds and microbes all existed inside of me, and did their work without my awareness or understanding of it.

I couldn't grasp how I was made of the same basic parts as the Moon, and Mount Everest, and the giant squids at the bottom of the sea, and the bamboo jungles and the piles of horse shit I used to shovel, and the shovel itself. Like Alice, something glassy inside me broke, but didn't shatter. It cracked open, and a billion pieces of me flew out.

TREE OF LIFE:
TAXONOMY OF THE GREAT WHITE GORILLA

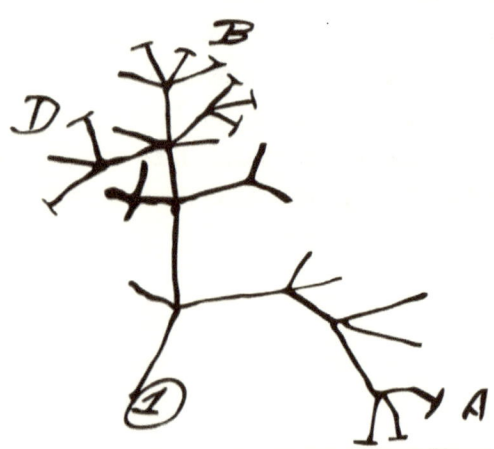

Charles Darwin's Tree of Life sketch, 1837

To understand the role of the great white gorilla in the global ecosystem, we must take another moment to consider their place in the Tree of Life.

The lush and bountiful Tree of Life is perhaps Earth's greatest achievement, brimming with an unfathomable variety of forms and colors, rituals and roles. It has been less than two hundred years since humans have begun uncovering the mysteries of the Tree of Life, and our work has just begun. As humans develop better tools for discovering and understanding Life, the diversity of living things seems to be ever-expanding, and in a constant state of change.

Change is the essential nature of Life. The struggle to survive and reproduce amidst ever-changing conditions and cataclysmic whims of the physical Earth require organisms to utilize their unique adaptive advantages. It is this sprawling chessboard of traits that distinguish species from one another and arrange us on the Tree of Life as competitors, beneficiaries, enemies, and friends.

Charles Darwin chose the symbol of the tree for a very important reason. Our connection to other beings is not linear, like bulbs strung in parallel on a wire; rather one connects to the whole via a series of branches, all of which eventually lead to the same single trunk, and are nourished from the same set of roots. We branch out by the ways we are different, but we stem from what we have in common. Those stems, like grandparents on a family tree, represent our adaptive heritage, and if you trace one species' roots back far enough, you find that all of Life shares a few key traits. We eat, we grow, we reproduce, we die. We all participate in the transfer of energy from one form into another, which plays out as a beautifully complex and infinite molecular dance; invisible to our eyes, but happening inside us and all around us.

After achieving the status of a global apex predator, the great white gorilla began viewing itself as separate from the Tree of Life: as an ornamental star placed on top, or as its divinely-appointed arborist. While this status could have been viewed as a sacred duty to steward and nurture the Tree of Life, the great white gorillas saw the Earth's bounty as a treasure chest to plunder, and its variety of life forms as subjects to dominate, exploit, or eliminate altogether. It is this false belief that has led us toward the ecological collapse crisis.

But all it takes is an afternoon watching a group of chimps at the zoo, who bond and fight and engage in complex social politics, to recognize that all of us in the Great Ape community share deep roots. It is particularly interesting to observe the dynamics of primate social hierarchies, mating strategies, and even intraspecies warfare. In fact, understanding our heritage as primates and observing the behaviors of other Great Apes provides us important insights into human nature. Most of humanity's quest to form "civilized" societies has been an attempt to curb, correct, or stifle our primitive instincts so that we may live together more peacefully, cleanly, and orderly.

And how is that quest going? Well, it depends on who you ask.

10
1861, 2019

I've been laying low for the last few days. I'm worried I have made myself too available. Can't forget the importance of the chase.

I know I still have his interest because the calls are still coming. More often than not he isn't calling to just chat. It's because he has a rant about some idiot "Lib" or "Millennial" experience that he's dying to share.

"I yelled at this Millennial dipshit who couldn't drive– total tech nerd. Doesn't even belong on the road. Couldn't make a turn on a red light to save his life. You should've seen his face as he frantically rolled up his window. His girlfriend will never look at him the same again."

"These fucking Libs," this, "these fucking Leftists" that. I grin and take it in silence; as mundane and ridiculous as it is, this is valuable villain fodder, and I can't help but laugh at times.

"It must be exhausting to be in your head," I tell him. "Don't you ever just let things go? Can't you just go about your business and not pay attention to them?"

"If they weren't in my way," he says, "but they are always there. Just leave me alone, get the fuck out of the way."

"The human population has doubled since you were born, so it's only downhill from here my friend."

He carries himself through the world with the pestering weight of a man wronged, with heavy steps and vigilant eyes that are blind to anything but evidence for his own grievance. The wrath sits in the soft skin inside his cheeks, tightening and acidic like sour candy, puckering his mouth into a permanent state of disdain.

There have been some hints that suggest Cam Benzin isn't simply loyal and generous– the little sentiments I have been attributing to his constant mentions of doing favors for his friends. It seems to be darker than that.

The phone rings. "Mr. Shaft" on the black screen. Green button.

"Good afternoon, Mr. Shaft."

"Good afternoon, Miss Distrella. What are you up to?"

"Walking home from Mallory Café. I wrote a few pages and read a few pages."

"That's funny– I was just heading to Cicero to get a cigar– thought I might see you there…"

"Why, Mr. Shaft, you aren't making a trip into downtown Mirage in hopes of seeing me, are you?"

"What? Of course not, don't flatter yourself. I meet the guys down there for a stogie once in a while. Some business meetings there too–"

"It's okay, you don't have to justify anything to me."

I can't help but smirk in my seat, tingly with female triumph. I'm glancing out the window of the café at his great-white-shark truck across the street. He gets out with a cardboard box and marches toward Mt. Mirage Cigar and Tobacco. He crosses the street with his usual air of angsty aggression. I can't help but wonder what is in that box. Surely he's not helping the manager stock cigars.

He speaks solely in vague terms about his work, and I've had this inkling before. It should make me feel a small sense of victory, shouldn't it? Watching my adversary down and out, and desperately trying to carry on with his head up while scrambling to conceal his situation? But it doesn't feel victorious. I'm surprised to feel myself hurting for him. I know exactly how bad things must be for a man like him to rely on help from others, or to be at the mercy of others' needs, running errands and favors, doing the bidding of someone else's desires or ambitions. I know because it's been my whole working life. It's most people's whole working lives, sometimes their personal lives, too. But I know enough about him now. This is not acceptable for him. I am overcome by an alien gut instinct: to lift him up, to help restore a man with talent and ambition to his rightful place in the world, to ensure the use of his skills and intelligence, and that maniacal engineer creativity. But as he walks past Mallory's big window on his way back to the truck, I squash that instinct like a roach scrambling past my foot.

"You sure buy a lot of cigars."

He stops short and looks over at me. The box is gone.

"Or were you donating cigars today? A whole case of them?" I give him the closed-lip smirk– the one you do when you pass someone awkwardly in a hallway, but with attitude.

"Needed just one today." He lifts his right hand to show a fat cigar in between his fingers. *A treat for a dog who performed his trick?*

"Got a lead on some upcoming political activity that may blow the winds in my favor."

Before I can say a sarcastic congratulations, his phone buzzes. He answers it as a crowd spills out from inside the café. An old Asian man, suddenly standing inches from Cam's face, calls out loudly to his family in his native language– I want to say Korean, but I'm admittedly too ignorant to know.

"*Đi thôi, đi nào! Đưa em gái của bạn đi! Chúng ta sẽ đến viện bảo tàng!*"

"Hey– I've got Charlie breathing down my neck– I'll call you back."

"Don't do that." I scold him but the smirk hasn't left my face.

"But it's such a beautiful language, don't you think?"

"I'm sure English sounds equally terrible to a non-speaker. Get used to it, Whitey: we are the great Melting Pot."

"I wouldn't eat out of that pot, there's probably cats in it." He laughs at his own joke as I narrow my glance and point to his truck.

"I believe your vehicle is over there."

He winks at me and struts off, clutching the phallic cigar between two fingers.

He speaks often of 'The Betrayal' from Kantian, as though it is some widely known public tragedy, but I've gathered few details about it in his ramblings before he moves onto another unrelated subject. It seems he was betrayed by a member of his Board of Directors, and it cost him millions of dollars. I don't think it was just that dollar loss, nor the loss of his company. I think it was something more.

To start, it appears that he is currently homeless. I thought the bed and the drawers of socks inside his garage were a bit strange. He described staying at Arnold's as a favor, to watch the cat and supervise the garden staff while he takes frequent business trips. But when a friend of Arnold's came to visit from out of town, instead of going to his own home, Cam stayed with other friends.

I was sitting around at his garage, smoking a joint and singing along to the Velvet Underground while he angrily rifled through a filing cabinet. He waved a stack of documents over my head; I went to grab them but he quickly withdrew and tossed them into his giant George Washington safe. "I built this thing from the ground up. Look at that– look at that market cap. For five years I didn't take a salary. And then–"

"Are you going to murder him?" I smiled. I lounged on the warm sidewalk and stretched out like a languid, stoned Cheshire cat.

"No no no, he must *live*. I know what he has coming. Things like divorce, broken children who end up addicts. These are the things that will really make a man suffer."

"Sounds like you've thought it all through, then. You want some of this? You need it more than anyone I've ever met in my life."

"It smells like shit. Put it out."

~

I'm sitting on the toilet, hunched over my phone in a posture that I imagine makes me look like one of those trolls that asks for a special coin before letting you cross under its bridge.

I stopped using social media back in college, after I returned from Australia to find that most of my friends had blocked me and a "Billy's Darling" smear campaign had taken place on Facebook that cost me my social life and earned me the unfettered disdain of every humanities professor. While I was on the *Siren's Revenge,* minding my own business in the middle of the Pacific, Billy Darling had posted a political cartoon mocking the Chinese Communist Party, reminiscent of the World War II-era depiction of Japanese people drawn by Dr. Seuss. (Google it if you must; it's not flattering.) It drew national outrage, especially when Billy laughed at the internet mob in his trademark easygoing way and refused to apologize. Multicultural and Ethnic Studies departments across the country organized a wave of campus protests to get him off the air, including at my school. My photo with Billy from the *Go America Go!* rally was unearthed on my Facebook account, and you can imagine how that went.

So I've sworn of social media, at least for socializing– but I recently made a secret account. *Hush–you hear me?* I don't want to be found out. My friends and relatives send me so many links to Instagram posts that it became exhausting… I simply had no choice.

I mostly use it to keep up with climate news and vegan activism, or to look at videos of babies with large dogs as nannies. Or for videos of country cottages with little ducks in a pond and sprawling wildflower meadows. And videos of freedivers who have made friends with sea lions and hermit crabs. And beautiful people cooking beautiful food on tropical, thatch-roofed verandas.

But this fateful morning one of my sisters sent me this photo filter that warps your face into Disney-princess-like features, and I was dumb enough to open it, and I
CANNOT
STOP
LOOKING
AT IT.

My eyes are bulbous and bright; my nose is effectively reduced to a pink dot and my lips are rounded out and shaded perfectly to match my smoothed-out, sun-kissed, dewy skin. It's even managed to make my hair shinier and several volumes larger. We're talking *Ariel* large. I purse my lips and bat my eyes; I fake laugh and reveal a perfect row of white little chicklets between strawberry lips. I've probably been on this toilet for fifteen minutes staring at myself.

Go ahead and judge me. I'm just being honest. I know I'm embarrassingly too old for this, and I truly believed– or at least hoped– that I was too smart for this. I know this is a fool's game; that it's crack-cocaine for a woman's mind. I know that I'm going to get off the bowl, flush, look in the mirror and be disappointed for the rest of my life. I don't even know why I opened it up. At least I'm not one of those people who actually post this stuff for the world to see. Then my real face would be a disappointment to them too.

The hypnotic enchantment of my fake face is interrupted by an incoming phone call.

Mr. Shaft.

"Mr. Shaft, good morning. How are you doing today?"

"You answer phone calls like the concierge at a hotel. What's with the customer service voice?"

Immediately I can tell he's in a mood. But he's right, I do use my customer service voice when I speak to him sometimes. It's disruptively polite and it throws him off; it's a stab of formality that says, *We are not as close as you want us to be.* I also do it when I speak to older people in general, without even noticing I'm doing it.

"Sorry, I worked late at Vero's last night. Sometimes it takes a full twelve hours to get out of character."

He finds that amusing, and it subdues his irritation for a moment. But it's short-lived.

"Did you pick up the new tire yet?"

"What tire?"

"You know what tire. For your car. It's at my buddy's shop waiting for you."

"Then can't you just get it?"

"What am I, your servant? You're an adult– allegedly. Besides, I wouldn't want you to feel *disempowered.*"

"Alright alright, I'll get on it."

"You keep driving on that bald spare and you're gonna find yourself a damsel in distress again."

Before I can conjure up a witty comeback, the ranting begins. He can't help himself.

"So I'm driving up Main, minding my own damn business, and as I'm turning the corner onto Cicero this filthy vagrant, total loon, jumps in front of my truck and starts slamming on the hood with his fists. You should have seen this guy– fat as all hell, belly hanging out the bottom of his dirty shirt, sweatpants half off his ass. You could just tell he smells like shit. He's yelling, 'You hit me, you hit me!' like those are the first English words he's learned and I just fucking roll my eyes at yet another one of these useless parasites trying to get his payday. I try to speak to him calmly but you know how these people are, he's probably wasted or dopesick or out of his damned mind, and it's just a waste of your time. I would have just moved on but too many people were watching, and I'm not about to get sued for a hit and run when I didn't hit shit.

"I ended up having to call my buddy at the police station to come over and deal with it, which I hate to do– I know he's got better things to do, and he's up to his ears in this shit. These people are all over the fucking place. All these people just draining our society, giving nothing and taking everything. We might as well just give them the drugs and let nature run its course."

It almost sounds to me like the man who constantly boasts of his superiority on the road might have made a mistake... but who knows, I was not there. He just as easily could have been dealing with a truly mentally-ill person, or a dangerous person, or just a standard jerk. Impossible to know.

"Do you mean like, let them overdose?"

"Sure, yes– absolutely. My sister did it years ago, and her death was the best thing that ever happened to my family."

"I... what did you–"

"She didn't want to be here, and we didn't want her here. She was draining everybody: our money, our time, our emotional capacity. It was slow torture. She spent a decade deceiving and stealing and doing god only knows what to get her next fix. And guess what? She met with

Palmetto's top therapists and went to some of the finest rehab facilities in the world– on my dime, by the way– and it did absolutely nothing. Zero.

"No amount of money could be successfully thrown at this problem. She could not be cured because she didn't have a *disease,* like all you bleeding-hearts like to tell yourselves. We had the same upbringing, the same problems. But I worked hard and made something of myself. She was just a useless, bored rich girl who became an addict because she couldn't handle reality. Our father wasn't around to give her tough love; just a mother who agreed with her over and over again, '*Yes, you're the victim, you're the victim.*' So when she finally overdosed, I cracked open a 20-year scotch, lit a cigar, and breathed a sigh of fucking *relief.*"

During his blustering I muted the phone, flushed, and washed my hands. I stare in the mirror at the disheartening, tired-looking face, and the flat, greasy hair. My cheeks are drained of color in disturbance at Cam's callous words. I assumed he was the worst person I'd ever met when I met him, but I still did not see that coming.

"Well… I can't speak to what sorts of problems you wealthy Palmetto folks deal with. But I suppose… I just wonder… exactly what conditions in our society are creating all these troubled people? Can we really blame uneducated people for being ignorant? Can we really blame poor people for having poor health? Can we blame the hopeless for wanting an escape?"

"That's my point exactly!" he cuts in; I adjust the volume so he doesn't blow out my ear drum. "You know what conditions are creating these people? *Coddling*! Sheltering! Over-mothering an entire society! The road to Hell is paved with melted participation trophies! This is what these radical Progressives want; a bunch of impotent, whiny, enabled *losers*, who rely on the state for everything and stand for nothing but their own fragility. It's the goddamned *Victim Olympics* out there!"

"But would you agree that some people out there really are victims?" I desperately search my brain for an example.

"Let's say a bunch of kids grow up with lead pipes in their homes' plumbing. We know, scientifically, that their brains won't develop properly. They won't have the same ability to succeed in life. So do we punish those kids for that? Who gets held accountable?" Things start to look up as he begins to rant about corporate corruption, and it seems we're on a path toward agreement and niceness again. *Well done, Nina.*

Just as I think we are in the clear, things take a distressing turn. Cam returns to his car story from earlier, but in his rage, his thoughts become incohesive, and seem to fall from his brain like hunks of heavy snow dropping from tree branches. In these moments I am not sure how to respond. I know that if I attempt to disagree, or point out a flaw in his logic, it will only make matters worse– a prospect that borders on frightening. I feel guilty to be tolerating any of it, but I suppose I have nothing to lose by hearing it; except perhaps my outlook for the day, which wasn't looking too sunny to begin with. I also have nothing to gain, except material for my villain, so I stand in front of the bathroom mirror in swallowed silence, and watch myself listen to him.

"Useless! Too many useless people, leeches of society, wrecking this town, wrecking this whole state! I wish some leader would have the balls to say the truth: we need to rid ourselves of them."

"But that can't happen. They have to go somewhere."

"But they don't need to be *here*– one of the most expensive, desirable cities in the country, in the richest state, in the richest nation in the world– and we have to deal with this? Why do they deserve to be here? To litter their filth on our streets and take over our beachfront parks, to scare off the dwindling number of small businesses and decent, hardworking, tax-paying citizens?

"Reopen the asylums, build more prisons; toss them on a bus and send them to so-called 'sanctuary cities' like that shithole San Francisco! Send them back to wherever they came from!" His ranting continues, and I continue to stare at the ruddy, droopy disappointment in the mirror.

I make one last attempt to bring the tone of the conversation down, back to the one group we both love to hate: the entitled Mirage housewives, who Cam calls 'the Blonde Breeders'. We talk about them like a rival football team. They push their $2,000 strollers down the esplanade in Lily Lime yoga clothes that cost more than my rent, they gum up the sidewalks on Saturday mornings and chat loudly over lavender oat lattes in the cafés where I try to work. These women seem to be dedicated to the sole purpose of creating more do-nothing, in-the-way consumers– the last thing the world needs.

"Fucking breeders," we laugh– and I'm relieved that the worst of this conversation has blown over.

"We need a war," he says. "We are long overdue for one. It would bring some much-needed perspective to the people of this country. I would enlist, happily."

I roll my eyes, thinking about him attending boot camp with his protruding gut, but then I absorb what he just said. "...You mean a *civil* war?"

"Yes," without hesitation. So much for moving out of sinister territory.

"Cam, it already feels like we are dangerously close to that point. I don't want it to come down to that." There is a hush over the line. We both know it. If there was a war, we'd be on opposite sides. "I don't want to let it come to that. I don't want to have to choose a side."

"Well, I recommend choosing the side you think is going to *win*."

"You know what the problem really is? The war you want to fight is not possible. The enemy you speak of is not stratified somewhere in our society. You're not going to have all the intelligent, aware, hardworking people on one side and all the self-absorbed fools on the other. You can't fight stupidity. You can't wage a war against cluelessness.

"The only way to fight ignorance is with education. And our country has gutted its education system at the behest of big corporations and the useless intelligentsia. I think we can both agree on that."

"But you're missing the point. You can't 'educate' your way out of cultural fracture and decay. You said it the other day, like some badge of pride: *We're the great Melting Pot!* – but we're not. We used to be. People used to come here, and they'd want nothing more than to embrace our language, our values, our customs, and *be American*. And our citizens were proud of who they were, proud of those values and customs, and taught them to their children, and held others in society accountable to them. But now we have embraced this idiotic notion that *all* cultures are equal, and *all* behavior is acceptable– and to ask someone to assimilate is demeaning and racist. Shame used to be a social force for good, that held us all accountable to decent, agreed-upon social standards– and now we are encouraged to place every weird behavior and vice as the centerpiece of our lives! It's an ugly, degrading lie— one that is going to kill us.

"*NOT ALL CULTURES ARE EQUAL*, period. Don't believe me? Go try wearing your little bikini and 'Abortion is healthcare' belly shirt in the Middle East or Africa! Go start a small business in Venezuela! Go petition for a workers' union in a Chinese factory! *WE ARE NOT THE SAME.*

"It's the culture, or rather, the lack of it, that's the problem. It's rotted us out. And it's not just multiculturalism and immigration, it's the American youth, too. They've been led to believe that they should be accountable for nothing and be given everything. They don't want equal opportunity– they want EQUAL OUTCOME. And the only way to achieve that is by stealing from the strong and exceptional; cutting the legs off the able and the capable, the producers of society. All the Left wants is a helpless, dependent population. Then their control is solidified, and absolute."

I search my brain for a moment. I know this one; I've been doing a little research in my spare time. This is known as the 'Great Replacement Theory,' commonly attributed to white Christian nationalist rhetoric.

In a moment of bravery and clarity, I decide to push a boundary, and call it out. "Isn't that sort of a conspiracy theory?"

"Let me tell you something, Sweetheart. I've been accused of being a 'conspiracy theorist' enough times to know, the only difference between a conspiracy theory and a quiet blip in the mainstream news cycle is a simple matter of six months to two years. Just wait, and you'll see. The type of man that jumped on my car today, he'll be the ruling class of this country in another five years if we stay on the path we're on."

"Let's say you're right. Let's suppose for a moment that this Leftist plan you speak of ends up a success: all the neo-communists, the feminists, the environmentalists, the LGBTQ activists and the immigrants, they all band together and take over the country. And then they turn on the white heterosexual male. They take away their freedom of speech. They threaten them in the streets. The ones who defend themselves get thrown into prisons without due process.

"I want you to know something. I want you to know that I'd be standing out there speaking up for you. Not because I like any of you. Not because I share any of your values. But because no one deserves that. No group, no race, no religion... no one deserves to be stripped of their liberty like that.

"I fight for the liberation of animals and the more I learn, the more I see the worst in people. And frankly, I hate them all. I resent the women pushing their strollers, feeding their babies ice cream from the milk stolen from another mother's breast. I resent the men who deny the world's troubles and hide behind neckties in air-conditioned offices. I resent the young do-nothings bent over their phones. I resent the generation of elders who shrug at the crumbling world they created while they feast on their pensions. My body carries an aching hate toward them, toward their ignorance, toward their sheer numbers, toward their power and relentless apathy.

"Their liberty shouldn't matter to me, but it does. Because when we disqualify the liberty of one, we open up the disqualification of all liberty. And above all, above friendship, or love, or even safety, I want liberty. And so do you."

"It is ironic to me that you speak of 'liberty' when you want the government controlling everything in our lives down to what kind of lightbulbs we use."

"I'm glad you brought that up actually. Because libertarianism has relied on two assumptions that no longer apply: environmental quality and a widespread acceptance of shared social terms. Globalism and capitalism have ruined both of those."

"So has multiculturalism. You just proved my point for me."

~

The day is ruined. At least it's a work day; it would have been ruined sooner or later. I descend the foothills and begin the long walk to Vero's. I cross the downtown streets, hands stuffed in my pockets despite the heat, and try to wrap my head around what I have gotten myself into. My stomach sits low and heavy, as if full of curdled milk. It feels as though a new territory has been entered; a sinister line has been crossed. This isn't just a fun little recon mission anymore. It's not cute, or funny, or exciting.

It reminds me of my first date with Dean. I met him while I was more or less living out of my car, and was visiting a friend at Miami University. (Which is in Ohio, by the way. I did not realize that when I had agreed to pay her a visit.) I was recovering from a broken heart of multiple varieties and insisted I was not looking for a date, but Dean persisted– and like a stray dog, I could not resist the beckon of free food. He was a real gentleman; opened doors and everything. He took me to a hip little Thai place on High Street and brought along a bottle of red wine. "I don't think I've ever had red wine before, but I asked the guy at the store and he said this one was good." As I inhaled the glorious contents of my plate and forked a few curious morsels off of his, he told me stories about serving in the war. He was grateful for an open and sympathetic ear, and described in great detail the living conditions of the grunts, the giant camel spiders and the sand in every crevice of their bodies; staying up for days in a row, having to shoot a pair of teenage boys who crossed over a dry riverbed that was designated as a no-cross zone; the IEDs hidden in the roads; watching a smoldering humvee with his best friend burning inside. He described the carnage so graphically, and yet so casually; I let my fork hit the white porcelain dish.

"I can't believe things like this still happen...I just *can't believe it*. I mean, you hear about it on the news all the time, in these abstract terms and so constantly that it doesn't register as real. I just can't believe your bravery, the things you've seen..." I reached out for his hand, my heart a puddle of red wine. My mind refused to comprehend that things like that happened anymore; as if suddenly, after the wars of our grandparents, we were done; we were all civilized now, and safe. I know how dumb that sounds. I'm just being honest.

I take a break from my walk to Vero's in the manicured grass outside the Mirage County Courthouse and pull out my notebook. I reread my previous notes about Cam, about our night singing in his garage and his slow breathing, but I struggle to add anything to it, afraid to record what I've heard on paper, to give permanence to his words. I watch a lively brood of children, dressed like miniature baristas and sculptors in grass-stained phony workwear, chase each other around grandiose geometric hedges. A freshly-groomed labradoodle fanatically darts toward her tennis ball to her owner's dismay, as her claws rip up the grass and stain her sandy fur with chocolatey soil. A couple takes cheesy engagement photos under a stone archway, staring blankly into each other's eyes in frozen, unnatural poses. The bride-to-be's tacky blue plastic nails sit long and claw-like on her fiance's cheeks. It wrecks the whole aesthetic of the photoshoot, if you ask me. You can buy all the overpriced manicures you want, but you can't buy class. And yes, of course, a cluster of homeless guys sprawl on the south end of the lawn, their territory formally designated by a ring of littered bottles and dumped-out packs. One of them sleeps completely zippered into a browned sleeping bag, and out in the daylight, it looks like a bodybag casually strewn next to the rose bushes.

Who the hell am I to judge anyone? I don't know anything. If I did, I wouldn't be in Mount Mirage with no money, no relationship, no connection to anyone or any place whatsoever, and pushing thirty. If I knew what was good for me, I wouldn't be talking to Cam; I wouldn't have walked into Klipspringer's in the first place. If I knew what was decent, I wouldn't have stopped talking to my father for no good reason, and my parents would know my address. Tyler wouldn't have needed to go all the way to Alaska just to get away from me. If I knew anything about anything, I would have just married Dean; I wouldn't be resentful of everyone with something as simple as a baby and a dog as unattainably rich and spoiled; I wouldn't have to donate fifteen hours a week to environmental causes to justify my existence. And if I wasn't a pretty-enough girl in her twenties with the option to cash in on my own vulnerability to avoid being accountable for anything, I could have easily ended up like one of these guys years ago. I could easily be the one in that brown bodybag.

I force myself to write down a few quotes from Cam's rant. My stomach churns at the words on the page. It may be time to make an executive decision.

"Hun, are you sure you've thought through what you're doing *he-yah?*" Debbie's voice is syrupy sweet as she fans herself with an ivory lace hand fan. Her modest sundress sits gorgeously on her body, her posture perfect. "I know he's quite rich, and *rath-uh* handsome for his age…but perhaps we are entering a dangerous or damaging place by being in the company of this *may-un?* There is, of course, your reputation to *consid-uh…*"

"I don't know, maybe he was just seeing red, like John used to get. Maybe he has no idea what he even said."

"Why on *Earth* are you making excuses for him?" Felicia snaps. She rips Debbie's fan from her hand and points it at me. "He's a monster; a racist, misogynist, bigot! A villain. *A villain!* You've known this! This is exactly what you wanted! Now you don't have to feel an ounce of guilt about using him. Rake his ass right over the coals. Now you know he deserves it."

The girls are cut off by an irate, vibrating black box; I pull it from my pocket and heave a dramatic sigh up to the heavens I don't believe in. "Oh, COME ON!"

It's Tyler, if you didn't already guess. I hit the green button, like an idiot.

"Alaskan Wilderness Police Force, Commissioner speaking. What is the nature of your emergency?"

"Wh–…Nina? Hi, it's me– it's Tyler."

"Yeah, I know. What do you want?"

"I'm just returning your call from the other day. You okay?"

"Yes, my mistake. A moment of weakness."

"It's not weakness if you just needed someone to talk to."

"That's exactly what it is."

We chat for a while. It's surprisingly pleasant to speak with him, to let some of my guard down for a moment. I tell him about the ocean correspondent job at Earth Defenders, and the latest developments with the power plant. He doesn't share much detail about where he is and what he is doing. He probably doesn't want to make me feel bad about how amazing it is. *Selfish bastard.*

"So, how's it going with the writing?"

"Oh, you know how it goes. You go into a creative project with an idea, and then it takes on a life of its own. You think you know where it's going, and then, *BAM!* – you get so much more than you bargained for!" I can feel myself sounding a little hysterical. Tears well up and I swallow them down.

"I'm not sure what you mean… are you still working on the same story you told me about? The movie, with the women?" Tyler's voice sounds calm, but concerned.

"Yes, but there's a bit more to it now. I have been presented with a unique opportunity, one that I simply could not refuse…"

I'm saying too much… I'm about to let the truth fall out…

"May I confide in you Tyler? I feel like I'm bursting inside with this story but I can't tell anyone. I feel like you're the only one who will understand what I'm trying to do, what I'm trying to say–"

But as I say those words aloud, I hear them, and I know that Tyler will not understand. I don't know who would. I hardly do.

I quickly hang up the phone, and as it trembles with Tyler's attempt to return the call, I hit the red button.

I stare at the blue-light abyss of my phone and open up the web browser. I type "Cam Benzin", chuckling to myself that I haven't thought to Google him sooner– and strangely, nothing comes up: nothing about Kantian, or his collectible muscle car, his many jobs and projects, not even a cheesy Linkedin profile photo. I glance back at my notes. The name "Michael Bauer" pops from the page– perhaps there is something more I can learn about Cam's father. I type it into the little bar, the magical Pandoran portal to the world, and what was supposed to be just a regular Tuesday takes on yet another unwanted layer, like a stinking, burn-your-eyes onion sliced open on the countertop. It isn't an old man's obituary, or a black and white photo that appears. It is a photo of Cam. I continue the long walk to Palmetto with my neck craned down, hovering over the blue light, stunned.

WILDLIFE POPULATION MANAGEMENT: ETHICS AND METHODS

This study, while focused on the great white gorilla, is ultimately aimed more widely at ecological conservation through the means of understanding– and potentially controlling– an individual species' population.

In the conservation realm, the topic of wildlife population control is rife with ethical dilemmas and competing interests. Decisions of wildlife management orbit around one central question: *What should we protect, and why?*

From this question emerges a battleground of competing entities: the rights and value of an individual organism; the value of a single population; the value of a species; of an ecosystem; of the global biosphere; and finally, the desires and interests of human beings. Each of these entities has an ethical camp arguing in their favor. Some animal rights activists, for example, believe the harm, confinement, or use of individual animals, even to protect other animals, is inherently immoral. Some ethical Darwinists believe in a hands-off approach to wildlife management, arguing that since humans themselves are animals, our activities are simply a part of nature's process; to interfere would be to "play God", to prevent Nature from running its evolutionary course. Some game conservationists care deeply about ecosystem health, for the utilitarian sake of having enough fish in the lake to fish, and enough deer in the woods to shoot. Socially-minded conservationists may place the most value on the rights of Indigenous subsistence cultures to continue their traditional practices.

What should we protect, and why?

The modern conservationists attempt a holistic view, and see human intervention as a moral obligation to reverse the widespread damage that has been done to wild places by human activity. Intervention may be a means to an anthropocentric end– for example, preserving natural resources for human use. Some conservational purists argue that we should preserve as much pristine, untouched wilderness as possible– not for human extraction, use, or even recreation– but simply to exist for its own sake.

What should we protect, and why?

Active wildlife population management may be considered for a variety of reasons. In some cases, a species that has entered a new territory is considered invasive (often introduced by human activity), and is systematically eliminated to preserve the native species and keep the ecosystem intact. Sometimes there is a disturbance that causes a sudden imbalance of prey and predators– such as the elimination of wild wolves in western farmland, and the resulting glut of grazers like elk and deer– and interventions are made to reestablish that balance to prevent greater ecosystem disruptions.

MANAGING THE GREAT WHITE GORILLA POPULATION

There are competing schools of thought on the pressing topic of preventing global environmental collapse, and the role of the great white gorillas in this crisis. It is the opinion of some scientists, intellectuals, and conservationists that we should utilize traditional animal control methods to rein in the GWG population. These methods include open hunting and lethal trapping, or for a more humane process, reproductive interventions: trap-and-neuter programs, or chemical sterilization in the GWG food supply.

The hunting approach is not only cruel, ambitious, and expensive– it also includes the highly probable risk of escalation and reciprocated violence from the GWGs, which may cause even more environmental destruction. Reproductive interventions are highly risky and cruel in their own right, and may take effect too slowly to prevent the worst of the environmental crisis.

Beyond the reproductive effect of castrating alpha males, there has been optimism that the resulting disruption to male hormones would be enough to successfully alter male behavior. In 2016 an ethology and communication study was conducted by Dr. J.P. Pandler on Western white gorillas in zoos around the world. Pandler's team of anthropologists and communication specialists set out to establish a 'Rosetta Stone' of the GWG's body language and verbal cues that could be deployed by outreach teams to wild populations. Pandler's results were a humbling disappointment: the male gorillas that had risen to the top of the social hierarchy in captivity were deprived of their instincts, therefore their behaviors had no practical applications in the wild; though reproductively still intact, they were effectively castrated by their confinement, and could not hold a candle to their wild GWG counterparts.

One radical proposal gaining mainstream popularity is that we have but one option to prevent a mass extinction: to eliminate Western white gorillas altogether before it is too late.

But this scientist refuses to accept the responsibility of deliberate extinction, especially in consideration of its process, which will inevitably be a brutal and violent one, with many risks to public safety.

Therefore it is the opinion of this author that communication is our only ethical and viable option to efficiently preserve what biodiversity we have left. Communication provides a pathway for creating a strategic alliance with the GWGs to prevent mass extinction and preserve Nature's bounty for future generations of all species. This method could channel the very traits that helped the great white gorillas take over the planet into preventing a collapse of their own doing. We have much to learn from the GWGs' intelligence, adaptability, and ingenuity, all of which can be utilized to provide solutions to the ecological crisis at hand.

11
Get Out of Town

We haven't spoken for a few days.

The nights have been sleepless. I can't stop thinking about Cam. *Michael*. Michael Bauer. Cam Benzin, Michael Bauer.

Cam Benzin doesn't exist on Google because Cam Benzin was born in 2017, when Michael Bauer died. It's a new kind of death– not a physical ending, but a layered killing of one's identity by means of the all-powerful, all-connecting, all-seeing Internet– a death we moderns call "cancellation". It is a social death of humiliation, perpetrated by infamy, mockery, and public scrutiny beyond the scale of a small town: the Internet. Global, inescapable, unerasable, permanent. A spiritual death by dispossession of one's vocation and dignity, financial ruin and the helpless anxiety of relentless exposure. Michael Bauer, Founder and CEO of Kantian Consulting, collector of classic American muscle cars, engineer of critical energy infrastructure technologies, handsome, wealthy and successful, popular in Hollywood circles and with California's elites, was booted from his company and his world in a highly publicized, humiliating and damning campaign, led by Giles Pion and an actress-activist named Cherry Boon.

Cherry was Cam's– *Michael's*– lover back in the early '90s. According to IMDB, Cherry played supporting roles in a few forgettable films in the '90s and early 2000s, and one lead role in an indie film in 2008. A magazine article from 2010 states, "Cherry's first love has always been acting and modeling, but she also has an entrepreneurial side. She started a feminist-themed makeup line called *For You Not Him* in 2002, which led her to take more interest in feminist causes, and in time, to become a prominent women's rights activist."

Cherry came forward in 2017, at the height of the #MeToo movement, to reveal that at the start of her acting career she was manipulated and pressured into a sexual relationship with Michael "Mac" Bauer after he had claimed to be related to a powerful film producer.

"I knew that if I denied him what he wanted," she shared on a video that she simultaneously posted to Facebook, Twitter, Instagram, and Youtube, "he would make sure I would never work in Hollywood again. My career, my dreams, my financial independence, were held over my head in pursuit of my body. Helpless and frightened, like so many young women in this world against the cold and universal force of patriarchal power, I submitted my physical and emotional being to a man with more power and influence than I had.

"His gaslighting began with a so-called 'rescue,' when I was with my friends in Venice and enjoying a peaceful sunset swim. Mac, a stranger walking down the beach, in his infinite male wisdom, decided that I had swum too far from shore for my own good. He swam out and grabbed me, touching and gripping my bare skin without my consent or understanding, and yanked me to shore.

"He had convinced me that he had saved my life– that I *owed him*– and the trauma of that day led to a toxic and abusive relationship, built on his sadistic desire to dominate and subjugate me, a vulnerable young woman who had just moved to a new city to pursue her dreams, all to make *himself* feel powerful.

"I haven't spoken to Mr. Bauer in many years, but he has left a stain on my life that has led to many self-destructive behaviors, a lack of emotional safety, and moments of crippling self-doubt– but it has also pushed me to overcome; to become a leader in the feminist cause, joining strong women everywhere to bring justice and equality to all. I want to thank the other brave survivors who have come forward to share their stories of sexual violence–"

There are many more magazine articles, interviews, and videos of Cherry after 2017. She wrote a book about activism through the lens of intersectionality, a belief that the oppression of 'womxn', queer people, people of color, Indigenous people, and climate change are all intrinsically connected. Cherry gave a TED Talk earlier this year. She is cast in a superhero film due to come out next year.

The nights have been sleepless– not solely because I can't stop thinking about Cam. But because of the rats.

The walls of our little cube in the foothills have been colonized by a tribe of very loud, rambunctious rats. They seem to have most of their festivities and fights a couple hours before sunup, and when I lay in bed I can hear them chewing and clawing behind my head.

In the little tapping of their claws against the drywall I hear the tapping of the buxom blonde's nails against the keyboard, the origin dream of what feels like a madness that's overtaken me, and I lay awake all night, listening intently to the dialogue of imagined characters and choosing the soundtrack of high-action montage scenes. My movie will be written, and produced. My girls will have their victory. The servers will be wiped clean, and the villain will go down.

The landlord is finally sending an exterminator today, and now I lay haunted by the fact that I have *become* the rat; I have sold out my vegan principles and condemned my furry little roommates to a gnarly, painful end. I wish it weren't so, but it's us against them; it's the value of a person's property– and the value of a good night's sleep– against their lives, and the scale tips against their favor.

I don't want to be around to see it.

Mr. Shaft

> Saw a girl this AM with a 'DESTROY CAPITALISM' t-shirt drinking a $10 drink from Starbucks. Want me to get her number for you?

11:12 AM

No thanks, I'm allergic to cat hair. Plus I'm picturing someone with more hair on her underarms than her head… not really into that.	11:14 AM
Hah, you were close! It was a white girl with dreads. So.. how've you been, stranger?	11:15 AM
I thought I'd give you a break from my wrath.	11:16 AM
What do you have going on today, Miss Distrella?	11:18 AM
Thinking about getting out of this town for the day. Thinking I need to.	11:19 AM
I am IN.	11:19 AM
I'll let you drive.	11:19 AM
L O L, let me. Good one. Meet me at the garage in an hour.	11:20 AM

My plan is to bring it up again, what he said, and have one last good row with him, and then be done. I should have enough material by now. I have been thinking so much about the villain character in the last several weeks that I've spent little time on the script itself. So here I go, charging back into the belly of the beast one last time– sword not drawn, but hanging there ready, quietly in the scabbard, in case I have to cut my way out. I feel like I'm playing with fire but I have so many more questions. For the sake of the story, I'm staying in the game. I'll tap out when I need to.

It takes me a long time, longer than I'd care to admit, to get ready. When it comes to dressing and behaving, I am between worlds, and I stand before the bathroom mirror a bit lost. In my upbringing on the East Coast I was considered the earthy one, the 'hippie girl', because I didn't bury myself under gaudy eye shadow, hairspray, and self-tanner. I changed nothing but which ocean I lived next to, and by comparison I became the diva, the high-maintenance one, the overdone girl compared to Tyler's backpacky, rock-climby, ski-lodgy girl friends, who wear nothing but mineral sunblock and tie-dye bandanas in their sun-dried hair (and somehow still look unattainably beautiful.)

The name of the game is to look appealing to Cam, but not to look like *I'm trying* to be appealing to Cam. I reach for what I always wear, a cotton sundress and a pair of sandals, and I listen carefully to Debbie's beauty tips as I attempt to style my hair and smear makeup on my skin.

I show up to his garage and the car that hung above us at our '80s slumber party is idling outside: a 1971 Plymouth Hemi 'Cuda convertible, black as night and one of only four of its kind in the world, and a bunch of other muscle-car-speak, all lost on me. I've learned a couple more words but I'm still indifferent to what they mean.

The engine is already running as I walk up. The thing is deafening; I resent the fumes entering the air. It sits there growling like some disgruntled, chain-smoking panther as Cam sorts out loose ends in his garage. The beast emits an old and ghastly smell, a smell of burning and poison, but it smells like my childhood, and nostalgia is more potent a drug than any hydrocarbon. It smells like Uncle Mick's old burgundy Cadillac that sat outside my grandparents' driveway on Easter. It smells like my father's sweaty shirt did at the end of each day, when I'd bolt to him for a hug as he walked through the door. It smells like the drive from the church to the reception in the robin's egg blue 1954 Chevy Bel Air Convertible on my sister Diane's wedding day.

Cam gives me a briefing before I am allowed to climb in. "Here's how I want you to get in the car." He demonstrates. I mimic his careful movements and settle into the passenger bucket seat. The inside feels and smells historic. I reach out to caress the little silver barracuda in the center of the wood grain steering wheel. The speedometer goes up to 240; the gearshift looks like the butt of a pistol. He wastes no time letting me fumble with the old seatbelt. "Use your thumb or you will pinch the skin on your finger." I comply.

"Can we stop for a cup of coffee first? I didn't sleep great last night."

"Sure, I could use one too."

We turn a corner and become caught in a tangled web of cars, bikes, and festooned floats and humans. "Shit, I forgot about the Summer Harvest parade. Let's just get out and walk."

It amazes me how all it takes is an excuse, something as simple as a parade celebrating crops, for people to let loose their inner freaks so publicly– especially in such a small and tightly knit city. Grown men are dressed up like wood nymphs, fairies, and foxes, with wings and bushy little tails that hang behind them. A troop of at least twenty post-menapausal women have squeezed their breasts and bellies into gold corsets and donned the appearance of demented Vegas showgirls, with huge feather plumage bursting from their shoulders and fanning over their heads. From a distance they look like a flock of frantic yellow peacocks battling hot flashes with their feathers.

A group of parade dancers are gathered on a corner drinking sports drinks and waiting for the festivities to start. They are all wearing matching thongs, some with the courtesy of fishnets and stockings, but most are bare-assed on this sunny Saturday morning. Most are women, or at least would identify as such. But there are also several men in the same costume; though, to their credit, all but one appear to have gotten waxed for the occasion.

A sixty-year-old man wanders around with a giant paper maché mushroom cap on his head and tiny red spandex shorts, and nothing else. I'm pretty sure that guy works at my bank. There are exposed bodies everywhere, old and young, wrinkles and flaps and rolls and hairs, sprayed and painted and glittered and strapped into shiny, plasticky, pleathery outfits. Ironically, the bulk of them would call themselves staunch environmentalists. Cliques of high school girls in the crowd are dressed in sixties-style fashions, with tye-dye and paisley crop tops in loud colors, high-waisted bell bottoms, big round sunglasses and plastic flowers in their hair.

Most of the floats warrant some artistic merit, so credit where it's due. With paint and plaster they have combined and transformed everyday objects into complex and beautiful moving scenes. This year's theme is "Honor Thy Mother," with the posters showing a plus-sized Black woman in a flower crown hovering elegantly over a planet Earth engulfed in swirly flames.

Despite the theme being a cause I hold dear, I find myself getting progressively angrier as I observe the joyous festivities. All I can see is irony: all the waste and consumption in the name of environmentalism. Cam has ruined me. I was already bad, and now I'm even more of a curmudgeon; a joyless kvetch. I should be locked away somewhere.

Felicia eggs me on. "These fucking people. 'Honor thy mother' with spray paint and toxic glue? Glitter in the streets? Don't they know that those are just microplastics that are going straight from the storm drains to the ocean?"

"Can't you just appreciate families having a nice time–" Debbie gasps with the theatrics of a drama major. "Do you see those people over there... *in thong under-waya*!? And that bearded *may-an*, he's dressed like the Chiquita Banana lady! This is a *family event*! The depravity! The sickness! Cam is right, we are a *cult-chah* in decay!"

The crowds gather to find their watching places along Main. I don't need to tell you who goes to parades. Day drinkers and families with little kids. Who else would be dazzled by all this glittered-up garbage? Children are everywhere, in costumes with rainbows, suns, and strawberries painted on their little cheeks. Little princesses, butterflies, farmers and sprouts. One kid is dressed like a potato– excellent. He wins the day. Sadly, many dogs are being led around in similar costumes, anxious and miserable, being pushed around in baby strollers or carried like infants in papooses. One obese bulldog is being pulled along in a wagon dressed like a ladybug, utterly dejected.

"Oh my little Nina, who has hurt you?" Cam grins at me and hands me a coffee. "Your face is twisted into knots. You're seeing it, aren't you?"

"Seeing what?" I try to neutralize my face, unaware of its previous shape. I don't exactly have a great resting poker face, or so I've been told. I have to make a conscious effort to hide how I feel. But over time I've gotten pretty good at it.

"You see what I see. The spiritual rot. The infuriating contradiction. The underhanded vulgarity of this place. I can see it in your look, you're seeing what I'm seeing. And something in you is repulsed. Something instinctive knows that this isn't all sunshine and rainbows. You know this isn't good."

Good Christ, please tell me that Felicia, Debbie and *Cam aren't all agreeing now???*

"I don't know what you're talking about," I recoil as he reaches to put his arm around me, but he pulls me to him anyway.

"I love it. It's kind of beautiful to watch. I'm seeing you wake up, in real time."

"That's a very arrogant point of view; that I'm somehow 'asleep' and you are the conscious one."

"It's only arrogance if I'm wrong, and I'm not. You see, all these people, the parents mostly, think that they're doing something righteous and noble by exposing their kids to this– that half-naked men wearing lipstick and fairy wings are a perfectly wholesome display, and their acceptance of it is a badge of honor; a symbol of their status as the utmost in tolerance and progressive ideals. But it's sick and self-centered, what they're doing. This is a parade of narcissists. In fifteen or twenty years, you'll see what all this deviant 'Pride' shit does to a generation of children, robbed of their innocence and conditioned into accepting perversion as normal."

"Cam, this isn't a gay pride parade. It's a summer harvest parade."

"Does it look to you like they're celebrating the success of this year's tomato crop?"

I chuckle at his obvious point, thinking of the gaggle of men in the matching thongs. I point to the kid dressed as a potato. "He gets it."

I fumble with the seatbelt again. "So, where are we going?"

He doesn't reply; only flips his sunglasses down onto his face like Doc Brown in *Back to the Future* and revs the engine.

I know how this is going to go. This thing goes up to 240 and a fanatical racecar driver is strapping in next to me. I'm not interested in any of this and I disapprove of it on principle; he knows that but seems prepared to convince me otherwise. You should hear the way he speaks about his abilities behind the wheel. Up 'til now I have used every opportunity possible to doubt him or quietly mock him– like with the incident on Cicero Street.

I want to believe that it was his fault. But today, something in my gut says to believe him, to believe *in* him– to sit back, let go and experience the fury of this man and his machine. I look around at the fine detail of the interior; the perfectly welded metal that surrounds us, the coat of shiny black paint that gives the car the look of perpetually being wet. Vertical slits on its sides look like gills; its broad grille and four headlights give it the look of a menacing deep sea creature. For the first time, I can see a machine as a work of art. It moves, it has use; but this vehicle is not just a mass-produced piece of equipment. I look at this car and I can see how Cam views himself. *This is him*; the soul of a man expressed as a machine.

I am certain I know better than all this, to get into this car and everything. But my curiosity silences the more evolved parts of my brain, and off we go.

We speed through town toward Cliffside Hwy 84. He moves around car after car with surgical precision, slicing his way between both space and time, avoiding collisions within frantic measures.

Everything is moving so quickly it stops looking real. For some reason I can't explain, this melty blurring of space and color relaxes and entrances me. Each time we hit a clear stretch we take off like a bullet being shot from a gun. We are the man in the cannon at the circus. We are a cartoon blur. And god damn me for not being able to prevent the thrilled giggle from escaping my body.

On a single lane stretch of the winding canyon road we get caught in a line of cars moving slowly. "Of course– look at the front of the line."

I lean over to search for the head of a winding snake of cars and trucks. A silver Prius.

"OF COURSE it's a Prius. When we drive past, look in the window. I'm going to go with female, Asian female."

I roll my eyes. "I'm going to go with white man, weenie white man."

As we exit the bend, the road opens up into two lanes, and the line of cars begins sorting itself into fast and slow. He weaves through all of them like we're in an episode of *Wacky Races* and slows down as we pass the Prius. A birdlike person with an asymmetrical haircut in their late twenties is hunched over the wheel. Impossible to tell in such a short time if they are a woman or man, but they are unmistakably Asian. *Damnit.*

We both shout, "A-HA!", believing that being half-right is the same as being right. I reach over and shove his shoulder as our laughter cuts through the roaring wind.

Once the line of impotent cars is behind us, he cruises smoothly into the valley. I catch my breath and glance over at him through a screen of my own hair. He doesn't register my gaze. I know that face he's making: Cam is DaVinci at the easel right now. He's Roark at the drafting table. I am staring at a man who is complete. I am staring at the equivalent of me swimming along the ocean floor.

The gearshift is just an extension of his arm, the growling engine an extension of his beating heart. They have melted down into a single, massive, violent creature; a shiny black barracuda; and I have been given the privilege of riding on its back. Without taking his eyes from the road he reaches out, and I accept his hand. We both squeeze hard– just below the threshold of trying to make it hurt.

It is midday on one of the hottest afternoons of the year, and we cruise across a treeless road into the yellowed valleys of wine country. So much for taking a shower. My hair is a windblown bird's nest and my sweaty thighs stick to the leather seat. By the look of his all-black outfit, I imagine he is also a sweaty mess. We grin and bear it; the day is still beautiful.

He pulls onto a country main street in a little wine town. People turn and stare as he paces the narrow streets looking for a worthy place to park. The town looks quaint and old-fashioned from a distance, but upon closer examination, faux-rustic modernity appears. The smell of smoked meat emanates from the steakhouse on the corner.

While he vets a half-dozen parking spaces, I quietly look up his car on my phone, adding all the adjectives I can remember. An article displays a sister of his car that sold at auction for two million bucks.

A cluster of middle-aged men approach us as he escorts me to my feet.

"What year is this one?"

"'71."

"Mmm. She is *somethin'.*"

"Custom-built. I can't even tell you the sweet, sweet pain this girl has cost me."

They start to talk in motorhead terms so my attention drifts to the stark difference between the mens' appearances. Cam dresses like a villain in a 1980s car movie; the solid black outfits, the slicked back hair and shiny watch, the patch-covered racer jacket. He looks like Val Kilmer. I giggle to myself. *For a person who takes himself so seriously, he looks like a fucking cartoon.*

The other men appear to be what Cam refers to as "neutered fathers." Goofy haircuts, Crocs and New Balance sneakers with high white socks, little-boy plaid and tan cargo shorts, shirts tucked in over big bellies.

One man's shirt says *"Squirrely's Pizza Challenge Winner!"* in bold orange letters with a cartoon squirrel eating a whole folded pizza. Another has a mascot of the local high school football team, a purple owl with giant muscles and lavender lightning behind it. Their mouths hang open and their eyes don't leave the car as they speak to Cam, who is clearly so aware of his posture that he looks like he's breathing at half his lungs' capacity.

I turn away to laugh at them. *Christ, I don't even know which of them is worse.*

He leads the way into an old farmhouse with a big rustic sign that says "G. Carlin Family Winery." Cam tells the girl at the counter, "We're here to see *so-and-so.*" I don't notice the name.

He stands at the bar and chats with the staff about the so-and-so they all know and the so-and-sos who worked with so-and-so and how great so-and-so is. He is very good at this, I've noticed, but I don't pay attention. I glance around at the place. A shelf is filled with black and white photos of an old man in military uniform, a Purple Heart in a frame, and dozens of military commemorative metal buttons.

We both want something cold after that scorching drive through the valley. We take two glasses of white to a dark room in the back. More old family photographs, old farm equipment hanging on the wall, big leather chairs for my thighs to stick to, oaken smells. A real masculine place.

His friend Dom enters, a chubby Irish-Italian man in his mid forties. "You must have something special between your legs. He doesn't take out the Cuda for just anybody."

"He hasn't even had a taste yet. Maybe I can get a helicopter ride."

I know– absolutely gross, isn't it? But this is how it works. Between waitressing, having an older brother and spending my childhood at Dad's shop, I feel like I've been training for this my whole life. This volleying back and forth of misogynistic quips and insults is a language to be studied, and with years of practice– and abandonment of self-respect– can be mastered. Doubt, hesitation and decency must be removed from sight and mind. It is a game of verbal poker. You're either dealt in the game or it does not recognize your existence.

As Dom and I go back and forth, I see Cam studying me like he brought me here with intention. The obvious motive is to show off the fact that he's with a much younger woman. But he's carefully observing how I react to this man's pig-headed audacity, how I carry myself in their offensive banter. And I'm batting a thousand.

"So Cam, you bringing this girl to Skip's this fall?"

"Which girl, hardware or software?" Cam winks at me. "Cuda's coming for sure. The rest is up to her."

"It would help to know what you're talking about."

"You haven't told her? It's the Palmetto Motor Club's Classic Car Show," Dom says with starry eyes. "It's Cam's Christmas. And this is an extra special year– the party's being hosted in Palmetto Hills at Skip Vodnyyvor's place."

"Oh yes of course, Skip Omnivore– who doesn't love that guy?"

Cam touches my arm. "It will be a huge show, with some of the most expensive and rare cars in the world, followed by a more intimate dinner with some very good friends of mine. Great people, who I think you'll love. Skip has very celebrated friends and is a wonderful host. Would you like to come?"

"YES SHE WOULD!" Debbie shouts into the microphone inside my brain. "Fancy cars, *Palmett-ah Hills*! Fabulous people! What will you *way-ah*?!"

Felicia reclines with a black cherry blunt. "All I have to say is, *Mac Bauer*." She blows skunky cherry smoke in Debbie's face. "*MAC. Michael Bauer*, bitch. Have we already forgotten? Who do you think these 'fabulous people' are? Bunch of fascist Nazis, that's who. Exactly how many movie villains do you plan on 'studying' until you become one yourself?"

I press the cold wine glass to my temple. "I work at Vero's on weekends, but thank you for inviting me."

"What are you, nuts? Get your shifts covered! Or quit! Palmetto Hills! Cam's *Christmas!*" Dom is flabbergasted by my hesitation. He's matching Debbie's energy. I look to Cam. I didn't consider that I just rejected his offer in front of his friend. He looks quietly disappointed in me.

"Nina, this isn't just a pleasure trip. These are great connections for you to have. You'll enjoy yourself, but you'll also have opportunities to network with very successful people. I'm offering this to you because I think it could help you."

"Stop playing coy, you little minx. She's going, Cam." He points at me. "You're going. Hell, I'm going too. More wine, to celebrate!" Dom exits with an empty bottle in hand. Despite the air-conditioner blasting us in the dark leathery room, I still feel sweat forming under my dress.

"He's kissing my ring so I'll put him on the list. I like to let him sweat it out, but he knows he's coming. It's a very exclusive event, you know."

"...It sounds exciting and all, and perhaps a great opportunity... I'm just not so sure I want to be introduced as your guest, as your...*date*."

"What?"

"I mean, it's a small town, I'm much younger than you, and I don't know you all that well..." He can't hide the hurt in his eyes with anger, though I can tell he is about to try. Before he can respond, I change course and grin widely. "I'm just kidding, snowflake. I'd be honored to be your guest. But as professional associates. Agreed?"

His lips part in a bleached smile. "You're the one who said 'date', not me." He pinches my thigh, and a bead of sweat rolls down the little valley of my spine.

"A sparkling rosé, to celebrate!" Dom uncorks the bottle and motions to a woman who brings in a plate of sliced cheeses and cured meats.

"Alright, two more names for the guest list. I'm texting Skip now." Cam looks up from his phone. "...But let me ask you something– and please don't be offended by this, but... are you able to dress up? Do you have a certain kind of clothes? Last time I saw you you were wearing some kind of hemp shoes..."

"They weren't hemp, they were just old— otherwise I would have smoked them by now. And yes, I'm sure I have something I can wear."

"Oh no she *doooesn't*," sings Debbie. "*PLEASE* ask him to take you shoppin'..."

Dom leans forward and his chubby cheeks are pushed upward as he rests his chin into his fists. He grins like a middle school boy. "Let's hear about the outfit."

Back to the same game. I am a tantalizing, shiny object, and it's time to dangle myself before them. "Well, I have a couple things in mind, but I think the best one is long-sleeved, black, fitted around the waist..."

"A dress?"

"Yes, high neckline in the front, but cuts very low in the back..."

They both nod.

"Elegant. Let's talk shoes. What about the shoes..."

"All I have are a pair of nude heels..."

"*Laaame.*"

"He's right, nude is boring," Cam says.

"I don't care about shoes. And I thought men don't care about things like shoes."

"Are you kidding? I *love* shoes. There is nothing sexier on a woman."

They start talking about shoes for too long, a minute or more, naming designers and describing styles.

"Are you guys 'foot dudes'? Is that what this is?"

"No, no, no— but a good pair of shoes elongates the legs and accentuates—"

"—Okay, I get it. But that's all I have." I have neither of these things, by the way. I will have to hit every thrift store in the county.

"A friend of mine runs a boutique in Palmetto Cove. I'll hook you up; I have a feeling you will benefit from a little makeover."

Cam leans over and shows Dom his phone. They both snicker.

"What is it?" I grab at the phone; I miss the first time, but like a cat hunting, I am able to snatch it from him after a few minutes of pretending to lose interest.

Skip Vodnyyvor

> I have a present for you.
> 2:22 PM

> I'm intrigued. Some more of those stogies? Good aged scotch?
> 2:22 PM

> Not quite. But it's 29 and goes down smoothly.
> 2:22 PM

> I like where this is going. Will it be nicely wrapped?
> 2:23 PM

> Most definitely. Add two guests to my party for the show. Dom will bring the stogies.
> 2:23 PM

> Excellent.
> 2:23 PM

"Don't get all offended. It's just a joke."

"Just so I am clear— you're giving me to this man as a host gift. Wouldn't I be worth more if you sold me at auction?"

Emerging from the air-conditioned, dark room at the Carlin Family Winery into the late valley afternoon makes the sweat on my body sting. The heat sits heavy like an invisible blurring cloud in the town, washing out the vision and gently ringing in the ears. The streets are deserted, the tasting rooms full. I pause in front of the door of the Cuda.

"Good girl." Cam opens the door for me and inspects the car closely as he circles around to his side. He lights a cigar in the driver's seat. The smell of its smoke carries me elsewhere, to dark poker rooms and a penthouse in Hudson Yards, and I search the streets, search the porches of the little buildings with longing eyes, with a desperation, a desperate desire to run.

"What are you doing? Get in."

"I… I don't want to go home."

"Why not?"

"A lot of reasons." His face changes; he hates responses like that.

"My house is lousy with rats. Well– I'm assuming dead rats, by now."

"*Gross*. I can only imagine what your place looks like on a bartender's salary in Mount Mirage." He takes a contemplative puff. He really does look like a cartoon villain; it's too good. "Tell you what. I'm going to get you out of there. Give me a week or two, I will ask around."

"Oh no, you don't have to do that…"

"And if nothing opens up, you can stay with me. I'm going to be housesitting for Arnold for a few months, starting next week. He's got plenty of spare rooms, a beautiful private yard. And a pool."

A POOL. Mount Mirage isn't like the California towns in the movies; only the *really* rich people have pools here. One of the greatest tragedies of Tyler dumping me was the loss of all pool access.

The heat runs from my head to my stomach, and the wine runs from my stomach to my head; I climb into the car and kiss him. "Mr. Shaft, why are you so kind to me?"

"The real question is, Miss Distrella, is why you're always questioning why I'm kind to you. Can't you just accept that I care about you, that I want the best for you?

"I see the real you, suffocated under your own idealism, and it frustrates me. I can see the untapped potential inside you, stifled by the misguided belief that you're a hopeless victim of social circumstances, or that your very existence is undeserved."

I think he's going to descend into a political rant, but he doesn't. He touches my cheek and I tilt my head back to prevent a tear from falling. "You're as special as you are beautiful, Nina. And who you are now is nothing compared to who you can become. Let me show you; let me help you blossom. Let me take care of you."

The engine lets out one big snarling roar and then subdues to a growl. He waits for me to buckle my seatbelt, per his previous instructions. We take off down the dusty lane, and the world blurs again.

PART TWO

THE FALL

12
The Smell of Metal

I suppose my fascination with men stretches all the way back to early childhood. I studied their vernacular, their work, their smells. Not just the smell of their bodies or breath, but more so the smell of the world in which they lived. Male spaces were hidden, untamed places, separate from where the women existed: garages, basements, forts; dirt, metal, wood. It seemed more honest than the colorful kitchens and orderly living rooms, the brightly-lit beauty salons and enticing shops of a girl's world. It was outdoor to indoor; feral versus sophisticated. The male territories were earthy, crude, visceral– *real*. The boys were allowed to say exactly what they meant, to get their shoes dirty and bloody their knees. On the playground and in the neighborhood, I stared at them curiously, stood in their groups and played their games, just to hear them speak and play; to see how they would act when a situation would arise. It started as early as my first memories, in my father's shop.

He ran a small boat repair shop in a European immigrant neighborhood of New York City. The ethnicities came in waves: the Huguenots and Germans settled there first; when the Irish came they beat them up; then the Irish beat up the Italians; the Italians and Irish formed an alliance to beat up the Jews. Then the Mexicans came and couldn't hide behind their brown skin, but they got relief when they started opening up restaurants and sharing their glorious food. No one dared to mess with the Russians when they started moving in, but they complained about their cold social discourtesy behind closed doors.

Dad drove over the Outerbridge around sunup each morning to get into the city from New Jersey. He was never meant to be a city boy, if you ask me. Harry Distrella is a soft-hearted man with a child's brown eyes, enviably capable of a deep satisfaction in things as simple as a freshly-cut lawn. He spent his earliest years on the streets of Brooklyn searching out enclaves of trees, dreaming all winter about visiting his cousins in the rural midwest in the summer. After high school he worked on boats and cars, and used his cash to build a motorcycle. He rode with some friends down to the Jersey Shore for the first time in the spring of 1983, and was both stunned and disturbed to learn that such a beautiful place existed a mere hour from where he was born. He fell head over heels for a beach girl with a tiny waist and big blue eyes, my mother. He bought the boat shop from his cousin when my mother got pregnant with my brother George, and they moved into a house in the Jersey suburbs to make room for their second child, which turned out to be two: my twin sisters.

My first memory is laying across the front seat of the pickup truck, my head on my father's knee, and staring up at the patterns of the Outerbridge's beams through the windshield. The morning sun flickered through the beams' gaps, stinging my eyes. I held a fluffy white blanket over them. Every time we went over that bridge I tried to imagine men building it, how it must start: the first girders and cantilevers reaching out into open space like the venturing green fingers on a branch of ivy. I imagined the bravery of the men who walked on the structure as they built it; man and metal, venturing out onto the current of cold air flowing above frigid water, trusting one another to perform their appropriate duty.

Dad's shop smelled like rusty metal, motor oil, and damp Raritan Bay air. He would start each morning by opening the garage doors and sweeping up loose nuts, crushed barnacle and shell fragments and bits of copper wire. He did his work, no matter how menial or tedious it was, with the utmost effort and concentration. He worked like a dog even though he owned the place; he took rude comments and complaints from his customers like a champion boxer; he never once grumbled about the long hours, the weeks without days off, or his seemingly tireless body. I would sit behind the front desk and watch him, play puzzle games on the clunky beige computer, and walk around the boats with George. Most were propped up in the yard, but I preferred the dock, always holding out hope to see a creature appear in the turbid, brackish water.

Dad's childhood best friend, my Uncle Mick, was a police officer, who would take two or three hour breaks from his beat to sit in the shop and talk to my father, talk to the customers, talk to anyone who would listen, anything to avoid going back outside to face the New York streets.

"You just wouldn't believe how much things have changed since Marshan took office," he said while my father was all but disappeared under a hull. "They've got the power now, the criminals. It's like there are no laws anymore. If we even touch 'em, we'll end up on the evening news. I gotta do my job, I got a right to make it home at night too, doesn't that count for something? Doesn't anyone care about a man trying to make a livin' anymore?"

My father continued his work. "Yeah, you should see the squeeze they're trying to put on us with these new franchise taxes, not to mention the ridiculous toll rate hikes. I might as well hand this place directly to the city."

"Fuckin' slime, Harry. They're trying to break us, I'm tellin' you."

I considered the boatyard a sort of home, and my time there as a sort of work. I would throw fits to skip school and go up to the shop with Dad. And he eagerly brought me along, even when he was busy. Dad loved us so much, he really did. He had a special bond with George, but he loved having daughters.

Late fall was boat winterizing season, and Dad would work around the clock. He would come home barely in time for a late dinner most nights, sometimes with a surprise behind his back: bakery cupcakes, little art kits with discs of watercolor paint that could be mistaken for antacids. He must have been so worn out, but he never showed it.

We would help Mom lift his spirits with a big hearty dinner: pot roast and mashed potatoes with half a stick of butter, carrots soaked through

with the juices that had dripped off the meat in the oven, flaky biscuits–
and we'd set the table in the "nice room" of the house, the dining room,
that hosted stacks of bills and school papers when not in use.

When we heard the pickup truck growl its way down the street we
raced upstairs to put our nice Sunday school dresses on and get back to
the front door before he opened it. He knelt at the door to absorb the rush
of little girls racing up to him and throwing their arms around him: one
around his neck and one for each of his extended arms. As the youngest
of the three girls, I always aimed for the middle. I would reach up and
kiss his cheek with a cartoonish *smack* sound. The meal was always good,
but you could measure just how good by how quiet we all were. It was
silly and lighthearted when we were that young. The lid of the pressure
cooker of life was off back then.

After boats, Dad's second love was cars. He could take a car apart
and put it back together. On weekends our relatives would stop over with
their car troubles and Dad would fix it, no questions asked. They'd chat
with Mom in the kitchen while she fixed dinner for everyone and he'd
crawl into the engine or under the driver's seat.

He always had metallic smells. The grease and metal seemed to come
out of his pores even on the days off, which were few and far between,
and those days were spent behind the lawnmower, which added a sweet
meadowy smell to his skin and clothes.

When we got older and started getting our learners permits, he'd call
the phone numbers painted on the windshields of cars parked on the side
of the road, or share promising newspaper clippings from the classifieds.
He came along to meetings with the owners and asked enough questions
to demonstrate that he knew cars and he knew liars.

He changed our oil, vacuumed the interiors, put air in the tires. And
when we started liking boys, he asked what kind of car they drove, and if
they knew how to change a tire or do an oil change.

When I complained to my mother, she defended his questioning.
"If you want to have a good life through the toughest of times, choose a
man like your father– one who is able to fix and build things, and enjoys
it– a man who is curious about how things work.

"A man can have all the money in the world, and it will be completely useless if *he's* completely useless. Those slick businessmen, with their white tennis shoes and European luxury cars, pay other men to build, fix, and maintain things for them. And guess what? If your father and I were stranded on an island with nothing but a string and a handful of paper clips, he'd have a shelter built and a fire going before the sun went down. That's what matters."

13
Kevin

I stare into the toilet bowl for a moment, and decide not to do it. I know where the drains go. I shouldn't flush them; it would fuck up some fish.

I hold the orange bottle in my hand, slowly twisting it so I can feel the weight of the pills rolling inside. I have so many reasons to dump them, the most important of which is that they don't work. I don't feel less depressed or less anxious. But I do feel a quiet pang of disappointment in myself each time I open the bottle.

The only difference I ever felt was in the first few months, and that doesn't count. I felt good because I put myself on a short and unsustainably rigid regimen to get healthy again. It was around 2012, after the Great Barrier Reef had broken my hope, Geologic Time had broken god, and John Laidir had broken my heart. Existential dread had crept through my body like a rainforest vine, twisting and curious, and wrapped itself snugly around my brain.

I convinced myself that my issues were merely physical, just a natural consequence of the stresses of school, of being broke and on my own. All I needed to do was to get healthy and then I could ditch the pills. I was not eating or sleeping, so I started going for long walks so I'd get tired. I started smoking pot to make myself hungry and to sand down the prickly edges of my thoughts. I unsubscribed from the dozen environmental and political email lists I was on. I made an effort to occupy my mind with things that weren't about the demise of the planet– no more videos about animals drowning in hurricanes, no more whales' stomachs full of fishing line, no more satellite images of rainforest fires and the sickening yellow smoke. I started walking dogs again, which forced me to leave the house. I skipped classes and sat in dark bars on sunny afternoons. I talked to ugly people with ugly lives and it put my life in perspective. It made me grateful to go home to my disgusting little room that stunk like the seafood restaurant where my roommate waited tables.

I would only keep a day or two's worth of food in the fridge. I didn't have the money for delivery, so I'd be forced to walk about a mile through the neighborhood to get to the grocery store. I took my time and tried hard to let myself be amused by my surroundings: a chubby kid falling off a bike, squirrels chasing each other from tree to tree, an immaculate front yard garden with a junkie sleeping soundly under the begonias. *It's not sad, it's funny. It's not a metaphor, it's a circumstance. It's the human condition and it's meaningless; it's nothing more than what it is.*

I'd get two apples, a head of romaine, a beefsteak tomato, a couple potatoes, a can of beans, a can of corn, tortillas, maybe a bar of chocolate. Then I'd walk home, take a few puffs of a burnt old joint, and turn the ingredients into something I could eat for a couple days. The food was as simple as it gets. The joint made it taste like a birthday dinner.

I wanted to dump the pills since the day I started taking them. I never expected them to be helpful. They were a wet bandage; a sloppy and unsanitary way to stop the bleeding. After graduation, I refilled the prescription and declared to myself that this would be the last bottle. I started taking them every other day, then every two days. Then one day I stopped, and like nature taking over an unused set of railroad tracks, everything crept back in again; the climate news, the urgent emails, the badgering student loan collection calls. But I didn't touch the pills. The full bottle remained tucked away in my cabinet– until I left Dean and moved to Mount Mirage.

Cam talks about it a lot, about "the Prescription Generation," given pills instead of parenting, pills instead of nutrition, pills instead of tough love and self-discipline. "Pills to calm, pills to focus, pills to sleep, pills to escape. There is no help for them. They have no way of coping with reality. First it's the ADHD pills and the anti-depressants. And then they get to college and take the party pills, the MDMA and their parents' Percs and whatever they can get their hands on. Their developing brains never experienced authenticity; always artificially stimulated, so that's all they know.

"Could you trust one of them to manufacture an engine, or drive a bus, or design a highway? Would you get into an airplane that was built by them, even if they become sober later? There's no fixing that sort of person. Their brains are broken before they are even grown."

I don't argue with him, and I wouldn't. I've seen it, and I'm kind of a walking example of it. And when I look around through his eyes, I can plainly see it: we are living in the land of rich-people-pills. I hear the waiters at Vero's brag about pills constantly. And we all know that guys who work in commercial kitchens love their uppers. I would bet good money that the manager is on something for every weekend shift, so pleasant and bubbly with each guest. And the guests are no different: I see the blank eyes of the women who sit at my bar in the afternoons, who speak way too slowly and have an eerie Stepford passivity in their tone of voice.

"But what about the cokeheads and the crackheads of the '80s? Most of them are still out there somewhere, working jobs, building things or whatever you said. Many of them are in positions of power if I had to guess– at least the coked half."

"Yeah, but at least back then we acknowledged that those things were bad. They weren't medically prescribed as treatment for a series of manufactured 'diseases'. They weren't accepted as part of a healthy diet."

Back in Ohio, it wasn't designer drugs and painkillers, it was opiates. Workers get injured and are given oxy. Then when the script or the money runs out, they get the cheaper stuff, the heroin or fetanyl that will eventually kill them. It's wild that no matter how much money you have or don't have, everyone seems to have the same problems. No one wants to be here. No one wants to live in reality.

I never dabbled with the ADHD stuff that all my friends loved in college. I saw it as half-cheating and half-danger. I fully bought into the dramatic *D.A.R.E.* speeches in middle school health class. I never trusted pills or powders and I also never trusted doctors. But when I dropped about fifteen pounds and stopped sleeping, I knew something needed to be done. I could blame it on my course material– how every lecture was about the intricacies of another ecosystem collapse, or about an Indigenous tribe being kicked off their habitat of 30,000 years in the name of market demand for double-plush toilet paper. I could blame it on the rupturing economy, Dad being forced to sell the boat shop and the neurotic meltdown phone calls from my aunt with my mother quietly sobbing in the background. I could blame it on my own weakness and inability to cope with the transition into adult life. But the cause didn't matter; it was upon me, and I needed to do something about it. I went to the doctor and took the pills he prescribed.

They make it slightly easier to sleep, much harder to come, and make days and weeks blend together more than usual. It's like you're walking through a tunnel continually, and the light at the end doesn't change size. It smooths out the rollercoaster so the lows aren't as low, but the highs aren't high either.

One of my biggest fears has always been ending up like the women men call crazy: an exposed human nerve, the man's worst nightmare; the "hysterical woman." I remember reading about Porcia in Shakespeare, the wife of Brutus, who stabbed herself in the thigh to show her ability to control her emotions. That's the level I strive for. I've worked at it for years now. I push down hard. I've perfected the technique for reabsorbing tears. Here's how you do it: you open your eyes as wide as you can, so the liquid has more surface area; then you tilt your head back slightly, as if to spill the tears back into your head. Then you think of something disgusting or funny– but nothing nostalgic.

I decide that flushing the pills is wrong, but I don't want my new roommates to discover them in the trash. So despite my better environmental judgment I dump them in the toilet anyway.

I moved in with Kevin after Cam's endorsement and a ten-minute conversation. It was rash, but I told myself a writer takes risks for a good story. Once I had agreed to attend the Palmetto Hills Car Show as Cam's guest, I realized I had committed myself to at least another month of the grift. I figured it could be interesting to say *screw it* and go all the way with it, to fully immerse myself in his world, and I couldn't think of a better way to do that than to live with someone he called friend. I also couldn't resist how cheap the rent offer was. I took a look online for good measure, and I laughed aloud at twelve-by-twelve studio apartments, with a hotel fridge and a hot-plate, offered for $1,650 a month. *No smoking, no pets. Overnight guests not allowed.* Where would I even put them, in the mini bar? In-budget options certainly would have included more rats, and then some. It turned out my cube place wasn't a bad deal in this marketplace.

Kevin spoke nonstop while he showed me around his place. It was hard to keep up, and he didn't ask me a single question about myself, which worked in my favor. I was impressed that a small space occupied by two men (previously three, hence the empty room) could be decidedly cleaner than my current place, where three women shared an equally compact space.

Kevin is energetic and, like Cam, is youthfully handsome for a man his age– unweathered by the exhaustion of family, marriage, or a demanding career. He works, but as a part-time consultant. "It's great. I make my own hours and travel all the time. You'll probably never see me."

Business must be slow, because he is almost always home, in his bedroom with the door cracked and the humdrum of a podcast playing. The skunky, pungent smell of the pot he smokes trickles into the hall. I wouldn't usually mind, except that I made the decision to quit smoking for the time I am here. I want to test Cam's notion of sobriety equaling some sort of cerebral superiority. Not that I would like to feel superior; Cam does that enough for the both of us. But I wouldn't mind feeling *better*, in a general sense. I also don't want Kevin to have anything to report back to Cam; it is obvious that he has the option to inquire about my living habits, and will likely take it. I've been keeping my room tidy, always making the bed each morning and putting the usual mountain of try-on outfits away, just in case Cam stops by, or Kevin pokes his head in.

On our first tour of the place, Kevin talked at a squirrely pace about his work, about his cars, about how much work he's done on the house to make it nice for the many tenants who have lived here. "This will be your room. It's the second biggest. I have the smallest one. Dale has lived here a long time and he's a hermit, so I gave him the best room. You'll see him poke his head out once in a while. The guy who moved out worked at a gym, and he left a few dumbbells behind in the closet. Let me know if you'd like me to take those out. Do you have your own furniture, or would you like to keep the stuff in here?"

The room's light was polar: pitch-black with the shades pulled, blindingly light with them up. A metal bed frame protruded from the far wall, holding a yellowed mattress. A black table and chair sat in the corner, and a single lightbulb in a wire prism was suspended from the ceiling. The room smelled ever-so-slightly of a male locker room: sweat layered under piney deodorant. It felt fitting for the male-centric environment I aimed to immerse myself in. "This will do just fine. I don't have any furniture. You can leave the weights in the closet too. I don't have enough stuff to fill it anyway."

Three days later, Cam and I were unloading the back of his pickup truck with my belongings.

Kevin and I have an arrangement where I get a steep break on the rent if I grocery shop and cook for the house. I decided not to tell them that I would be cooking vegan; I figure if I make the meals hearty and flavorful enough, they'll barely know the difference. I've made double "cheezeburgers" with smoked carrot bacon and garlic fries, spicy three-bean chili with buttery sliced avocado and cornbread, shepherd's pie with lentils and cashew creamy mashed potatoes, and fudgy black bean brownies with whipped coconut cream. They eat enormous portions rapidly and cheerily, like teenage boys who just returned from football practice. Their voices light up at the smells that waft upstairs from the kitchen. "Oooo-*eeee*! Is that garlic bread I smell?"

"With *neat*balls!" I shout from my post. I roll the little pink balls with breadcrumbs, herbs, and a walnut-based "parmesan cheese", and plop them into the sizzling oil. I sing along to the oldies music playing throughout the house– Kevin hooked my phone up to the bluetooth sound system. I have somewhat-ironically let myself enter the character of a doting mother: I wear an apron over a gingham sundress that I found at the thrift store, and I've tied my hair back with a green ribbon. The plant-based meat is the best brand from the store, made with beet juice to give it the characteristic bleed. The outside of the "neatballs" crisp up beautifully, and the little beads of coconut oil inside melt down to create a juicy and tender ball of flavor. I watch their reactions to the food adoringly. I am proud of the progress I have made as a vegan cook, and very grateful for the sponsorship to eat full meals.

Dale gives me a silent grateful nod, straightens his tie and runs out the door to go to work. He works the front desk at one of Palmetto's most posh hotels. It's entertaining to picture this video-game maven who rarely makes eye contact charismatically greeting five-star guests. It's amazing what putting on a uniform and getting into character can do.

Kevin lingers behind and helps himself to another square of brownie as I clear the table. I pour him a glass of vanilla soymilk to wash it down. In the few short weeks I have lived here, I have come to enjoy his company and our mealtime conversations. He seems to have a much more open and progressive mind than Cam. He's told me stories of traveling with an electric car expo around Southeast Asia, which has made him an outspoken advocate for environmental protection. Between his pro-environment and pro-pot stances, I am surprised he and Cam are even friends.

"You're really a great cook," he says with a full mouth. "I'm impressed."

"Thank you," I beam at him from the sink. "Do you mind that it's all plants?"

"I might have, but you're really making the most out of it. I was a vegetarian for a short while if you can believe it. But I never ate this good."

"Really? What made you decide to do that?"

"I saw this video on Youtube about the government culling wild horses to protect grazing land for livestock. But then a few weeks go by and you know how it is, you go out with the guys and you're called a pussy if you order a salad. But with this food, I feel like I'm eating like a man should."

"*Like a man should.* Isn't that funny, that we think a meal defines us in some way? Like if I eat the same number of meatballs as you, am I less of a woman?"

Kevin laughs with a mouth full of brownie.

"It's all the mind-body connection we were talking about the other day. A man may think if he doesn't eat meat, he's internally accepting on some level that he's not capable of killing. And scary as that may sound to you, all men want to know they're capable of protecting themselves and others, even to that point. It's innate to us.

"But look at you, barefoot in your little dress, ruler of the kitchen. You're all woman. It's really nice to see— a fine and rare sight these days. A woman happily at her station."

"My *station*?"

"Naw come on, don't take it like that! You know what I mean— cooking, singing, nurturing. Look how naturally it comes to you. You will make a fine mother, and a lovely wife to a lucky man." He smiles at me and wipes milk from his mustache with the back of his arm.

"I appreciate the compliment, but I won't be a mother. I hope to find a partner in life, but I doubt I'll get married either."

His face darkens, and he looks at me with deep concern in his eyes. The concern is genuine, and it enters his voice. "Nina, don't go down that road. Listen to what you're saying. You don't want to be a mother?"

"I have many things I want to do in this short life, and motherhood isn't one of them. What is so wrong about that? What do you mean 'down that road'?"

He shakes his head. "See, this is what feminism has done to women. You're going to wake up at forty and realize you're an empty shell. What fulfillment can your career give you that motherhood can't?"

"Wait a minute… you're in your forties, aren't you? You have enjoyed your career and adventures, haven't you? Are you an empty shell?"

"I have enjoyed them, and I still have time to be a father. I'm not on the same timeline as you. It's not fair, but it's life. And besides, the female instinct to be a mother is stronger than a male's instinct to be a father."

I can feel Felicia getting ready to jump out of one of my ears and pounce. Debbie listens quietly, a little smug, hands folded neatly in her lap.

"You should really think about this carefully. Just picture the next twenty or so years of your life— the 40s, the 50s. Those decades get lonely real fast. You only have a few years left to find a good husband and have healthy children, while you're still young and beautiful. I'd hate to see you waste all this potential and abandon your own nature just because you've been told a career can replace family. Or worse, you'll try to do both in equal measure and end up divorced and miserable, with broken children..."

Sheesh, what an indictment.

"Well it's not just a career; it's travel and adventure, financial stability and independence, hobbies and academic pursuits…"

"Do you really think those are going to fill the hole of love and companionship?"

"Well, I still picture a life partner, and definitely some pets along the way…"

"Hun, may we please discuss this?" Debbie chimes in after waiting patiently for the right moment. I look down at my soapy dish, and let her say her piece.

"He does make a point, darlin', about the timeline. Men can become daddies in their sixties if they want. But if you're gonna do this, which I hope you will still *consi-duh*, perhaps you ought to start thinking about it now. I know you wanted freedom in your twenties, but do you really want to keep livin' this way… *forev-uh?*"

When you say it like that, absolutely not. But–

"First off, the planet has way too many people as it is, so this conversation should be a non-starter." I'm surprised Felicia has kept quiet this long. "Why are we even entertaining the ideas of this sexist dick? 'Women have stronger instincts to be mothers'? John and Dean talked about fatherhood way more than you ever thought about motherhood. You never even played with dolls. And then to tell you that if you don't have kids you're *wasting your potential?*"

What potential? Does he mean the neatballs?

"He's saying that you have good instincts and you'd be good at it, is all," Debbie says.

"And what about the *potential* of your career? What about the *potential* of your movie, that's going to empower women everywhere? If you change your mind about kids later, that's one thing– though I obviously think you shouldn't. But this is 2019. You are a free woman. You can have it all."

"Sweetie, she means you can *do* it all. But why would you want to? Why should you have to work *and* keep a home *and* raise children?"

"Well she would find a progressive partner who shares equally in the work."

"I don't mean to be rude, but that's just not at all likely. Men don't have the same instincts and skills–"

"Here we go with the bullshit gender norms again! Why don't you go back to the 1950's where you belong?"

"You don't have to be so rude! You see? This is why she's alone!"

I've been running the sponge over the same dish for god knows how long. Kevin seems pleased to see me considering his words. He takes it a step further. "Tell me Nina, why don't you want children?"

"I have many reasons–"

"So let's hear them. All of them."

His tone changes from concerned to slightly indignant, and his arms cross his chest. He wants a list. My cheeks feel hot and I try to gather my thoughts.

"Well, I guess there was a time when I did want children. But when I look back at what I imagined motherhood would be like, it was very romanticized, like a 1950's appliance ad. I kind of pictured what I'm doing right now: pleasantly cooking and humming to myself; quiet story time with little ones huddled around me by a fireplace; making a house a home; tender affection from my husband. I didn't think about the physical cost, the nights without sleep, the years and sacrifices I would make. I didn't think about how much I treasure my own freedom and independence. I didn't think about the financial cost, and that it would probably be impossible to provide a good standard of living for a family these days without a second income. I saw myself as a young, healthy mother, with a big community around me, like my mother had when I was a kid. But what time would that have left for education, or for professional experience, or for finding out who I truly am?"

"Those sacrifices are worth it, and possible if your husband has a good job—"

"That's another thing," I cut him off, an important lightbulb going off in my head. "If I was going to do it, I would really want to do it right; to stay home and really focus on the family, like you said. But the thing I would fear most of all is the surrendering of my freedom to my husband. If I didn't work, I would be relying on him to support all of us. There is no economic value placed on domestic work. The choice to become a homemaker is a surrendering of your financial destiny to someone else."

"That's why you find a good man to take care of you," he softens again. "That is why the structure of marriage exists. 'What is mine is yours,' as it goes."

"That is so much pressure to place on a man," I muse aloud, rubbing the sponge in a circular motion along the inside of the chocolatey mixing bowl. "To support yourself is hard enough in this world. But to support another adult, *and* children? That's a lot of pressure. And somehow, it seems that it's only gotten harder. It's a lot of pressure... the kind of pressure that can break a man, push him to make bad decisions—"

"You're right, it is. Which is why men *used to be* treated with respect. They weren't just walking ATMs with their balls chopped off, taking orders and having their needs ignored. There was a system in place for a reason, a sacred system. And today's media and society are trying to tear it down."

I dry my hands on my apron, and sit across from him at the table. My plan was to enjoy a brownie after all that work, but there is a discomforting knot in my stomach. I can't pinpoint anything in particular that he said that was untrue. But something still isn't right.

"A sacred system. I think you're seeing the same romantic Frigidaire ad in your head that I saw. It wasn't all pleasant and perfect back then. The repression of the '50s led to the cultural chaos of the '60s. People don't seek change when they are content. Maybe the same media that is tearing that system down are the same ones who created the illusion of its perfection? Or maybe the media is just following the shifting cultural tides and not making the waves themselves?"

"It's simpler than all that. All you have to do is follow the money," Kevin grumbles as he stands to bring his plate to the sink. "If you encourage women to join the workforce, now you have double the labor pool. Now they have twice as many people paying taxes to the state. Plus there's supply and demand in labor– now they can pay even lower wages, and like you said, now it takes two incomes to support a family. Now you've got working parents who need to pay for daycare, who need nannies or house cleaners, and need a whole slew of consumer products and services to save time and energy. They've got us right where they want us."

"Wow, I've never thought about that. Double the workforce." I decide to opt for the brownie after all. "But what if, in a future version of the family, two parents are working shorter weeks? Or what if they each work half-time, and stay at home half-time? Maybe the health insurance industry will change, so people don't have to work full time to get healthcare?"

"Do you really love working that much?"

I almost spit out my bite. "HAH, no, I can't say that I do. I definitely love having my own money. But I also hate having to pay for everything."

"So would it be so unthinkable to stay home, and put all that effort and time into the welfare of your family instead? When you and your friends see a stay-at-home mom, how does it make you feel?"

I snicker again. "It's one of our favorite kinds of people to talk shit about."

"But why?"

"Because– because she's–"

"Less than you? Looked down on for doing something 'lesser' than making money? For contributing to society in a different way?" There is disdain in his voice, but again he corrects himself. "You know what, it's honestly not even your fault. You're the product of a culture, Nina– a broken culture. We used to value mothers and motherhood. And maybe if you felt valued for doing the things you do, you'd feel differently. So thank you for dinner– and please don't stop making your magic in the kitchen." Kevin rests his hand on my shoulder, and gives it a little squeeze.

He rises and I'm looking forward to finishing my dessert alone. He looks back at me as he opens the door to the garage. "Let me ask you one more question, Nina. Are you on birth control?"

"...Yes..."

"The pill, right?"

"...Yes? So?"

This feels inappropriate, like Kevin has overstepped a boundary, but when it comes to conversations like this I will answer any question I am asked. I don't know how to refuse a response, or press pause on the conversation, without immediately feeling like I've inadvertently given the worst possible answer. So the truth just comes out. It's strange, because I've always called myself a good liar, pretending to be a mysterious heiress in a bar just for the thrill of it. But now I'm wondering if any of that was even remotely convincing. Maybe people were just humoring me. Maybe I looked like a complete jackass.

"How many years have you been taking it?"

"Since I was about eighteen. Right after I lost my virginity."

"Eighteen. So for over a decade you have been taking a daily pill that chemically convinces your body that you're pregnant. Over 4,000 pills. Over 4,000 days of your life."

If I'm being completely honest, I didn't even know that is how the pill works. "I guess so. I mean, I have missed days..."

It's a big number. Four thousand pills is a big number. It sits heavy and I know it instantly; I'm going to flush those things too. I was planning to avoid intimacy until my screenplay is done anyway.

"Mind-body connection. Imagine how many ways that has affected not only your body, but your mind too." He disappears into the garage.

~

I finish cleaning up the kitchen. I am grateful for the mindless busy work as I run through Kevin's arguments in my head, with the irritant chatter of Debbie and Felicia arguing in the background. As I imagine myself doing dishes and mixing things in bowls and scrubbing toilet seats for the rest of my life I become angry – until I remember that no matter what, I'll probably be doing that for myself anyway. Takeout is greasy and expensive, and I wouldn't trust a stranger to be cleaning my house even if I could afford it. So Kevin is right? I give my efforts to an employer instead of my family? And I have to come home and be domestic anyway? *What the fuck kind of deal is that?*

But no, the difference is that the checks go into *my* bank account every other Friday. But– if I were married, my husband's money would effectively be my money. But does it really ever work that way? How can it ever really feel like your money when he's making it? How can he not resent you over time for spending all his money, and how can you not resent him for resenting you, while you're keeping his home and children and cooking his meals? And with kids, it's more than a full-time job; it's 24/7, weekends, nights, holidays, with no vacation days and no quitting. For 18 years – longer if you have more than one, and today it's more like 25 before a kid is half-decently adult. *Christ... What am I even talking about?*

I have wandered upstairs to my room without noticing, lost in thoughts that circle around each other and lead nowhere. I sit on the bed and stare at myself in the closet mirror. "That outfit looks ridiculous," Felicia sneers. "You're playing into a pathetic male fantasy. You're in a slave's costume."

"Dear, I think it suits you," Debbie says sweetly. "You chose it and I think you know deep down that you like it. You were so happy down there until you over-thought it. Your brownies looked divine, by the way! Was that coconut cream–"

Can everyone please just SHUT UP?

The frustration creates a pulling sensation that runs from my forehead through to my gut and down between my legs. I reach for my phone to alleviate this tension the old-fashioned way.

Now look, before you judge me, just know that this isn't a regular thing, or a thing that I'm proud of, or excited about. I wouldn't exactly call myself a connoisseur, either. I still go to the same website that Henry Ribbit sent me on AOL Instant Messenger when I was barely twelve years old. He sent a link and told me it was something he "really wanted me to see." From sixth to ninth grade, the sun rose and set out of Henry Ribbit's ass; that desperate, hormonal, journal-his-name-in-your-notebook kind of infatuation. So my heart fluttered and I eagerly clicked the link.

The video was called "Rough Teen G–ngb–ng Leaves Her Red and Raw". I'll never forget that name; *red and raw* is just so distressingly graphic. There was no soft opening; no couch or kissing or conversation. The clip was mid-scene, where three men were inside all parts of this girl all at once, and at least four others were standing around her, gripping at her breasts or attempting to direct her hands or head toward them.

I was in my final week of sixth grade. I had never seen a man naked before. I had never been touched, or kissed, or had any perception of what sex would look or feel like. I was raised on Disney depictions of love, and there was no space yet created in my head for sexual fantasy or physicality. I was still a full year from my first menstruation. I had barely even noticed my own naked body yet. But here this was, this scene, this girl, getting penetrated in ways I didn't know were possible or desirable, getting slapped and choked; *red and raw.*

After a few moments of stunned observation I quickly closed the browser window and began to quietly weep; fearful and horrified. But a feeling arose between my legs– a sensation I had not before experienced– and just like that, Henry had won. Well, I can't even say it was Henry who won because I never slept with him, never even spoke to him after that. I would still follow him around school like a timid stalker, but couldn't look him in the eye. I guess you can say no one won.

Those first few times… Nothing has ever felt like that. I don't know if anything else will ever feel like that. Maybe it's not supposed to be that good. Anything too good will ruin your life.

I open that same old Henry Ribbit website, and start in the "female-friendly" category, where it looks like real couples, and there is some fairly convincing tenderness or sincerity. I choose one that I recognize. It's this girl sleeping in this pair of plain white underwear, and her boyfriend wakes up next to her, and the sight of her is just driving him crazy. He starts caressing her legs, and rubbing her ass over the white underwear, and then running a finger along the seam and just under it, and she's just laying there– and it's really bothering me the way she's laying like that, with her ass in the air and her back arched and everything, and all I can think of is how no one could possibly sleep like that, that they'd get a crick in their neck in the first few minutes– and there's no way she could still be sleeping with him touching her like that, the big faker. I can't get into it, which is a shame because her boyfriend's got these big juicy lips, and it's nice to watch him use them on her, on her breasts and stomach and everything, but I'm too far gone thinking about what a faker she is, and I'm too annoyed to enjoy it. I'll just be thinking that she doesn't deserve a guy with big lips like that.

My mind starts to wander back to Kevin's words; to what Cam would say; to what Tyler would say about what I'm doing, about living in this house, about cooking for men for money, about this gingham dress. I need to dig deeper, to turn off my thoughts and speed up the process, so I take a different tack and search for something more hardcore. I see a video titled "Becky Can't Pay Rent". Now there's something I can relate to. The still shows her with two men; I guess she has two landlords. I tap my phone's screen, and lean back on the pillows.

They're talking. Just one of the men is in the scene. He is ugly and early middle-aged. I can't hear what they're saying; I never watch it with the sound on. You only need to make that mistake once. Hear the wrong nasty talk or phony moaning and you can't unhear it; that foul sound will be rattling around in your head for weeks.

I hover over the red bar at the bottom of the video and jump ahead.

3:25– He's yanking pale breasts out of a purple bra. *Swipe*– 4:22– Her lips are touching the base of his body; you can see the cherry-colored lipstick through the curling pubic hair. Her eyes strain to look up at the camera. He's got his hand behind her head and there is a jerky bounce, like she tried to retreat, but he holds her firmly in place, gripping her hair from the scalp. She has great hair, shiny and jet black, bunched up tightly behind her head in his grip. I feel a momentary stab of envy at her hair, at her alabaster skin and slender body. This always comes, and I always tell myself the same thing: *Yes, but she's doing* that *for a living, and you are not.*

Swipe–5:26– Her head is bobbing so fast– *How does she breathe?* I wonder how much practice she's had. Her skin is so perfect; she's too young to be this good. It reminds me of the girls on the field hockey team sophomore year, who would brag about doing it on the long bus rides to away games. I remember overhearing one girl, who was one of the prettiest girls in school, boasting about how much power she had over a handful of seniors. "Like if you start, and then stop doing it suddenly, you can get them to promise you anything, *anything*, if only you'll just keep going. I could get them to dump their girlfriends, quit the football team…"

I pause the video and start to touch myself. It's frozen on another close-up of her looking at the camera. Her eyes are brilliant and bloodshot and colored like mine. Black tracks of makeup are beginning to form underneath from a buildup of moisture in her eyes. The sheen gives the eyes a swollen glow. *Swipe–6:41–* Not one, but two more men have appeared and already have their pants off. The camera is on their lower halves, and the back of her head, and the shiny black hair. One of them lifts her by the throat to his mouth; before he kisses her he slaps her face a few times. He's holding tight and saying something sinister as her face turns pink and I'm glad I can't hear him. Their tongues appear through their kiss and the original "landlord" grabs his tenant and places her on the couch, upside-down so her head hangs over the edge of the seat. *Swipe–8:52–* The video freezes and buffers. I don't care to describe the freezeframe, but I will say that her eyes are looking at the camera again, but are obstructed by trails of saliva and mascara, and the airways of both nostrils are blocked by flesh. I feel disgusted; then the warm, familiar, shameful moisture under my dress and I try to swipe ahead on the red bar, but the image is frozen. I am aroused enough to continue on my own; I drop the phone and close my eyes. I picture Tyler taking me in the closet in that burgundy skirt, but that prompts a sob in the back of my throat as I remember kissing that man with the terrible breath. I quickly redirect my mind to other images I've seen, things I'd never, *ever* want to do and men I'd never want to touch me, but I've been assured many times by *Cosmo* magazine that you're safe inside your own fantasies and that there are no rules.

I like the ones where the guy is simply overcome with desire. He comes at her like a hurricane with so much passion that all she can do is receive him, and her eyes get all wide and she has that sort of deer-in-headlights, dumbfounded look on her face. She is *his*; there is no say in the matter and he's going to do to her what he wishes. It sounds hot, even romantic, in the context of a romance novel scene. But the live version of that scenario is much more extreme. It involves a lot of smacking, spitting, worse– much worse. You don't know what you're going to get until you've already seen it, and once you have, you can't unsee it. And what's worse, you might actually come to like it. And then that lives somewhere deep inside of you now– a small, harmless thing, like a dead cockroach under an old fridge in the garage. It's a harmless thing– until its body feeds another cockroach.

As my body tenses up to climax I see an image flash that I almost always see in these moments: the freckles on John's stony shoulders, and my nails desperately digging into them, raking up eight raised pink lines over his flesh. It's excruciatingly involuntary; the image appears on its own accord and I accept it with begrudging, helpless pleasure. If he ever knew this, I would die. But I'm sure he wouldn't be surprised; I can see him smirking now– *arrogant bastard*.

The pleasure melts me down and I sink into my blankets, languid, lulled, void. As I drift into the sweet vacuum of sleep, I'm jerked awake by my buzzing phone. I wait for the second buzz of the voicemail.

"Hello Nina, this is Piper Hammick from Mount Mirage Earth Defenders. I'd like to set up a time next week for an interview–"

14
The Hunt

I rounded a corner and came to a screeching halt behind a tall shrub. No time to catch my breath; a gazelle knows better than to pause when a lion is behind it. The sun was going down but my dress was such a bright white that I'd still be visible for a while. My leg muscles shook. My veins were electric, lit up by the pulsing adrenaline.

I fled up the path that led to my dormitory building, Courtship Hall. The sweat on my body caught the wind and gave me a chill despite the heat. I darted into a courtyard, desperate for a repose from the steepening path. As I stumbled over a tree root, I felt a debilitating grip on my arm.

"A-HA!"

It was sharp and relentless; a piercing set of teeth to the prey's throat. He yanked my body into his, squeezed hard, draining my lungs, and pulled my head back by my long tangled hair. He gave my ear a playful lick instead of saying something cliché. For someone more animal than man, spoken language was seldom necessary. The touch of his tongue ignited fury inside me. I kicked and thrusted my body about as he carried me to a bench in the courtyard. The campus was otherwise quiet. Midterm examinations began in the morning.

I managed to land a fist to the side of his head as he laid me over the bench. He laughed wholeheartedly, and considered acknowledging my efforts with an encouraging word. But instead he simply grunted as he removed my shoes and threw them into a nearby flowerbed, pulled up my dress to take what he considered his. My body was heaving with anger at my powerlessness. I leaned forward and managed to grab a handful of dirt; I chucked it behind me into his face, just in time. My chance for escape came as quickly as my previous moment of defeat. I wriggled away, letting out a squeal of elated relief as he rubbed his eyes. He chuckled again, admittedly impressed.

"So that's how it's going to be, li'l missa?"

I flew past the dining hall and the sports fields. My dress was stained with streaks of dirt and grass. Courtship Hall at last came into view; I was painfully close to a door to which I had a key– but I could hear him gaining ground behind me. John Laidir is a smart man; he had removed my shoes knowing the bare feet would slow me down. The pavement was still warm from the day and recent rains had washed rough gravel over the paths. I was certain that anyone who stepped out of their room could hear my heart beating from their doorway. It was a lost cause. I could almost feel his breath behind me. The thrill of the hunt gave him a burst of energy, though I told myself that the physicality of his arousal should have slowed him down. It did not.

He tackled me into the grass and pinned me down on my back. I defiantly stared him right in the eyes, which were green, but in these moments took on a hunting shark's blackness.

"*I'll never stop fighting!*" I thrashed to free myself.

John laughed again. "I think it's so cute Nina, I really do. Plus it turns me on– clearly." He rubbed against my leg as I squirmed around in the grass.

"Please… at least take me to your room," I begged. "I don't want people to see me with you."

"That's too bad, li'l star. It's too late for that." The accent belonged to a Northeastern boy, bogan and thick as the Queensland air, challenging for an untrained American ear to understand. He leaned down and kissed me with infuriating tenderness, narrowly dodging chomping teeth. "I simply can't wait until then. Plus a nerdy little bird *loike* you'd be lucky to be seen with a man like me."

"Your confidence is all in your head. *You're pathetic!*" On an impulse I tried to spit up at him, but he dodged it. It returned back to Earth and splattered on my neck.

"Oh, I'm the pathetic one, ay? You just spit all over *yahself.*" He released himself and brushed over my face. "Give 'im a kiss, Nina."

I giggled and gave an exasperated groan as I swayed back and forth, attempting to move my head away. John moved along with me, with that smug shit-eating grin that he always gets when he wins. The sun was finally down and the air instantly cooled. Our bodies had become silhouettes in the grass from the windows of Courtship Hall.

"I've fallen for a monster!" I swung and kicked my legs around. "*Get off!* I'm not going to do it!"

"Come on now, you're just making this *hahder* on yourself. Don't make me pinch your nose now, I'll do it."

I looked back into the shark eyes with a penetrating gaze, bright and glaring as a sunflare, and slowly parted my lips. My body flooded with warmth. As I felt his massive body relax, I reached around and pinched him hard on the leg. He jumped up onto his knees; I tried to escape from under him, but was promptly re-pinned. "Enough of this. You lose, I win, every time. It's *ovah*. You had no chance and you never will have a chance."

No chance, huh? I broke an arm loose and smacked John in his boulder of a head. He responded by wrapping me into some sort of humiliating wrestling pose, with all four of my limbs rendered completely useless. He spoke calmly, as if I were the crazy one in this situation.

"Are you going to be good?"

"NEVER!" I wriggled and writhed, and jerked my head around. Nothing.

"Are you going to be good?"

"...Fine. FINE!"

At the first release of a free arm, I cracked him hard in the forehead. I laughed in a big burst, tickled by the comical *smack* sound of the blow, only to be wrestled back into the same position as before.

"Are you going to be good?"

The same story repeated twice more. I was filthy, sweating, and utterly exhausted.

"Are you going to be good?"

" "
...

A long silence; a moment to consider my options. "Yes... yes, I'll be good."

John lifted my arms above my head and held them firmly against the ground with one hand. His kisses were hesitant at first, awaiting an attack, but when it didn't come his mouth became more fierce, more focused. He used his free hand to lift my ruined dress. My resistance had made my muscles tense, and it intensified the sensation for both of us. My body betrayed me; the inconvenient, unhideable truth of my attraction ran down my leg.

The surrender made me go limp beneath him. He felt it and released my arms, freeing them to wrap around his broad and stony back. The adrenaline drained from my body and the exhaustion put me into a drug-like trance. I could feel his satisfaction as he worked over me, a delicious victory for the scoreboard. *Bastard.* I lifted my head and bit at his freckled shoulder. After he felt my body's final shake of pleasure, he loaded me over his shoulder and carried my limp body to his bedroom.

∾

Alright alright– no need to start in on your judgment. I beat you to it. I am very aware of how this looks, how I am the world's lousiest feminist and a traitor to women everywhere. You can save it, because I hate myself more than you ever could.

I've spent countless hours berating myself for the things I tolerated from John, years interrogating myself about moments I should have drawn the line and didn't, moments I should have left but stayed. By and large the worst part is how much I enjoyed it. I put up a good fight for a long time, and not just physically. We also had verbal fencing matches, not only in private, but at social gatherings and in the lunchroom, never raising our voices but publicly slicing and degrading each other with carefully chosen, cutting words.

It never ended; we were always in an intellectual battle or a physical one, wrestling and rolling in front of our building or in some back corner of the rugby fields. I would fight relentlessly to the bitter end, and my eyes would turn wild. It was as stimulating as it was cruel, and the stakes seemed high, especially to me. I can't explain why it mattered so much to me. With John and me, everything was a power struggle: who was more intelligent, who was better looking, who could outsmart the other one, who could cut the other down more thoroughly. In the physical realm, John had the obvious advantage; but when we competed over intangible things, winning meant destroying what the other thought of themselves. The disdain, abasement, and power struggles made way for tremendous pleasure. Perhaps I have answered my own question.

In the beginning we both loved it. He was bored and enjoyed the rarity of a worthy adversary; someone who would hit back, who would take blows and bend, but refuse to break. I was looking for any excuse to focus on something other than what I was supposed to be doing. John and I were disruptive, obnoxious, and passionately in love, but desperate to keep it a secret– first from ourselves, and then from everyone else– though I don't know who we were fooling. We made scenes, showed up late to things, sneaking in separately to hide our togetherness, or didn't show up at all. We thought we were so important… Where did that come from? I guess I've never thought about that until now.

It's been many years since I've seen him, but he still frequents my dreams. He was the first and last of his kind in my romantic life: rugged, forceful, feared, well-liked. Charming and almost terrifyingly masculine; a primeval brute with a brilliant mind– but you wouldn't know it at first. John is deeply hidden behind his brawn. Sometimes I'm convinced he purposely presents himself as a howling baboon because he's a cynical man who knows what works in this world– but then I ask myself if I am giving too much credit to a howling baboon. And there he is, in my head again. I guess you could call him a master manipulator. He'd probably love it if you did.

A business major with great ambitions who emerged from the rugged inland mining and cattle country, his confidence was outward and unflinching. John sees the world as a physical thing. Everything is measured solely by its strength. And so by that measure, in his mind, he's above all of us. "Why do people love diamonds? Because they're the *hahdest* damn things on this earth. Toughest thing in the damn world, and rich cunts wear 'em 'round their necks."

(I'm sorry. I don't know how to say John's words without saying John's words. But John would never say sorry about that. Not in a million years.)

After spending all that time aboard the *Siren's Revenge* with Captain Don, I should have known better. I should have been inspired and focused. I was on campus with a job to do and not much time to do it. Don secured a grant for me to stay in Australia and work on campus for another semester. The coral reef study was one thing, but the plastic pollution issue had opened up another can of worms, adding layers of complication and consideration. As the data rolled in, it needed to be reviewed, processed, and converted into plain English so a case for action could be made to decision-makers.

I spent long days in the computer lab, frantically watching Microsoft Excel tutorial videos on Youtube. (If you don't know what these applications are, either together or separately, consider yourself a member of a lucky generation.) Processing the data was hard enough, but the results also disturbed me; the videos and photos we took of the expanses of ghostly corals were haunting. I longed for an escape from reality, from my own brain. For a man like John I was ripe for the picking.

At first I only saw– and heard– him from a distance. We lived in the same dormitory building, so we frequented the same dining halls and watering holes. His reputation preceded him: the drunkest guy at the pub, a shameless womanizer, a barbarian with scabbed-over knuckles. At social gatherings he was always surrounded by a large crowd of people, a drink in each hand and the front of his shirt darkened with spilled liquor and sweat. He seemed inhuman, a bellowing ape with sophisticated vocal chords. (See? Howling baboon.) I didn't think of him as a real person, only a comical archetype of the Australian male meant to entertain and frighten the visiting Americans.

There was a time when I was certain I couldn't possibly love anyone else, and many more times when I've been certain that he is the single worst thing that has ever happened to me. The passing of time does not make anything clearer; as you continue down the road, the parallel stripes of black and white in the rearview mirror only blend further into a mound of gray.

What I do know for certain is that, unfortunately for me, no one else in my life knows me well enough to give me any worthy advice.

John Laidir- DON'T ANSWER

> John, I'd like to video call soon. I have some news, about a job. Are you free this weekend? — 10:12 PM

> Yer– I'd like to see your face lil star. Wear something nice — 10:26 PM

> Fuck you — 10:26 PM

I get home from a Friday night Vero's shift and send him a message. It's his Saturday afternoon. "Free, doing chores" he says. I take a deep breath and hit the little blue button to start the call.

"Nina, what *ah* you *wearing?*"

"My work uniform."

"It's just awful. A high *collah* and a loose *sweatah?* Simply terrible. No wonder you don't make any money."

I roll my eyes, and then fight an instinct to grin as a lightbulb appears: *How didn't I think of this before? John is another rich well from which I can draw toxic male villain material.*

"And why are you naked?"

"I'm not, I've got me boxers on. Be reasonable, Nu– do you really expect me to be doin' chores with clothes on? On a weekend no less?"

He looks more or less the same, except around the eyes. John's eyes always had the sharp coldness exclusive to a certain shade of green-eyed people, but the distress around the eyes is telling of his previous few years. During our time in love I watched John slide from macho campus alpha-male to desolate addict, mostly from a distance of nearly twelve thousand miles through a computer screen, as we attempted to stay together while I finished my degree in America. But he's since cleaned himself up, and has found success in the business world. Sociopaths always do.

"Let me show you my new house plants. I'm a regular *Doctah* Greenthumb." He carries his laptop across his blank canvas of a condo, furnished with one recliner chair, white walls and a four-foot pile of dirty clothes and junk shoved into a corner– his version of "cleaning". He shows me an array of tropical plants with the pride of a new father. "See this one? I propagated this little cunt *roight* here."

"Jesus John, some things never change– look at that mess! What is wrong with you?"

"*Yeh* well I need a woman to take care of me." John giggles like a child who received the intended reaction to a ploy for his parents' attention. The man is an Olympic medalworthy mess maker. For the brief time we cohabitated I was up to my eyeballs in filth. One image in particular will never fade from my memories: a steady stream of tiny black ants emerging from a conglomerate mountain of John's underwear, fast food wrappers, and a black video game controller covered in a shiny, sticky goo of some kind.

After the plant tour he settles into a chair on his balcony and begins his ritual of rolling a cigarette. I can hear the cacophony of Queensland birds, and a small part of me longs to be there. What can I say? I've already told you plenty of times, I'm an idiot.

"Looks *loike* you're in a new place since I last seen ya. Doesn't exactly look like an upgrade."

"It's better, trust me. I've actually moved twice since we last talked…"

John lights up the cig and glances out at his empire. "I reckon you're the problem, ay. You're too preachy. You always get along with people at first and then they get sick of your preaching. You don't let yourself enjoy anything and you take enjoyment from everyone else, sittin' on your high horse."

"You have no idea what you're talking about…" I start to sweat a little, remembering the protest signs and posters I had displayed around my previous place; the sticky notes reminding my roommates to recycle in a slightly threatening tone; the photo of an emaciated polar bear I taped next to the thermostat. But John doesn't know all that, nor does he need to.

"*Yeh* well look at me, I'm a *homeownah* now!" He gives me a more thorough tour of his place– the bouncing camera rattles my brain– and he plops down onto his mattress, which I'm impressed to see has a sheet on it. "An' how's that li'l pussy of a boyfriend of yours? Did he help you move all them boxes? If he's even strong enough." John flexes his biceps and does a little somersault on his mattress, fully re-entering his old schoolboy charm without a hint of irony. I'm just glad he has boxers on this time.

"Let's not talk about Tyler right now."

"Ah, I see— he finally ran off, didn't he?" *Smug, smug bastard.* "I called that, like a year ago I called it! I tol' you he was no good. What a vegetarian little pussy."

I have a momentary urge to defend Tyler, but I choose not to. He rolls another cigarette in his bed. Pale gray smoke emerges from his mouth as he speaks.

"Listen li'l girl, you need to be getting your act *togethah.* You're almost thirty for *fahck's* sake– and you're bartending to rent a li'l shithole room? All you've done for the last five 'r more years is indulge yourself in passion projects. How much *didje* make as a janitor for them elephants, when you were datin' the fat cop?"

"Don't–"

"You've done nothing to actually help yourself move forward. But if you'd just apply *yahself,* you will be successful. We've been through this. You need to start getting yourself sorted."

"I told you, I've needed time to write–"

"Look, you gave it a red hot crack. I'm proud of you for taking a risk. But you've clearly failed. You haven't produced anything of substance in at least a year. An' I've read some of your other work, and it's *jest* more of your preaching. No one's taken you seriously and it's your own fault, 'cause as usual you expected way too much from the public."

"Yes, I certainly realize that now."

"So d'you want to be a single thirty-year-old woman dragging herself *loike* this? I won't have it. Look at me– I'm livin' in a palace, movin' up the company ladder, and I'm a self-taught master *gahdenah*."

"And let me guess– I only have a couple of years left to lock down a man, while I'm still 'young and beautiful'?"

"Yes! Exactly."

Debbie uses her parasol to trip Felicia before she can slit John's throat. I sigh in lieu of a response.

"So, tell me about this job opportunity. What have we got? Where are we in the hiring process?"

"I have an interview tomorrow. It's a paid job at the environmental organization I have been interning at for the last year and a half. And John– it's my *dream* job. It's writing about ocean issues, and I imagine it involves traveling…"

"*Yeh, yeh*, righto. And how much does it pay?"

"Not sure– probably not much, but it can't be less than what I'm making now."

"Hah *yeh*, I reckon minimum wage is more than nothing. But now I see why you wanted to talk. We need to get you ready for the negotiating table li'l missa."

Oh god, here we go. A lecture is imminent.

"Now listen here. These environmental, intellectual *toipes* are keen to take advantage of women like you. They're gonna guilt the shit *outcha*– tell ya they're all *grassroots*, an' it's all about the *cause*, not the money. They're gonna prey on your compassion and desperation. But guess what? Those cunts in *chahge* are makin' six figures, an' drive new cars, an' I bet they even have swimmin' pools in their *backyahds*."

"These are passionate, dedicated activists, and I admire them," I say. But John is probably right. Every time I reach out to him I think I'm sharing an update or a brag– *Look at my new job, look at my new boyfriend, look at how great I'm doing!* – but really, I'm almost always looking for advice, or a pep talk, or John's special brand of tough love.

"I want you to do somethin' for me. Think back on every job you've ever had. As tough as you talk about yourself I'm damn certain you can't think of a single time you vehemently *ahgued* for your wages, or stood up for yourself when they sidelined ya or took advantage. I bet you smiled and said *sure mate, no problem!*, and maybe ya grumbled to yourself as you walked away, or called your mum to complain that night, or maybe cried in your *cah* on the way home."

"John, what the *fuck*–"

"It's *alroight*, ya see– it's your fault, but it ain't really your fault. You see here this is the problem. You don't see your career as a business transaction– a means of funding your health, safety 'n *loifestyle*. You see it as an extension of your personal values or political beliefs. But that's why you're always broke. It's all business; gotta be all business.

"And it's not just you. I'm speakin' in broader terms too. It's not a woman's nature to be aggressive in that way. Your hearts are bigger an' softer. It's why you're drawn to the social sciences and righteous causes. You don' belong in the hostile business world. We are seeing such a struggle today because everyone is rejecting the instincts and interests that come naturally to them simply for the sake of defying the norms that have arisen for a reason– it is our nature."

Did Kevin, John, and Cam all have a conference call or something? Are they all subscribed to the same misogynist podcaster?

"Alright, so maybe there is a pattern of instincts, but are people not individuals? Just because a generality applies to a population doesn't mean a person will fit into that mold. No one is trying to force people into roles that don't suit them… I feel like the goal of modern society is the exact opposite. That was '80s feminism, when women put on shoulder pads and mimicked men in corporate offices. I don't want to mimic men's behavior because I don't approve of it. But I also want to be free to pursue what comes naturally to me, whatever that may be."

"So what comes natural to you is working two or three shit jobs, and renting out shithole *apahtments* with people who can't stand your preaching?" John cracks himself up. "Wow, I almost sold ya short there! You're *roight* Nina, you're clearly on the path to achieving your wildest dreams in the hopeful year of 2019!"

His mocking laughter hits down to my bones.

"*Please*– stop– I already know I'm down. I don't need to hear any of this because I already know it– I'm living it. I know where I am and what fucking year it is."

"Well listen my little girl– I know you think it does, but it doesn't bring me any pleasure to say any of this. But I know you need to hear it. I don't want the love of my *loife* struggling like this. And everything I'm faulting you for is also what I love ya for. When I think of you and the reason you struggle I think hey, this girl is just as pure as the driven snow. Your strengths are by all means my weaknesses. You struggle because you want to save the whole damn world. You're a *sweet-haht,* you always have been. You are creative and carin' and you always see the best in the people you love."

And there it is– the part of John that trips me up every time. Am I just an insecure sucker, so desperate for a compliment?

～

It started with a bicycle. A rusty, squeaking, barely-any-brakes bicycle that I had adopted from the campus swap center. The university had a large international student population, so there was a lot of coming and going. The center was a repository for furniture, books, clothes, and housewares, and was open for students to take what they needed. That swap shop supplied my entire existence for that semester, from clothes and sheets, to half-used shampoo and soap bottles, to my trusty rusty form of transportation. One morning I reached to unlock my bike off the rack outside of Courtship Hall, and it was gone. Why someone would steal that bike of all bikes is beyond my comprehension. I was already running late to my session at the marine science lab after a long night haunted by coralline nightmares, and in my exasperation, my face reddened and my eyes welled up with tears. I looked around desperately and listened for the squeaking sound.

"Oi– ya look like a lost doe. What is it?" John was leaning against the building and sifting a pile of tobacco into a neat little line on its square paper.

"It's nothing– it's– my bike. Someone stole it, and I'm late."

"Cabbie, you two-bit bloody *CUNT!*" I shuddered at his thundering words as John, who was shirtless, shoeless, and with the freshly-rolled cigarette hanging out of the side of his mouth, stormed off in a hurry.

Did he just call me a cabbie? And a... c-word? I was flabbergasted to the point of laughter. The absurdity of the interaction reversed my upset and I headed toward the dining hall to grab breakfast. I was already late for lab, no point in showing up now.

As I walked the path back to Courtship Hall with my backpack full of mangoes and mandarins, I heard a disturbing crack come from the other side of the building. As I turned the corner, a young blonde man was limping toward me, bloodied and whimpering. A pair of pretty Aussie girls in floral sundresses and ballerina buns hurried over to escort him to the med clinic. Behind them, John was in his original spot against the brick and beaming at me. My bike was laid out on the grass before him. "Here ya go, li'l girl. I believe this piece of shit is yours." The cigarette flopped up and down as he spoke, still stuck to the same corner of his lip, but now the end was streaming smoke.

"How did you find– why did you–"

"What a piece'a shit to be sookin' about, hay. What are you riding that thing for, anyhow? Decent-looking bird like you surely could score a nicer *boike*, if you tried.

"And to answer your half-questions, I knew Cabbie had taken it, that whingy little *fahck*. He and I are in a sort of territorial battle at the moment. No one fucks with a chook who lives in my roost."

Although I was relieved to have my bike back, I let him have it. "So you think you can just beat the snot out of people like that? What kind of animal are you? I didn't ask for your opinion about my bike, and I certainly didn't ask for your help. And what the hell is a chook?"

He laughed at me. "Well lookee here! The little American has a mouth on 'er! Someone's gonna find herself an old maid, talking back *loike* that. An' I'm still waiting on a thank you."

"Don't talk to me that way. Who the hell do you think you are?"

"I'm the king of this campus and you'll do what you're told. Say thank you."

I picked my bike up off the ground. As I walked toward the rack I grumbled to myself, "What an idiot, 'king of the campus'..."

He stepped in front of me, legs spread over my front tire. "What's your name, li'l miss attitude?"

"It's Lilith Mississippi Attitude, M.D. Please get out of my way. You smell like cigarettes and it is giving me a headache."

His abdominals tensed and rippled with his laughter. He looked at me stumped, like no one had ever spoken to him this way before; like a bull listening to a mouse yelling insults at it. He looked me over, probably searching for something to insult.

"*Alroight* listen here, miss. You new around here?"

"Born and raised actually. Can't you tell by my accent?"

"Enough with the sass, I'm try'n'a help ya. This *boike* really doesn't look safe, and I don't want you on the bus at night. I've got a ute. If you ever need a ride into town, you knock on 6B, *roight*?"

Now I was stumped. '*I don't want you on the bus at night?*' *What is he, my father?*

"I– thank you for the offer. I won't take it, but thanks anyway."

"I bet you never even made it off campus on that stupid thing. You ever seen a Queensland rainforest?"

TESTOSTERONE: THE GREAT WHITE GORILLA'S DEFINING HORMONE

Testosterone is the primary hormone of the male sex, and the key marker of a *Gorilla-industria violentus* who has risen to the alpha status of great white gorilla. GWGs exhibit notably higher levels of testosterone than other males, which manifest in characteristics that often lead to reproductive and social success. Understanding the function of this androgen gives us important insight into the GWG's behavior.

Testosterone, or 'T', drives the development of male characteristics, both physical and behavioral: dictating muscle mass, bone structure, body size, hair growth, and grunt tone; as well as traits like dominance, aggression, courage, and libido. High-T males are physically larger, stronger, and more aggressive, giving them the competitive edge to rise to alpha status against lower-T males.

TESTOSTERONE'S EFFECT ON DEVELOPMENT

Testosterone is biosynthesized in the gonads via cholesterol, which may explain the GWG's insatiable appetite to consume high-cholesterol foods like eggs, mammalian meat, organs, and fat. While testosterone is present and necessary in both sexes, it is typically found at rates seven or eight times higher in males than females.

There are several periods during the male life cycle when testosterone production is pivotal, including during gestation, infancy, and most notably, puberty. Testosterone plays a critical role in a male's reproductive success: it guides the development and growth of male genitalia and the production of semen, and provides both the audacity and sexual drive required to risk injury, social humiliation, and even death to pursue mating opportunities with healthy, high-status females.

ECOSYSTEM CRISIS AND ITS EFFECT ON TESTOSTERONE

In review of the existing literature on the subject, combined with a review of recorded observations in the wild, this study has discovered that for the last fifty years, a true GWG has– to the delight and relief of many scientists– become increasingly rare. This is believed to be primarily due to a precipitous drop in testosterone rates in the global *Gorilla industria-violentus* population. Ironically, this is hypothesized to be, at least in part, a consequence of their own doing. Some population ecologists have nicknamed it a global "self-neutering," but as mentioned in the wildlife population management part of this study, it is not considered to be happening quickly enough for it to have a significant effect on mathematical climate models.

The current ecosystem crisis brought on by the great white gorilla is deeply complex, and not yet entirely understood. Some consequences are more apparent than others: for example, droughts and fires are easily seen and measured, but their secondary consequences are not. The extinction of a species may be visible, but the effect of its disappearance on its environment may take months, years, or decades to unfold. Similarly, we aren't entirely sure what exactly is causing this steep drop in GWG testosterone rates, but studies are beginning to reveal that the waste products created by the Western white gorillas' rapid consumption of natural resources may be to blame. These waste products come in many forms and can be found in soil, water, and even as particulates in the air throughout the world. One commonality in these wastes are endocrine-disrupting qualities– which could hinder the production of hormones like testosterone.

Low-T males exhibit symptoms including smaller genitalia, low sperm count, low energy, reduced muscle mass, increased fat, diminished sexual drive, erectile dysfunction, social dysfunction, anxiety and depression.

A NEW DOMINANCE: ALLIANCE OF ALPHA FEMALES AND BETA MALES

The endocrine-disruptive waste products created by the GWGs have not solely disrupted the development and socialization of males. Females are also experiencing hormonal dysfunction, though at lower rates.

One response to heightened rates of female infertility, combined with a shrinking pool of appealing high-T males, is for females to forgo reproduction and male bonding altogether, and instead to take on more dominant social roles in gorilla troops– a behavior that appears to be increasing their testosterone rates. There are now all-female Western white gorilla troops, in which females choose and replace their alpha frequently. In contrast to the physically violent way males compete to overthrow an alpha or to remove members of the troop, females utilize social warfare, in which individual females are singled out and psychologically destroyed by their competitors through humiliation and isolation.

Submissive, low-T males have been observed joining troops led by high-T females, hopeful for opportunities to reproduce in the absence of alpha males– though observations show that female-led troops still tend to nest and travel close behind GWG-dominated troops, in case the need for protection or desire for reproduction arises.

15
The Interview

2012

"Nu, how many pups 're we gonna have? Five? I can see five– or six, even– depending on how much money I get."

"Christ, John– *six*? What about my career?"

"What career? I know you love swimming with them fishes but, what is it that you even want to be?"

"I don't know, I've always seen myself becoming a person who talks about animals and places– someone who has a TV show on National Geographic, or makes documentaries and writes books. To tell people about amazing animals and ecosystems, and wild parts of the world. And how humans have managed to survive through it all."

"So do that. It's a long shot, because *fahcking* everyone wants to do that. But you could at least pursue it."

"But after what I've seen, and what I've learned? What a frivolous thing to do, when it's all about to be destroyed! I can't do it. How could I be so selfish? It would be like leisurely painting a picture of a seaside village as I watch a wall of lava roll down its mountainside. I have to do something. Or I'm a bad person."

"But it's a wall of lava, Nu. Might as well sit back with a cold one and enjoy the show. What do you expect you can do?"

"Maybe get a few people out of harm's way? Build a boat? Divert some of the lava into the ocean?"

"First off, your attempt to divert lava into the ocean would probably cause a huge explosion and kill everyone. Won't you feel stupid, after all that forethought.

"But really, what you should be doing is saving yourself. What do you owe those people? Who the hell are they? What about you? All you know is that you are you *roight* now. Who's looking *aftah* Nina?"

"I just don't think I could live with myself if I wasn't making an honest effort to offset the environmental impact of me just existing as a human. A Western human no less, who uses like five times the resources as—"

"Then you should just kill yourself. That's truly loving the world. Think of all the resources you'd save. You'll be a huge hero.

"I'll speak at your funeral: 'Here lies our *dahling* Martyr for Humanity, Nina Di-something. For Nina so loved the world that she sacrificed her own *loife* so another person could eat and have clean *wahtah*, or better yet, for no humans at all, but for the trees and rocks who don't even know they exist. Each breath Nina chose not to take in her remaining fifty or so years have now been donated to someone who needed the air: the corner *panhandlah*, the shoe model, the insurance salesman. Nina's beauty, her talent, her vision, all spared in the name of the souls who truly deserved to live. May she rest in peace."

～

The Mount Mirage Earth Defenders have one of the nicest office spots in town, up the hill but still adjacent to the heart of the city. From the big windows of the conference room your eye can follow the palm-lined path of Main Street to the ocean. The lobby looks out to the east side of Money Park. Yes, it's called Money Park. I don't know if it's named in honor of money itself or after a man named Money, but it's as beautiful as you'd expect a park with such a name to be. No money trees, though. Believe me, I've checked.

I rarely get to go to the MMED office. I submit the newsletters to Piper online and show up onsite to events and protests. At the front desk I am handed a large brown sticker name tag with a line for my name, a line for my pronouns, and a line that says "I defend the Earth because__". The faces are all familiar at the office but most of them don't know my name. I get it, though. They're on the payroll, and I'm not. Someone in charge decided their net contribution is worth something of value. And today is my day to prove mine.

I have taken John's advice and I'm dressed more or less like a man: dark pants and the white collared shirt from my Vero's uniform. My hair is slicked back in a practical low bun like a chick in the military. But I have kept two elements of Mount Mirage crunchy-granola-looseness in my getup: sandals and an antique starfish hair barrette that I found while rummaging around an old shipwreck on one of Don's reefs.

The goal is to look serious and professional, but still fit the Earth Defenders brand. I fill out my name tag, pausing for a moment to consider whether or not to use "she/they" on the pronoun line. I certainly look the part today. *I defend the Earth because__*. I write in: "the sea is worth saving".

I sit across a long redwood table from Piper Hammick, who is a familiar face; another woman whose purple hair and brassy yellow roots I recognize from the last power plant protest, and a man in a lemon tunic who I've never met before. He reminds me of an old buddy of mine, a guy I waited tables with back in Sand Dollar, and I smile at him, feeling a sort of unspoken ease or kinship. But I am mistaken; he gives me a brief wince as if he smelled something that stinks coming from my direction and shuffles in his seat. *Okay, then.*

Piper begins. "Nina, thank you for meeting with us today. Before we begin meetings in this space, we like to pause for a one-minute moment of silence to acknowledge our occupation of Indigenous land. Let us take the next sixty seconds to recognize our privilege and reflect on the suffering and genocide that led to our place at this table today."

"It is also National Latinx HIV/AIDS Awareness Day," the tunic man says. "Let us acknowledge that also." He passes me a card with a QR code.

"In case you want to donate," he says coldly. They wait for me to scan it with my phone and enter my payment information.

We begin our silence – staring at each other at first, but I close my eyes out of self-conscious discomfort.

"… Should we pray?" Debbie whispers. "Maybe it'd be polite if we prayed."

"We don't pray," Felicia retorts. "Pray to whom, by the way? Christian *God*? Magical white man in the sky? I'm sure the genocided Indigenous people would *love* that. Also, stop giving a shit about being polite."

"It was just an idea, you don't have to be so defensive. Dear, it's felt like quite a while, hasn't it? Is someone timing this?"

"Open your eyes, dumbass."

I shove Debbie and Felicia into the back room of my mind and I waste no time. I pass out copies of my résumé, samples of my writing, and photos and charts from my coral research, all printed– very expensively– on recycled paper with plant-based ink.

"I've been studying marine science formally since college, but you could say that I've been a student of the ocean since I was a child. So much is at stake when we consider the threats that face ocean health: it is the home to most of the life on this planet, a source of solace, beauty and adventure; a confluence of nature and human needs and interests. It is a frontier, yet it is our mother. It is the centerpiece of billions of human lives and livelihoods.

"Answers to many of the existential problems we face today may be found in the ocean. It has much to teach us. Those who live on it and in it have much to teach us. I can tell those stories; not only tell them, but frame them in such a way that brings people hope, and excitement. I can –"

"*Yeaahhhh……*" The purple haired person grins consolingly, and the word "yeah" elongates for an uncomfortably long time. "That was all very nice, like, *wow*– but– the position in ocean correspondence has been filled."

Felicia slams her fists into the back of my eyeballs. "Then what the everloving FUCK are we doing here? Why are they doing this to us?!"

Debbie whispers, "Maybe we should cry?"

Before I can respond or cry, Piper interjects. "*But...* we brought you here because we think you'd be great for a different position."

I pause. Felicia pauses. Debbie gasps and desperately fans herself.

"One that will make the most of your amazing passion for the ocean and bring about real, serious change."

I'm listening.

I wait. Felicia waits. Debbie waits.

The lemon tunic guy, whose energy has just completely flipped, leans forward. His dangly earrings jingle as he rests his hands flat on the table, a big smile across his face, like he's about to reveal a prized, juicy secret. "Are you familiar with *disruption activism?*"

"I guess it sounds self-explanatory, by its name," I muse aloud. "Do you mean like protests, marches, things like that?"

"Yes, sort of like that— but a little more strategic, and more targeted."

Piper opens a folder and lays a series of photographs on the table. "Here are some sites of great importance to the Palmetto elite, and to the Mount Mirage community as a whole. The first phase of this campaign is already underway: public disruptions. These aim to garner the most attention possible to bring public awareness to the issue."

From the pile, Piper brings center photos of the fountain at Money Park, the annual Diversity and Culture parade on Main Street (formerly the Thanksgiving parade), the art museum, the high school football field, and Camus Junction— the main entry point to both major highways in and out of Mount Mirage for commuters.

"So what would be happening at these places? What would my role be, to organize volunteers? To report on the event?"

"Honey... You'd BE the event!" the man says. "You would be one of the disruptors! Making it happen! On the ground! Like the Monkeywrench Gang!"

"So, what exactly would I be doing?"

"That's where it gets really cool," says the woman with the purple hair, who looks close to 40 years of age. "I'm Purple, by the way. I use they/purpleself pronouns." She points to the middle line of her name tag. "I also go by 'Purp' for short." She, I mean *they*, points to a rainbow infinity symbol pin on their shirt, which they explain symbolizes purpleself's pride in purpleself's autism diagnosis. They has– have? a purple plushie sitting on the table with purpleself. It is no particular animal or shape– just a lumpy foam pillow with anime-style eyes and a little grinning mouth. It feels like the eyes are looking at me.

I can hear Cam in my head, ranting about slippery slopes. *"Oh sure, let them identify however they want– men can be women, girls can be boys, we can all be both, neither, and something else all at once. I'm telling you– it's never just a simple thing; it always escalates. Soon you'll have people identifying as animals, and inanimate objects, and demanding that you 'respect their identity.'"*

"Come on Cam, that's ridiculous."

"I'm telling you, it's never enough with these people. You'll see."

Purple continues. "Disruption activism is about taking real, direct action to stop these things from happening. Kantian Consulting thinks they can just come in and build a nuclear plant close to one of Mirage County's poorest neighborhoods, on sacred Indigenous land? They think they can just buy our politicians and sell off our future?" She– I mean purpleself– slams their fists against the conference table.

Am I missing something? Did she say what we'd be doing? Debbie and Felicia glance at each other and shrug.

"So– would I be doing anything illegal, or dangerous?"

"It's about non-violent civil disobedience. Think of Martin Luther King Jr., or Malcolm X....or Jane Fonda! Heroes of their movements!"

"All of them went to jail. Should I expect to get arrested?"

The panel hesitates, each looking to the other to jump in and take this one.

"I mean yes, it's possible. But Nina, think of it this way–"

An instinct has kicked in and I am standing. As silly as it may sound, the first thing that has come to mind is my days working at a pet shelter back in Ohio. We didn't adopt out animals to people with criminal records. The only thing I want in this life– more than a man, or a job, or a house, or anything– is a couple of dogs. To disqualify myself from lifelong dog ownership for a minimum wage gig is out of the question.

"I'm not sure I'm the right person for this. I've already got a bartending gig to pay the bills, so maybe I can just keep interning until the right job comes up…"

Piper jumps in. "Nina, before you decide, let me ask you something, and this is really important. I want you to consider, what will it be worth to achieve success, all your dreams, if you're on an unlivable planet? Will you care that you got handcuffed for a few hours when millions of people are starving to death from floods and droughts?

"How will you, or any of us, sleep at night, knowing we could have done more to prevent this global catastrophe from happening? How will we face our children and grandchildren, knowing what we know about the state of the climate crisis now? How will we face our most vulnerable communities, who did the least to contribute to the problem, but will suffer the most dire consequences? How will you face the ocean that you cherish so dearly, when it is devoid of life, filled instead with plastic and toxic waste?"

I have sunk back into my chair, heavy; heavy and paralyzed, all the old feelings from the Great Barrier Reef weighted on my chest.

"We chose you for this for a reason, Nina. We know your passion and commitment to the cause. You have an amazing opportunity here, to be a leader, to be a hero. To make a real difference, to stand up for the silent; to use your privilege as a force for good. And we haven't even told you the best part."

The tunic man smiles and passes me a job description. At the bottom in bold is a number; a number I have never seen on a paycheck before; never even close; not even half; never in my life.

"Due to the urgency of the situation, we have received backing from a very special donor for this project– someone who has inherited a family fortune built on exploitation and extraction of natural resources like fossil fuels. They are very motivated to make this happen."

Felicia tugs my ear. "Wait a minute…are you hearing this? A rich heiress… wants to use her wealth… to disrupt the assets of powerful people? And is recruiting a team of scrappy, marginalized people to carry out the mission?… Do you SEE IT?"

I do see it. This is my movie. I have somehow found myself inside the plot of my own story. *Is this a dream? Am I on some sort of hallucinogen, and the entirety of the last six months has just been a weird trip? Am I going to shortly wake up in an ayahuasca circle, covered in my own puke?*

"You are welcome to take that paper home and think it over for a few days. Our next disruption will be at Camus Junction next week, and we've got a big one coming up that we are very excited about. We'd love for you to participate in that one."

"Yes… maybe I can go as an observer first, and then decide after that. Where will that one be?"

"It's going to be a blast! Lots of press, big names and *big* money."

Debbie pulls the hem of her skirt up to cover her eyes. "Dear *Lawd* in Heaven…"

"The Palmetto Hills Car Show."

16
The Lecture

"Now Nina, you jes' sit *roight* there 'n' listen to me now. You really *fahckin'* need to hear this, you really do."

I lay still, and waited.

"It's high time you grew up. Seriously cunt–" I fidgeted in my position on the ground, antagonized at the word. "Exactly! Look at ya now. It's jest a *fahckin'* word! You make the bigges' commotion over every li'l thing. It's childish nonsense."

I went to bite his arm to free myself, but my head dropped back to the dirt defeated, nowhere near accessing flesh.

"I just wish it didn't have'ta come down to this, where I'm pinnin' ya down in your *noice* li'l outfit, to be able to talk reason to *yah*. You should also consider that if you struggle, you're only rubbin' more dirt into your clothes, 'n more bugs in your hair, so you ought to jes' listen to what I have to say. An' Aussie insects, you know–"

"Alright, ALRIGHT, I'm fucking *listening*! Just say it so you can get off of me–"

"Well I would if you'd stop *intah-rupting*," John said with phony exasperation and a smile in the corner of his stupid Neanderthal face.

"You're twenty years old, an' real *loife's* about to hit you fast. You need to accept that your idea of the world is in the clouds… whatever shows 'n nonsense you've been watchin', whatever fantasies you've been actin' out with your sisters on the front lawn, it ain't real. You need to face the world for what it is, face reality.

"There are bad people in this world Nu, irredeemable, evil, sick an' broken people. An' everyone else is flawed as hell, yourself included. All *koinds* of people out there, who'll *hahm* ya, exploit ya; and there's a million forms of mayhem out there jes' waitin' to crush ya.

"There are real, unfixable problems in the world– because of human *naychah*, and because of the nature of existence itself. It's not anyone's fault; Nature's a beauty but a cruel bitch. You can't be pretending you can fix the world, or worse, pretending that these things don' exist an' fail to protect yourself.

"I seen how you walk aroun', not lockin' up your *boike*, joggin' at dusk in them li'l shorts, signing up to live on some boat with a strange cunt you never even seen–"

"He's affiliated with the school! Can you please just admit that you're jealous of him?"

"I would *nevah* admit to something *loike* that," John stated proudly, and quickly flipped me onto my back so he could access my armpits. I wailed and writhed with tickled laughter, desperate to catch my breath after John's massive body had been pressed over my lungs for the last several minutes.

"*Please*! I can't– *breathe*!" He returned me to my stomach and held me down as before. "Were you a wrestler in high school, by chance? Though I feel like you're too much of a homophobe to do something like that."

"For *fahck's* sake woman, don't change the subjec', I'm not done with you. An' I'm no phobe– whatever you said, I went to a boy's boarding school. I seen more naked blokes wrestlin' and beatin' each other than there're porns about it. I just think parades about who you like'ta *fahk* are dumb on principle– an' I want to be able to call me mates fags when they're bein' fags."

"But can't you see how offensive…" I was out of breath; I groaned in lieu of a reply so he could finish his speech and dismount my aching body.

"Now– I want you to really *considah* somethin'. Twenty minutes ago, you and I were laughing, havin' a fine *toime*. Suddenly, you were yellin' at me, then you're crying."

"Because of YOU! You–"

"Sobbin' like a little child who didn't get 'er way. Upset, furious– an irrational hotpot of emotions. How you gonna behave someday when your boss yells at ya in a room full of people? Or when a coworker humiliates ya? How are you gonna handle it when your landlord tries to evict you, or the dog you wanted from the pet store is bought up by someone else?"

"I would *never* buy a dog from a pet store!"

"As usual, yer lookin' *roight* past the point. Jesus cunt, who raised you?"

"I'm sorry I wasn't raised by a pack of wolves like you!"

But when I considered how I had behaved in those last twenty minutes, it didn't stack up with my personality, or a lifetime's evidence of my behavior. I wasn't the irrational one. I was quiet and withdrawn; the one who looked before she leapt, and kept to herself. John was right; I *had* changed. What was it? Was it my epiphany on the *Siren's Revenge*, or the Queensland heat? Or falling for John?

It was John. Obviously John. He was the reason I had started yelling; the reason I started crying; the reason I was laying in the dirt and being forced to laugh like a hyena on cocaine. His very presence could get a rise out of me; he brought out an emotional capacity I didn't even know I had. His words either sent me to heaven or sliced me open. *Is this what love is? Or is this how a cold case movie starts?*

"It's you," I said abruptly, still unable to bridle my emotions. "IT'S YOU! And you know it too. This isn't who I am. You make me like this. YOU!" I squirmed with a renewed strength, committed to freeing myself so I could land a punch somewhere soft.

"Ah, passing the blame, I see. That's another thing you've got to get a handle on– blaming the whole world for your own problems 'n your own shit *behaviah*. Though I have heard that love'll make you do crazy things, hay. I reckon I've driven a few birds crazy," he chuckled and sighed at cherished memories of ruining other girls' lives.

"One last thing before we wrap up here. An' by wrap up I hope you know I'm carryin' ya to my room. Now, I know that your professors at uni, an' the books you read, an' the movies you watch, they've all filled ya head with ideas: ideas about people, about love an' the world, about the way things *should* be. But you need to understand there is a huge rift between any *idea* of what's true and what's really true. That's why them academic cunts are so hated by real workin' people. They have some theory about how things should or could go, an' they try to bring those theoreticals to *loife–* but they're just ideas, you understand? There's always gonna be some unintended consequence, some variable they didn't account for. We've gotta be dealing in what *is*, not what *should be*. You understand?"

17
Stay Lady Stay

My room is a mess; clothing and little bottles of goo are strewn about everywhere. To prepare for this big car show– and, in no small part, thanks to Cam's passive-aggressive critiques of my "unkempt" appearance– I have begun the long process of giving myself a makeover. A haircut, pore-declogging clay face masks, clean shaves of the legs. Scraping the dirt out from under my chewed-down fingernails and inside my belly button, scrubbing old stains off my clothes and shoes with baking powder and peroxide. I have let many things go for a long time– so long that I stopped noticing them. But Cam notices everything.

I took Debbie's advice and asked him to take me shopping. I had to tell him the truth, that I really didn't have a single thing to wear to any nice occasion that wouldn't completely embarrass him. He was thrilled for the opportunity. I chose dresses and blouses that were sophisticated, yet girlish– conservative, yet sexy: lots of white and cream, powder and navy blues, steel gray, corals and periwinkles. High necklines and midi hems.

I've spent hours standing in front of the mirror in my new clothes, posing, admiring the shape of my body complemented by rich colors and flattering patterns. I stroke and smooth the luxurious fabric down my thighs, talking to my reflection in the mirror; channeling both Debbie's and Felicia's opinions, flipping between coaching and harshly berating myself.

"You are a walking contradiction– look at you! Filthy hypocrite."

"This is just a *social experiment,* for a work of art with noble aims. You are just in character."

"It's supposed to be nice– it's what rich people wear. There's nothing wrong with enjoying what is obviously nice."

"YOU ARE AN UNPRINCIPLED WHORE! You look like a rich man's kept wife!"

"You look...beautiful. I didn't know we could look this beautiful."

To reduce my carbon footprint (and because I've been dead broke) I have been wearing clothes from thrift stores for the last five or so years, and it's been mostly fine. But I look at myself in the mirror in these clothes and I feel elegant and important; I feel a sense of *authority*, like I'm in control of my own life...which is a rather hilarious illusion, because I didn't buy them.

I haven't dared to wear my new clothes yet, at least not in town. Cam and I have made escaping on micro roadtrips a bit of a habit.

Last week I drove along Palmetto Cove in the rain, prepared for a slow and painful shift at Vero's. The shops and al fresco patios were empty. Palmetto only receives a handful of rainy days each year and it brings town to a screeching halt.

"Nina, what are you doing here?"

I see my manager and an unfamiliar face removing glassware and silver from the patio.

"I'm covering Ryan's shift...or aren't I?"

"Oh I see– this is my mistake. Ryan was let go a couple days ago. We hired a replacement and I just assumed he was taking all the weekday shifts. Sorry about that."

"No problem, I'm happy to go home." It's about time they fired that guy. He was clearly selling Adderall to the customers.

I turned and walked out with a spring in my step. I could have used the money but the place would be empty anyway. I took my phone out of my bag and dialed Cam as I strolled languidly down the sidewalk in the drizzle.

"YO."

"Yo. Turns out they don't need me at work tonight. How wonderful is this rain?"

"I know. So what's your plan?"

"My plan was to work, dumbie."

"Right– well I'm bored. Been on the phone all day. Want to get out of Dodge and hit the valley? We can go to Dom's restaurant for dinner. I'm sure he'll be happy to see you."

"Sure, why not."

"I'll pick you up."

I drove home and stood in front of the mirror before changing out of my uniform. I always button the white collar to the top, because I like the boyish and preppy way it looks. My hair was fastened neatly in a high ponytail, but had frizzed from the rain. Without the apron around my waist, the gray sweater gave my torso a squared shape; I turned to the side and saw that the layers almost entirely hid the curves of my breasts. The khaki pants were tight after many rounds in the wash, but the sweater covered my behind. I could hear all their words echoing in my head:

High collar and a loose sweater? Simply terrible. No wonder you don't make any money.

Shouldn't you expect that as part of your job? It's just good for business.

I like it actually. You look like a Catholic school girl.

For the longest time, when I walked down the street and a man told me to "turn that frown upside down," I actually smiled– not because I was afraid or because I felt obligated to indulge him, but because someone noticed me. If I saw a man staring at me on the subway, I made eye contact with him, not because I wanted him, but because it excited me to see him suddenly get nervous and shy away. If a husky construction worker called out, "Nice ass!" as I walked by, I increased my pace to a strut and turned my head back to shout, "Thank you!" because I genuinely saw it as a compliment, and again, because I relished the fact that he noticed me.

I adored the attention, I craved it; I dressed for it and sought it purposefully. Male acknowledgement was a red stamp of approval and in some phases of life it was the only way I could see myself.

I'm aware it wasn't healthy, and certainly not feminist. I don't want a positive self-image to require male validation. But after reading about the subject, and watching some videos online, I've learned that this has been wired into me. It's textbook patriarchal structure; they have us right where they want us, seeking their gaze, hinging our happiness on their approval.

So after I left Dean, I decided to shed it all. I made myself invisible to men so I could wean myself off the juice. I dressed in bulky sweaters and wore my hair slicked back in a bun. I stopped wearing makeup in an attempt to become comfortable with my face as it was. I stopped shaving to become comfortable with my body as it was. And you know what? Not only did it work, but it was total bliss. For about two months. I was at ease, but felt sloppy, and out of touch with some part of myself. Comfy, yet void. I looked in the mirror and didn't see anything. Just a person. Which was nice... for about two months. It got old faster than I would have thought.

I suddenly realized how long I'd been staring at my reflection and quickly changed into a pair of jeans and a fitted sweater. I barely slipped the sweater over my head when I heard Cam's knock on the door.

"Hello Miss Distrella." I watched his eyes move up and down my body. "I like those jeans. They fit you very well."

I said "thank you" with no emphasis in my voice, not flattered nor bothered, like I was reading aloud from a technical manual. I turned to run up the stairs for my coat and gave a quick scan over the room to be sure that it was tidy in case he decided to follow behind me. "The view from behind is even better. Great jeans."

"Consignment chic, baby."

I was lying. The jeans were new.

We climbed into the pickup and headed up the winding road into the mountains that would drop us back down into the valley. Cam had mentioned before that Dom and his wife Carmen have a little Mexican restaurant.

We pulled into a strip mall that looked like it had been built around the restaurant. The faded adobe bricks stood apart from the tacky orange new ones that comprised the nail salon, laundromat, and pharmacy surrounding it. A man on a ladder was carefully peeling back plastic film from a tall sign, revealing each letter very slowly. "I..L… G..A..T..T..O.."

The place was charming inside, and smelled delicious. Colorful *papel picado* hung along the ceiling, and various artistic renditions of black cats were displayed on the walls. The waitresses had plastic red roses in their hair. But there was a decorative sign on the hostess stand that said "*Cucina*" with red grapes. You'd think someone would have caught the spelling error.

"Well look who it is," Carmen said as she wrapped Cam in a big hug. "It's great to see you buddy, it's been a few weeks."

She glanced over at me and reached out her hand. "You must be Nina, nice to meet you."

The women I've met while in Cam's company have all had the same reaction to my presence: a polite stiffness masking either cold resentment or utter confusion. In my experience, older women do not enjoy interacting with younger women, especially in the hyper-competitive environment of wealthy circles. And I don't blame them. In this patriarchal world, a woman is forced to derive her power from her desirability to men, and men worship youth and beauty. My age is threatening. Even if they are more beautiful than I am, which they almost always are, my age still gives me an unspoken upper hand. Their husbands stare at me and comment on my looks; it makes me anxious and justifies their wives' icy resentment. The only thing that somewhat levels the playing field is that I am poor, but it's not the most tasteful topic of conversation. My best defense is to dress modestly and try to avoid eye contact with their men, but because the women refuse to look at me, I'm left with three equally lousy choices: stare at their turned faces, stare at Cam, which makes me look like a child, or let my eyes wander aimlessly around the room and mentally depart the group conversation, which makes me look like a bimbo. But maybe I was overthinking it this time. Carmen didn't raise an eyebrow, or subtly look me over. She placed a basket of chips and salsa on the table.

"Can I get you two some drinks?"

I hesitated. I didn't want it to seem like I need to drink every time we go out.

"What, you're not going to have a drink?" Cam rested his hand on my lower back as we sat down.

"Are you?"

"Sure, I'll have a beer. Carmen, you know which one I like."

"I'll have the same." *Shit. That makes me seem young too, doesn't it?* I had also forgotten about my plan to remain sober until my screenplay is done.

"Nevermind. Water is fine." *Way to go– now you look like an indecisive fool.*

"Good to see you again, Nina," Dom gave me the same up-and-down as before, with the same childish grin on his face.

"Same here, friend." I know he's a pig, but I kind of like the guy. His sense of humor reminds me of the guys that used to hang out at Dad's garage.

"I see you finally caved and changed the sign. How much did it cost you?"

"Don't bring it up, Cam– you'll just upset her," Dom sighed.

"We had to change it." Carmen slammed down her tray, the beer bottles trembling. "Not to mention the window decals, the menus, the wraps on the van, our social media pages and website, our t-shirts. ¡*Podria matar a algien!*"

"Thousands, thousands it's cost us. Many hours, many phone calls and missed sleep. They were threatening to go to the press; they dropped some national names. We even received some death threats online. All for one stupid word."

"What word?"

I was playing dumb. I had heard about this from Purple at MMED, who was leading the charge. She– I mean, they– asked me to proofread an op-ed she– *crap, sorry;* I mean *purpleself–* submitted to the *Mirage Beacon.*

"*Under the guise of the Spanish term for 'black cat,' this restaurant is blasting this offensive slur out into our communities to intimidate and further marginalize Black-identifying persons– not to mention the problematic masculine gendering of the cat. The business should be boycotted by all allies in the community until they publicly apologize, and either change the name or close down for good."*

"My grandparents opened this place in 1955," Carmen sighed and sat next to Dom at the table. "They were both born and raised in a little town called Caborca. He made her a pair of shoes, when they were little kids. That's how they met. She was crying because she could not run on the hot pavement without shoes to play with the other children. He made her shoes out of old bike tires. Seventy-eight years, that's how long they knew each other. That's how they met."

"They're like a Mexican Mary Sucre and Tom Carpenter," mused Debbie. "How *romayan-tic!*"

"They moved to Mirage County together to start a family and life of their own. This restaurant was their greatest accomplishment: it employed and fed the whole family, gave them a stake in the community, brought them stability and respect. *Mi abuela* named it 'El Gato Negro' after the family cat, a stray that had wandered in the day they bought this place and never left. They saw that cat as a blessing from God despite its dark color– black cats are usually considered a bad omen, *pero Abuelita* knew that the cat sought a good life here, and so did they.

"Sixty-four years of serving the neighborhood without problems until some white liberal *chismosas* with so-called 'Ethnic Studies' degrees from MMU decide the name is racist. *¡Racista! ¡Soy* fucking *Mejicana!*"

"What a fascinating misunderstanding, don't you think, Nina?" Cam assumed a cartoonish pondering pose. A bus boy arrived at the table with a basket of garlic bread.

"So naturally," Dom smirked with his mouth full, "the white man wins out, once again. A toast to my boy, Chrissie Columbus!" He and Cam chuckled and clinked the necks of their beer bottles.

"Actually, he's your boy too, Nina. Congratulations on your victory, too!"

Seeing my confused and embittered look, Cam elucidated. "They're becoming an Italian restaurant now, as a nod to Dom's heritage."

"That's not set in stone yet," Carmen interrupted. "We might just do both kinds of cuisine. We're testing the waters. We thought we could save money with the Italian spelling, 'Il Gatto Nero.' Just a few letter's difference…but that didn't work either. The whole thing is a mess." Carmen slumped dejectedly; Dom stroked her back in a husbandly way.

I ordered black bean tostadas, Cam ordered veal parmigiana. The food was good– at least mine was.

"So how's the writing business going?" Dom said.

"I actually just had an interview for my dream job… at least, what would have been my dream job. But they gave it to someone else. You know how it is. Talent and merit don't matter in this world, it's all politics. It's all about who you know." I shook my head like a middle-aged man listening to talk radio.

"Especially around here," Carmen refilled my water glass. "Best to be aware of what kind of people you choose to associate with. It can open windows or slam doors."

I glanced around at where I was. *Great. Right on track.*

"I am not really a group person. I try to associate with as few people as possible," I shrugged.

"It can be a good thing though," Dom said, "the networking thing. It's kind of an essential part of life. I'm proud of how many people we know in this town, and what we can get done. As much hate as we've gotten from strangers about this whole 'black cat' thing, we have received an equal wave of support from our neighbors and friends. I made a few phone calls and got hooked up on all this new stuff we had to buy for the restaurant. If you want to get somewhere in life, you need to participate in society."

"Where exactly is it that I'm trying to get?"

Cam shook his head. "Do you see what I'm dealing with here? Maybe you can get through to her."

"Maybe you don't want to be part of any group because you spend all your time around people you can't stand."

"You mean everyone?"

"What kind of job were you applying for?"

"It was a writing job, for a… small media company. A column on the environment."

"Well there you go! I bet you're hanging around liberal Ivy-Leaguers: angry feminists, doomsday climate nuts and perpetually-offended queers. Sounds like a real positive crowd."

I usually don't say anything to Cam, but since it's Dom, I attempt a debate. "I just don't understand why you have to make *everything* about identity. It's queer this, Black that, fag this, lib that. It's harmful, and offensive. Why do you have to constantly make it an issue?"

"We're not making it an issue, they are."

"But can't you hear the tone of disdain when you speak this way? Where does it come from?"

Carmen jumps in. "I'll tell you why I moved out of Mount Mirage. Yeah, it's a beautiful place and all that. But it's the stifling so-called 'progressive' atmosphere. I couldn't take it anymore. It's gone so far that it's collapsed on itself, and circled back around to the other side; they've become so obsessed with their ideals that they've become a mockery of them.

"First off, *they are* the sort of people who make everything about what color their skin is, or who they sleep with, or what they have– or don't have– in their pants. I'll give you the perfect example. We were members of the Mount Mirage Chamber of Commerce. They started a 'woman leaders in business' group and asked me to join. I went to the first meeting. And all these women, these rich Mirage County women with $500 hairdos, and nannies at home raising their kids and cooking their meals, sat in a circle complaining about how hard it is to be a woman in business. And they kept looking at me and another Latina woman and saying, 'and it's so much harder for you, women of color! It's so much harder for you.' And they kept calling us Latinx– what the fuck is that? They never asked us if we wanted that word, or how we felt about it, they just started calling us that.

"So the group elected to make a pact to support women-led businesses, but even before that, women-of-color-led businesses first. I raised my hand and said, 'Then how am I supposed to know if someone is giving me business because my food is good, or if someone is giving me business because they feel sorry for me?' And one woman said, 'What should you care, as long as you're getting paid?' I told them they were a bunch of *putas racistas* and got out of there. They all hated me after that. Not one of them has ever 'supported my business,' even before that. Not one.

"You see it on the news, and in every movie and TV show: the enemy to people like me is supposed to be the poor and middle class whites, the 'rednecks' and 'white trash', the voting block of so-called white racists. But you know who has consistently been a pain in my ass my entire life? Rich white people, that's who. Rich, over-privileged, bored white women, who sit on boards and committees and condescend to people like me, who pretend to know what's best for everyone. The women who have been completely silent through this whole *gato* mess. *Chismosas blancas*."

～

Still getting ready to leave for the weekend. I have about twenty articles of clothing strewn across the bed, because today is the big day, and I've convinced myself that if I look nice enough, the Earth Defenders won't recognize me. I've got a big derby hat and cat eye sunglasses that make me look like that iconic 1960's Barbie doll, or Meredith Blake. Cam's going to love it. Felicia may burst into flames.

Per Piper's recommendation I biked to Camus Junction at 7AM last Monday to preview the Earth Defenders' civil disruption campaign, to decide if all those zeros on that job offer would be worthwhile. The junction was as busy as you'd expect. Early-morning commuters were stopping for gas, coffee, and greasy breakfast sandwiches before hopping onto the freeway. From above, the alternating cross-sectional lanes entering and exiting overpasses and underpasses looked like a star pattern in a mechanical ant colony. There are poorly designed intersections in this world, and then there are good ones. Camus seems to be a pretty good one. People were getting where they needed to go. They were waiting their turn. No one seemed to be running late today.

I'm actually quite familiar with the flow of the morning commute here, because I've sat atop a rock outside Camus Preserve and watched it many early mornings after nights without sleep. I've tried to explain this to Tyler, but he doesn't get it. He thinks solely nature in its purified, humanless form is an appropriate venue for thinking. But anyone who's grown up in or near a big city knows that it is amongst absolute human chaos that has been funneled into sanity, especially from a comfortable but small distance, where a person can really disconnect from the world.

So at Camus Junction it goes like this:

From 6-7:30, you've got the rush of the trucks: the real-work workers, the guys who climb telephone poles and build houses and fix pipes. The next wave is from 7:30-8:30, and it's a mix of customer service workers, high school seniors in their first cars, and school buses. Then 8:30-10 is everyone else— the office people and retirees mostly. I don't know if that is how it is everywhere, but that's the flow at Camus Junction.

Right at 7:00, ranks of MMED protestors, dressed in matching green t-shirts that say, "NO PLANET NO ECONOMY" assembled along the roadside, and upon a red light, unfurled a giant green banner that read "Stop the Invisible Hand Power Plant" and took their places across the entrance of the freeway. At the green light, the trucks inched up to the line, honked, and flashed their brights. The activists did not budge. I could see Purple's hair from my secret watching place. Several protestors sat down in the road. Madness ensued pretty quickly. The lines backed up as far as the eye could see in all directions, all limbs of the star full in a matter of minutes; box trucks, beat up old pickups filled with guys and equipment, flatbeds with other vehicles strapped to their backs.

My stomach felt sick; it begged me to either do something, or to look away. *This is the wrong time; it's the wrong crowd. These guys are just trying to get to work. What does this solve? What does it prove?*

Angry and desperate drivers at the front of the line left their vehicles and began shouting at the activists, but only Purple seemed to respond. The others were silent, solemn in their stubborn indignation and polyester neon green shirts. Sirens began to reveal themselves in the cacophony of horns and I felt relief that this counterproductive display was about to be over. By the time the police arrived, a group of the blocked drivers had teamed up to drag the protestors off the road and hold them to prevent re-entry. Upon being touched, the activists hung like dead weight, or curled into balls in the street like frightened pill bugs. It was pathetic. I knew some of these people.

"Thank Heaven Almighty, the *po-leece* have arrived!" Debbie clapped. "Our heroes in uniform, here to restore *ohr-dah* to society!"

"Yeah, great," Felicia scowled. "Hopefully no one gets shot for being–"

The three of us were stunned into silence as four of the drivers were restrained into handcuffs.

The drivers? The real-work workers?? The guys who climb telephone poles and build homes and fix pipes???

Some sick part of me coped with the outrage of this scene with laughter; cackling, grotesque laughter that made me feel instant shame. I couldn't watch another moment; I rode off, convinced that no amount of money was worth that. And I've done plenty of crappy things for money.

They asked me to join the big disruption at the car show tomorrow, but I told them I would be out of town... which is technically true. We'll be staying at Cam's friend Skip's for the weekend. It's gonna be *bad*. If this event is full of people like Cam, the activists will be lucky if they come out of this alive.

They have been studying a map of the car show layout. Cars will be displayed in various categories: antiques, hot rods, muscle, custom, classics, et cetera. Arranged in the center will be the Winner's Circle, a collection of cars that have won various award categories. "Skip basically chooses all of them," Cam said. "Every member of the committee is either trying to do business with him or in the running to join his next international yacht excursion."

I carefully pack my new clothes in borrowed luggage. I'm wearing prescription-strength antiperspirant, borrowed from a busboy at Vero's. I've been a nervous wreck leading up to this day and figure I will need it. All I've desired in the last 48 hours is a big fat joint, something to take my mind elsewhere, to take the edge off– but I've somehow adhered to my weed embargo since moving in with Kevin. It has made days feel longer, doing chores more arduous, and food less appealing. But the boredom and mental clarity has led to some great writing. Act I of my film is just about done– but I'm struggling with the setup in Act II. I'm not quite sure yet how the climax is going to unfold.

I've chosen a bold look for the drive: a replica of the crimson jumpsuit that Sally Grossman wore on the album cover of Bob Dylan's *Bringing it all Back Home.* If you don't know what I'm talking about, look it up right now. I know you have your phone in your pocket. Why pretend? Why not know things when you can know them instantly?

This is the best clothing purchase I have ever made; a childhood dream come true. I had a poster of that album cover on my wall for all of high school. I even bought a pack of cigarettes just so I can hold one in my fingers and stare emptily into people's eyes the way she looks into the camera. I've been practicing in the mirror. I'm not ashamed of it either.

I don't know why, but since puberty I've been secretly obsessed with that sort of iconic image: the beautiful young woman sitting coolly in some gorgeous, ungodly setting, well-dressed and flawless, surrounded by crystal vases full of roses and great Danes and gold sconces and expensive scotch, and she is completely unimpressed, utterly detached…stoically touching her suited man's shoulder, gazing into the distance, her mind obviously elsewhere. The Lana Del Reys of the world. The Rose-from-Titanics; the Sofia Coppolas, the Melanias. There's something so deliciously indulgent about a fantasy of misery, don't you think?

I don't expect men to understand, and frankly, I don't quite understand it either. But it's a real thing– there's something seductively, self-destructively tempting about being that woman; about being an exquisite wild animal in a gilded cage.

I step outside with my cigarette and pose for Cam as he pulls up. "Polished up like a ruby, look at you. I am stunned, speechless."

"You're not capable of being speechless."

"Fine, you're right. You look fucking delicious." Cam grabs me by the waist and kisses my cheek. "And that perfume… so elegant. I knew you had good taste hiding under all that hippie shit."

"Isn't it lovely? It's Italian. Fresh but still kind of earthy; I think it suits me. So did you get my reference or what?" I wave my cigarette and do the pose again.

"You're putting that album on for the drive… but don't even think about lighting that cigarette in my car."

"And compete with your cigar smoke? I'd never dream of it!"

He is wearing all black, as usual, and a pair of aviators. They look good on him. I preserve my hair by wrapping my head in a silk scarf, one of those fancy-looking ones with the nautical patterns. I don't even know who I am anymore.

You are in character. For a work of art. With noble aims.

"Are Dom and Carmen meeting us there?"

"They can't make it. The restaurant transition has been a disaster, it's been really hard on Carmen. I told Dom I'd get him on the list for next year."

We take off for Palmetto Hills and "She Belongs to Me" overcomes the growl of the Cuda and the whipping wind. As we pick up speed and he reaches over for my hand, all my fears and concerns are gone… at least for now.

～

Tyler

Hey, I'm back from Alaska…	11:18 AM

I accepted a job in the city. It's not where I want to be of course, but it could pave the way to finding a field job later on. It's just so hard to plan for the future when it feels so uncertain… I just feel like I shouldn't be waiting to be in the place I want to be, like there is no time to waste.   11:27 AM

Maybe we could get together and talk before I go?	11:40 AM

I see the grizzlies failed to eat you. Too bad.   11:52 AM

On the final stretch of the drive, Cam attempts to brief me about the weekend, but between the Earth Defenders meetings and my own Googling, I have a good sense of what I'm walking into. Palmetto Hills is not a place you go; it is a place you "get into." If Mount Mirage is filled with millionaire peasants, Palmetto Cove is the noble court, and Palmetto Hills is the billionaire kingdom. In other words, we are climbing a hill to enter Hell.

I brought along my well-worn copy of *People's History of the United States* to peruse in hopes of sparking some interesting conversations. He sees it sticking out of my bag.

"Imagine a world in which the most rich and powerful were truly the brightest, most talented, and most productive or useful members of society. Would they, then, be worthy of their riches and power?"

"But they aren't, and never will be. So the question is irrelevant."

"Why is it irrelevant? Your kind envisions 'Utopia' all the time; it is the basis of all your arguments for social change, is it not? That constant corrective action is imperative to work toward an ideal?"

"Yes of course, so?"

"So– what if the ideal was to exalt the best, the brightest, the most talented, productive, and useful, to the benefit of both the individual and the society alike?"

"That's already the American ideal. But–"

"But what? The system's flawed and produces imperfect results?"

"Yes exactly, to say the least."

"You're not seeing the irony of your own paradox. The mistake you progressives always make is that you think the answer is to invert the cultural ideal, to shame the strong and revere the weak, but that inevitably reverses social behavior. If you idealize the best, people race toward the top. If you worship the underdog, people race toward the bottom."

"But like you said, it's a flawed system. The top is not filled with the best, and the bottom is not filled with the worst."

"Explain to me how you're going to create a perfect system in which greed, corruption, incompetence, injustice, and cheating will all be eliminated. Take your time, think it over. You can present your master plan at dinner tonight– there will be enough money and power in the room to make it happen."

"Looking forward to it."

Felicia, who is dressed in our MMED shirt with the sleeves torn off, is cracking her knuckles. "Let's see how smug you are by this time tomorrow, fucker."

"Well, hey now, maybe this is actually a fine *oppahtunity*," Debbie offers. "Maybe we could make a nice Powerpoint presentation? I personally like the Savon template best..."

Skip Vodnyyvor's driveway is a mile long, the entrance of which is sealed by a decadent wrought iron gate with gold accents, including Skip's initials: SVV. We drive slowly through a manicured jungle so lush that I almost forget where we are going. While Felicia bitches about the drought, I daydream of an old fantasy of traveling through South America with John.

"*Yeh* look, I'm not too keen on coming to America," he said, "but I reckon after I get my first few companies set up I'll come grab ya. We'll get your folks' blessing and hightail it south before we marry back at home. I'd love to explore the Amazon jungle with you before I get ya pregnant."

"Oh John, I'd love that! But promise me we'll still travel after we have children, too? I want them to see the world."

"Yeh of course Nu, our kids will be worldly as."

"And can we make a stop in Belize? I've always dreamed of seeing the reefs there."

"Sure thing, Nu, sure thing. Whatever the most precious li'l *crea-chah* on God's green earth wants, she gets."

Skip's jungle tunnel opens up to an estate that looks like it was designed by Ponce de León, or perhaps a druglord with archaic taste. It truly feels like we have been transported to South America, to some exotic land that has been conquered by Spanish royalty. But from the giant carved wooden doors a little pink man appears, furrowed and adorably sympathetic like a flaccid penis, and I remember exactly where we are.

"Baby, you are looking *hot*." Before I can take offense, Skip gives Cam a rambunctious hug. "Look at that leather jacket, and tight ass!"

"Thank you Daddy– but I know you just want a piece of her."

Before I can say "now just a minute, you chauvinist *pricks*!" they both walk right past me to look under the Barracuda's hood.

"Best in Show this year, without a doubt," Skip says. "Speaking of Best in Show– you haven't introduced me to *Lay Lady Lay* over here." Skip scans me from toe to temple and gives Cam's shoulder a squeeze of horny approval. "This conflict-free diamond in the rough is Nina Distrella. Nina, meet Skip Vodnyyvor, our fine host and my dear friend."

"*Mister Tambourine Man*, how do you do?"

He brings the back of my palm to damp wrinkly lips.

"Look at you, beautiful creature. Simply beautiful. What a weekend Mr. Benzin is about to have. Won't you look divine standing next to him in the Winner's Circle tomorrow!"

"...The Winner's Circle?"

You mean exactly where the disruption will be? You want me to stand there? Oh yes, I'd love to; happy to do it. I just need one thing: a new face. Could you get me a new face by tomorrow? This place looks like you have at least one plastic surgeon on retainer. May I have a new face? A new life, too, would be great.

"How many cars make it to the Winner's Circle?" I consider lighting up the cigarette I've been holding since we left, but without realizing it I have snapped it in half.

"There are ten winners in various categories, and Best in Show sits right in the center of them all. The committee was gracious enough to nominate my old Cobra over there, but I'm thinking this should be Cam's special weekend. He's shown me more loyalty in the last few years than my own family– and Lord knows much more than my ex wives!"

"Come now, Skippy– don't make me blush."

"I wouldn't dare! That's this little red rose's job. Mm-mm-mm, what a time; what a weekend, old friend. Looks like things are finally looking up for the both of us." Skip plucks a fragrant Hong Kong orchid from the landscaping. "Make me the happiest man in the world, would you, and place this in your hair?"

I am exactly half-disgusted, half-enchanted; I hold the orchid to my nose and the scent is breathtakingly sweet. I take one more intoxicating whiff, and tuck it into a barrette in my hair.

"Heaven, heaven in red. Oh Cam, do I envy you! Now, Miss Nina, how about you go join the ladies for a nice pampering on the terrace this afternoon? They've got the masseurs and manicurists cued up poolside, and buckets of champagne waiting. We gentlemen have to be pampering our other ladies for the show tomorrow– and by that, I mean supervising a team of men to do it while we smoke cigars and run our mouths!"

"Now now, Skip, I think you know me well enough to know that I insist on polishing up the Cuda myself."

~

Do you remember your first buzz? Sixteen or so, sipping a stolen beer, or passing around a bottle of peach schnapps; that initial anxious thrill of doing something wrong, the giggling and the looking around saying, "no no, we shouldn't!" before you take that first sip; and it's sweet and bitter and stings, and you feel it go down to your belly all warm, and then it kicks in; that first buzz, that dreamy feeling that suddenly washes over you, the feeling of something wonderful but not quite real; that feeling that the world is yours, and you're so alive, more alive than ever, and you love everyone and everything, and all your troubles are just a laugh, a nod to a far-off problem that you can hardly see on the horizon... Do you remember that first buzz, that very first time?

I floated through the whole afternoon just like that– childlike in my vacant state, completely removed from my own life and reality, and dropped into an existence I never would have thought to dream of. I cautiously approached the grotto of kept women who were being polished and groomed to be displayed next to their men's cars at tomorrow's show, following behind a maid like a child clinging to her mother's ankle on the first day of kindergarten. I was surprised to be warmly welcomed and not evaluated suspiciously like other Palmetto women had done– perhaps because no competition was necessary here. We've already made it; we're already in the Winner's Circle. Or maybe it's because they had been drinking since ten.

The initial disgust at the excess around me was carried away on a flying carpet of champagne bubbles. I gorged myself on Thai mangoes, Hawaiian pineapples, pastries taken from the oven only moments earlier by a Parisian baker. When no one was looking, I tried a piece of brioche. I know it has eggs in it, but I could not resist the scent of it. I don't know why I was sneaky about it, either– as if these women would know I was vegan, or care.

A team of handsome young men and women dressed in white massaged my body, soaked me in sweet-smelling oils and concoctions that made my skin glow and my hair silken; they manicured my fingers and toes, they waxed my eyebrows, lasered my underarms, my legs and bikini line…and even in spite of the pain I floated, positively floated.

And look, I know. I'm just being honest. I thought I was better than this, I really did. I knew what I'd be walking into, and I thought I'd be unable to stand it. I pictured myself making a statement, boldly saying no to all of it; expressing sheer disdain and disappointment at this perverse display of material excess in a world with starvation and drought and extinction. I thought it'd make me insufferably sad, and angry, and unable to bear it; I thought I'd be pushed to the point where I'd stand up and make some heartfelt speech about what has real value, and integrity, and the hollow sin of luxury. But the truth is that I didn't do any of that. The truth is that I fell right into it, and enjoyed the hell out of it. I ate it up– just like you would have done. I hate myself, and so should you.

It's also worth mentioning that Felicia was absolutely silent all afternoon. It's possible that it was Debbie's doing, but I've got too much on my mind to ask questions.

"That robe is so big on you, it makes you look so *comfy!*" The woman was smiling and sincere. She motioned toward the open lounge chair to her left and extended her arms, revealing bare quarters of her forearms and wrists. "I'm so tall, everything is too small on me."

"It really is cozier when it's all big like this…no offense." I squirmed around in the very fluffy, very white robe, and took a seat next to her. I was grateful that she broke the ice. "That is honestly the most beautiful blanket I have ever seen."

She had it draped elegantly over the arms of her chair. None of the other women had one; it was clearly an expression of her taste. It seemed to compliment the shades of her skin, her eyes and hair– even the vibrant greens of the gardens seemed illuminated by it. Thin gold threads were woven into bright tropical colors, which were countered by geometric patterns of black and white. It had the charm of old-world tribal patterns somehow complimented by abstract modernity.

"Oh thanks, I love it too. I got it in Seychelles."

"Wow, what brought you there? Seems like a unique destination." Full disclosure I had no idea where that was. Apparently she frequents one of the most exclusive resorts of this tiny hidden gem, nearly 1,000 miles off the east coast of Kenya.

"Just for fun, to get away from the routines of life, you know?"

"Oh sure…" She handed me her phone. I scrolled while she narrated over photos of dreamy exotic landscapes: infinity pool overlooking turquoise ocean, clawfoot bathtub filled with flower petals in a deep green jungle setting, foreign cityscape seen from a balcony breakfast table.

"That was a yoga retreat in Bali; that was a business trip to Milan; *Ooh!* – that was an arts and fashion festival in Dubai– I got this bracelet there." She jiggled her wrist and the bangle danced around.

Glancing at my awed expression, she said very plainly, "You could do all this too, you know."

"No, no I don't think so." *If you only knew who I was, you wouldn't condescend to speak to me. I am an intruder,* is what I wanted to say. *I am white trash. I am an imposter and a fraud.*

"You see, that's the problem. You won't even let yourself envision what is possible for you. What if you fully embraced the wildest possibilities for your life? What if you allowed yourself to truly dream big? What if the only thing preventing you from meeting your ultimate potential is your own self-limitation?"

Maybe it was the first few sips of the classy champagne, but I began to float on her words, and my mind's eye indulged itself on gaudy visions of the future. There I was, galloping at full speed, bareback on a shiny chestnut mustang from meadow to forest's edge; working on my latest novel at a Swiss ski lodge in the feathery snow; diving off the bow of my sailboat to visit my beloved coral reefs, which were in no danger at all, but full of life.

"So how do I do it? What is your secret?"

"You see, I've been able to emerge from humble beginnings and achieve the life of my dreams through the power of manifestation. And now I help inspire other women to do the same."

"What does that mean?"

"It means that your own vision and attitude have way more power than you think, and if you can expand your mindset into one of possibility, opportunity, and abundance, you can draw those things to you. Like a magnet.

"Take this weekend, for example. I haven't seen you at Skip's before, so maybe this is your first time. Consider what brought you here, and the mindset that led you to this moment."

That's easy: resentment, bitterness, a desire to eat the rich...

"Just think of the conversations you may have here, the people you might meet and the connections you may make, and how that could lead to incredible possibilities! The only real limitation is in your mind!

"Do me a favor. When you go upstairs to get ready for dinner, stand in front of the mirror and repeat this ten times:

'Love, money, and success are drawn to my energy.
Good things love me, and can't get enough of me.'"

Pollen winked at me. "Trust me."

Mr. Shaft

Hope the ladies are treating you well. Skip won't shut up about how lucky I am. I'm inclined to believe him. — 2:47 PM

I'm in heaven... getting all polished up. And everyone's been very nice. Blow the car a kiss for me. — 2:52 PM

Thinking of you... Your beauty put that orchid to shame. See you at dinner. — 4:02 PM

One of Skip's maids leads me up to the room I'll be sharing with Cam for the weekend. Each guest room is furnished around a theme, and ours appears to be Polynesian, with colorful photos of reefs and women scantily clad in traditional tropical garb, and a glass coffee table supported by the white skeleton of a large elkhorn coral. *How ironic.* I wonder if Cam asked for this one.

Before she leaves I request some water; she points to a gold mini fridge. I open it to encounter a row of little striped bags in various colors, filled with gourmet candy, and a row of opalescent bottles labeled 'Locke Water'. I look into the mirror and think of Pollen's mantra.

Love, money, and success are drawn to my energy.
Good things love me, and can't get enough of me.

I say aloud, "Disappointment, debt, and failure are drawn to my energy.

Idiots love me, and can't get enough of me."

Not going to repeat that ten times, but it gives me a nice laugh. Then I think back to her photos and I have some kind of foolish, superstitious fear that she has the Universe figured out and I don't, and if I don't reverse the spell I just cast, I'll be living paycheck to paycheck for the rest of my sorry life.

I quickly say Pollen's mantra, not once, not three times, but the full *ten times,* which takes longer than I think, and by the end, I'm angry at myself for doing it. I am a sucker.

I sit on the edge of the California king bed and stare at a square package sitting by the pillows, wrapped with a dark Caribbean teal silk ribbon. "Please don't get offended," the tag says. "But such an amazing gift deserves the very best wrapping." I assume he is referring to the thick white paper and plastic tape, but upon opening it his words take on a new meaning.

～

The table seats twenty.

It is set up on the lawn– or rather, on a giant Persian rug on a patch of hardwood floor on the lawn. The decor on the table brings out the rich colors in the rug, with small vases of carmine and orange flowers, sprigs of fragrant greens, and candles in tinted glass jars. A structure has been set up around the table to host a string of warm, starry lights. Antique lanterns of various shapes and sizes have been hung in the surrounding eucalyptus trees. Cam escorts me to my seat, marked with a gold leaf card, which is next to one head of the table but not next to Cam. He smiles at me and whispers, "You'll do great," and takes the long journey toward the other end.

What?

Debbie is startled. "He's not sitting with us? Dear *Lawd*, what do we do? Do we discreetly pull the host aside and explain to her there's been a mistake?"

"Nah, I like this." Felicia is calm– almost too calm. "This is a classy move. Mix the guests up and let them have at it. I love it."

"I suppose she has a point," Debbie ponders aloud. "It's like that lovely successful girl said this *aftah-noon*. Think of the conversations you could have. Maybe this is our first manifestation!"

"Oh, for fuck's sake," Felicia mumbles.

The crowd drifts around the table and the seats slowly fill in. Skip occupies the seat next to me at the head of the table, and the surrounding six seats are all the other men's dates and wives. *Ah, that's why.*

"It's my birthday!" Skip squeals and does a little dance in his chair. I'm thrilled and relieved to see Pollen seated on my other side. I am sitting stiffly, but the women are chatty and pleasant; we laugh in unison at Skip's jokes. Skip's wife Patricia looks stern yet pleased at her end of the table, like a queen in court, surrounded by the husbands in descending order of her preference. Cam sits to her left.

"Don't the new bottles look excellent? Beth here designed them... though I helped a little, didn't I?"

Beth returns a fond glance to Skip. "Yes I couldn't possibly take all the credit. It was your vision!"

The LockeWater bottles stand on the centerline of the table like little soldiers. Servers have begun pouring their contents into tall collins glasses at each place setting, followed by another procession offering white, red, or sparkling wine. The server in me can't stop thinking about how long it must have taken to set up this table. *And the cleanup...*

"Patricia was concerned they'd throw off the aesthetic of our little banquet here, but I think they add an exciting touch."

"So you're in the bottling business?" I ask, somewhat incredulously. *Didn't think one could buy estates like this with water bottle money.*

"You could say that," Skip says as he slurps down a Kumamoto oyster. "I like to call myself a 'water magnate', or rather, that's what the *Palmetto Press* likes to call me!" Skip's vague familiarity becomes clear. His company is on the Earth Defenders' hot list of villains. Skip buys up land with springs, lakes– any place in which he can privatize water rights.

"What does a water magnate do, exactly?" I am trying my best to control myself, though Felicia is stomping on my lungs.

"We are explorers, primarily– seekers of the planet's finest sources of freshwater. We traverse the wild and remote to bring people a taste of the exotic, pure, and extraordinary."

He sounds like an ad in an airline magazine. *Spoken like a $250-an-hour marketing consultant.*

"That is quite a brilliant business plan," I smile with fake praise and forced sincerity. "You privatize something that belongs to everyone, and then sell it back to them!"

"Hmmm... that begs a very interesting philosophical question, doesn't it?" Servers silently place the first course in front of us, fill in open spaces on the table with baskets of bread, and fill water glasses with the contents of the opal bottles. It reminds me that I have a double shift at Vero's on Monday.

Skip elaborates. "One could suppose that all of Earth's natural resources belong to everyone– effectively, rendering them the possession of no one. What would be the practical application of such a philosophy, one could wonder. Who gets to use what, then, and in what measure? Does that bring us back to an old tribal model of 'survival of the fittest,' in which the spoils of the Earth go in proportion to the biggest and most warlike? If that were the case, Pollen has chosen the ideal husband– Jeremy would most certainly provide!"

Pollen giggles and waves a flirtatious finger down the table to one of the foulest-looking creatures I have ever seen. If you're a member of my generation, I'll describe him like this: he has the physique of Shrek, the haircut of Lord Farquaad and the charm of the pink fire-breathing dragon. He looks like a medium-rare piece of prime rib come to life. The folds of his neck are wet, and presumably have mushrooms growing in them, competing with the skin tags and sparse curly hairs for the best real estate. This probably goes without saying, but he has food on his face, and is chewing with his mouth open.

The 'power of manifestation'. Right.

"Well," I muse, redirecting my disgust back to our conversation, "perhaps if Earth's resources were shared by all, instead of garnered in excess by a few, there would be a mutual sense of concern and stewardship. And perhaps those with ancestral connections to the land have the best knowledge to steward those resources."

"That is certainly a lovely thought! I like a woman with an optimistic heart." He touches my hand consolingly, and patronizingly. "But I like to think of myself as performing an important service. Considering the modern state of things, I see our possession of these water resources as an invaluable act of stewardship. We have the resources and expertise to monitor and protect these places to ensure the water is kept safe from pollution and misuse.

"In the old world, it was a somewhat more applicable strategy that rights to resources belonged to those who were there first– though that is when conquest was the global norm; the rule was, if you want to keep your land, you best be able to defend it from whomever wants it.

"But we live in a post-origins world. Humans have moved around since we discovered our own two feet, and we will always move; it's far too late to try and reset the course of tens of thousands of years of human venturing.

"Consider this as well: the remote springs we own are out of the reach of nearly the entire human population, therefore we are providing people access to pristinely clean drinking water. And of course, such a service is deserving of compensation. Like Binley over there – Binley, darling!"

Skip waves to a stuffy-looking man down the table. The table is called to attention and the side conversations pause to listen to Skip's question. "Binley owns Hume Oil and Gas. Binley, how would you characterize your service to mankind?"

"Easy. We light the homes and businesses of over fifteen million people. We fuel their commutes and vacations. We employ over 25,000 people."

I can see in my periphery that Cam is smiling at me, but I don't acknowledge his glance.

"What about you, Finch?" Skip says.

Finch's mouth is full; he washes his bite down with wine and asks, "Come again?"

"What value do you provide to the world? We're taking a little poll, aren't we?" Skip winks at me again. "Finch co-owns Sinclair Meat, and sits on the board of Bourlag AgriCo."

"Well," Finch says, "we have fed millions of people for over 100 years. We started small, but now we operate in 66 nations and have built extensive networks to move perishable food through complex supply chains. We employ more than 100,000 people, many of whom live in rural areas without many economic opportunities, and we give them health benefits and opportunities for education. We also provided tonight's main course, thanks to our partnership with J. Wayne Ranch."

As if on cue, the procession of servers arrive, delivering trays of the main course. It smells absolutely divine, if I am being completely honest. I didn't give up meat because it doesn't taste good. But I begin to internally panic; I have not mentioned my dietary preferences to our host. "Don't worry darling, I am vegetarian too," Pollen says. "Chef is very sensitive to these things."

Two plates are placed in front of us and my mouth waters. By far, the most appealing piece of tofu I have ever seen, breaded like a piece of Southern fried chicken. A whole head of romaine has been marinated and grilled like a steak; crunchy, juicy and full of savory, smoky flavor. A medley of sweet potatoes, orange and yellow and purple, are drizzled with truffle oil. Summery sides are passed around the table: warm corn spoonbread, grilled broccolini with fragrant garlic and chili, heirloom tomato salad, all prepared to complement their textures and maximize their flavors. The chef appears tableside to describe our dishes to us. He explains that unlike the afternoon's international spread, everything here is local and specially chosen by his team of buyers. I try desperately to mimic Pollen's slow and ladylike dining technique with little dainty bites, though I want nothing more than to shovel this food into my face like her porcine husband is noisily doing.

"So, do you all believe your compensation is proportionate to your contribution, as compared to the thousands of workers on the ground who actually drill for that oil, or service the power grid, or slaughter and dismember these cows?"

Pollen places a hand to her lips; there is an abrupt rattling of cutlery and plates. "Dismember" may not be the best word to say at a dinner table. I stifle a shit-eating grin, and take a crunchy bite of grilled romaine. *Whoops.*

Binley takes this one. He's got a British-countryside quality, like he spends his summers pondering old literature in a mahogany study with a pipe full of cherry tobacco. "I envision it like the human body," he says. "Individual cells, while cumulatively essential, are generally mundane, and to an extent, are expendable, and relatively easy to replace. Organs too, are essential– but cannot perform their duties without the electrical prompts of the brain.

"All the cooperation of the cells, tissues, organs, all fall on the orchestral power of the brain. So it sits up above, in its protective case, and is given the lion's share of the body's energy. The brain needs oxygen, water, and nutrients, and relies on the cells of the body to deliver. In turn, it guides the body to keep the whole operation alive. It is quite a responsibility."

"And quite the metaphor! Cam, dear, did you know that Binley was such a poet?"

"Unfortunately yes, I did. Sometimes I go out on my balcony at night, and there's Binley down on the lawn, reciting me sonnets in the moonlight. It's been quite awkward."

Binley gives a sour look to Cam and shakes his head. Cam sips his drink and leans forward to make eye contact with me. "But– we have an actual poet at this table. Nina here is a writer, and a promising one at that."

My cheeks flush hot. *Please,* please– *don't ask me to recite a poem; please don't ask me to recite a poem...*

"Oh, how lovely!" a woman across the table says. "I love poetry. I love the real sing-songy, rhymey ones."

Of course you do.

"Nina," Patricia turns the nineteen heads to her end of the table. "We'd love to hear a poem, if you'd be so gracious."

"Oh, I don't know... I'm more of a–"

"It's my *birthdaaay!*" Skip pinches my shoulder. "See if you can top Binley, I'm sure you can. Perhaps a slam poetry session will spontaneously erupt!"

"Dear god, let's hope not," Cam utters.

I take a deep breath, and close my eyes for a moment. Not to brag or anything, but I can be damn quick on my feet when I need to be. Felicia smirks, Debbie giggles, and I begin:

> "At the top sits the brain,
> given quite a head start,
> but the unspoken hero
> is our true friend, the heart–
>
> "She attempts to share blood
> as the toes become colder,
> but the vampire of all
> is the body's shareholder."

The table erupts into surprised applause and laughter. "Well, look at that!" Skip raps on the table and a few of his precious water bottles shake.

"Cam, what a little treasure you've found! What a weekend for Cam. What a night for Miss Nina!"

"That was awesome!" Pollen touches my shoulder.

"Well done, young lady."

"Thank you–" I nod, pink-faced, but glowing at my own cleverness. I glance down to Patricia's little male kingdom, and Cam is beaming at me, giving me that "dad at his daughter's college graduation" sort of look.

"What a weekend for Cam..." Skip forks a scallop. "What was it again? The vampire is the body's shareholder? Excellent! Hilarious!"

"You know, right after the '08 crash, Jack Welch declared that 'shareholder value is the dumbest idea in the world.'"

"Yeah, easy to say after he made his millions at GE."

"No one ever finishes that quote. He said that *sole* emphasis on shareholder value is an obviously poor business strategy. He said to focus on products, customers. Things that hold up long-term."

"Well that's the problem with this young generation. Everything's short-term thinking, short-term gains."

Oh, you mean the generation trying to sustain the planet through two centuries of short-term industrial greed?

"Yes and now with all these trading applications on their phones, the integrity of the stock market has been whittled down to a stump. It's going to have serious consequences, you mark my words. You're going to see concerted efforts of bored teenagers taking down companies they don't like."

"That's ridiculous."

"What really concerns me is this cryptocurrency nonsense. I've had several people attempt to explain it to me, and it sounds indistinguishable from a Ponzi scheme."

"That's because that's what it is. Young people are whining about their student loans while they throw their cash down this space-age black hole. It will skyrocket and then crash; it's only a matter of time."

"How is that any different than the regular stock market?" My voice cuts through this old man dialogue like a dandelion that's popped out of a city sidewalk.

"A fair question," says Finch. "The stock market has gone through its ups and downs over the generations, and has been manipulated irresponsibly. But in principle it has always been rooted in real, tangible assets: businesses that sell real products or deliver real services. Real estate, natural resources, valuable goods.

"But as I understand it, cryptocurrency has no basis in reality. It's as if young people have spent so much time on the internet that they have come to see it as a real place."

"It's going to replace the stock market in 30 or so years."

"Nonsense, absolute nonsense! Pass the butter."

"Don't you give him any more butter. Your cholesterol—"

"So help me God, woman— I'll tell the whole table the Gustavia story!"

"...Fine, give him the damn butter. But just so you know, I'm selling your boats when you croak."

"I'm living forever. I have to; I'm not going to let Steve wreck forty-five years of what I've built at Sinclair."

"I think the same thing. I mean, look around this table. We're all on our second acts, except maybe Benzin and the poet. I don't know about you all, but my children are morons... one's an Ivy League Marxist with a quarter-billion trust fund and the other two sit on some program called TikTok all day."

"Jack!"

"Well it's true. I have no one I can trust to pass this all on to. Who is going to hold up all that we have built? Do we really think we have a fighting chance against the Chinese? They're re-colonizing Africa as we speak."

"Oh the doom and gloom! On my birthday!"

"He's right, though— we all know it. It is very possible that history will consider us the last generation of the American Empire."

"The whole West is going to shit."

"And the strangest part, what I truly can't understand, is that the young people seem to be *happy* about this."

"It's the universities, we've known it since the sixties. They're all being taught to hate their country, hate Western society, and hate themselves."

"Is this true, poet? Do you hate yourself?"

Thirty-eight eyes turn back to me; my mouth is full of food.

"Oh, sure… but I think all poets do."

That breaks up the tension of the conversation a bit. I am killing it tonight. I take another big bite, and wash it down with Skip's imperialist water.

Plates are cleared. A four piece band begins playing. Dessert and port are served. I subtly spoon a chocolate pot de crème.

Debbie has been on cloud nine all night, reveling at the sophistication of this multi-hour, multi-course meal, and enjoying her self-assigned role of policing my etiquette.

"Make sure you're using the right fork!"

"Sit up nice and straight! No elbows!"

And I've enjoyed it too, if I am being honest.

An unreasonably large cake is wheeled out for Skip, and we sing. All the women refuse a slice of cake but are served anyway; they take subtle forkfuls from their plates. After a while a few couples rise to dance to the band. Cam appears behind me. "May I have this dance, madam?"

"Are you serious?" I laugh uneasily, incredulously. Cam's eyes flash with hurt.

"You know, I like to joke, but I can be a gentleman."

"Only if you lead, and go slow– I don't really know how."

"As it should be." He takes my hand and leads me to a spot near the cellist. The cello's tones are brooding and sentimental; I am carried off to far-away visions from the cottagecore Instagram, imagining myself waltzing inside the images: the first snowfall dusting an endless sea of tall pines, warm gingerbread and steaming cocoa, picking wild summer strawberries…

The rhythm suddenly sounds familiar. "Wait, is this… a Meat Loaf song?"

Cam grins. "Made a special request to the band." His hand rests on my waist and I feel a gentle pressure. I rest my head on his chest, and I think about tomorrow to the tune of "For Crying out Loud".

∾

I've been to plenty of motor shows with Dad, George, and Uncle Mick: car shows, boat shows, air shows. It's always hot as hell, and full of old guys in baseball caps and t-shirts, and has at least one old military helicopter or boat that kids can climb inside and pretend they're steering. I would always go along, not particularly interested in anything, but eager to partake in fair food without my mother around to say no: the frozen blue and red slushies, the footlong hot dogs and cheese fries, and greasy funnel cakes coated in Scarface-levels of powdered sugar.

There are no kids at the Palmetto Hills Car Show. There are no funnel cake stands, or balloons, or cooling stations with giant misting fans. But one staple has held: old guys in baseball caps. It looks less like a fair, and more like the polo scene in *Pretty Woman,* with tastefully dressed people mingling on the grass, sipping cocktails from real glassware. And just like Julia Roberts, I am the tacky whore in an elegant disguise.

A few booths are set up, not to sell anything, but to fundraise for local charities: the Mirage Child Protection Alliance, the Mirage County Police Foundation, the H. Caulfield Memorial Church Food Pantry, the Palmetto Pet Rescue Network. Each booth has volunteers eager to give out pamphlets, free keychains and pens. Sign-up sheets sit on clipboards and under branded paperweights, hopeful to collect email addresses. I've spent countless weekends of my life as one of those "tablers" for various nonprofits, and it is one of the most draining experiences imaginable: all that smiling and phony kindness, while you're trying to explain animal abuse to someone who just wants a free foam stress ball shaped like a corgi.

A huge white canopy is set up behind the cars with hors d'oeuvres and a full bar, plus free bottles of LockeWater. Posters hang behind the bar in the opalescent color, bearing Skip's appalling slogan: "WATER IS WEALTH".

The restaurant and terrace of the Palmetto Hills Polo Clubhouse is open to members only, of course, but all car show guests may peruse the lobby. Over 100 cars are arranged in their respective categories in alignment with the Earth Defenders' recon map. Cam and the other men drove off early this morning in their prized possessions; the rest of us enjoyed a morning yoga session by the pool and a breakfast made to order. I had chia-banana French toast with scrambled tofu, coconut bacon, and a small mountain of tropical fruit. The other women watched me ravage my plate with a mixture of fascination and fear on their faces. I snuck off with a Madagascar vanilla oat latte to reread my notes from the night before. (Don't you want to strangle me right now? I realize all this stuff must sound as pretentious and frivolous as you can possibly get. It's an outrage that any of it exists, isn't it? But if I told you that it's no better than the fair food at the old boat shows, I'd be squarely lying to you.)

Last night on the dance floor, right at the crescendo of our Meat Loaf song, Skip cut in.

He whispered something to Cam– I only caught "birthday present."

"Are you finding your way alright, my dear?" His cold hand could be felt through the fabric of my dress and raised goosebumps on my arms. "I was quite impressed with your wit at the table!" He pulled me close, and kissed my forehead. "Take good care of my Cam, won't you? He deserves someone like you."

I returned to the room before Cam last night, grateful for a moment to sort through the day and mentally prepare for the next. Felicia was drafting a sexual harassment police report against Skip while Debbie twirled in delighted ecstasy, reliving all the glorious moments of the last twelve hours.

"Take good care of Cam, won't you?"

I had already made up my mind.

When Cam entered the room, there was a long pause. Our eyes both drifted to the bed, the *one* giant bed, and the box sitting on it, which was closed but had clearly been opened.

"...Having a nice time so far?" Cam asked shyly.

"I am… everyone has been very nice."

"I knew you'd think so…"

...

"So." Cam broke the silence. "Tomorrow is going to be a long day; let's get a good night's sleep. There will be a party back here after the show."

We both seemed to loosen with relief, and proceeded getting ready for bed.

"Cam? You know, I was thinking– and I hope you don't mind me saying– but I think it might be a nice thing for you to return the Best in Show spot to Skip. It's his birthday, and he's the host, and–"

"You don't think it should be me?"

"It's not that… but, maybe the gesture will mean something to him, and he'll think of you later on. I am sure he has connections related to Invisible Hand, and–"

"Wow, thinking ahead. I love it. You're right. I don't want to be in the spotlight anyhow."

We exchanged a fond glance, and I breathed a sigh of relief to be freed from the spotlight too. He emerged from the bathroom in a white t-shirt and boxers. "Besides, lately I've felt like I don't need a title to know I'm the best." He gave me a satisfied kiss and passed out on his side of the six-foot-wide bed.

I thought this car show would have a bunch of those half-naked models standing next to the cars– you know, the ones that all regular women despise. But this place is truly classy. The women are mostly dressed like me; like Audrey Hepburn or Jackie O; like Lana Del Rey in her "National Anthem" music video. I take my place next to the Cuda, next to Cam. I am wearing a cream dress of embroidered lace, with puffy sheer long sleeves that taper into smocked cuffs. The Cuda's jet black paint matches the accents on my shoes and the ribbon in my hair.

I've never felt so damn good about myself, in my shiny new clothes, with my shiny new hair and my shiny new pores. I feel like I'm outshining the car. I shake hands and pretend to listen to the "so-and-so" stories. Mostly I'm just staring at people's clothing through my sunglasses. Everything is sharp and crisp, neat angles and dark as night black fabrics. Everyone smells amazing, especially the women. They walk by and the scented halos around their bodies pass through me like resplendent ghosts.

My usual resentment is distracted by an involuntary sense of aesthetic appreciation– for the clothing, the cars, the architecture of the clubhouse and the gardens. Everything is immaculately curated and classic in design; it evokes an emotional reaction that I can't fully explain. If select cars were removed, this scene could be taking place twenty years ago, fifty years ago, maybe even a hundred years ago. My mind drifts over time, from the self-driving Teslas to the muscle cars and minivans, back to the original "horseless carriage," the Model T; to the bicycle, the steam locomotive; to the cart and carriage and chariot; to the horse and the mule, the all the way back to the humble foot of man. It all happened so fast. And it's only getting faster. *I'll give this to humans: we are selfish and greedy, and we push to extremes– but hell, we have created some incredible things.*

I catch what almost feels like a sob in my throat; a sense of nostalgia for times that aren't mine; a longing to hold onto something I can't name. I think of Main Street; the old buildings are so beautiful and ornamented, full of charm, intricacy and imagination. Everything that has been rebuilt, renovated, or replaced, is ugly: geometric, bland, and soulless. Chunks of Main remain nostalgic and appealing, but if you walk another ten feet you're surrounded by minimalist corporate logos and windows without shutters. *Why is everything new so ugly?*

"Every single human being on this planet is born capable of the greatest good and darkest evil," Captain Don once said. "If you want to change the world, call on people to consider their legacy. Ask them to apply their brilliance and ingenuity to improving the world instead of taking from it. It doesn't have to be a selfless thing, when you think of it in terms of legacy."

Suddenly aware of the time, I hide under my derby hat and sunglasses, and try not to look around. It must be a horrible thing to be psychic; to constantly know that terrible things are about to happen, but still be forced to exist in the present. Our position in the American Muscle section sits in the periphery of the Winner's Circle. It is arguably the "coolest" section, but all day I've seen Cam glance toward the center, clearly disappointed. But then I glance upon the profile of a familiar face, disguised in the white attire of the clubhouse staff. Another one appears, and then another, like whiteheads appearing on your nose before a date.

Here it comes.

I am paralyzed by a sharp but heavy pain in my gut; suddenly I'm thinking of everything stupid I have ever done– even things I don't remember doing, but *might* have done, or *thought* about doing– and I'm embarrassed by all of it, by every choice I've ever made and every word I've ever said. I'm embarrassed by my entire life. I don't know what I'm more ashamed of: being here as a guest, as Cam's guest, or being associated with the people about to ruin it. The truth is collapsing on my head; I really am the Millennial poet who hates herself, who spends $30 a week on coffee and lets elephants descend on a garden party.

"Do you know how many cars these pompous Boomers probably own?" Felicia tries to talk me down from my guilty panic while Debbie sobs in a dark corner on a velvet chaise lounge. "Owners of meat-packing plants and oil companies? That's who you're feeling sorry for right now? Sticking it to these people is literally OUR DREAM! Don't go soft on me now! You know they deserve it!"

"You're not saving the world, you're just ruining her reputation… hurting your own cause, ruining our chances of *ev-ah* being happy!" The sobs are histrionic. "We *wuh* SO CLOSE!"

Their drama is cut off by a loud thump. I turn to see a protestor standing on the hood of one of the Winner's Circle cars. "THE COMBUSTION ENGINE IS DEAD–"

He is tackled off the car before his sentence is complete– but while everyone's attention is turned on his distraction, another activist dumps a bucket of orange paint all over Skip's Cobra… a convertible.

The shouts of outrage, shock, and calls for security are drowned out by their chant, coming from all over the lawn, perhaps twenty or more strong, as they descend on the Winner's Circle:

"OIL IS DEAD, AND YOU ARE NEXT,
NO MERCY FOR THE ONE-PERCENT!

KILL OUR PLANET, KEEP THE REST?
WE'RE COMING FOR YOU, ONE-PERCENT!"

～

"They are terrorists, plain and simple. They should be prosecuted as such."

"I can't wait to hear what Steve Sung has to say for himself about this complete failure of security by the Club. Surely the Board will can him."

"No, I think it is more complicated than that. There is no way those kids pulled off that stunt without at least one inside horse. I think this was orchestrated by a member of the Club."

"I think we all know who that would be..."

Skip's afterparty was canceled and replaced with this brooding discussion. The drawing room is filled with last night's dinner guests and the other Winner's Circle drivers. Skip's staff, overwhelmed by the change of plans and the volume of food and drink they prepared, are dropping fresh trays of food throughout the room every few minutes. No one is really eating, except me– and I am hyper-aware of that fact, fearful of looking at all suspicious. I strategically nibble just a bit off of the closest tray, and wait patiently for the next one to be dropped off, so I can do it again.

Skip paces out on the terrace making calls. Cam is also gone; I haven't seen him since the incident began. He hit the ground running the moment he heard that thud; he was one of the hands that yanked the first protestor off the car, and he assisted security with detaining the others. I was ushered back to Skip's with some of the other women, and we all quietly retreated to our rooms until we heard the caravan of cars pulling into the driveway. But the Cuda wasn't there.

"I just wish I could yank the bull ring out of that little punk's nose. How much do you want to bet that he grew up in Mirage County, probably went to private school and goes to MMU?"

"I told you, that's what they're teaching them over there!"

"It starts with the parents– these kids have been enabled to the point of malignant narcissism and sociopathy. The neo-liberal parenting technique of 'do whatever you want' is causing real psychological harm. I've read a couple of books on the subject."

"But how can't they see that they are actively hurting their own cause? None of us honestly want to destroy the natural environment; in fact, Dan and I have given tens of thousands to conservation projects over the years.

But we also recognize that people need to be able to drive their cars and heat their homes. We–"

"This isn't about energy and the climate! Wake up! Didn't you hear their chant? They want a new world order, French Revolution-style. They want to kill us!"

"Don't speak that way, there are ladies present!"

"Don't patronize us! This isn't 1808, we can handle ourselves."

Another woman attempts to muffle audible sobs.

"Look, we've all had a trying day. But we must keep in mind who we are up against. This is the most spoiled, overstimulated, helpless generation this world has ever seen. You know how they fight? By crying and shaking, by policing your language and weaponizing their hurt feelings. They don't have the wherewithal to enact some social revolution; they're all anti-gun and mentally fragile. Hell, just shut down the cell towers for a few hours, and you've already won."

"Yes, but to your point about how they fight– it is an insidiously powerful strategy, if they manage to be successful. Today they're ruling the lecture halls, tomorrow they'll be ruling the administration buildings and boardrooms, and then the legislative chambers. That's the biggest threat of all, if you ask me. Tyranny of bureaucracy. Censorship. The end of free speech. That's what they'll go after. That's how they'll win."

"That's giving them a lot of credit. Weren't you there today? All I saw was the irrational rage-fit of a three year old. They're all emotion, no substance. They've been convinced that Western society, capitalism, white males, are all evil– and need to be burned to the ground. I think they're taking it literally."

"Burned down, and replaced with what?" Again my voice is disquieting in this setting.

Felicia interjects inside my head, "A better, more just world? Sounds dreadful…"

"That is the most important question." Cam has appeared in the doorway. He has an orange smear on his jacket. "Replaced with what…

"If we can take any lesson from the wars of the twentieth century, it should be that the road to Hell is paved with good intentions. The thought has always been the same: 'If only *we* had the power, we'd get it right. *We'd* make it fair. *We* would create a better world.' But it is never that simple, is it?

"The system is torn down; a vacuum is created, and from there it's jump-ball. Who will win the battle to govern, the egalitarian lamb, or the Machiavellian psychopath?"

"What about an egalitarian psychopath? Or a Machiavellian lamb?"

"A contradiction in terms, my dear." He motions his head toward the door. "Join me for a walk?"

I am working hard to prevent myself from visibly shaking. He knows; he must know. Maybe he thinks I am the inside horse. The traitor. Maybe they all think it. I am going to jail, aren't I? He's leading me to the police ambush.

"Interesting discussions over the last couple days, don't you think?"

"Yes, it's been quite thought-provoking. So… is Skip okay?"

"The Cobra's interior is ruined of course, but the car will be alright. He'll be alright."

"Looks like you got to be part of the action today," I poke at his orange stains.

"Not just today. There will be lots of cleanup to do after this. Stains can be stubborn…"

"Sometimes you sound like a mobster when you talk in vague metaphors like that."

"I'm no mobster, just a janitor."

That one makes me giggle. "No breaking legs for you then?"

"I find people tend to break their own legs, if given enough time."

We cross the lawn on a cobblestone path, to one of Skip's award-winning orchid gardens. I don't particularly like orchids. There is something alien about them; they almost look like monsters, with beautiful colorful faces, staring without blinking, luring bugs into their mouths.

"I just wanted to thank you again for coming with me this weekend. It's been a tough year, and even with all that's happened today, I have enjoyed being here with you. It's been a pleasure watching how you have carried yourself, and how you've participated. You just seem to fit in a way I bet you never would have imagined. It's like watching one of these flowers blossom…" He pulls a box from his pocket, and hands it to me. Inside are a pair of gold earrings in the shape of tiny bear paws. "I remember you mentioning how much you dreamt about making friends with a bear…"

"I adore them! Thank you, Cam." I immediately put them on. "Do they look nice?"

"Oh yes, they suit you. This whole place suits you. Natural beauty standing alone in a human place."

"I want to thank you for this weekend too; I am sorry about what happened, but I've still had an exceptional time."

"Let's stay another night or two. Skip will appreciate the company." I nod enthusiastically. "Look at you. Did you ever think your people would be found in a place like Palmetto Hills? I feel like in another world you could have been one of those idiot protestors!"

"Hah! Ha…haha! …*hah…*"

~

I lean on the rail of the balcony in the gorgeous dark teal lingerie he bought me and stare at the distant city skyline. I feel removed from it. I close my eyes and imagine it is empty, it is gone. It's not mine and it never was. I didn't build it. It's not my problem. A warmth fills my body as he slides in behind me and presses me into him.

I feel it– the warm gentle crush, the chocolatey luxury of letting go, of giving up on it all, of exiting the toiling, burning world represented by this jagged heap of metal and concrete in the distance. I start to sway and delicately apply pressure against him. He holds my throat in one hand and pulls my waist in with the other, his lips pushing against my ear.

"You belong to me tonight."

I surrender myself to this moment, suspended in the luxuriant abyss of lust, able to evade the inevitable. I can let go of all of it. It's going to get so much worse before it gets better, if it gets better at all. Look around you. It's too little too late. Let it wash over, and enjoy it. I tried, I did what I could. I'm going to surrender myself to this. I'm not going to live forever but before it all goes down I'm going to live.

He turns my chin and our open mouths are hungry.

GREAT WHITE GORILLA MORPHOLOGY AND MATING

After millenia of migration, adaptation to new ecosystems and food sources, and interbreeding with other subspecies, Western white gorillas have a wide variety of phenotypic expressions. Therefore, despite their name, not all great white gorillas have white fur.

Certain physical characteristics have allowed *Gorilla-industria violentus* to be so complex and ecologically successful. Like all the Great Apes and most Old World monkeys, gorillas have opposable thumbs. This advanced manual dexterity allows for tool use, climbing, grabbing and pulling, grooming and advanced communicative gesturing.

Opposable thumbs, in conjunction with advanced intelligence and physical strength, has led the great white gorillas to tremendous success in resource gathering. One morphological marker of the GWG is a pronounced and rounded belly, telltale of their success in gathering abundant food resources. Fascinatingly, this belly is often out of proportion with the rest of the body; an individual may have muscular or thin limbs, but will still retain this abdominal protrusion. The belly may be so pronounced that a GWG's side profile may even be mistaken for a pregnant female's.

Previous studies have shown no evidence that this is a sexually-selected trait by females; it is instead believed to be attributed to the Western white gorillas' diet, rich in corn and oils extracted from various plants and seeds.

Females utilize anatomical clues to determine the reproductively-fittest and most dominant males. Typical indicators of health and genetic fitness are sought by females, with great emphasis on features like size, strength, and quality of fur. Females generally seek older mates, preferring males who have access to abundant resources and will provide for offspring.

It was previously believed that all alphas share certain distinguishing physical commonalities, like the unmistakable silverback gorillas, or the large cheek pads of alpha orangutans. But upon closer observation this study has uncovered a variety of "alpha archetypes," which may lead to a new understanding of the GWG's complexity.

1. Physio-alpha – "Old World Alphas"

This alpha archetype is most widely known, and is consistent with many other social structures throughout the animal kingdom, in which the physically biggest and strongest individuals rule social hierarchies and garner the best mates. The highest levels of testosterone are present in these males, which influences both physical traits and levels of aggression. Physio-alphas are easily identifiable by their large size and muscular build– particularly in the width of their backs and shoulders. Exposed skin (not covered in fur) is usually darker from time spent exposed to sunlight, particularly on the posterior of the neck. Indicators include an extended brow ridge, thick fur, and deep grunting vocalizations.

Although this group is most targeted as the cause of ecological damage, study observations have shown that this group has lost much of its social power in recent generations. While they are the most physically appealing to females, physio-alphas may still struggle to attract mates if they are unable to garner and retain resources– which has become more appealing to females than physical strength and protection alone. High testosterone levels also make this group more physically aggressive and volatile, and those who are unable to control their aggression may scare away mates or find themselves in dangerous social conflicts.

2. Opes-Alphas – "New World Alphas"

Derived from the Latin word *opes*– meaning wealth or resources– the opes-alpha derives his high status from the stockpiling and control of natural resources, including food, water, territory, and minerals. (Fascinatingly, the minerals most valued by females serve no practical use, but are simply shiny or colorful. It appears they are primarily used to signal their status to other females.)

This resource-hoarding adaptation has persisted across many generations, leading to an entire class of males who have inherited stockpiles of resources from previous opes-alphas. Due to this abundance, physical work to retain food or other needs is unnecessary, therefore these males live in what appears to be a self-imposed captivity. They are often visibly weaker than their counterparts, however, opes-alphas may use their free time to build muscle to imitate the appearance of physio-alphas.

One interesting differentiation between true physio-alphas and the mimicry of opes-alphas is visible in the hands. True physio-alphas will have strong hands, with rough and calloused palms from physical work, whereas opes-alphas have soft palms and notably cleaner hands and fingernails.

Physio- and opes-alphas both find mating successes and failures, but in different ways. Females may struggle to choose between the physical protection offered by physio-alpha males, and the resource security offered by opes males, as both are important for raising successful offspring. Opes males have further tipped the scales in their favor by using their abundant resources to control non-dominant males to provide protection on their behalf. Where physio-alphas once dominated social hierarchies by force alone, opes-alphas have changed the dynamic tremendously– or rather, female preferences have, which drives male behavior. The Achilles heel of the opes-alphas comes from deep seated instinct: this resource-driven approach is very new, evolutionarily speaking. Females may choose opes males for their resource capacity, but millions of years of evolutionary wiring still draws females to physio-alphas. This study has uncovered an astounding number of cases of females tricking opes-alphas into raising physio-alpha offspring.

The most astonishing finding so far is the emergence of a new trend in non-dominant males, who previously had mixed success with mating. It appears that some of these males are mimicking the social and even morphological traits of dominant *females.*

Those who are mimicking female social traits appear to be trying a new mating strategy, in which they present themselves to females as subordinate. There have been no findings thus far showing that this strategy is proving successful in the long term.

Those who are mimicking the physical attributes of dominant females appear to be seeking the protection and benevolence offered to females by dominant males. Instead of a mating strategy, this appears to be a survival strategy in which subordinate males, successfully disguised as females, may be offered resources and protection from other males. Again, there are no findings of success in this strategy so far.

18
Cave Paintings

2011

The description of this memory will be no different than a photograph taken at the foot of a tropic mountain. There is no possible way I can do it justice with my words; no way to make any definitive sense or shape of it. There is no way to truly capture the spirit of this handful of my life on a piece of paper: what it looked like, felt like; what the air smelled like in the jungle, or in the recesses of the cave. I can hardly recount the feeling in my own fading memories. I can only attempt to paint a picture with a limited human vocabulary. If you'll indulge it, let loose the dreamy, drunken mind of your inner twenty-year-old. I think that will help tremendously.

Many of my childhood daydreamings placed me deep inside some distant jungle, making friends with large, wild beasts. Formidable creatures feared by man, natures and temperaments unknown, would be disarmed by my relentless kindness. Offerings of food from an open hand would draw them in, and a gentle stroke to their fur would indicate I meant no harm. We would learn to walk together, play together, and trust each other. The befriended beasts would take me into the uncharted folds of the forest and share their secrets.

That was my time with John.

John was feral; an untamed, uncivilized, wild animal. He grew up without the invisible guardrails that guide most of us through the civilities of society: gratuitous things like courtesy, punctuality, clothing, plumbing. He was in touch with his most primal instincts, and he acted on them without subtlety or hesitation. John's complete disregard for any social rules made him both loved and feared. He fed off of both reactions.

After our incident with the bicycle, I did not plan to take him up on his offer to "see a Queensland rainforest." I had hoped to avoid another interaction with him altogether. But one night around 2AM I found myself knocking on the door of dorm room 6B.

The faint strip of light under his door was the only one in the hallway. "I'm sorry to bother you," I said through clenched teeth, my jaw tight with pain. "But I think I need a ride to the hospital." The room was a filthy, dark cave and stunk like male. If you grew up with a brother, or have a son going through puberty, or had a boyfriend in high school, you know this is more than a smell. It's viscous in the air.

"*Yeh, roighto,*" he reached into a pile and shook out a tank top with a half-nude woman on it. "What is it?"

"I'm not sure, but it feels like my stomach is on fire, and I've just thrown up a lot of blood. Please hurry…"

Without hesitation John escorted me to his "ute", a rusty 1983 Ford Ranger. It reminded me of my dad's old truck, bright red with a thick white stripe around the middle. There were fast food wrappers and empty tobacco pouches everywhere, and cigarette burns in the ceiling. I tried to hide my disgust, aware that he was doing me a favor. "So my bike's a piece of shit, huh?"

It turned out I had a stomach ulcer. Apparently that's what months of drinking coffee and rum instead of eating real meals will do to you. "How long's it been goin'?" John asked as I slid back into the passenger seat.

"A while… I thought it'd just go away on its own. I don't really trust doctors."

"I wouldn't either if I was you. American docs always lookin' *ta* make a profit off ya. You in pain?" I cradled my stomach like a pregnant woman. "Have some'a this." John took a joint from behind his ear and lit it. I paused and stared at it burning in his fingers. At the time I still had a

1990s-family-sitcom view of pot: it was for the bad kids in denim jackets, not nice girls with potential. But I was hurting. I took it and gave it a long drag. The coughing fit made John laugh. "Amateur hour."

He pulled out of the hospital parking lot in the opposite direction of campus. I considered asking him where we were going, but didn't feel the need to. I hadn't been in a car in months, and the motion felt smooth. The night sky stunned me into silence with black endlessness and cool moist air. He played music and rolled down the windows, and I melted into it. I felt both perfectly present and simultaneously in some faraway dream.

"So what brought Lilith Mississippi Attitude to the best plot'a land on the globe?"

"M.D., don't forget," I smiled. "I guess you could call it the desire to be as far away from my own plot as possible." We drove out of town, up some winding mountain road that turned the small city into a twinkly quilt of white and yellow lights. We talked all night with our feet dangling over the cliffside, about anything and everything: what we got into trouble for as kids, our majors, Captain Don, our laughable cultural differences. I asked him repeatedly to slow down because I could hardly understand him through his thick accent. "I'll slow down if *yah* stop talkin' through that nose! American accents are that nasally!"

He surprised me with his knowledge of world history and philosophy, but my own ignorance failed to catch any errors hidden in his confident declarations. He was more than happy to educate me. He was obsessed with history's most ruthless conquerors: Alexander, Attila, Cyrus, Napoleon. I knew nothing about them, other than the recognizability of their names. "They were bad men, that's all I know."

"That's not how I see it."

We feasted in a McDonald's parking lot while we glared into the sunrise, and just like that, we became inseparable. Our smoke-infused drives out of town quickly became a nightly ritual. We snuck away from parties and slipped separately out of Courtship Hall to meet at the truck. We fell behind in our coursework and I ignored Don's messages, marking them as unread to return to later.

We didn't become intimate, or even hint at it, for at least a month–a detail that nonpluses John to this day. "I have *nevah*, I mean *NEVAH*, spent more'n an hour with a fertile bird without try'na fuck 'er."

"That can't be possible. You have plenty of female friends. You know everyone on this campus."

"Know 'em, sure, but they aren't me friends, Nu. Why would any bloke have a woman as a friend?"

"What? We are just people. What do you think we're doing right now?"

"Yeah I guess you *moight* be the first, ay. You're the only woman I've met who's ever had anything interesting to say."

"You're an asshole– or should I say, *arsehole*?"

"Don't go provin' me wrong now."

We spent late nights in his dank, dark room, laying in sheets that were so cold from the blasting air conditioning that they felt damp, laden with his scent, listening to music on Youtube. Our eyes squinted at the lyrics rolling across the screen of his laptop. We wrestled, cuddled, and enjoyed the inner world of our altered, sleepless minds in silence. It was and will always be a cave I can retreat to in my mind; a place where the outside world ceases to exist.

The first night we kissed was one of those nights. It had been an uncomfortably long time, of us just being friends. The electricity was unbearable. We were stoned, sprawled on the bed and daydreaming in the dark. I smacked his head. He started to tickle me and pinned me down. Our faces were close; I licked the tip of his nose. A giggling wrestling match ensued; he pinned me up against the cold wall, his hand around my throat. And finally, mercifully, we tasted each other, and the electricity became a lightning storm.

First John took me to various local spots on our drives: creeks, meadows, foothill lookouts. But one day he showed up to the campus refectory where I worked and demanded,

"Hang up the apron. We're outta here."

"What? John, I can't just leave–"

"You're *roight* actually– make us a coupla' *sangas* before ya knock off."
He reached into a basket by the register and pulled a handful of seran-wrapped cookies. "Make mine two."

"Two *what*?"

"Two sandwiches… *Fahck* Nu, do I have to explain everything?"

I'll never forget that drive into the Paluma rainforest, how the landscape slowly opened from the manicured little city into long expanses of open grasslands dotted with droopy-eared cattle, to the sudden wild envelopment of the jungle. From stark country sunlight we were chilled by green shade and the paved highway narrowed into rusty orange dirt roads. We stopped at a shack along the Bruce Highway to buy fresh mangoes, mango ice cream, mango candies and cold drinks. The dense canopies held a layer of damp, earthen air inside. John rolled his window down and I followed. I'll never forget the first time he reached across the center console to take my hand– not to hold it, but to wrestle back the blue tobacco pouch that I was withholding. But after I lost the battle and he rolled his smoke, he reached back over and took my hand in his.

We hiked along a barely-maintained trail and he pointed out poisonous or thorny plants. "My ol' man's farm has bush like this on its skirts; well, a bit drier. I'll take ya there, you will love it."

"I would love to see it– and I'd love to meet the man who raised you."

"Oh, well I did spend summers with Sully, but Mum mostly raised me. At least when I was small. I did most of the raisin' myself."

"How old were you when they split up?"

"Jus' *foive*. Got ugly– Mum don' take shit 'nd Sully don't either." John looked out across a ravine and chuckled to himself. "Used'ta *fahck* me up real good. I don't blame him, I was a real rebel. And Mum used to fuck him up! She's a real tough bird, has to be in her work."

"What does she do?"

John held a branch back so I could cross under it. "She's the director of a mining camp southwest of here. When I was a lad, the place doubled in size o'er a few months, then doubled again. Coal boom has been bringin' blokes in from all over the world, even cunts from America. An' Mum looks after 'em all. Takes her work real seriously– sees it as a duty to the country." His description brought to mind images of Rosie the Riveter, a woman called to duty in a national time of need, and in answering it, proved women can do everything men can. I liked the sound of this woman. I didn't even consider the fact that the coal miner is the nemesis of the coral reef. All I could see was a tough single mom; the boss of a compound full of rugged men. *Now there's a woman I could really respect,* I thought.

"Pay's good too, that sure don't hurt. Mum loves her diamonds. Those rocks added a whole other dimension to 'er whoopings." *Or perhaps not.*

John told stories of his childhood days at the mining compound, where he was always showing off to earn the respect and cheers of the miners. He would mostly do this by beating the other little boys who resided there. Even as a child he was thickly built and hard-headed. Because of the particular culture in such a place, John's behavior was encouraged, his reputation a point of pride for his mother. It wasn't until he knocked the teeth out of a new miner's daughter– who had been mistaken for a boy by her Buster Brown haircut– that he was sent to Saint Yowie, an all-boys boarding school. There, from a swirling vortex of testosterone, dining hall politics, and unfettered rage emerged the beast of a man that sat before me, perched on a rock beside a waterfall, scratching himself with his foot like a dog.

"I thank God *e'ry* day that I came up at Saint Yowie. That place really toughened me up."

"Oh, the playground fight club at the outback mining compound wasn't tough enough for you?" I laughed and settled in front of him on the rock. The view of the water dropping off sharply just below my dangling feet was beautiful and unsettling, just like the creature wrapping his arms around me. I reached behind my head to stroke his hair as he pulled me in closer to him.

"*Yeh* well at the mines I was a big fish in a puddle. A school full of discipline cases was the perfect environment to really stretch me legs, see how powerful I really am. Gave me the confidence and skills that will make me a success in the business world."

John gave his usual speech about building a business empire so he could be free, travel the world and then be the patriarch of a big family. I listened as the water trickled beneath us and spilled over the waterfall.

"So– what're you going to do when this is up?" His right foot sailed across my legs, to scratch the inside of his left thigh with his toes.

"When what is up?"

"Your time at uni, idiot– at my uni, in my country. How long are you staying?"

"I have not done a good job on this research, thanks to you and your joints. There is no way they'll pay for me to stay another six months. So at semester's end I'll go back home to finish school, I guess." I looked up slyly. "Are you saying... you're going to... MISS ME?" I splashed him and then looked in horror to realize the mistake I had made. He grabbed me, dunked me to within an inch of my life, stole my swimsuit, and then made me sing the Australian national anthem before he would give it back. Which means I stood in that damned creek, furious and naked, LEARNING the Australian national anthem for about fifteen minutes. If that even was the anthem; John might have completely made that song up for all I know. I never looked it up.

"Well, I'm glad you got to come here, an' learn about this place. You got to see some of the true beauty of it too, I reckon, thanks to me."

I rested my head on his shoulder.

"I will show you the beauty of my country, if you ever dare to come."

"Don't count on it. But I have always wanted to tour through Central and South America. I figure it needs to happen before I'm thirty because I'll be having kids after that. So I'll come to the States and see ya."

"Maybe I'll be married by then."

"Well I'll be sneaking you out the back door."

"You're that ruthless that you'd take another man's wife?"

"'Course I would. Depends on the man. I'm assuming this is some American cunt, this supposed husband of yours. Why would I have loyalty to someone I've never met? My loyalty is reserved for the people I care about. See that's your problem– you care about the whole world and so you're loyal to no one."

"You just made a very big statement out of nothing. So because I wouldn't sleep with a married person and I care about other people, I have no loyalty and am somehow less morally upright than you?"

"Look bub, I love your foolish pure *haht*, I really do– but it's that impractical. Do you think anyone else in the world would give you the benevolence that you give them? Look around you and stop romanticizing. You read too much literature and not enough history. You can't love them all; they don't want it and they especially don't deserve it. If all you do is try to love humanity as a whole, you'll neglect the people who're actually in your *loife,* and you'll end up haggard and alone."

"That's not the first time you've used 'you'll end up alone' as some kind of threat. Why should I be so afraid of that?"

"*What*? Look at yaself in the mirror lately? You're like a li'l sack of grain!"

John picked me up over his shoulder and tossed me back into the river. The water shocked my body. I leapt into his arms, wrapping my legs around his shoulders and trying to use my bodyweight to push his head under the surface. Our laughter echoed into the canyon at the futility of what I was trying to do.

"Oi– shut up Nu. Look down there."

John pointed to a crystal pool beneath us, the third large pool in a series being fed by the waterfall. I looked below and considered how the endless battering energy of the waterfall could be so quickly stifled into still serenity– until suddenly two brown ovals appeared in the blue. "Are those…"

"A rare *soight*! Yes li'l missa, the legendary platypus– beloved, wet, and elusive, just *loike* your li'l fannie." He began to tickle me and my shouts echoed through the ravine, scaring the little creatures back into their blue world.

"I barely saw them! You *asshole*!" I began to swat at him, futilely as always, and he responded by pinning me down on the rock and planting a bruising hickey on my neck.

"There, you're stamped. Now everyone will know that you're my property."

"Your *PROPERTY*?" My attempt to free myself to get even ended with John's lips devouring mine. I fell still as his kisses moved from my mouth, to my cheeks, across my forehead and down to my bruised neck; to my forearms, the tips of my fingers– every part of me suddenly alive, alert to his touch, each square inch of my skin impatiently waiting for its turn to be touched, caressed, *stamped*.

My body seized as he entered, tightening around him before releasing into hypnotic tranquility. He took his time, pausing to control his own desire; we scarcely glanced away from each other's eyes, only to take in the sight of our bodies, gorgeous with youth, Queensland sun, and subtle hunger. I desperately gripped the wide freckled shoulders as the waterfall's gushing harmonized with the sounds of our exalted pleasure.

All was right in the world that afternoon: two naked, giggling creatures in the green depths of Paradise. I carried our clothes in my bag along the trail until I dashed into a bush at the distant sound of fellow hikers, which turned out to be a flock of rainbow lorikeets. John remained comfortably in his nude until we reached the truck.

We remained in a lustful stupor until the towering trees were slowly replaced with rolling pastures and then buildings, and we had reached the highway back to campus. The cab of John's truck fell silent, and the cozy air of pheromones was replaced with an unnamed tension.

As we rolled toward the marine science lab I checked my phone for the first time since we left:

> What are you wearing tonight? Make sure it's maroon, and NOT blue!

> Picking up drinks. Want your usual? Bottle of Bundy and pineapple juice?

> Where are you?

"Why is everyone asking me about tonight?"

"Biggest footy game of the year's happening *roight* now," John sighed. "Biggest party of the term comes *aftah*."

"I'm shocked you would miss that– did you forget?"

"No, I stopped going to games after they kicked me out the league for *foighting*. But my presence at the *pahty* is important. One might even call me an essential guest."

"Drop me off here!" I blurted out, suddenly realizing this was the first time I would be exiting John's car during daylight hours, no less with mussed-up hair and a strawberry-sized hickey on my neck.

"Yer going to do lab work *now*?" John scoffed. "Classic nerd." He drove off without waiting for my response, probably realizing the same thing that I just did.

I decided to pop into the lab; since I was there I might as well. Spending my recent nights with John had me sleeping late into the day and missing deadlines. I was too afraid to check my emails, anxious to acknowledge that I was letting Don down. I also hadn't logged into social media in months to avoid learning what was going on at home and uninterested in answering a barrage of questions from my friends and family. The building was quiet. *I guess even the science nerds care about this rugby game.*

I glanced into a tank of soft corals in the lobby, with a few yellow tangs circling around aimlessly. Tangs have a dopey look about them that makes them always appear happy. They intermittently flapped their little pectorals as they hopped around the tank. I envied their blissful ignorance, but then again, they were in a tank in a science lab only a handful of miles from the world's largest reef.

By the time I returned to Courtship Hall, the courtyard was teeming with people, kegs, speakers and maroon pennants. The crowd was cheerful and rowdy, a common sight on an Australian Friday afternoon– but the game had prompted an even earlier start to the drunken merriment than usual. People were sweaty and sloppy. Among the crowd John stuck out even more than he usually did, chugging rum straight from the two liter jug and spilling its golden contents down his chest. I snuck into the dorm to get ready, swiping a small bottle of rum on my way inside. I quickly washed the creek water and John's kisses off my body, attempted to bury his "stamp" with makeup and braided my hair to the side to cover it. I was empty-stomach drunk by the time I emerged back into the courtyard. I poured another cup and stumbled sheepishly over to Clarissa and Sophie, whose calls and messages I had missed earlier. I had been a ghost the last few weeks and they were reasonably standoffish. As I attempted to make an excuse for my absence I jumped at the sound of a metal bottle cap hitting the rim of my cup and splashing into my drink. Suddenly thirty people were singing at me, forcing me to remove the cap and slog the too-strong concoction down:

> *"Here's to Nina she's true blue,*
> *She's a pisspot through and through,*
> *She's a bad bitch so they say,*
> *She tried to go to heaven but she went the other way!*
> *She went DOWN, DOWN, DOWN, DOWN!*
> *SKULL! SKULL! SKULL! SKULL!"*

When I emerged from the rim of my glass, half-ready to puke, I saw that the tosser was– who do you think?

"Check this out, lads," John swatted at my braid. "Our li'l Yank missed the match to get herself rooted." My eyes burned a laser hole through the center of his forehead. "What *kina* loose gumma lets a bloke give her a suckin' on like that?" I shrunk under the blinding spotlight of laughter.

So that's how it's gonna be, huh? Two can play that game. After escaping the circle of banter at my expense, I "skulled" another glass and made my way to the dance floor. The last light of day was fading and the world blurred under the courtyard's diagonals of colorful string lights. Though in a drunken fog it was clear to me how things would be from then on; the pitch and yaw of that single day would play out over and over again, the heights ever higher, the lows ever lower. John continued to drink like it was the end of the world and I, swaying clumsily and gripping his shoulders tightly, feverishly kissed Cabbie, John's territorial rival. And so began our descent toward Hell.

〜

Cabbie was a notably bad kisser– tonguey, sloppy and drooly, and somehow grinding his teeth against mine. But I persisted, if only to assure that enough people would see it, ensuring John would find out, if not witness it himself. He would have no choice but to ignore it and suffer the blow to his ego in silence. John had a reputation to uphold, which certainly did not include falling in love– especially not with an American, an inferior class by his standards. John was a man's man who regarded the other sex as an object of lust, a symbol of status, or a foreign and irrelevant entity to be ignored.

Both of us were forced to come to terms with the unfortunate reality that we were ashamed of our affection for the other– me a science geek and a Yank, and John a redneck and a brute.

Of course our story did not end that night; in fact, the opposite occurred. We became even more passionate and affectionate in private while becoming ever more ruthless in public. I did not expect or want this to be the case. I kissed Cabbie to even the score and then I wanted nothing more than to never see John again. After refusing Cabbie's persistent, salivating invitation to spend the night at his dormitory, I returned to my room, drunk, foolish, ashamed of myself. I did not approve of my behavior; I had made the classic mistake of playing right into what John had said about me. I 'skulled' two glasses of water and slipped on my robe and shower shoes. Clarissa was in the bathroom brushing her teeth. We locked eyes for a moment and she spit in the sink. "Are you okay, Nina? I haven't seen you much at the lab and you never answer my texts. Sophie says you quit your job at the refectory. I don't want to pry, but–"

"I know, I'm sorry," I leaned against the stall door, deflated and exhausted. "Can we get lunch tomorrow and talk?"

"Not at the refect, I guess?" A little toothpaste foam sat in the corner of her smile. I was lucky to have her and Sophie as friends. They both traveled extensively with their families as children, so I think they were handling the experience of being away from home better than I was. As I rinsed the evening off of me, and vomited up rum and a blob of blood over the shower drain, I thought about America for the first time in months. I wondered if my parents understood why I hadn't called.

More water, a multivitamin, handfuls of dry cereal. I rifled through my pack and upon finding a highway mango began to look for a decent method of slicing it.

A commotion began to stir outside, then in the hallway. "*Foight!* In the courts!"

I could see the courtyard from my window. I peered out, knowing who would be engaged in a brawl post-midnight. I smiled to myself, admittedly flattered. But I felt a pang of guilt. *Poor Cabbie,* I thought. *He doesn't even know why this time.* I'm sure John has made some less-than-elaborate excuse. But when I glanced out at the brawl, the bloody face was not Cabbie's.

It was a boy named Tommy, a fellow study-abroader from the suburban Midwest. He came for the semester with his girlfriend, who had immediately ditched him upon arrival for the broad-shouldered, rugged and accented Australians. She showed no discretion with her new pursuits and it devastated poor Tommy. He spent his evenings following her around at a distance like a stray dog hoping for scraps of food, and asking anyone who would listen for their advice on getting her back. Over time those willing to listen dwindled, as it was both a pathetic sight and a clearly hopeless prospect, until Tommy was more or less outcasted and incredibly lonely in a foreign country. Sophie, who sat with the former couple on the flight over, shared that they were high school sweethearts, and Tommy was both a football star and homecoming king. This made his situation seem all the more pathetic– a young man's confidence and self worth ripped from him through his heart.

Of all the people John could've taken his anger out on, why poor Tommy? John was more apt to take on a challenge, not to pick on the weak. He had Tommy on the ground and was going for the third or fourth blow to his face when a group of boys from various dormitory halls pulled him off. John was wild and upon breaking free began swinging at them, landing a few blows before even more boys joined in, placing him at a tennish-to-one match. He had clearly done this before and was not deterred by his odds. As the group got their advantage I closed my blinds. *I've seen enough.*

Water, more dry cereal, and I curled up in bed with the *Geologic Time* book Captain Don lent me when I departed the *Siren's Revenge*. I was still too intoxicated to read without feeling nauseous so I simply stared at renderings of underwater creatures from the Precambrian. They were ghastly and nightmarish things, curled and segmented bodies with tentacles, spindly legs, soulless eyes. I tried to close my eyes but the room began to spin and I cringed at the thought of puking up more blood. As I finally started to drift off, a knock at the door brought me immediately to my feet.

John was a grotesque sight: busted lip, black eye, shirt ripped, wet, and stained. No shoes, as was his usual custom. He had a sizable gash on the side of his head. One end of it entered his hairline. Blood had crusted over and was turning from crimson to brown on his temple. Enclosed in his swollen and bloody fist was a bouquet– a term I am using very loosely– of flowers and grasses that had clearly been ripped from the campus landscaping. Clusters of dangling roots still clung to soil, which had fallen in a trail along the hall floor. I tried with all my might to hold back a smile, but the sight was hilariously absurd, and quintessentially him. I sighed and cursed the gods, the Universe, Charles Darwin– whoever was responsible for making me love this vile beast– and whatever forces were making me feel even more in love with him in this moment.

"You gonna lemme in 'r what?"

He raised the flowers up and a clod of dirt fell to the floor. I willed my smile into a contemptuous scowl. "The *fuck* I will!" But as voices emerged from down the hall I yanked him in by his wet shirt and slammed the door.

"But I got you *flowahs*," John slurred and plopped down on the bed, glancing at my open book. "Those'ah some *noice* li'l fishes you got."

"Shut up. Just *shut the fuck up*. Look at yourself! What have you done? Why did you do that to poor Tommy?"

"I won't expec' you to understand, but I was looking out for the kid." He raised the arm with the stolen landscaping to silence me so he could continue his thought. Another clump of dirt landed on my sheets. "There's a code that men must live by. Man's gotta have a certain level of respect for hisself. The way his bird's up'n left him, then shoving it in his face, is unacceptable as it is. But his reaction to it? Can't have that.

"It's a man's duty to make sure other men 're being men. I'm a leader 'round this place and I take me job seriously. Lad needed a *noice* whooping, to knock some sense into 'im. Once I had him on the ground, I told him what I was doing and what for. Told 'im that he'll thank me someday soon, and— *aghhh, FAHCK– easy, woman!*"

I was scraping the crusted blood from his temple with a damp towel. "Oh hush, take it like a *man*," I taunted. "I don't need your dirt, sweat, *and* blood in my sheets. Now hold still." As I nursed his wounds and mouthed him off for his behavior, his words, and his entire personality, he just sat there quietly, choking the stalks of his flowers in his monkey grip and smiling triumphantly.

"Why are you looking at me like that? Aren't you listening to a word I'm saying? I'm telling you how much you disgust me."

"*Yeh yeh*, I heard ya. But you're dead wrong, li'l missa. You love me." He threw the mass of weeds and dirt to the floor and grabbed me by the arms– of course, to prevent me from swinging them in protest– and kissed me with his busted lips.

"*Get off me!* You are *filthy!*"

"Stop pretendin' *loike* you care. You love me, little girl– and you love me for exac'ly who I am – blood, dirt, rums an' all. Stop lying to yourself."

"Why are you so damn sure of that?" I squirmed.

"'Cause you're spewin' venom from your mouth but your *haht* moved your hands. You grabbed first aid an' towels and went *roight* to work on me, even as you told me how terrible I am. You could'a ran out the door and nursed up Tommy– but you took care of your man instead. You got instincts; *foight* them as you might, you got 'em. An' that's why I'm love with *yah*– you filthy dago Yank."

I didn't try to fight him this time. I laced my fingers behind his neck and tasted the iron of his bloody kiss. I ran my fingers through the sweaty hair and pulled this filthy, cruel, despicable creature into bed with me.

We slept heavily into the afternoon. I missed my lunch date with Clarissa and John blew off "shoulder day" at the gym. My world had disappeared into him; the dark cave of his bedroom, his scent, his truck and the thick clouds of the joints we smoked. My obsession with John transcended my remaining months in Australia and my flight home. My only focus upon returning to America was to get through the next year of school and raise the money for a one-way flight back to him, so I could meet his parents and get married. I was stamped.

∾

2019

I didn't plan to go to Arnold's to see him tonight. He asked me to come, to celebrate a successful meeting with one of Skip's associates, but I told him I wasn't feeling too well. I went home and tried to focus on writing. I felt restless and the words wouldn't come. I started pacing my new bedroom at Kevin's place, avoiding boxes stacked along the walls. I got in the car just before midnight.

When I arrived to Arnold's, the house was dark inside. The lanterns by the door were flickering with fire and a spotlight cast its impression on an old Spanish style fountain behind the patio furniture. I approached the fountain and watched a stone lion's mouth drool water into a ceramic pot painted with flowers of orange and violet. The pot overflowed into a large square pool below. The water's surface was littered with magenta flowers from the surrounding bougainvillea bushes that conceal the giant stone wall. I stared at it for a while, irritated by its beauty, the beauty of this whole place, hidden behind walls and eucalyptus trees. *All this water, this energy, this aesthetic beauty and artistic expression. For what? For a man who's never even here?*

I went inside and followed the scent of cologne and cigar tobacco to the bedroom, where Cam lay half asleep to the sounds of a documentary film about a famous American plane designer. I crawled into the bed behind him and held my body to him. I smelled the back of his neck and ran my fingers through his hair. He half-consciously pulled me forward in

276

front of him and wrapped his body around mine. The warmth, the scent, the force of being held– I'll just admit that I came here because I needed this, the human contact, desperately. In these moments the stone exterior is gone, and I get to experience the man beneath.

It's been several months that I have been listening quietly while this man says horrible things, expresses his indifference for the suffering of others, his warlike bitterness toward a world that's rejected him, his desire to take back what he calls his. And I've spent an equal measure of time being welcomed into his world, as he divulges his life's achievements and shortcomings, his hopes, the sources of his anger and his fears, his friends, his undying devotion to the combustion engine, to his sense of personal power found only in velocity, to his unshakable belief in himself. I turn to face him and place my head to his chest; the beating heart is loud. He kisses my forehead, the top of my head, my cheek, over and over.

I have made a horrible mistake. All of this is a mistake.

With every word I write, I betray him further, which I would not mind if I were less intelligent and could not see past the revulsion of his words. But he has opened himself to me enough to allow me to put together the puzzle pieces of his life. Underneath the frigidity and callous exterior resides a sensitive little boy who has had his sense of love and meaning stripped away like layers of paint chipping off a neglected wall. A childhood empty of love, a town full of dysfunctional people, being born of a generation trapped between two antithetical worlds... it all has created a man who is deeply alone. And what have I done? Added myself to the long list of people who have wronged him, underestimated him? If he finds out what I have been doing, I may take the last shred of humanity he has left inside him. But there is no future for me and this man, there simply can't be. The only thing I can do now is be honest here, with myself, and to be sincere in my affection and appreciation during these pure human moments that we occasionally share.

Am I experiencing Stockholm syndrome, or is this a test of the tensile strength of my sense of empathy? I look at him the way I look at the dog who draws blood from a defensive bite: he is an animal, chained to his place in the world, frightened and hungry for love and belonging; hungry to lead a pack that does not exist and will never exist, because all the other wild dogs have been captured and are rotting in pounds, or have been domesticated and weakened, or are chained in some other yard in some other place with flies chewing off the tips of their ears. Humans are not unique because we have figured out how to melt and bend metal or because we manipulate the laws of physics to suit our desires. We are ragged, ruthless, instinct-trapped animals.

I weep silently as his breath slows and the gentle snores come, and I say aloud, quietly but with fervor, "I am sorry. I am so sorry."

19
Stolen Valor

I think the hardest part of what I'm doing right now is that I am alone in it. I can't disclose what I am doing and what I am going through with anyone in my life, and I'm starting to feel the weight of it. Part of digesting any idea is being able to vocalize it, hash it out, and get feedback from someone else. The dogs and cats I petsit can be terrible listeners. Parrots can be helpful, but they usually just tell you what you want to hear.

I constantly remind myself of the greater purpose of what I am doing. This is not about me, it's an experiment in understanding, compassion, and empathy– the principles I have touted for the last few years. It's all being put to the test. I am being tested.

The trial of it does not make it any easier. But as a writer it is important that I try to let myself feel the true depth of the dark moments, to let myself sink into the mud and let the vines overtake my body. I lay in it, look up and ask myself: "Can I still see the light? And if I cannot see it, does that mean it ceases to exist?"

The isolation from my usual network is a painful reminder that our surroundings do dictate, at least in part, our attitude toward the world. I have never felt a stronger sense of "too little, too late" when it comes to preserving the integrity of nature (or rather, humanity's ability to survive its degradation).

I thought the experience at Skip Omnivore's gated mansion would have reinvigorated my sense of righteousness and urgency, but it muddied the waters even further. I indulged myself beyond my own comprehension, enjoyed the company of monsters, and shared a bed with the enemy. How do I face Piper and the Earth Defenders now? How do I face Tyler, or Paula, or the mirror?

"Humans are pack animals," John berated me over a video call. "What are you doing isolating yourself *loike* this, you bloody idiot? Don't you know that depressed people can't be doing shit like that? You're swirlin' around the edge of a downward spiral."

"Mind your business, ape," I looked down at my fingernails. "I need the solitude to write and think."

"*Yeh* well this film better be good. What is it about anyway? Some stupid girl shit?"

"It's the story of a bunch of women who stick it to a man like you."

Autumn is supposedly waning, but it's still hot and dry. Mount Mirage doesn't really have seasons, or weather for that matter. Every day is more or less the same; something new may be in bloom, or a few hopeful clouds may roll in, pregnant with rain, but only to deliver someplace else.

The Earth Defenders' stunt at the car show made the papers with mixed reviews, depending on the political leanings of the publication. Six of the protesters were arrested, but were promptly bailed out by an anonymous donor. Their most recent disruption took place at the first MMHS football game of the season, where they dumped black paint all over the field, and demanded that the school athletics program stop taking sponsorship money from Invisible Hand.

"NO FOOTBALL ON A DEAD PLANET! NO MARCHING BANDS ON A DEAD PLANET!"

I've been submitting the newsletters online but I haven't answered their calls about the job offer. What could I possibly say? I've crossed over; I am the enemy now.

Cam has invited me to dinner tonight. It will be my first time out with him since the car show and our weeklong escape at Skip's. "It's just a casual thing, very casual. You can wear your garage sale clothes."

"What if I feel fancy?"

"You might feel out of place."

"I always feel out of place."

"Then you might as well be comfortable."

"No, no way. Absolutely not."

The motorcycle's engine is not quite as threatening as the Cuda – but I know better. Cam is wearing a denim jacket covered in patches. Something looks off– he doesn't have his usual manicured look. But then again, he did say casual twice. "Please get on, Nina. I promise I'll drive slow. We'll be late…"

"But… My brother…"

I haven't told Cam this story, or Tyler, or anyone except John, and it's only because I was drunk off my ass, mourning my final night in Australia. We were up all night, laying in our usual wrestling spot in the courtyard outside of Courtship Hall, and in my vulnerable state, I asked him to pass me his cigarette. I took a long drag. "I want to tell you, John. I want to tell you about George."

"I've been waiting," he said. I rested my head on his chest, and we stared emptily at indignantly grand stars.

"I think it's why I fell for Dean– they were the same age, and went through the same thing. They watched the Twin Towers fall, right at the start of their senior year. It was obvious to them, what they needed to do. My mother protested fiercely; I remember her shattering Grandma's gravy boat at Thanksgiving. My father fell silent, and seemed to stay silent until George was gone to Boot Camp. There was so much uncertainty about what would unfold with the war, if it even was a war, and how long it would last, and how bad it would be. I know Dad was proud of him, but still didn't want him to go, so he chose to say nothing at all. The two of them would go on drives. They wouldn't let me come. I wonder what they talked about, I've always wondered. I see why you love these cigarettes– I feel… I feel… like I hope this night is purgatory, and I'm trapped in it forever. Will you roll us another? Kiss me–

"George had many skills, thanks to Dad and the garage. He went to the same Boot Camp as Dean, if you can believe that. But they never met. Dean was sociable, good at leading men, and George was always quiet, and skilled with his hands. They had him repair vehicles. He was due to ship out to Kabul in the spring. He was ready, he felt good; that's what he said to Mom on the phone. But less than a month before, he suffered a spinal injury that warranted two surgeries. I only heard about it through my parents; he wouldn't answer my calls, until two days before he died. He texted me and said, 'I'm in Heaven already'. I immediately called and he answered. I could tell he was on drugs.

'They are like God's answer– finally, after 2000 years of silence, He has spoken again.'

'What's God's answer? What do you mean?'

'The pills… the pills… they make me feel… I am on God's porch, and there's rocking chairs and everything, and the scenery is simple and beautiful, and we just rock there, Nina. We just rock all the time and talk every day. And He's like that friend– that friend you haven't seen in six months or six years but you call Him up when you're having trouble with your girl. And He's such a good listener– He just sits there, and lets you rant and question yourself and everything. And He just listens– quiet but He is speaking without saying a word, because He already knows me… You see we're all being guided, quietly guided through this life– and I'll be with my brothers soon– I'll be on that plane…'

"He started on an incoherent tangent– I couldn't follow it. But I sat there and listened, until he suddenly cut off. I guess his phone died."

John rolled me my own cigarette. I climbed over him and tasted his mouth; he flipped me onto my back, but I pushed him off to continue my story. The cigarette was blurry, lightheaded heaven. I suddenly understood every cigarette John ever smoked. I became desperately sentimental; I wanted to hold every man in the world in my arms, all the soldiers in the trenches smoking the same sloppily rolled cigarettes in all the wars, I wanted to hold them to my chest and sing to them like a mother, to tell them it would all be okay, and that they are loved– their mothers love them, and their sisters admire them, and their romantic aspirations and wives cherish them– we are all here, praying for them, waiting for them to come home.

"He was caught with something beyond what he was prescribed for the pain. My parents never revealed what it was. He was slated for rehab the same date as his flight. I think it was too much for him, the disappointment in himself, the medical bills, the guilt, the painkillers. He crashed his motorcycle into a tree. They found all matter of substances in his blood. They said it was remarkable that he could even sit upright to ride in the first place."

I sat up, and then lay back down over his chest. "Do you believe in Heaven, John?"

"*Yeh*, I reckon I do. He's still a good bloke, don't worry. He's up there. I got mates up there too. The mines pay good, too good for a young man out in the middle of nowhere with nothin' to do. Man's gotta have a purpose, gotta *provoide*, gotta be challenged and occupied. Or our demons get us."

Cam's pleading eyes prompt me to hesitantly swing my leg over the bike; he puts the helmet on my head a little brusquely in his hurry– and I cling to his back desperately as we pull away.

The back room has been rented out at a nice seafood restaurant in Palmetto Cove. There are old nautical charts on the wall, a wooden helm, a bookshelf with early editions of *Moby Dick* and *Two Years Before the Mast*. I immediately feel more out of place than usual in my kid's XL Old Navy sundress, bought second hand. *Why did he say casual, twice?*

"Cam! We thought maybe you weren't coming!" A drunk but composed beautiful woman wraps him in a hug. Her husband, a tall salt and pepper gentleman with a similarly expensive-looking spray tan as Cam's, shakes his hand. He's got that effortless, mindless charisma one needs to be a successful politician or an infomercial star.

"I'm Roger Wilkes," he says as we shake hands. "A very firm handshake! Very respectable handshake!"

"Thank you, Roger."

As the drunk wife hugs me I see Wilkes lean toward Cam's ear. "She's perfect," I overhear him whisper past the chardonnay-scented embrace.

No one is seated at the table, but all mingling around it. Cam takes my hand and leads me around for the so-and-so talk. Everyone is very old and stuffy. We are clearly out of place here. Something is off. Waiter approaches us. Cam orders a cheap beer. *Suspicious.* "I'll take a scotch on the rocks. Make it a top shelf one. *Doble, por favor.*"

I sip and tune out for a while. But I am brought back from the post-credits scene of my movie by the word "Airborne."

"It's just so encouraging to finally have a politician in my corner, for once," Cam says. "Someone who sees the value in our service and what we've been through, and will ensure we are taken care of." The old people nod approvingly.

It appears I have been hit in the side of the head with a road sign. I'm smart in a way that hurts like that– ugly truths hit me all at once, and so does booze. It's suddenly clear as day: The rack of uniforms in his garage. *He's pretending to be poor. He's pretending to be a vet. I am a prop in a garage sale dress. I am Cam's anti-trophy wife.*

An old couple is staring at me. I have been asked a question. "I apologize, come again?"

"They asked what you do." Cam senses that I've caught on, and he winks, like this is a fun little prank. But then he watches me skull down the rest of my drink, and his face changes to pleading: *Nina, dear god, please–*

I smile warmly at the old people, and speak in my most down-home, good-girl voice– my waitress voice. "I was born on my family's farm in rural Idaho, where I spent my days playing in the woods with my eight siblings and helping my parents care for the farm's animals. After marrying my high school sweetheart," I smile lovingly at Cam, "we were stationed in Mount Mirage. I'm just a humble waitress for now, trying to save up for our next steps, but I volunteer at the local animal shelter, take a swim class at the rec center, and sing in the choir at H. Caulfield Memorial Church. But now that my love is home safe, and the night terrors and binge drinking and sleep-fighting have slowed, I am looking forward to starting our family." I nestle under Cam's arm and look up to him dutifully.

"Did you say you sing in the Caulfield choir? We're part of the congregation, I don't think I've seen you before."

I pause and stare at the old woman, caught but unfazed. "You should come to our women's group," she says. "We meet Sundays after mass and every other Tuesday night. We're a great little circle. We discuss the Bible, drink coffee, and chat. A lot of the young women have benefitted from the council and mentorship of the elders."

"How lovely! Would you pardon me for just a moment? I have to powder my nose."

I walk past the bathroom, out the door, and vomit into a bush in the darkness. My heart pounds. I consider my options. Cabs aren't cheap. Too far to walk in my uneasy state, though a ten-mile run in the dark sounds pretty alluring right about now. I decide to call Kevin to pick me up. "It's urgent... please Kevin?"

"Are you alright? Need me to beat anyone up for ya?"

"You have no idea. If you come get me I'll make you any dessert under the sun."

"You don't need to do that... I mean, I'd never turn down a banana cream pie. Be there as soon as I can. Hang in there."

I begin walking down the street so Cam doesn't get smart to my disappearance and try to beckon me back inside. I only put my phone back in my purse for a moment until I pull it back out again.

"Yes, hello– this is Nina Distrella. Yes, uh– she/her. May I please speak to Piper Hammick? Thanks.

"Hey, Piper? Yes, I'm doing well, thanks. Do you have time to meet at your office this week? Yes– I am interested, and I'd like to negotiate your offer. I have some information that's going to take this campaign to the next level."

Kevin and I walk into the house after a quiet ride home. I was grateful that he didn't ask me to explain. I storm into the kitchen and take out the coconut cream, vegan butter, graham crackers, sugar, vanilla. I start furiously peeling bananas. Kevin enters the doorway and leans, watching. "You're so sweet. You really don't have to do this right now."

"Yes I do." I look up, all teary-eyed but holding them in, and I fall into his chest, throwing my arms around him. His arms fold down around me and envelop me in the scent of man and pot smoke. He lets me linger there for a long time, saying nothing, asking nothing, and I finally whisper, "I'm so glad I have this place. I feel safe here. You're the best."

"I'm very glad you're here too," he says. "You've been... it's just real nice, having you here."

"Thank you. Thank you."

PART THREE

THE WINTER

20
Stella

2012

I couldn't bring myself to enjoy my time living in Sand Dollar. College is advertised to be a golden age of a young person's life, and with a vacation destination sparkling in the backdrop of my senior year, I should have been carefree and thriving. But I wasn't. I was back in survival mode, and worked myself numb so I didn't have to mourn the Great Barrier Reef, or think about Captain Don on the *Siren's Revenge* all alone, or think about Alice with Burt's baby, or think about John. John and I weren't getting married. As far as I knew, John was in prison. Or dead.

I had moved into a crumbling one-bedroom apartment with my friend Amie and we were both barely scraping by. She worked at a seafood restaurant outside the city that gave her ringworm on more than one occasion. To the delight of her cat, she came home smelling like warm shrimp every night. I was happy to take the futon so the smells of the two of them could be sealed off by her bedroom door.

My barely-decent grades were a product of bullshitting and doing the bare minimum. I was bitter and drained from working so many hours, and I resented my friends who were forwarding their bills to their parents' addresses. I found it easier to spend my few free hours alone, walking the beach and sketching little sea specimens I saw, or writing sappy poems in my journal. Until I met Stella.

I was cleaning up Sea Dog's Pizzeria one night, wiping down tables and refilling the pungent parmesan shakers. No matter how much bleach and all-purpose cleaner burned my nostrils, the place never felt clean. It had a sleazy quality, a greasiness, like the orange oil that dribbled out of the pizzas was misted into the air. It was a quiet night and the dining room had emptied out early. I was looking to quickly wrap up my six hour shift and cut my losses. A pathetic $34 in tips burned a disdainful hole in my pocket. Stella and Chuck remained at the countertop. They were strangers, but had both come to see my fellow waitress Brittany, who was leaning over the counter and chatting with them. She was a sickly girl with thin blond hair and a slouching posture, always looking at her phone, her lips always slightly parted. We didn't have much in common to talk about, but luckily for me, she was very popular, and always had friends stopping by for her to talk to.

I had seen Chuck many times before. He came to the restaurant almost every evening, and always sat at the same table by the window, which Brittany would set for him in advance. Without him needing to order she would hastily grab a beer from the fridge with a frosted pint glass, ladle him a cup of Italian wedding soup, arrange a plate with a doily and three packets of crackers, and bring it to the table when she greeted him. She knew how he liked his three rotating dinners prepared, and she'd place her hand on his shoulder as they spoke. His hand would travel up and down the sides of her waist, and her giggles carried through the restaurant. After he left, Brittany would lean over the countertop and count her tip with starry eyes.

Chuck unsettled me, and I went out of my way not to make eye contact with him. He was in his mid forties, and Brittany was nineteen. She wasn't a student, and as it turned out, she had no plans to become one. "I'm just not into that stuff," she said when I asked her what her major was, assuming she was a late-bloomer freshman. "I don't really want to do anything. So I'm just going to keep working here until something else comes along. Chuck says I'm the kind of girl who doesn't need an education anyway."

"What does that mean?" I looked at her fearfully.

"I think it means he thinks I'm hot." She blushed and didn't look up from her little wad of cash.

I hadn't met Stella before, but I had seen her around campus. She was not the sort of girl you could overlook. Stella was a short and squat Italian girl with an enviable air of confidence: raucous, bold, and full of gusto. She dressed scantily on top, sweatpants on the bottom, and every part of her five-foot body seemed to be working together to hold up her pair of enormously disproportionate breasts. She carried them proudly, and they sat naturally high on her chest as she marched around campus at a Manhattan pace. She seemed unaware (or at least uncaring) of the effect she had on others, and while she wore her hair big with lots of hairspray and gel, she never bothered with makeup and stylish clothing, unless she was going to one of downtown Sand Dollar's clubs.

"Stella's an environmental science major," Brittany called me over from across the dining room. "Have you had any classes together?"

How can you be an environmental science major and use that much hairspray?

"I don't think so, but we probably will," I said. "I'm studying marine ecology."

"Wait, I know you. Aren't you also a clerk at the campus bookstore?"

"That would be me."

She looked me up and down, and then at the dining room disgustedly. "Nah nah girl, you're workin' too hard for not enough. How much money d'you make tonight?"

"$34, plus $2.14 an hour..." The cash laughed at me from my pocket.

She shook her head and picked her phone out of a designer handbag. "That's insane. You need to set your sights higher, lady. Time is money. You waitressed a lot?"

"Yes, for a few years, unfortunately. Why?"

"I work at a fancy place downtown, and my girlfriend quit last weekend because the GM dumped her. You're coming to work with me, where you'll make the big money. It's a great place, great food, great clientele. You'll love it. I'm texting him now." Her long plastic fingernails melodically clicked against the screen of her phone.

My ears perked up at "big money". *She's right, time is money. If I could earn more per hour, I could work less and have more time to be a student, be a person.*

The journey from my apartment to the restaurant took about an hour. The drive began with picturesque coastal pleasantries: tourist families dining outside at the local pancake house, bridges over expansive estuaries of green, gray and shades of blue, flocks of gulls flying overhead. But as soon as you're on the straightaway into the city, the panoramic views of the estuarine channels and tidal flats become obstructed by enormous billboards, scarlet and black with big flashy letters, advertising the casinos' attractions and shops.

"YOUR BEST BET TONIGHT!"

"DIAMONDS ARE FOREVER! TRY OUR ELITE DIAMOND SLOTS"

"SAND DOLLAR'S MOST EXCLUSIVE CLUB"

The final exit from the freeway takes you below an overpass, which was decked with one final billboard: a young woman's legs extended from a red plaid miniskirt, and a bronzed male hand, weighted down with a shiny wristwatch, rested on one of her thighs. A banner across the top read, *Because College is Expensive,* and on the bottom banner, *Find your Sugar Mate today! www.sugarmate.com.*

Something about that billboard haunted me. I guess it made me think of Chuck's hairy hand on Brittany's frail little thigh. But I'd soon forget it after driving down the main drag of Sand Dollar toward the Seaside Pleasures Hotel, where I'd take the long walk through the casino, past the shops, and the pier to Lotusia.

I hated Sand Dollar, but I adored Lotusia. It was everything Sand Dollar wished it was, but was absolutely not: elegant, tasteful, whimsical yet refined. It was like entering another world. And after passing the many depressing sights of the casino to reach the restaurant, I was grateful to escape through the giant wooden doors with the gold-plated dragon knockers.

The main dining room was a large dome, with red and gold paper lanterns hung at varying lengths from the high black ceiling. The booths along the walls had plush burgundy cushions and Chinese silk pillows of rich turquoise and gold, and the floor tables surrounded a central communal table of black mirage marble. Gold tree-shaped candelabras grew out of the center of each table, and the tips of the branches held tiny lights. It created the effect of a starry night sky across the dimly lit restaurant.

Stella volunteered to be my trainer, but the manager insisted I should be trained by a more experienced and "professional" server. A young-faced woman, small but authoritative, met me in the loft one afternoon to begin. She carried a binder half the size of her body.

"Good afternoon, I'm Shoshana. Welcome to Lotusia," she said in a beautifully articulate waitress voice. "I will be your trainer. This," she held up the binder, "is the Lotusia bible. Every recipe for every drink and dish can be found in here, as well as the floor plan, procedures, and staff information. In the next month, you are going to learn all of it. You will be tested on the ingredients of every dish and every specialty cocktail, and to complete your training, you will serve a table of the restaurant managers. Do you have any questions before we get started?"

I stared at her blankly. It seemed like way too much for a restaurant job. "Did you say a test? And a *month* of training?"

She smiled. "Welcome to the world of fine dining service, my friend. This is not the wing joint or sports bar. You will be expected to perform an elite level of service, where your intellect and appreciation for fine details will be crucial, and if you can handle the pressure, you will be compensated handsomely. How much did you make in an average shift at your last job?"

I was almost embarrassed to say. It seemed she could see that, so she continued, "I know. And I know the nights of brushing off insults from the cook and the bartender, dodging sexual advances from your customers, competing with passive-aggressive servers. Welcome to a better place. I can't promise that you won't experience *any* of those things, but it will be balanced by a higher quality atmosphere. Shall we sample some menu items?"

My face felt warm, my eyes watered. I felt like a patient in a hospital bed, and she was the nurse who, in my delirium, I would mistake for an angel. We settled in at the table with the binder, and a young man in a navy changshan approached with a bento box and two colorful cocktails. Each tiny portion of food in their little square compartments looked more like art than food. I was ready to learn anything and everything Shoshana had to say.

I spent more time studying the Lotusia bible than my ecology and biostatistics books. Why depress myself any further? The truth was clear: the reefs are screwed. The animals are screwed. The human race is on its way out and will take everything down with it. So who cares what I focus my energy on? Lotusia offered me hope and immediacy: rent money, fancy food scraps, the opportunity to connect with fancy people with deep pockets. Shoshana taught me to approach each table differently, reading the customers' every feature and word, and come up with a strategy for a version of yourself that would yield the best results. I was the cute and innocent struggling college student, the elegant food expert ready to divulge the deepest insights into the menu, the foodservice ninja who was practically invisible at the table, the girl "who might be interested in meeting us for drinks later"... whatever it took. I entered the mindset of an actress, dashing from table to table and rapidly switching between characters, always with dollar signs in my eyes.

One Sunday morning, I grasped my coffee mug tightly and set myself on autopilot through the motions of getting to work: pleasant coastal drive, flashy billboards, underpass, *Because College is Expensive. Find your Sugar Mate today!*, Cringe. Parking garage; tingling smell of toxic fumes. Elevator and carpeted walk into the casino. Slot machines dinging and flashing lights. Seniors with fanny packs, obese folks in baggy t-shirts, and hungover twenty-somethings feeding the machines. A few baccarat tables occupied. Tingling of the nostrils from the cigarette smoke. *So many people gambling at 9:30am. But why?* Shopping plaza; smell of leather handbags and chemically floral perfumes. Long hallway with giant windows overlooking the ocean and the boardwalk. Grey sky and seagulls to match. Giant wooden doors with the gold-plated dragon knockers.

I worked the lunch shift with a guy named Ramón on Sundays. It was the slowest shift, reserved for the newest servers. Ramón and I got along like two peas in a pod. We had similar family lives and similar feelings about the world. He had graduated two years ago with a philosophy degree and had the same outlook about humanity that I did.

But this Sunday I was greeted by the sound of Stella dropping a bunch of freshly polished forks on the floor. "*SHIT!*" I rushed over to help her pick them up. "I just polished these little fuckers. Ugh, sorry. I was up all night last night."

"Where's Ramón? Is he sick?"

"Not as sick as me! I'm hungover as fuck, *and* walking bowlegged." Her eyebrows jumped at me. "But really, he had a last-minute family thing and I owed him one. So I'm joining you on the loser shift today. I really am exhausted though, so you can take most of the tables. You'll break a hundred bucks, easily."

"I'm fine with that. Are you okay? What do you mean you're walking bowlegged?" I understood what she meant, but I wanted to hear her say it out loud. Stella had a way with words and I try to never miss an opportunity for a good laugh.

"Oh you know, the evening ride. I had to be extra limber to accommodate my less-than-limber partner. The ol' steed has seen better days."

"Is he… disabled in some way?"

"Oh no, he was just stiff from dancing at the club all night. But he has fallen in love with the blue pills, so even after too many drinks, a particular *stiffness* was persistent. I'm spent!"

I laughed. "Sounds like a lot of work."

"Well you know, hard work pays off. He's taking me on his yacht to Saint Martin next month. I'll give you first pick of my shifts. Well— second."

"Whoa, that sounds fancy. Did you meet this guy while working here?"

"Yes, technically," Stella grinned to herself and started setting the silverware in a perfect pattern around the table. "I met him online, and invited him to come by for a drink one night. But I've decided to stop bringing guys I meet online near Lotusia; not good to mix business and pleasure, you know."

We started our route to set up the restaurant, weaving through the fifty-four tables of the giant dining room. I was first with the towel and sanitizer, then Stella followed with the crimson cloth napkins and the perfect pattern of polished silverware.

"So... have you been together long? Do you mind if I ask how old he is? I mean, if he has a yacht..."

"Yeah, he's up there. He says he's 46, so I'm guessing he's about 52." Stella was tickled by my obvious wince. "Hah, I know it sounds a little *gnar*. But maybe that's just 'cause you have never been with an older man. The idea used to give me the creeps too, but I've warmed up to it.

"Older guys are so excited for the opportunity to bed a young piece of ass, they'll treat you like a queen. They're established and accomplished, and they know what they want 'cause they have an extra two decades of mistakes under their belt. They see you as a rekindling of their youth, a symbol of a fresh start, or a fantastic escape. They take you places, buy you things, dress you up and pay for spa treatments. They worship your body. And some straight up give you cash." She removed a wad of hundred dollar bills from between her breasts.

"Wow. How do you meet them?" I knew the answer. I saw the bronze hand and the red plaid mini skirt.

Because College is Expensive....

"It's that Sugar Mate website... I'm sure you've seen the billboard on the way in. You can't miss it. That company must be cleaning up in this town. I've got two 'daddies' right now, and some guys just want to meet for a long weekend. We're in the perfect spot for it, nice college girls in a casino town."

"Don't you feel like a... like a—"

"A whore? Oh yeah, sometimes, sure. I get looks when I'm sitting with an old guy at a lounge that say, 'You don't belong here and there is only one reason why you could be here.' And to be fair, they are right. I'm there because I'm more or less on the clock. But what use does their opinion serve me? I know who I am. I was brought to the community college to take physics and calc classes when I was thirteen years old, and my parents are barely literate. I'm going to college for free as they foreclose on my childhood home. I've looked around and I know how it works."

This little speech may read as defensive or irritated, but it really wasn't. Stella was calm and matter-of-fact as she spoke. I think that's what really drew me in. She was as smart as she said she was. She looked around at the world and saw the same hopelessness I saw. She was an environmental science major.

"This is as easy as life's going to get for us, being young and beautiful like this. That's just the honest reality. We might as well apply smart economics to it. I didn't create the rules, I'm just making the most of 'em. I hope you know that you're young and beautiful, and full of potential too. But there's a tiny little clock strapped to our necks, ticking down our best moments and our best options. We have a short window of power in the scheme of a lifetime, so we have to cash in fast."

If I heard young Stella say those words today, I would tell her she is wrong. Perhaps I would tell her that she is degrading herself irreparably, and wasting her potential– or that we perpetuate our own exploitation and disrespect by participating in the commodification of our bodies and our sexualities. I would tell her this today, because today I sit on a real mattress with a full stomach and a savings account, albeit a small one. But her words flowed through my lean and despondent flesh and stuck there. The math made sense; so did the necessity of it. Stella was cynical but honest. And she was making the very most of the cards she had been dealt, playing the game as she believed it to be designed.

She and I spent many afternoons and evenings together after that lunch shift. She traded with Ramón for the Sunday lunch "loser" shift with me, and she nursed her hangovers while I raked in cash. After work we'd spend half of our tips at happy hour at the Lotusia bar or the restaurant next door. She introduced me to her roommates, who also had big gorgeous hair and sweatpants, and they let me borrow their tiny sequined dresses to wear to the clubs. We got ready over the course of several hours and several shots of sweet liquor, singing and dancing to Lady Gaga songs and gathered around a giant mirror at the base of a Marilyn Monroe shrine.

Stella taught me how to order cherry palomas "up" and how to flirt your way into concerts and VIP sections. And one night, after tasting the sweet burst of the second tequila-soaked Luxardo cherry, I signed into my new Sugar Mate profile on Stella's phone.

21
Forms of Fire

Christmas Eve, 2019

The gate rolls open, and as it closes behind me, the world is gone. It is comforting and claustrophobic. I imagine this feeling is not unlike that of a princess in her sprawling, enclosed estate, or that of a prisoner in a cell that has, against all instincts, become home.

A dense line of eucalyptus trees forms a secondary wall outside the property. Inside, it looks similar in style to Skip's: the compound of a successful conquistador. White concrete walls, Spanish clay tiles on the roof, ornamented bars over the windows. The impossibly heavy door, plated with metal, sits between two sconces holding lanterns that burn real fire.

It's Christmas Eve, but you'd never know it. Arnold has been gone for months, and Cam is not a religious or festive sort of man. There are giant palms along the cobblestone path to the house, broken up by immaculate ceramic planters holding large bushes of clustered purple flowers. Hummingbirds bicker in a manicured grove of olive trees. This miniature citadel's high adobe walls have been overtaken by thick green vines.

A dry creek runs through the property, and if you follow its path, you'll be led to a trio of guest cottages and servants' quarters that are much more spacious and lavish than any place I've lived in my adult life.

I set up the fire pit and sit beside it with my notebook and a hot cup of coffee. I try to focus on writing, but I keep peering up at the flitting hummingbirds. I have named my screenplay *Gasoline.* Its climax has become clearly formed in my mind, more brutal and shocking and satisfying than I ever could have hoped for. The translation from my brain to the paper is the art and the struggle. But I am pacified by my surroundings; too out of place to take on the emotional struggle of my main character. She's fighting against a greedy capitalist world, and I'm once again bathing myself in the luxury that belongs to it. I throw another log on the fire, dump the coffee in the gravel and raid the liquor cabinet.

Up to a month ago, this story was my world. I slept, ate, and breathed it. I shirked important financial and social obligations to work on it, believing that I was finally taking stock in myself as an artist. I lost Tyler over it; lost my friends from Paula's women's group. But I haven't added a single useful word to the script in weeks– since the fire.

After the "anti-trophy wife" incident, my plan was to withdraw from Cam entirely so I could focus my energy on his takedown. I was sitting at Mallory Café the next afternoon, furiously translating my villain notes into a dossier that I could share with the Earth Defenders. The day was uncomfortably warm for November; the wind too warm to provide relief. It whipped paper napkins and plastic wrappers along the corridors of Cicero St.

Everyone in the café seemed to share my restlessness. There was a lot of movement, conversations were muted, the staff moved cautiously to avoid spilling their trays as people shifted around. I kept glancing at my phone, expecting to hear from Tyler. His messages finally stopped after receiving no replies from me, but last night I finally reached out again, with no response yet. I angrily shoved the thing into my backpack.

Suddenly a sound filled the room, forcing heads out of books and menus. It was a muted buzz, accompanied by an orchestra of dings, beeps, little musical tunes, and one duck quack. We all fell silent at once, and took a moment to absorb the sound: fifty or so phones beckoning their owners at once. Some patrons glanced around anxiously before reaching into purses and pockets. I reached once again into my backpack.

Mirage County Alerts

> **EMERGENCY ALERT:** Thunberg Fire- Flames moving quickly through Camus Pass in the Mirage Mountains, pushed Southwest toward Mount Mirage by high Santa Ana winds. Evacuation orders are in effect for all residents between Camus Pass and Timothy St. Stay tuned for evacuation notices and other alerts. Click here for more information...   3:28 PM

The silence quickly fell into a buzzing chatter: uneasy whispers, people shuffling to get to-go cups and containers from the counter. I sat still, gazing at my phone. *No; you're not going to panic, and you're not going to call him.*

As I finally settled back into my villain report, a familiar cigar smell wafted through an abruptly opened door.

"Hello my dear. Let's get dinner."

Without saying a word, I began packing my things. I stood to put on my coat.

"You won't need it. It's warm."

I looked out the window as his truck raced through the downtown streets. In the distance over the rooftops, a trail of smoke could be seen filtering out of the mountains. It was a baffling, unnatural shade, somehow both orange and purple at once.

"Are you afraid?"

Yes.

"No."

"I for one am excited to watch it all burn. Should teach the Greens a well-deserved lesson."

"And what would that lesson be? 'You were right about climate change'?"

"No. Poor land management. This whole, 'let nature be pure and grow out its pubes' attitude has turned those mountains into a tinderbox. The County has been forbidden from clearing, cutting, and doing controlled burns for decades, all over excuses for the preservation of some lizard, or 'the sovereignty of the land to govern itself', or something equally ridiculous. A bush fire was bound to happen, and with that lack of maintenance and these winds, they'll be lucky if it doesn't reach downtown. You can blame your hippie friends for that."

"My, what? Hippie friends, what?" My face reddened. "I don't have any–"

"I'm just saying, if you actually care about what's good for nature, and humanity for that matter, you're rooting for the wrong team."

"Team? This isn't a football game, this is life. People could get hurt. Maybe act a little less excited."

"Not the people I care about." The truck rolls through Camus Junction toward the foothills.

"Cam… why are we driving *toward* the fire?"

"Because I have something called loyalty. And ethics."

Cam proceeded to make about a dozen phone calls, always ending with, "I'm on it," "I've got it," "Roger that," "Don't worry." We drove up Timothy Street, which I had never been on before, and Cam pulled into various drives to secure gates, throw patio furniture and potted shrubs off of decks, move vehicles, and take photos. "For insurance," he said. He entered one house and brought out a cat kennel. He sucked on his ring finger. "Damn thing bit me."

"But why would–"

"They're out of town," he said. "A lot of these are vacation homes."

"What's the patio furniture thing about? Why would that make a difference?"

"Those chairs and cushions are flammable as hell." He glanced back at the house, and then up the hill at the dense chaparral. "It does upset me to think about the wildlife. Fire is a natural thing. Destruction is part of nature. But when you don't let it burn when it's supposed to, if you don't work *with* nature– when you sing *'Kumbaya'* and refuse to acknowledge its power over us, and its indifference to our existence– this is what happens."

We parked on a slope and he completed another round of phone calls, answering questions, giving assurances. I sat patiently, and the truth of it is, despite our proximity to the fire, I felt safe.

"Want to see something?"

"Always."

Night had fallen by the time we reached our destination.

I didn't realize where we were until I climbed out of the truck. Then I saw my sitting rock. We were at my lookout spot above Camus Junction.

"This... this is my spot. How do you know about this spot?"

"It's just a spot." We looked out over the junction. It was quiet. Cars were ambling along at reasonable speeds, waiting in line, taking turns. "You're looking the wrong way." He turned me around. There was a disturbing red halo over the mountains' silhouette, and for the first time, I could see flames. These foothills were no longer the gentle green and brown giants that watched over the city like humble kings; they had become erupting volcanoes, hellish and angry, spitting out white flames and orange smoke, staining the whole sky.

I turned back to the highway below. No one was panicking. No one was speeding. If everything wasn't tinted orange, you wouldn't know the world was ending.

"Jesus, I thought climate change was going to make everyone crazy," Felicia said, crossing her arms. "But this is how it's going to be? Quiet acceptance? Shopping at Target? People are even stupider than I thought. We deserve to be wiped off this planet."

"You know," Debbie raised her dewy face from her handkerchief, "considerin' the global direness of this situation, it sure may be good advice to keep a big strong *may-un* around... for protections and such."

I glanced up at Cam.

"You see? This is what always happens," Felicia growled. "This is what white women do. We finally inch close to our independence, and then at the first sign of danger, we crawl back to the patriarchy."

"Yes, *but*," Debbie asked cautiously, "if a man's willing to run into a *fi-yah— for us*... is it really *that* terrible?"

Felicia's eyes were wild, but she spoke plainly. "I'd rather go down in flames than answer to a man."

I look at the clock. Ten to seven. The stars are hard to see with the light of the fire. It crackles, tamed and contained, in Arnold's round stone pit.

It melts the ice in my drink. I keep sipping the cold liquid and rereading the same scribbled passage over and over again, of the main character and the villain together, dancing under lantern-lit trees...

I keep looking up past the line of palms, toward the front gate— eager for the flash of headlights, or the rumble of the engine. It has always been a fantasy of mine— I don't know why— to be the beautiful woman waiting for the man to come home. I made some sort of great vision out of it, and I attempted it with Dean. I'd freshen my hair, wash myself meticulously, spray on perfume. Hours in advance things would be put away, cleaned, prepared for the arrival. I would choose undergarments specifically— sometimes playful pinks and knee socks, taking on the girl-next-door look so proliferated in his favorite pornos and coming-of-age films. Sometimes I'd wear a pretty powder blue set under regular clothing that would be revealed as a surprise; sometimes it would be a pair of black stilettos and red lipstick, and nothing else.

I would choose an activity that offered a veil of spontaneity: reading a book, stirring a pot on the stove, fake-sleeping in a flattering position on the couch by the door. Anything to demonstrate that I was classic, that I was iconic; that I was a possession worth prizing.

But it never went the way I imagined. I would get stuck in my phony position for over an hour because he picked up overtime without telling me. Or sometimes he would come in and not notice me, tired, spent from a long day out in the world, and would retire to the bathroom or the garage. The reaction was never once what I wanted it to be, but each time I failed I tried harder. I sought it like a madness.

Then the desire died suddenly, subtly, the way a season changes. You wake up and you look out the window and nothing is different. The trees haven't turned yet. But your body knows. It's not the same. There is a new electricity in the air.

The chemistry, the attraction, the charm— gone. Gone in an instant. What was left was a sensation of cold emptiness, concrete and hollow, like an empty silo that once held the nourishment of a village. And I am feeling it all over again, but more acutely, because now that silo is filled with rage; a rage that must be kept quiet, kept tame and contained like the fire in this pit, until precisely the right moment. The veil has been lifted. He almost got me. Another clever twist in a very twisted story.

But this space inside me didn't just occupy feelings of intrigue and infatuation for this man. I am worried there was more in there that has been lost: the desire to be creative, the desire to make a difference; a desire to change people, to struggle for the sake of an ideal. The ability to remain hopeful. *Hope.* Hope that the prophets of science are wrong; hope that we can change in time; hope that people are learning; hope that a transition to a sustainable society will be a peaceful one. Gone. Gone like the last warm ray of summer.

Am I this easy to defeat? This is all it took to break my spirit? Or is this just the moment of honesty that tears a person down before they discover their true purpose? I attempt to push myself to see outside of it, but the struggle is constant. There is no more space in my mind for anything else. I watch everything that meant something to me slipping through my desperate grasp like handfuls of dry sand.

I enter the house, a little stumbly with a buzz. The latent cigar smell warms me, brings me back to our afternoons cruising into the valley in the car; the good old days when this was just a playful ruse; justified research for "a work of art with noble aims," and I was still free from my own weaknesses– or at least I was still telling myself that convincingly.

Quarter to nine. I don't know where he is, and it's not my business to ask. I stare at my phone and begin the brainless, pathetic act of scrolling on Instagram: a woman thumbing through a leatherbound book in a mahogany library; a woman eating a croissant with jam on an urban European balcony; a woman in a field picking flowers in a white dress. "Who the fuck are these women? How do they have the time for this? Who is filming them? Their *boyfriends*? Like that Brad guy following around Dolphin Trainer Bozo? AH–!" I throw the phone into the couch cushions and drain my watered-down drink.

I return to the firepit with my notebooks– not just one notebook, but *all* the notebooks– the cardboard box of notepads, folders, napkins and receipts that comprise the entirety of my thoughts, ideas, and manuscript of this ridiculous, overwrought, derivative screenplay. Pathetic. *Pathetic*! *This is how you've spent the last eight months of your life? On this box of bitter lunacy?*

I consider throwing it in, and a huge, ugly Harley Quinn smile takes over my face. I picture the words melting, the ink bubbling and the paper blackening, and I feel a freedom that I haven't felt since the first time I jumped over the gunwale of the *Siren's Revenge* for a swim.

I grab a random paper from the box, crumple it into a ball, and throw it into the flames with a shrill, delighted shriek. The paper catches instantly; my heart swiftly drops; I go to grab it, desperate, only to withdraw my burnt hand. It is overtaken by the flames and gone, gone as quickly as the impulse to get rid of it. An idea… a thought… *my* idea…something of mine…swallowed and gone forever.

I'm immediately sobered; frightened by my own behavior. I return the box back to the trunk of my car. I grab another random slice of paper from the pile; one that's deeply wrinkled from being crumpled and then rescued several times. I sit by the fire with it, and read it aloud:

"If you want to be justified in hating something, invite it into your life: welcome it into your thoughts, learn about its hopes and fears. Imitate it and attract it to yourself. Let it speak, and listen: ask it questions, ask it anything, ask it what it is and why. Make it feel at home with you. Let it into your arms and heart; laugh at its jokes and hear its stories, press it against you and warm it with the heat of your body. Make it laugh, give it a meal and observe how it eats. Live amongst it, watch it groom, rest, play, mourn, enjoy; observe how it comforts itself, how it cares for itself, how it hurts; what it desires and what it is willing to do to get it.

If you still hate it, then and only then, you are justified."

22
God and Captain Hook

"My friends, welcome. On this beautiful winter morning, I'd like to talk with you about the many forks we face on the road of life."

I cross my arms. *Of course you do.*

Then I remember that no one has forced me to be here; I woke up early, put on these nice clothes, walked into this chapel and sat in this pew entirely– and bizarrely– of my own volition. And I just happen to have exactly the kind of predicament this old man in a robe is about to discuss. So perhaps I should shut up my pompous inner voice and listen for once.

The big "Roger Wilkes for Governor" fundraiser is only days away, and the plan I have set in motion has taken on a life of its own. In ruining Wilkes' campaign, I am also ruining Cam's chance of being reinstated at Kantian Consulting– and, equally likely, ruining his life. But Cam crossed a line at that seafood place that can't be uncrossed. It's like some big fancy drape has been yanked off my eyes, and I can finally see the last few months for what they actually were: me being distracted by nice meals and road trips, distracted by male attention and mischief, shaken up and frightened by wildfire, all while forgetting that this man represents everything I stand against. I lost myself, and sold myself out...all in the name of a story I am failing to write. Maybe I'm not even a writer at all. Writers are cowards, if you ask me. I'm a woman of action: an activist on a mission to protect the planet from greedy, self-interested, cis-straight-white-male chauvinist-capitalists like Giles Pion, Skip Vodnyyvor, and especially Cam Benzin. For all I know, Cam could have known I was an Earth Defender all along, and was the one seducing *me* to extract valuable information about the power plant fight. *That bastard!*

I haven't been sleeping well since I had my big meeting with Piper and Purple at the Earth Defenders office. Once I had revealed what I knew about Cam, I watched their faces light up at the gift I had provided them: this unassuming man, who has been hiding in the shadows of this whole Invisible Hand operation, is now going to be the centerpiece of its takedown. I questioned myself at night, if the punishment really fit the crime, until I got my Earth Defenders welcome packet in the mail: health insurance, dental and vision, a membership card to the Mirage Athletic Club, and a high four-figure check, the first of many.

I haven't been able to face him since I cashed the first check. I told him I'd be honored to be his date to the fundraiser— as that's part of the plan— but that I have a nasty and persistent case of the flu that I must focus on curing before the big night. I quit Vero's cold turkey and I've been hiding out at home with Kevin, cooking comfort food and playing board games. He has been a lifesaver; such a good listener and always making me laugh. I might even call him my best friend. *Only* may be a more honest word.

I know I am doing the right thing, in the end. I still don't really understand nuclear energy, despite Cam's many lectures, but if the scientists and experts at MMU and MMED say that it's bad, I trust them. They say it's a distraction from the necessary changes we need to make in the energy system to save the planet from destruction: wind and solar farms. Micro-grids. Electric appliances, vehicles, planes. Community-owned energy resources and lithium-ion battery banks. Less per-capita energy consumption. Transition to plant-based diets. Less reproduction to curb our carbon legacies. Rewilding nature and condensing the human population into urban areas to make room for intact ecosystems. Of course, I don't plan on doing that. I've got my sights set on a cabin somewhere deep in the woods, away from everyone.

But enough nights without sleep will bring a person to do stupid things. I've been regularly calling John for advice, telling my story to drunk strangers in bars, and even reading the horoscope section of the local paper, if you can believe it. And now I find myself in a church for the first time in a decade. But I'm here, so I might as well listen. I uncross my arms, and straighten my slouch.

"We have entered a special new year," the pastor continues, "a new decade, the Year of our Lord 2020. A turning point, full of potential and promise, and equally ripe with challenges and tensions. An election year; another crossroads for the soul of our nation and community.

"Hopefully we all had the opportunity to spend the Christmas holiday at home with our families, resting our hearts and minds from the trials of the year, and praising God for the past twelve months' many blessings and lessons. And now after our festive repose, it is time we look ahead— out across the horizon of the new year, refreshed in Christ's renewal of our spirits and hope, and we ask ourselves what path we will walk on this next chapter of our journey."

Is he talking directly to me? I feel like he knows. But how could he possibly know.

…Does he know?

"We live in a time and place unique in all of human history: a time absolutely rife with choice. Want a loaf of bread? There are two aisles of varieties to choose from. Want to watch a film, hear a song, buy a shirt? Let us hope you have something specific in mind, or you'll be browsing the web all day. Want to change your name, change your hair? Quit your job and find a new one? Meet a date for tonight? *Click, click, click.*

"It is our historically-informed norm to equate choice with autonomy, and autonomy with freedom, and freedom with happiness. And what American would ever argue that more freedom is a bad thing?

"But the wisdom of both history and the Scriptures reminds us that too much of anything tarnishes the human spirit. Excess of any kind pulls us away from God, and into our own selves. Excess is the unique challenge of our time. It is hard to escape it, let alone resist it."

All I can see is myself at the pool at Skip's, surrounded by servants pouring drinks and massaging my scalp. *I am going to Hell for sure.*

"To exemplify this new reality, consider the fact that for all of human history, all of *living* history up to the post-industrial era, the main concern of all living things has been to avoid starving. We now concern ourselves with the constant temptation of overeating. I am sure, after the delightful marathon of Thanksgiving, Christmas, and New Years, there are many belt buckles fighting for their lives in this very room. I, for one, may or may not have a button loose under this robe."

The congregation chuckles quietly. I glance around, surprised to see that while most of the pews are topped with white and gray hair, there are a handful of couples about my age.

"We are given many choices in this modern world; many opportunities to shape our lives in the ways we wish. But how many of these choices genuinely benefit us– the deeper versions of us, our immortal souls? How many of these choices are simply surface level, providing us a distracting and mollifying *illusion* of choice? We are humans, after all– social beings of habit and culture– therefore we inevitably find ourselves swimming in the cultural currents in which we reside.

"Romans 12:2 tells us:

'Do not conform to the pattern of this world,
but be transformed by the renewing of your mind.
Then you will be able to test and approve what God's will is—
his good, pleasing and perfect will.'

I quickly grab one of the little pencils out of the back of the pew in front of me, and one of the donation envelopes. *"Roman 12."* I want to remember that one. As soon as I heard it, I had a vision, clear as day: me living in my cabin somewhere deep in the woods, far away from everyone, feeding a horse and planting a garden.

"You have been given this tremendous blessing, this tremendous *responsibility*: to be modern, to be here and now. How will you use your gift of choice? To uplift and please your Creator, or to uplift and please yourself? Will your choices lead you to visceral, fleeting pleasure, or to lasting honor and fulfilling moral duty?

"Continuing in Romans 12:

'For by the grace given me I say to every one of you:
Do not think of yourself more highly than you ought, but rather think
of yourself with sober judgment, in accordance with the faith God has
distributed to each of you.

'For just as each of us has one body with many members, and these members
do not all have the same function, so in Christ we, though many, form one
body, and each member belongs to all the others.

'We have different gifts, according to the grace given to each of us. If your
gift is prophesying, then prophesy in accordance with your faith; if it is
serving, then serve; if it is teaching, then teach; if it is to encourage, then
give encouragement; if it is giving, then give generously; if it is to lead, do it
diligently; if it is to show mercy, do it cheerfully.'"

~

This looks like an AA meeting. The church basement has old but clean carpeting and bulletin boards on the walls, advertising spaghetti dinners and bazaars, the choir practice schedule, and missionary trips abroad. About a dozen chairs are arranged in a big circle beside a table filled with home-baked goods covered in saran wrap, and a few plastic tubs of grocery store cookies from the women who didn't have time to bake. On the end of the table, like a king surveying his kingdom, sits a giant coffee urn and his court of paper cups, creamer, and sugar packets.

The woman from the seafood restaurant is here, the one who called me out on my "I sing in the choir at H. Caulfield Memorial Church" lie, and she approaches me as I pretend to intently read something on the bulletin board. "Nina, isn't it? Nice to see you again."

"Oh, yes hello– nice to see you too. I thought I would try out this women's group you spoke so highly of."

"I'm glad you did. Come, sit next to me."

We grab coffee and I put a raspberry linzer cookie on a tiny paper plate. A fat woman in a periwinkle sweater calls the group to attention, and the old birds all settle into their seats like hens sitting atop their eggs. There are welcoming remarks, announcements, and a couple prayer requests. The woman next to me speaks up and starts gesturing toward me, and I sink into my chair.

"Everyone, I'd like to introduce you to a newcomer this morning. This is Nina, and she sings in the choir."

"She sings here? Judith and Gwen are in the choir."

"I've never seen her before," Judith says. *Shut up, Judith.* "Do you mean she just moved here from another congregation?"

"Didn't you say that you were part of this congregation, dear?"

My face is hot, caught in the headlights of my lie. "I'm sorry– I meant to say that I am a new member of the congregation. Or, er, a visitor, I guess. The truth is, I used to sing in *a* choir, when I was a kid. The truth is, I haven't been to a church in years. I stopped believing in god a long time ago. After learning about Geologic Time, and how complex and infinite the Universe is, the Christian view of god felt like a simplistic, pacifying lie– something you'd tell kids to get them to behave, or to make them feel better when something bad happens.

"It was disorienting, like how it felt to realize Santa Claus isn't real, and that no matter how much you try, Christmas will never be the same; the magic is dead. And you realize your parents and everyone who you looked up to and trusted have been lying to you your whole life. I was angry, very angry, and lost. I guess after a while I stopped caring about life, because all at once it had become meaningless, and I resented the countless hours of my life I had spent praying to nothing." My speech slows down as I continue to think aloud. I close my eyes a bit as I speak, almost like I'm praying.

"It's like one minute, I'm sitting on a boat, looking at the stars, and it all looks so big, and I can see god up there above it all, outside it all, looking down at me, giving me life as a carefully chosen gift; caring where I was, what I was doing, what I was thinking about; and the next minute, the sky seems somehow bigger, and the Universe is expanding faster than I can comprehend, and there's nothing beyond or outside it, and it doesn't give a damn who I am or what I'm thinking about, or whether I live or die…

"But over time, I have found a way around it. I have come to understand that we all are simply matter, made of the same basic material– all things on Earth, and in the Universe– and so we are at least a *part* of something. And I can worship the Universe itself, as the mother of all things; and maybe I've got no soul and there's no heaven, but all actions on Earth have a ripple effect into the world, and when I die, my parts will break down into their most basic parts again, and will be reabsorbed into the endless cycle of Life, and in that way, we are all eternal, and all one."

The women stare at me in horror, as if I have just lit the Bible on fire, swallowed it, and then let out a sulfurous belch. Except for one woman with gold-rimmed glasses, who pleasantly responds.

"While I am quite sorry to hear about what you went through, I see these things as more or less one and the same," she says. "You still view yourself as an eternal being, whose actions have consequences. You therefore have a responsibility in life, and in death, to act morally. You feel a kinship with your fellow man, and all fellow beings– all of Creation – yet the key difference is where you turn your head in worship. You worship the *created,* 'the universe itself', as you said… but why not worship its Creator?"

"Because the creator is not a white man in a robe on a cloud in the sky," I retort, instantly guilty at the irritated condescension in my tone.

"No one said he was," she chuckles. "It's true that we, as mostly European-rooted Christians, use the word *God,* and the Bible tells us that he created humans in his image, so we see him in a form that we can comprehend: our own. But that isn't some absolute; it can be interpreted in many ways."

"And that's another thing– why is god a 'he', anyway? Wouldn't the creator of all things be a mother, not a father? Isn't that just us participating in the fundamental domination of men over women?"

A few women sigh in tired exasperation, but a couple of them lean in with their paper coffee cups, interested in how this conversation is going to go.

"I'm glad you brought that up," another woman says. She looks like the second-youngest person in the room, around 35. "Because I came to this group with that exact same question. I had just left my husband– or rather, *life partner,* as we chose to call it– and I was completely lost.

"We thought we had figured life out: we were super-progressive atheists, with an egalitarian marriage and plenty of disposable income to travel and pursue our hobbies. We had the time of our lives in our twenties. Then we started talking about next steps in life, about having children. I became much more interested in the prospect of family than he was. I mentioned I wanted to stay home for a potential baby's first few years, but I was earning a lot more money than him– like, *a lot* more– and he said it was out of the question if we wanted to maintain our lifestyle. I was willing to sacrifice a couple of the vacations and hobbies, but he wasn't. I suggested he try to advance in his career; I offered to support him through additional schooling. He refused, saying he was happy where he was, and that he didn't want any more responsibility."

"This is all sounding like a pretty good case for god being a woman," I grin.

"Well, let me finish. For a while, I gave up on having kids, and tried to accept my life as it was. It was an objectively great life: I had a lucrative career, a beautiful home, and a partner who I loved. But something was profoundly missing– and no promotion, or fancy restaurant, or trip to Bali could close the gap. One day I realized I was smoking pot every day after work. Every single night, like clockwork, as soon as I got home; like I didn't want to be fully conscious for the hours when I wasn't distracted from my own thoughts.

"Then, as a five-year 'anniversary present', Kyle wanted to open up our relationship." Another chorus of disgusted sighs and groans emerge from the circle. "He gave me this lecture about how marriage and monogamy are 'Western concepts built on a system of women's oppression', and that I deserve to be free… and since we were always obsessed with being equals, that *he* should be free too. That was the last straw."

My mind flies backward, like a skipping stone in reverse, to Kevin's speech in the kitchen; to Tyler's speech when he dumped me; to that first night at Klipspringer's Steakhouse, and Cam's lecture about men around here pulling this sort of stunt all the time. I thought he was being dramatic, or just a dick.

"So I felt pretty done with men after that," the woman continues. "I got a place on my own, traveled, and spent a lot of time on social media following the 'you don't need a man' types. I pictured a life on my own, being a tough single mom with a career, and I began to sort of worship that image of myself. I started looking into getting a sperm donor. But then one night I saw an *actual* single mom at the grocery store, a girl I went to high school with. She looked a full ten years older than me. The kids were all over the place. I thought of God for the first time in like twenty years– like he had placed her in my path to say, 'Now let's just think this through.'

"So I went from thinking: *I don't need a man!*– to, *Well, even if I don't need a man, I still want one, and that's alright*– to, *You know what? I want a man, I need a man, a man needs me, and my children need both of us.*

"This maybe isn't great to admit, but I started coming back to church to look for a man. I wanted a solid partner in life, someone to take care of me and to take care of. I realized how deeply I was craving *wholesomeness* in my life; and a man with values to share it with, who wants these things genuinely. So I came here, and listened to the sermons, still resenting the maleness of God, but eventually I realized that men who become fathers– which for all time up to now, was the default– *must* be expected to be strong, and must be willing to take the responsibility of leadership of their family, because what is the alternative?"

"*Us* havin' to do it," a large woman with her arms crossed over large breasts grumbles, clearly speaking from experience. "Us having to fill yet *another* role. And how can you be attracted to a man who nervously looks to *you* for answers in times of crisis, or when big decisions need to be made? How can you respect a man like that? I know I can't."

The woman beside her giggles, shaking her head. I guess she knows the woman's husband. "If you don't have a man at the head of the table, then *you're* the head of the table, and then guess what? You're stuck spending your life with a man who is weaker than you, who takes orders from you, and will eventually both fear *and* hate you. Good luck with your sex life."

"Harriet!"

"I'm just saying. We're all adults here, are we not? How old are you, girl? Twenty-three?"

I straighten my posture. "It was just my birthday, on New Year's Day. I'm thirty."

A chorus of '*Ahhs*' resound through the circle, as if I had just cracked the case of why I'm here.

"Wait… can we go back to the whole patriarchy thing for a moment? It sounds like what you're saying is that you're all in support of a social structure that puts us at the bottom. I can't understand it. Why does it have to be a power struggle, anyhow? Why can't there just be two heads of the table?"

"There can, in the sense that you can treat one another with equal measures of respect, and each have your own responsibilities and zones of influence in your household. But there will always be moments where someone needs to take charge, or be the decisive one, or to speak up."

"And it's not the bottom," another woman says. "You're looking at it the wrong way. Wait, I have the perfect Bible reference…let me just find it…" She starts madly thumbing through a worn Bible filled with multi-colored sticky notes.

"I guess I should have expected this," I sigh. "I remember reading all those misogynistic Bible passages in Women's Studies class freshman year. 'Women shouldn't speak,' 'women should *submit* to their husbands', that we're nothing more than a hunk of rib…"

"Yes," the old woman next to me chimes in, "there are certainly many, let's say, *outdated* passages in the Bible. The Bible talks about slavery too. Deuteronomy is full of nightmarish old-world rules about women, sex, and marriage. We must take the context of the authors in their time. The world was a different place; humans were a much rougher bunch. We have come a very long way in the last two or three thousand years. But one thing has not changed: the nature of our being. No amount of advancement and refinement will prevent us from being sinners by design, still bound in our human bodies with vestigial instincts that need to be reasoned with, and overcome. No amount of technology or social change will alter the fact that *we,* as women, are the bearers and nurturers of children, and that men are physically bigger and stronger than us– and therefore we must order our society around those facts, always with the top priority of what is best for children." The circle of hens nod ardently. "What environment creates the stability, warmth and nurturing that children need to thrive?" Before I can answer her question, the others chime in.

"Functional, safe, and stable households."

"Parents who are in love!"

"Two parents. Solid marriages."

"A healthy division of responsibilities and work."

"Daddy winning the bread, and Mama baking it."

"Speaking of baking, hats off to Marie for the rugelach! My God, these are good! Can I bring a few home for my grandkids?"

I roll my eyes in frustration. "All this talk about kids, but what if I don't want them? What does it matter then? What if I have bigger things in mind?"

"What bigger thing is there, than creating life? Than building a family, the next generation of humanity? Participating in a community, building a legacy?"

"Jeez, I don't know– healing the blind? Stopping climate change? Curing cancer?"

"Oh, so you're a scientist?"

"Well not exactly, but–"

"So you're a doctor?"

"No– but I'm smart. I've been told I'm smart my whole life, that I'm full of potential. And I don't want to waste my potential on a life of dirty dishes and socks and household drudgery! I don't want to be miserable!"

"What brought you here this morning, dear?"

"...I'm... I'm in the middle of an existential crisis!– And I'm...well frankly–" I shrink with the weight of my own admission, "*fine*– yes, I am miserable."

The hens nod knowingly, satisfied with the wisdom of their seniority, grateful that they aren't my age any longer.

"You see," I swallow a lump in my throat, "next week, there's this fundraiser…"

"Found it!" the woman with the Bible announces. "Starting at Ephesians chapter five, verse twenty-two, and skipping around a bit:

'Wives, submit yourselves to your own husbands as you do to the Lord. For the husband is the head of the wife as Christ is the head of the church…

'Husbands, love your wives, just as Christ loved the church and gave himself up for her to make her holy, cleansing her by the washing with water through the word, and to present her to himself as a radiant church, without stain or wrinkle or any other blemish, but holy and blameless. In this same way, husbands ought to love their wives as their own bodies. He who loves his wife loves himself.

'After all, no one ever hated their own body, but they feed and care for their body, just as Christ does the church…each one of you also must love his wife as he loves himself, and the wife must respect her husband.'

"You see?" she says. "It goes both ways. You cherish and respect each other, and yourselves. You submit to him, and he is responsible for you and your childrens' wellbeing and protection. You serve him, but he serves you too. He loves you as Christ loves the church, and so you value yourself as holy to him, and present yourself to him as such. Have you ever been loved like that?"

"I have not. Well once, maybe. But I ran from him, as fast as I could, and moved all the way out here."

~

The road up to Camus Preserve was part of the burn zone of the Thunberg Fire, so the shock of seeing it is lessened by the preview. The tall grasses are usually green and lush this time of year, revived seemingly overnight after the early winter rains, and the clouds hover purpley and heady over the mountains. It gives the foothills an Irish resemblance and tricks the senses, for winter is when everything seems to come to life here; the summer is golden and stifled and dead. Once you transcend the grassy foothills, you enter the chaparral of the mountains, full of fragrant sage and rusty-colored manzanita trees. The canyons are shaded by live oaks and protected by a ubiquity of poison oak, the sheen of their red and green leaves a testament to their oily power to destroy you.

I pull onto the gravel strip on the side of the road to begin my pilgrimage into the preserve, with no destination in mind, but hoping to get lost for the day. I do my best thinking between miles two and six of a long walk.

There are two problems with my plan. The view is more depressing than I could have possibly hoped for. There is no green at all, only the char and gray-brown of devastation, and some orangey burnt pine needles. The fire swept over everything. I assumed there would be patches of burn areas, but *some* life would remain. It looks like the elephant graveyard from *The Lion King*. The stark sunlight and cloudless sky somehow make it worse than it'd be if there were clouds. It's unforgivingly harsh, like fluorescent lights on a tired face with no makeup.

Problem number two is the car that has just pulled in the patch of dirt ahead of me, a lagoon blue 2017 Hybrid Subaru Crosstrek covered in National Park stickers. Tyler.

"Oh, for CHRIST'S *SAKE!*"

Before I can restart the engine and make a run for it, he knocks on my window.

"Hey there. Guess we had the same idea."

I nod, and continue tying my boot.

"Do you want to go check it out?"

"I already did," I shout through my closed window. "I'm leaving."

"Then why are you putting your boots on?"

I step out into the bright winter morning. I'm still wearing my church clothes; my dress is the color of the sky– pale, washed out blue with a high neckline and midi leg. I've tossed the tasteful cream shoes with a feminine little heel into the back seat, and the hiking boots and wool socks look ridiculous with my dress and beige trenchcoat. The stiffness of the fabric restricts my movement; I surrender to it and walk slowly, deliberately past Tyler without a glance toward him and toward the exposed path.

We silently weave up the hill and get to the first crest, with a view of the burnt-up wasteland ahead. I stop short, exasperated and pissed.

"You've ruined this. This is ruined. I came up here to think, not to hear your boots crunching along behind me. I'm just gonna go–"

"Wait," he pleads, "maybe I can help. What's on your mind? Maybe talking about it will–"

"Why would I want to talk to you? Have you forgotten? You broke up with me, Tyler. Twice. How many more clues does a person need to–"

"Look, I know, I know that I've hurt you and I'm sorry. I just… miss being friends. You know me in a way no one else does. And I'm kind of worried about you. The last time we talked… I just want to know that you're doing okay."

"How I'm doing is not your business anymore. We aren't friends and we never were. We were a *couple*. That's something entirely different. And how am I doing? How I'm doing is…I'm not doing great, okay? I'm in the middle of this– I can't even begin to explain it. But I've screwed a million things up, and I can't pump the brakes on it."

"Well I was going to say let's go for a long walk here, and we don't even have to talk, you can just think for a while; and then if something comes to mind, you have someone to bounce an idea off of. But looking at this place… it's just depressing the hell out of me. I don't know if I can stay here."

"Me too. I can't believe it's just…gone. I can't talk here. All I can think about is our climate-apocalyptic future."

"Me too. What if we just go for a drive?"

The scent of the car is all too familiar; the smell of damp polyester tent fabric, and dirty gear soaked in campfire fumes. "So," Tyler attempts to break the silence, "why are you dressed like that?"

"What are you even doing here? I thought you got a big-boy job in the city."

"I came home for the holidays, and with the fire going on, decided to stay a bit longer. Turns out I can do most of my job remotely."

"Neat."

We sit on the bluffs at Point Camus. Below the bluffs are a short beach and a wide stretch of solemn ocean. Perched surfers float over the rolling waves; bored by unbroken swell, they glance back toward the mountains. Pelicans skim the surface of the water in military precision. One leads the group, and one trails behind. I quietly ponder the nature of winners and losers, and whether or not the American ethic is indeed a lie. *Are we just born into a lot in life, or can some really claw their way to the top out of sheer discipline and will?* Tyler and I stare forward, but after a moment he turns and looks at me. I don't return his glance.

"Nina, less than a year ago you sat here with me, and you wept as you held your battered copy of *The Grapes of Wrath* to your chest. You wept for the suffering of the displaced farmers and the downtrodden workers, and the generations of inescapable poverty that built California, and you said to me, 'I don't deserve to be here.' You said Mount Mirage was the promised land, promised to those shoved to the West, shoved off the safety of their farms and out of their own self-sufficiency, but the promise was a lie. You said they sent the backbone of this country out here in droves with fairytales of hard work and sunshine and fruit trees. And when they got here, the walls and fences were already built. They suffered and toiled to get here, and when they finally made it, they weren't wanted. You wept for them; you felt their suffering inside you. And you felt guilty."

"Yes, I did."

"And then you wept over the meatpackers and factory workers in *The Jungle,* and the ill-fated couple in *The Pearl,* and the deaf man in *The Heart is a Lonely Hunter,* and the prisoners in *Not About Nightingales*– and you said that you felt guilty for all the downtrodden everywhere; that those stories were just a microcosm of what has happened all over this country, all over the world, for century after century; a neverending trail of injustice and hardship."

"Yes, I did."

"But you accomplish nothing for them by forcing yourself to suffer. Nothing. You don't bring justice to the past and you don't create less suffering in the future. It's just suffering on top of suffering. If anything, you should be living life to the fullest, making the most of every gift you have been given, and in your appreciation of where you are and what you have, maybe that's how you honor those who worked toward a better life."

"That is probably the smartest thing you've ever said." I can't help but giggle a little. I wonder what the hell he thinks I am up to.

"I don't know what you're going through, or what you've been doing, but I just want you to know that I am always here for you. If you need someone, someone to talk to–" He touches my hand; it feels warm and gentle and familiar. I let it rest on mine.

"You are right." I turn my hand so our fingers can interlace. "Tyler, I could really use your help with something. Will you be here next weekend?"

"Actually," Tyler lights up with a wide white smile, "I'm heading home Wednesday to prep gear for a very exciting trip. I am taking a couple months off work to go bicycling around Eur–"

"Oh Christ, you almost had me!" I stand up and wipe my hand on my dress. I point my finger in his face. "*You*...Tyler, do you *really* want to know what I think about you?"

"Yes, I guess..." he looks somewhat frightened.

"It's not going to be nice. But it will be honest."

"Alright, I want to know. You have a right to say what's on your mind."

"Fine. Good." I turn to the ocean. "But I warned you."

A gallon of water dumped from a bucket is not the same gallon of water that dribbles out of a watering can. The streams from a watering can are controlled, and steady. They don't drench and run through; they sit and soak. Tyler used to scold me for watering my houseplants by dumping a cup of water on them. "You dump that water into that little pot and it just runs right through, taking the soil's nutrients along with it," he'd say. "You have no patience."

I speak to Tyler, but deliver my sermon to the ocean. "Tyler, up until quite recently I thought you were the one. But I also thought a lot of things that I am not so sure about anymore. To your credit, I am suffering, yes– I am suffering deeply. I felt so connected to this story; I felt almost a sense of duty to it– to the people it was for. I hoped that people would see the film and feel a moment of satisfaction, or relief– that it would challenge the powerful and leave them exposed. I saw it as my one little mark to avenge the suffering of the people on which our empire was built. And I thought I could go out there and see it firsthand, to acknowledge it, so I could describe it accurately. I thought I could hear it all in their own words, and then I could write it down.

"At first, I thought I was in character, the way I used to chameleon my way around my tables when I was waitressing. And I thought, maybe if I just opened my mind a little bit, and I allowed myself to connect with them, I would better understand why things are this way, or maybe I'd even have an opportunity to teach them something.

"I put myself into this character, this world, for what feels like too long– and in doing so I have burned my own identity. She doesn't exist anymore. And I honestly don't know anymore if that is a good thing or a bad thing– because I ask myself, well, how old was that particular version of my identity? Is that who I was when I was in high school, or even college? What would the little girl version of me think of who I've been, or who I am now? Is there any continuity between us whatsoever?

"And how is it even possible to be changing this much, all of the time? Am I just some plankton, floating in whatever direction the current is moving? Don't I have a backbone, a sense of my own principles, my own concrete ideals that ground me, that contain me in some way?"

Tyler is staring at me, squinting his eyes in concentration– either in an attempt to follow what I am saying, or to at least *look* like he is.

"I did get what I wanted: I heard it in their words. I've heard from everyone, on all sides; a line has become a circle and now the compass is spinning out of control, like in *Pocahontas*. *Jesus*, can't I go ten minutes without referencing a goddamn Disney movie?!" I blush in the realization that I told him that this dissertation was about how I feel about him, and I've just ranted for several minutes about myself.

"I thought I moved to Mount Mirage to start over and reclaim my life, and grow into the woman I want to be. But really I was just running away, like a scared little girl. And when I look back on our relationship– when I think about how I behaved with you, and how I dressed, and what I tolerated… We were like boys; like a pair of little boys playing outside. It was fun and exciting, and maybe admissible when I could still say I was 'in my twenties.' But at some point, it's time to look in the mirror and accept that we've grown up. And when I look at you, Tyler, I am afraid that you are eternally, incurably, Peter Pan."

His eyes sink to the dirt; I continue before he can respond. "I certainly get the appeal of never growing up– it's everyone's dream, really. But some dreams aren't meant to be achieved; they're meant to be enjoyed in their ethereal, untouchable form, detached from the cold consequences of reality. And not living in reality, well– that option is only available to a very select few. You are one of the lucky ones, I suppose. I guess I am congratulating you. You have won the lottery of human existence. And I'm not all that far behind you, in the big scale of things. But even still– I am not convinced that Neverland is the paradise we make it out to be. Look at how your father–"

"Please don't bring up my Dad," Tyler whispers.

"Sorry; I am just saying that life is long, and we don't know what's going to happen in the future–"

"Yes, exactly– we don't know. But we can make a scientific guess, based on what we see now. And things don't look good; for the planet, for humanity, for America. So why would we tie ourselves down with obligations and responsibilities to things that rest on broken foundations?"

"Because 'we don't know what the future will bring' has been true for every generation that has ever come before us, and every one that will ever come. But we have a choice in front of us. Like you said, we can use the gifts we have and make the most of our lives, or we can spend it running."

"Running from what, exactly?"

I think of Don; his words etched into my gray matter like a tattoo. "Running from what is *real*. Running for the simple sake of keeping our feet from touching the ground, and becoming real.

"I thought that was the last thing I wanted, but I've changed my mind. I am on a mission now. I want to become real– a real woman. I want all the real things in life. Which means, I won't settle for less than a real man."

"Wait, are you saying that I'm not really a man?" There is defensiveness in his question, and hurt in his eyes, but he looks out at the horizon as the words leave his lips, perhaps admitting to himself there is some truth in my accusation.

"You're thirty-three years old, Tyler. Your body is a man's. But a scared boy lives inside; a boy who has led a blessed life that maybe has actually been a curse, a world in which a man was never needed; a boy who never had to lead, or fight, or struggle for anything real. It is not my desire to ask you to grow up, and it is not my duty to convince you you should. The urge can only come from inside you."

I stare at him for a long time, while he stares at the ocean.

SOCIAL IMPRINTING

Social imprinting is a form of developmental learning in which juveniles learn certain behaviors, attachments, and preferences from other individuals. These imprints on the psyche– especially if learned from a young age, with consistent reinforcement from multiple individuals– are often permanent, and often impossible to reverse.

Observations of *Gorilla-industria violentus* suggest that young males don't mature solely from biological processes; social imprinting is a critical part of their development– more particularly, what they learn from other males. Females, perhaps by virtue of their reproductive role, appear to have more innate, clearly defined social functions through the extensive dependency of offspring. Males have far less reproductive obligations than females, at least by what is mandated by nature. Their assumption of responsibility to support females, assist with offspring, or serve useful roles in the troop is primarily a product of their socialization.

Social imprinting for young males begins at infancy, typically with the father. (This further emphasizes a female's need to find a reliable mate who will stay to co-parent offspring.) The male progeny of a great white gorilla is much more likely to become an alpha himself than other young males. A family troop led by a great white gorilla typically has a consistent male socialization strategy for its members. Young males congregate and learn both good and bad behaviors from one another, secondhand from their fathers. If there is discord in male behavior, it is up to the troop's GWG to set the example and put subordinate males in their place. This appears to be a cornerstone factor of troop stability and healthy function: if the alpha is dysfunctional, the subordinate males follow suit, and both the females and juveniles suffer instability and vulnerability to attack from other troops, or from within. It is therefore the responsibility of a GWG to set the social tone for the troop's males and vigilantly enforce the social order. Both young males and non-dominant adult males appear to benefit from a great white gorilla who has learned to channel and control his aggression, assert independence and self-reliance, and maintain his physical strength to serve and protect their troop.

The dwindling population of true alpha males has increasingly placed beta males or alpha females at the heads of Western white gorilla troops. Without the mentoring and social imprinting of a successful older male, young males experience confusion about their roles within a troop and what behaviors and functions are expected of them. Groups of young males are increasingly observed breaking up into subtroops, causing destruction, disorder, and violence– or individual males are wandering off on their own, reducing their chances of encountering a mate, and increasing their risk of isolation, starvation, or predation.

23
For Crying Out Loud

Just when you thought I couldn't sink any lower, I have taken up an obsession with cigarettes. I've been buying expensive European slims and sticking them in a vintage opera cigarette holder I recently bought from a headshop.

"Yeah, that looks good– you'll be like that Audrey-something– like Tiffany, the breakfast lady," the stoned guy behind the counter grinned.

"Yup," I held the thing and stared in the mirror. "I wish I had her neck."

I am sitting on the porch, ruining two and a half hours of primping and preparation by marinating in a cloud of blue cigarette smoke; my own little pocket of air pollution, my big contribution to the world. It's really perfect. I am turning the Mirage Earth Defenders' dirty money into toxic, stinky smoke, like a little fossil-fueled, industrial machine; a smokestack in a red Bob-Dylan-album-cover jumpsuit; a beautiful thing transforming an ugly thing into something even uglier; smoke wafting and swirling out of my flared nostrils… I am the Devil Herself.

Last night I received my biggest Earth-saving check yet; a downpayment for my services, to be rendered today. And you know what I did? Some force I can't explain took over my body, and without thinking I got into my car, filled the tank with premium gas, and drove out of town, up the foothills, down into the valley, to that little phony farm town with the wineries and the smell of smoked meat, and I walked into the steakhouse at quarter to nine on a Thursday, sat in a dark corner, and ordered top shelf scotch and a $148 J. Wayne Ranches grass-finished grade A tomahawk steak, medium rare. The whole place smelled delicious, haunting. I drank fast and wrote nonsense in my notebook. It had been years; at least five years since my mouth tasted anything that once had a heartbeat. I was good and drunk by the time the meal for two came to the table, the table of one– one sad, confused little girl, who feels like she's a little girl, but she's thirty and sprouting crow's feet.

I stared at the little pool of translucent red juice on the plate; the huge lump of garlic butter like a rosemary-flecked glacier, swirling and spilling its entrails atop a caveman-sized piece of seared flesh; the subtle, elegant curvature of the bone that stuck out beyond the skillet and cast a shadow over the golden mountain of mashed potatoes. I cut a slice, carefully, surgically; I held it up to my eyeline. I stared at the striations of the tissue; the magenta raw protein inside; on the outside, the thin stripe of gray amino acids and sugars that had been transformed by an underrated miracle: Man's control of fire. I touched it to my lips and then licked them; tasted the salt and the butter, the ferrous heme and the char, hoping to draw the line, desperate to be repulsed– but it was as though the spirit of a starving prisoner overtook my body, finally freed– and I ate with the vigor of my last meal on this earth. I had mashed potato on my face. I ate an entire loaf of sourdough and a large ramekin full of whipped butter. Silverware, glass, and ceramic clanked and rang from the dark corner of the restaurant and resounded through the dining room. I could feel the eyes of a huddle of staff watching me, impatient to close down the restaurant, but bewildered and fascinated by what they were witnessing.

I took a moment's repose to catch my breath and take another swig of scotch. I assumed I was the last patron in the place, but I overheard a man's voice a couple of booths down– an ugly sound, toadlike and mean, cutting through the low hum of folk instrumentals played overhead. He was uttering a simple word that floated sinisterly through the air, each letter puffed out from hot breath and slowly dissolving, like the caterpillar's vowels from *Alice in Wonderland*: T-O-M-O-R-R-O-W.

"Yes, fine, after tomorrow we can discuss that. If tomorrow goes as planned, then you can make your case. But I want you to understand, the media storm is going to take up most of my time. I won't be readily available for a while after that. You understand? Good, good. Oh yes, I've got them lined up and waiting; this is going national, not a doubt. We'll talk in the morning. My camera people will meet you at your office, please be discreet."

I was still and silent as the cow on my plate; frozen with my fork and knife in hand. I heard the phone hit the table. "What kind of name is Purple, for fuck's sake…"

"What did she want?"

"Oh, some nonsense about closing down some restaurant. The fat bitch is crazy, absolutely nuts. Make sure I only have to deal with the Gloria Steinem lookalike with the glasses from now on."

I was suddenly overcome with the urge to use the restroom. I rose carefully, placing my cloth napkin defensively over my plate and glass to signal to the waiter that if you take this plate you better take me with it, and I inched my way toward the kitchen. I didn't have to be subtle; the pair of men were already buried in their phones again, and wouldn't have noticed if I sat in one of their laps. The face on the right was clearly the source of the croaking voice; the other was unmistakable, illuminated grotesquely by the box of blue light he hovered over. The man from the paper. The most hated man in Mirage County. The current CEO of Kantian Consulting, Cam's betrayer. The one and only, Giles Pion.

I was certain it would have made me ill. I assumed that my body no longer housed the appropriate microbes or enzymes to digest thirty ounces of beef and a quarter pound of butter in a single sitting, and that my evening would potentially–hopefully– end in the hospital; or at the very least, wrapped desperately around the toilet. But no such luck. I woke up perfectly fine. Not even a hangover. Apparently the expensive stuff is worth it.

"Wow, look at you! Why are you so dressed up?" Kevin ambles up the walkway with a stack of mail and his keys. "And since when do you smoke cigarettes? With a baton?" He laughs and waves the smoke away with the pile of envelopes, and wraps me in a big hug. "You look very beautiful, by the way."

"Oh, thank you Kevin– thank you. I am just waiting for Cam to pick me up, and I guess I'm a bit nervous."

"Wait, Cam?"

He looks up to point his ear toward the growl of the Cuda rolling down the street. Cam flings open his door, walks over to open the passenger side, and yanks off his sunglasses like a movie star would. "Get in, gorgeous."

I rise and wave to Kevin before I disappear into the car.

"Why aren't you dressed?" I fuss at the dark circles under my eyes in the mirror.

"Relax, we're making a stop at the garage first."

The garage doors are closed. I enter the door to a sea of boxes, containers, and stacks of loosely sorted items. It's clearly a rushed job; like an earthquake suddenly shook everything off the walls, but in a semi-orderly way. The bed is still set up, and perfectly made.

"You're... moving?"

"Something like that. Got into a dispute with the owner, and I'm not paying him another dime. My luck to get into such a fight at the close of the month. All of this junk is going into storage, just for a few weeks until I find a new palace."

I glance around the wreckage while he changes clothes and fixes his hair. A yellow paper, that has been crumpled and then re-smoothed, is calling out from the chaotic stack on his desk– *EVICTION NOTICE*. But you would never know it. Cam isn't his brooding, aloof, usual self. He is whistling. He's chipper. Today is his big day; the day he has been working for for the last two years. All he has to do is smile, and shake hands, and semantically imply that he's a combat veteran without saying the lie outright; and in his big campaign speech Roger Wilkes is going to announce that Cam will be the best man to lead Mirage County's transition to nuclear power. And when Wilkes gets elected governor, which I suppose to Cam is inevitable, Cam will be reinstated as the head of Kantian Consulting–

at least, that's what he thinks is going to happen today. But just before that speech, the carefully-placed protestors will overtake the soundboard and lights; Cherry Boon will appear onstage, and the torment of the last 730 days of Cam's life will be displayed for all of Mirage County's elites and decision makers. The room will erupt in a chant; Cam will be called a rapist, a predator; a danger and disgrace to all who associate with him— all at the hands of his original betrayer, the man who took his company.

Last night while I sat up late on the toilet, praying futilely to the heathen vegan gods for debilitating, punishing diarrhea, I looked up Pion on my phone. He went to a private high school in Los Angeles and spent most of his career in real estate. I saw many photos of him posing with LA politicians at charity events. He appears to have no background in energy whatsoever; no connection to Mount Mirage, or to Cam.

I pick up Cam's old photo album and start rifling through it. In my periphery I can see him behind stacks of boxes in the mirror, combing back his brassy hair. He is wearing dress blues. I wonder if he is taking his time to avoid coming out and facing me. I look back through the photos of Cam as a boy, when he was still Mac Bauer: at an airshow, posing next to an old plane; bent over a Chrysler engine with George Peterson, "Big G," his motorhead mentor. Photos of him posing next to various cars, laughing, with groups of people holding glasses, his arm around a pretty girl with feathered bangs. Photos of him in a rock band, of him wearing a jean jacket over a white t-shirt; of a group of his friends at a football game. I get to a section that is older-looking and more faded: an old farmhouse, empty land; cows, a group of dirty-looking children. "Cam, who are these Dust Bowl children in your photo album?"

He steps forward in his uniform. He looks into my eyes, hopeful for mercy, and I give him nothing. My skin is on fire; my heart is a war drum. I want to lash out, but I remember Cherry's coming speech, and it soothes the pure hatred I feel, and allows me to remain calm. He gives me a look— recognizable as pain— an acknowledgement that he knows; that he is ashamed. I hold up the photo book. "Are you sponsoring kids in Appalachia or something?"

"Appalachia has mountains, genius." He points to a tall boy in overalls, about twelve and standing up a little straighter than the others. "That one is me."

"I thought you grew up in—"

"My mother won sole custody when I was ten, just to spite my dad. But having me around was a burden; she had re-entered Palmetto society and had no interest in being a mother. So she sent me to a fancy boarding school— you can guess how well that went. So I was sent to Kansas to live with my aunt and uncle. They had nine kids. I actually came to love it. It's where I learned how to properly suffer."

"How come you've never mentioned it before?"

"I hitchhiked back to California right after my eighteenth birthday. In the long run of life, eight years isn't much."

He goes for his shoes and I continue flipping through the album. More cows, kids playing, big outdoor picnic. One boy begins to stand out— pockmarked, pudgy, and always near Cam, but subtly— either behind him or drifting in the background, and looking in his direction. The sour face is unmistakable. It is the toad man from the restaurant.

"Let me make a phone call real quick and then we'll go." Cam walks outside. I stand motionless over the open album, like it's a loaded gun.

"Darlin', this is all gettin' to be too much," Debbie fans herself, "I think I'm gonna faint— and then die…"

"Please do," Felicia says. "That being said, I'm a little lost. So the guy with Pion last night, he is Cam's *cousin*? And Pion is in bed with the Earth Defenders, to demolish his *own* company's chance at controlling the region's power supply? What the fuck is happening?"

I glance outside. Cam is strolling around on the phone, caught up in his conversation, laughing, truly happy for the first time since I've met him. I duck under the small window on the door, and stand before the safe with George Washington's face on it. I try Cam's birthday. Nothing. I stare at George Washington. I try 7-4-76. Nothing.

"Did you know that George Washington was one of the oldest signers of the Declaration of Independence? He was 44; the same age I was when I got

my first multi-million dollar contract with Kantian. Most of the Founding Fathers were in their twenties and thirties, believe it or not. We always think of them as these crusty old men, but they were young, and passionate– full of life, and eager to build something."

44-17-76.

Click.

I peer out the little window. Cam is talking to the landlord. The man is red-faced and angry; Cam is just listening calmly, a grin narrowing his lips.

I open the heavy safe door. Guns, bullets, armor, cash. The shoebox sealed with the cartoon pie sticker. Cherry pie. *CHERRY PIE.*

The box has a handful of old Polaroids, love letters on girly stationery, with sloppy cursive and lipstick kisses, ticket stubs from a Motley Crüe concert, an old gold tube of Revlon lipstick. At the bottom is a faded newspaper article from 1989, "Aspiring Actress Rescued from Riptide by Aspiring Racecar Driver." There is a small square photo of them. Cherry was beautiful, with high-waisted white pants and a faded denim jacket– and he was handsome, with pale skin and shaggy black hair. He wore a black tee that read *Black Knuckle Motors.* They made a handsome couple, iconic, like Tom Cruise and Kelly McGillis in *Top Gun.*

Nineteen-year-old Michael "Mac" Bauer was walking down Venice Beach at dusk and passed a group of young women at the shoreline, who were dancing and giggling with cans of beer in hand. As one of the women waded into the surf, he continued his walk, but recalled nervously glancing behind him, as there was a riptide and few people on the beach on this cloudy evening. He heard a shout, and saw the water disrupt with struggle. He immediately stripped off his jacket and jeans and swam out toward the distressed voice. Cherry Boon, eighteen, had taken in a big gulp of sea water and fainted; Bauer carried her to shore and gave her CPR until she was resuscitated. After saving her life, he asked Cherry, who had recently moved to Los Angeles to become a famous actress and model, if she'd like to get a cup of coffee with him. They've been head-over-heels for each other ever since. "It was like a movie! I came to LA to be in the movies, and then I found myself living in one," Miss Boon said. "He's my hero."

"I didn't know she was an actress," Bauer said, "but that made me feel all the more glad I was there to save her. We need people in this world with big dreams."

～

"Ready?"

My ears are still ringing from the roaring motor and the whipping wind. We stare ahead at the little circle of protestors in the distance, marching around the gated entrance of the ranch, being watched like hawks by police and security.

"Cam, wait. Can you pull this?"

I point to the back of my neck at the zipper. He pulls it down. "Got an itch?" I pull off my sleeves and let the top half of the red jumpsuit fold open over my lap.

"What are you doing? This is not the time to–"

"Let's go to that place you mentioned one time, the place in Palm Springs with the private pool and the massages. Or let's go to Skip's. Let's go somewhere. I don't want to go here."

"Don't be nervous," Cam laughed, "you're going to do great. You have impressed me at every turn. I wouldn't have brought you here if I didn't think so. You're ready."

"Sometimes I feel like you look at me as a project, like a crappy old car that you're rebuilding."

"No, I don't see you as a project. More like... an investment." He rubs the little bear paw stud in my ear. "You are clearly in a transitional phase of your life, and I am happy to be helping you to mature. I can provide you the benefit of my connections, introduce you to the right people and help you move your career and your life forward. But I hope you understand how much more than that you are to me." He takes my hands in his.

Dear god... don't—

"Since that first night at Klipspringer's, you have just caught me. The way you challenge me, and hear me; the pure and open way you look at the world... I never thought I would again, but– I have fallen in love with you, Nina."

I lean back and widen my eyes so the tears won't fall from them. "Then let's get out of here. You don't need any of this. You don't need to prove anything to me. Who cares about some company, wrapped up in all this political mess? With your brilliant mind and your tenacity, there are a million things you can do. Let's go somewhere. I have a bunch of cash– my – my... *uncle* died, and left it to me. I'm buying. Who cares about Kantian?"

Cam withdraws his hands and stares ahead coldly. "Imagine you built a car– not *fixed* a car, not *re*built a car– I mean *built* the thing, piece by piece, painstakingly, every day, for years– choosing every individual part, inspecting it for imperfections, understanding it intimately; understanding exactly what it is meant to do, and where it fits in; spending countless hours and dollars; and it's a mess, for a very long time– and you think, *Jesus*, this is chaos; all these tens of thousands of individual parts, with their own purpose, their own issues; it's never going to meld all together and form something cohesive; it's never going to run, for each part to simultaneously accomplish its own purpose, and yours, all at once– until it all finally comes together, and you're standing outside of it, looking at it– and it's yours; your vision, your diligence and commitment embodied into a physical thing, and then it *runs...*

"And you're in the driver seat, feeling the engine respond to the lightest pressure of your big toe; angling at the slightest movement of your hand on the steering wheel. And it's counting on you, to steer it, to feed it; it begs for the grinding sound of the starter, your hand at the stickshift; it wants to run; it wants you to wax its paint and let it be as proud of itself as you are of it. And then– someone takes it from you, and fills it with cheap ethanol, and drives it on jagged gravel, toward a concrete wall. Wouldn't you run after it?"

He projected his words outwardly, as if to not only me, but to the whole world– including himself.

I sigh and thread my arms back through the stiff red garment. He pulls the zipper up to the base of my neck and kisses me there; I shudder. We roll along a corridor of uniformed men, through the gates, and up the hill.

The farmhouse at J. Wayne Ranch sits about a mile from the freeway. The six hundred acres of pastures are lush from the winter rains; the cows seem to hover up and down the hills, the tall grass hiding their legs. They wander hungrily beside the cliffs with ocean views that you couldn't afford in two lifetimes. The "farmhouse" is a log cabin mansion, with river rock chimneys and the smooth gray lines of clay chinking slithering between two stories of richly stained redwood logs. An enormous American flag dances on the sea breeze from the west side of the home.

The fundraiser is set up by the barn, which has been opened up, emptied of all animals and manures, and manicured into a staging area for the event staff and sound equipment. The barn doors are draped with translucent white curtains, opening up to a stage, tables sprawled beyond it onto the lawn.

On the left side of the periphery are drink and hors d'oeuvres tables; on the other, a pen of Texas longhorn cattle, on display to honor the Mirage County chapter of the Longhorns Club. "I looked up the Longhorns– did you know that they didn't let in women, non-whites, or non-Christians until the '70s?"

Cam hands me a drink. "Yes, God forbid white Christian men have a space for themselves. Imagine if I were to show up to a book club for Latina atheist lesbians and say, 'You know, it's really unfair that you don't include *me*.'"

We stare at the large beasts, the bulls' impressive horns curved like braces.

"Cam, do you believe in god?"

"What? Of course not." He waves and nods at someone by the stage, and extends a bent arm for me to grab so we can saunter in that direction. "I don't have room for magical thinking in my life."

"That's what I've always thought, too."

"Yes, I know. Your cold, rational sensibility is one of your finest attributes. And of course, your ass."

We are sat at Table 1, right in front of the stage, with Wilkes and his wife, who talks like a twenty-year-old at a college football game. She is bragging about how "super cool" it was to go backstage at some concert and "get hammered" with the band.

"So...do you have kids?" I ask, hopeful to get this forty-something woman to act her age.

"Oh yeah, my sons are beautiful– my pride and joy! They're at their friends' houses," she says, winking, "*for the weekend*. Wanna take some shots?"

"No thanks, I've got an empty stomach."

Another pair arrives at the table. "Good afternoon," the woman says. She is composed, elegantly dressed and healthy-looking; clearly comfortable with her mature age, without the need to dress youthfully or cake on makeup. "My name is Marla, and this is Dennis." Dennis nods and pulls out a chair for his wife. He's got an unassuming allure, rooted in looking both manly and responsible– a real Atticus Finch vibe. His beige suit and round glasses fit him well. I find myself blushing, surprised to find this look, the "returns home after a long day at the accounting firm and grabs his pipe, robe, and newspaper" look, to be quite sexy. Mrs. Wilkes rolls her eyes at Marla and gulps her wine.

"Hi, I'm Nina. Are you a big supporter of Roger's campaign?"

"Oh yes, he's been very supportive of our work," she says. "We are the founders of the Mirage Child Protection Alliance. Roger has been working with us to include our message in his campaign platform, and he's kind enough to allow us to speak today."

"What kind of work does your organization do?"

"Well, as I'm sure you know, California is America's laboratory of progressive social engineering. Over the decades this state has become more and more radical in its ideals, and in practice, it has become like a runaway train headed downhill. The home base of these radicals is the school system. It starts with public school and culminates in the universities. And one of their central goals is the dissolution of the American nuclear family."

"Oh, my— and why would they want to do *that*?" I'm playing along, but inside, Felicia and I are laughing. Gotta love a couple of conspiracy theorists; though I'd generally expect them to have greasy hair and wear sweatpants, not perfectly-pressed suits.

Dennis chimes in. "Well, it was explicitly described by socialist intellectuals in the 19th century, and then taken up by American social Marxists in the 1960s. Their premise is that the nuclear family is a form of privatization– and in their worldview, everything should be public– meaning, in practice, under State rule. Where did you first learn things like manners, morals, what is important in life? It started at home, with your parents. They want those things to come from the State. They view the family as a form of enslavement, and call for the 'abolition' of children from their parents. First they were denying it; then they said it was true, but it's a good thing. And now– now if you dare to disagree, you're a scary right-wing 'fascist'."

"To put it lightly!" Marla giggles. "We've been called every terrible name in the book."

"Because it is so expensive to live here, most families in this state have two working parents and rely on the public school system to raise their children. Most parents have no idea what kind of depraved and damaging things their children are being exposed to, from a very young age."

Felicia scoffs. "Oh, you mean like, '*Don't be a racist bully*', or, '*Chris Columbus wasn't exactly a 'nice guy*'?"

I continue my phony curiosity. "So what is it that they are doing in the schools?"

"They are indoctrinating young children into their postmodern ideology from an extremely young age, in which everything is relative, or is a social construct, or is based in an oppressive hierarchy. Concepts like, '*gender is a social construct*,' and '*every white person is innately racist*' are being taught to kindergarteners. They're intentionally creating confusion, guilt, and fixation on things that children have no business worrying about. It is mass theft of innocence."

"Kindergarteners, really? How old are kindergarteners again?"

"Five. By the time parents are finding out, the damage has already been done. Our mission is to expose what is going on in California's schools and empower parents to protect their children."

"Wow," I shake my head. "Seems like an uphill battle in such a blue state."

"It is. But any worthy battle is a difficult one." Dennis pulls out his wallet. In the clear plastic holder sits a photo of him, Marla, and their six children. "I was an only child and grew up around adults– then went to college, then law school– so I never thought about kids. But once I had them, and saw the magic of them– it changed my entire worldview."

The little chocolate-haired brood is smiling, laughing, and looking in different directions at each other. It isn't one of those khaki-wearing, forced photos you see in the homes of families where everything looks perfect, but you can tell they all hate each other. They look genuinely happy.

"They're beautiful. So, if I may ask, why don't you move to another state? A place that aligns more with your values?"

"This is our home," Dennis says. "We could leave, but that would be a form of cowardice, don't you think? Isn't it better to stay and defend the place you love, and the people in it? It's not just our children we are worried about. It's a whole generation, our whole community– our whole country. California leads this madness, but it has seeped into education all over."

"We decided a long time ago to homeschool, so we could stay," Marla says. "More and more families are doing it."

"Of course they do– look at the cross around her neck. What a bunch of wackos," utters Felicia.

"I think they're kinda sweet," says Debbie. "Wholesome and principled. You don't see much'a that these days, feels like." She sighs wistfully.

The spread is decadent country food: brontosaurus ribs and steaks, pasta shells sailing in a sea of bubbly yellow cheese, biscuits and mashed potatoes with deep brown gravy. I am surprised to see all these elegantly dressed people eating like this. I throw a rib onto my plate and dump mac and cheese on top of it. "What are you *doing*?" Cam says, his eyebrows distraught.

"I don't know, these smell good."

Everyone settles into their seats with their plates. The emcee leads with the Pledge of Allegiance; the group stands and turns to the giant flag at the ranch. I place my hand over my heart. I have not done this since the Billy Darling rally; I listen to the words carefully as I say them:

...and to the Republic for which it stands, one nation, under God, indivisible, with liberty and justice for all.

The emcee leads a short prayer, sharing blessings over the abundance of food and joyfulness on this occasion, asking god to protect our country and its service members, the usual. A little girl is brought forward to sing a patriotic song. She is dressed up in a tiny yellow chiffon dress, with a big yellow bow in her hair– she looks like a marshmallow peep. Her parents are glowing as she sings beautifully in a little mouse voice.

I have not been privy to the name of the heiress who is bankrolling today's catastrophe, but now I wonder if she has any connection to Giles Pion or to Cam's evil toady cousin, or if she even exists at all. Maybe it's been these two trolls the whole time, I don't know. What I do know is that the Earth Defenders have a small fleet of "marine research" boats that they often use for social gatherings and fancy donor stewardship, and they will be using them today to infiltrate the ranch from the shore. Handsomely-paid protesters, led by Purple and Cherry Boon, have probably already climbed the cliffs, and are army-crawling through the tall grasses at this very moment, hopeful not to be noticed by the cows.

" –but of course these same environmentalists can't be bothered when it comes to the homeless encampments that have overtaken downtown, who burn trash in the park and leave human waste of all kinds right next to our sewer drains!" The emcee rolls on with his intro, getting lots of laughs and applause. "From my time working for the EPA, I can tell you: there are no real environmentalists in DC, or in any city for that matter. Have you ever looked at a satellite image of a big city? You think the people living in that steaming pile of gray concrete and metal know anything about nature? I'll tell you who the real environmentalists are. The country folk, and the outdoorsmen, like my friend Roger Wilkes here. The farmers, ranchers, hunters, trappers, fishermen. These are the people who have a bona fide connection to the land and the ecosystem. They have a genuine interest in keeping wildlife populations healthy and intact. And most of them live simply, and don't entertain themselves by going to the damn shopping mall every weekend. Sorry, Linda– no offense!"

Mrs. Wilkes smiles and gives him a silly 'oh come on' gesture, flashing the many gaudy rings on her left hand as the audience eats it up, and she returns to her drink. After the emcee butters Wilkes up for another five minutes, he calls up Marla and Dennis to the stage to introduce their organization. They don't read from notes, but you can tell they have thought through their words.

"There are more than 70 million children in the United States, and yet, in today's public discourse, we are increasingly concerned about the needs and desires of America's adults. Our culture has forgotten its children.

"The divorce industry puts the needs and desires of the adults first– not the children who are often forced to live in two homes, endure custody battles in courtrooms, and deal with their parents bringing home strangers.

"We have come to venerate the image of the high-power executive woman, and encouraged generations of young women to put their career ambitions above their families– then we dumped our children into daycare centers and the public education system, leaving our babies to be raised by strangers.

"When we legalized homosexual marriage in 2013 locally– and 2015 nationally, we were thinking only of the rights and desires of the adults who wanted to marry. But what about the children, who are exclusively born to a mother and a father? Can two same-sex parents do the job of two heterosexual parents? In some aspects, sure. But in the most fundamental aspects, no. In just a few short years, we have normalized the commoditization of birth through surrogacy and the selling of gametes.

"Our entertainment is filled with nudity, profanity, and gore. Public spaces are filled with highly suggestive, bordering on pornographic images, because that's what sells to adults. But does any regulator fight for the right of children to retain their innocence?

"Modern culture tells us that children are a financial and social burden, and abortion is the 'compassionate' thing to do if a child will be an 'inconvenience' to his or her parents. Young adults perceive children as a luxury item that they cannot afford; a hindrance to their busy consumerist lifestyles.

"We see these messages and more in our cultural institutions, most obviously in Hollywood and the music industry, but also in fashion, consumer goods, the universities, and the legal system. 'Put yourself first,' is the anthem of our modern society, touted with promises of happiness and personal well-being, meanwhile record numbers of people are taking antidepressant drugs— especially women. When did we cross over? When did we stop putting family first?

"With so many things working against them, it is no wonder that today's children are anxious, isolated, depressed, and confused."

I am distracted by Marla and Dennis's disturbing speech. My first and most prominent thought was shared with my inner Felicia: these people are overzealous schoolmarm types; aggressively Christian, aggressively moralistic squares who will wag their finger at anyone short of Puritan sainthood. But something has jumped out of me, and transported me elsewhere, back to the innocence of my own childhood, in recognition of how different the world was only twenty or thirty years ago— the sweet, sweet Dark Ages, before the internet was in every home and in every pocket, beckoning to us like a metallic siren— demanding our attention, feeding on our focus and ambitions; demanding we watch what it has to show us, the whole world, the good and the absolute worst— and insisting we see it, insisting our innocence be taken from us. All those mother hens that warned about the evils of the internet were right. The same bunch were right about rock-n-roll sixty or so years ago.

"Women are the moral watchdogs of society, and we have abandoned our posts— in exchange for the trappings of wealth and power— only to discover in the end how hollow and empty life is without family," Marla continues.

My mother was my age when I was born. She already had three children, and had been viewing the world through the lens of maternity for seven years. She protected us from the world as every good mother does, a fierce mama bear surrounded by doughy, fuzzy little cubs, willing to face sacrifice, depravation– anything to ensure we were safe and cared for. What responsibility do I have that could even remotely compare to that? Why is it that I think having a dog is too much responsibility and money at thirty years old? Why is it that I've stopped thinking about being a mother altogether? When did it happen? How am I this old, with so little to show for my time on this earth, and yet I have looked down on motherhood as a selling-short of my potential?

I am brought back to reality by a momentary emergence of a copper dot: a beautiful head of red hair in the green grass in the distance, to the left of the stage. My heart surges; I look around. No one else has seen them yet. To my right, the longhorn steers amble around slowly in their pen. Marla and Dennis are in the final part of their speech: *Vote for Roger, support our charity, restore moral order to society.* I feel the human warmth of Cam's hand. He squeezes mine; his palms are sweaty with joyous nerves. He is ready. I am not.

"My foot is asleep, I'm just going to go stand in the back," I whisper in his ear.

"Take a video of Roger's speech on your phone, will you? The angle will be better from back there." He squeezes my hand again, and raises it to his lips.

"Sure thing. Good luck, Cam."

I walk past the food table and grab a cold slice of watermelon. I stand behind the rows of tables, leaning on the longhorns' gate, holding the watermelon rind to my forehead. It is cool and forgiving. I see Purple. They are here. Someone is letting them into the back of the barn.

*What do I do? Felicia, Debbie…*someone? *John? What do I do? Who am I? Am I three people? Am I a hundred different women sloppily melted into one, like a candle made out of old crayons? Or not even a person at all?*

And then it hits me; an answer so perfectly obvious, so poetic in its delicious, decisive irony, that I officially decide that God is real, and He's got one hell of a sense of humor. I look up to the sky and give him a nod, take a refreshing bite of watermelon, and let the juice run down the sides of my mouth as I get to work.

24
Villain II

I have been searching everywhere for the villain of my story. Is it Cam? Is it John? Is it Roger Wilkes, Giles Pion, the Toad man? Is it Skip Vodnyyvor and his natural resource mogul friends? Is it all the One Percenters, the Boomers? Is it America, my father, God? Is it all white men collectively, all men collectively, all white people collectively? Is it Western civilization, the wave of conquests over thousands of years that have colonized the world and remade it in the image of modernity?

I keep searching, wandering down roads that go nowhere; sprinting at first, and then slowing to a trot so I can glance around, and then meandering until I find myself at a dead end.

As soon as I have a lead on a good villain, I find a secret window, or trap door– I peek inside and find a whole other world, one that I couldn't have seen coming, a whole other story that insults my belief in my own creativity: devastating scenes of terrified children ducking in corners, of young faces nodding to bad advice, of men working sixteen hour days, shiny with determined sweat. I find misguided intentions, betrayals, hollow promises; games with scribbled out rulebooks and rigged decks; I see worlds upside-down, and sideways– versions of reality that make me question everything I know, that make me think the social conditioning I have been whining about for years is actually a funhouse mirror, showing me a version of myself that is far smaller than I am, in a world warped and misshapen; and the whole storyboard is a reflection, and is exactly backwards.

I'm just looking for someone I can oppose; someone I can blame for the things that have gone wrong for the hero of my story. But the hero's face, too, becomes continually blurrier. What if there is no villain? Is there, then, no hero?

Our humanity rejects the possibility of such a scenario. We are a species of stories; stories are the bricks by which we have built our entire civilization, our entire identity as human beings. Stories need heroes, and especially need villains. Someone must be blamed. Someone must fall so someone else can rise.

With each dead end I encounter, it is becoming increasingly harder to ignore the very real possibility that the villain is me.

25
Flat II

I wonder if "Girl Releases Longhorn Cattle Into Fancy Political Event" will get as many hits on YouTube as "Escaped Elephants Trash Zoo Garden Party" before it gets taken down. It's a shame, really– so many people are trying so hard to get famous on the internet, and I just keep wandering into these things.

… Kidding. I see that it's my fault. I see that now. Hindsight equals 20/20– got it. So it's time to go.

That's all I know, for right now. *It is time to go.* I want out of this town, for real this time. It's been pretty and all, but Paradise is filled with poisonous flowers. Cam was right: I never belonged here in the first place, and I'd have been better off chasing something real, instead of airbrushed photos of palm trees and surfers and margaritas. I'll figure out the details later– the where, the packing, everything– a little later. For now, I am tired. I'm just going to grab my go-bag and see if I can stay with Paula until this thing blows over. Then I'll go. Because this is what I do. I run. I make a mess, then run.

I'm relieved to find Kevin's house empty. No explaining; I'm clear for now. One last thing– I open up my laptop and log into the Earth Defenders' e-newsletter software. The keys rhythmically fold beneath my fingers, and I crank out the best damn piece of writing I've maybe ever done. I attach the photos I took on my phone of Cherry's poetic love letters to Cam, and the newspaper article, and I casually add that Giles

Pion and a media mogul have been working with MMED's leadership to influence both the election and the fate of the power plant. This might be my favorite part:

> *You are subscribed to the Mount Mirage Earth Defenders' newsletter because presumably, like me, you care deeply about their mission to defend the natural environment from human greed, corruption, and pollution. It has always been my belief that no cause can be more noble than this— for what good is an economy, a society, the arts or culture, without clean air or water, or healthy soil to grow our food? What good is anything that humanity has built without the natural buttress on which we all stand?*

> *It has always been the greatest of human endeavors to allow our descendents access to a better life and world than we have had. With a cause as righteous as this, it is no wonder that the Mount Mirage Earth Defenders brought in over $20 million in fundraising last year alone.*

> *As you know, their latest focus has been the prevention of the Invisible Hand Power Plant's transition to nuclear power. In a recent newsletter, our Executive Director was quoted as saying, "This is an existential fight for our community's safety and the sovereignty of the Indigenous lands on which this monstrosity will be built."*

> *In last Earth Day's newsletter she was also quoted, saying "The immediate transition to a carbon-free economy is an existential fight for our community's safety and the sovereignty of the Indigenous lands on which our society has been built."*

> *While nuclear power has no shortage of cons, it is an unquestionably carbon-free source of energy. The United States already operates close to 100 nuclear reactors, the most of any nation on the planet. Together they have a capacity of nearly 100,000 megawatts, or about 20% of the electricity generation in the country. If carbon is an existential threat to our community and way of life, as our Executive Director has claimed, wouldn't this benefit of nuclear energy, at least in the short-term, outweigh the risks?*

Three groups of MMU graduate students partnered with the Earth Defenders in 2015 to complete a lifecycle analysis of three proposed renewable energy projects: wind turbines off the coast, a series of ground-mounted solar arrays and battery storage centers to power all county municipal buildings, and transitioning all county vehicles, including police, fire, and public transportation, to electric vehicles.

A lifecycle analysis accounts for the full environmental impact of a product or activity, from start to finish— from the harvesting of the raw materials needed to build it, to manufacturing, transportation and installation, to lifetime use and then disposal. Each student group focused on the net carbon cost of each of these initiatives as their graduate project, and they found that not only would two out of three of these initiatives be significantly net carbon-positive— meaning, they would put more carbon into the atmosphere than they would save— but they would also be extremely costly for the county's taxpayers, and cause energy prices to rise by as much as 42% in ten years.

The grad students were thrown under the electric bus, so to speak, at their thesis defense presentations, by their own mentors and professors who provided them the tools and methods to complete the analysis, and the study results were quickly covered up and forgotten. The Earth Defenders moved forward with influencing Mirage County to approve all three projects, citing new projections and colorful charts that boast a carbon-neutral city by 2030.

A similar life-cycle assessment was submitted to the County by Kantian Consulting for the installation of two nuclear reactors, which cited a report from the United Nations' Intergovernmental Panel on Climate Change that reported nuclear's average life cycle emissions are similar to wind energy, and significantly less than solar photovoltaics. The economic cost, while steep upfront, would cheapen the cost of energy over the reactors' 40 plus years of operation.

So again, wouldn't the immediate benefits of carbon-free nuclear energy be worthy of the up-front costs, if we are in a desperate race against time to prevent global carbon emissions from raising global temperatures even a single degree celsius? At the very least, wouldn't it be worth considering?

It only takes a few minutes of Googling the MMED Board of Trustees and reviewing the organization's public financial records to see that even the most wholesome of causes can be disfigured.

You see, a whopping six members of the MMED Trustees are major shareholders in the renewable energy companies that have been promised contracts by these projects. Four members of the organization's leadership team are relatives, spouses, or otherwise connected to the consultants, contractors, and County bureaucrats who are pushing these projects forward.

And let us not naively overlook the greater reality of this fight: the victor will wield influence on the power supply of the region for decades to come.

We often see nonprofit charities as exactly that– grassroots, mission-driven, and money-disinterested entities that work outside the rules of capitalism and corporate greed. But our rosy lenses fool us; the Earth Defenders have just as big an interest in power and money as any other corporation or governmental body.

I wish it weren't true, and my heart is broken, as I am sure yours may be to hear this whistle blown. But I take comfort in the reminder that we are all inescapably corruptible beings. We are just human, after all: primates with big brains and busy fingers, and insatiable arrogance. No matter where I look, the same rule applies: When any entity becomes too large and powerful, and therefore becomes too centralized, it corrupts its purpose.

-Siren's Revenge (she/her/blueself)

I got some clothes packed, my water bottle, computer, and of course, my box of screenplay notes. I am in the bathroom collecting toiletries, imagining myself throwing the *Gasoline* box into the glowing cauldron of a volcano, to lift the curse on myself and finally be free, when I hear the front door open. I hope it's Dale; I could see the upset in Kevin's face as I left this morning. I assumed he knew I was seeing Cam. But I don't have the mental energy to discuss it right now.

I pop onto the bed for a moment and close my eyes, but I keep seeing Cam's face... the hope he had in his eyes right before the purple and orange heads of hair emerged from the grass. I grab my phone and flip greedily through the cottagecore hashtag on Instagram. I want to wear white flowing cotton dresses and straw sun hats with big cream ribbons; I want to pick wildflowers and stick cherry tomatoes and sprigs of rosemary into soft bubbly focaccia dough; I want to drift along a lazy creek in a wooden rowboat followed by a trail of yellow ducklings, and snuggle up by a fire in a log cabin with my husband. I want Mary Sucre's life; I want a Tom who loves me, and all the simple, wholesome, *real* things. I just want the real things. And Felicia be damned, I do want a husband. A husband...

"Well hello there, sleepyhead," Kevin leans against the doorway. I scramble out of bed.

"Hey, I was just– packing– to stay at a friend's for a couple days."

"A friend's, huh? You mean your man?" He steps toward me. I smell tequila and lime on his breath. His face is changed.

"He's not my–"

"It's okay, this is my fault. I should have made myself clear. My intentions." His words slur. "Cam's not my friend anymore. And I'm not your friend."

"What? Kevin, of course you are–" I go to touch his arm. He grabs my shoulders.

"You need a man, like me– I just need to show– I am the man you want...and it's okay–"

He grips me and pushes me against the wall, yanks my head back by my hair. He whispers, "*I know exactly what you like.*" He covers my mouth in a wide open, tonguey kiss, sour and fermented. The back of my head is ringing from hitting the wall; I am stunned like a fish that has been slammed against the ground. He squeezes my cheeks in one hand and brusquely slaps me across the face, grips at my breasts and presses himself to me. I finally get a handle on myself, and shove him away with the full force of my body. Tears swell in my eyes, and I back away from him slowly.

"Kevin, *please…*"

His face immediately changes again, back to someone I recognize; he is frightened. "Oh God– Nina, I– I just thought– I thought maybe you wanted me to– I overheard, on the speaker–"

The speaker? Overheard? And suddenly it dawns on me: that night with the brownies, the night we had talked about children and marriage, and I was listening to music on the speakers– and then I watched porn to calm my nerves… *Oh dear God…*

I grabbed my bag and flew out the door.

I'm very good at this. My heart beats its fists against the cage of my ribs and the sweat seeps out my pores, but I tell myself the familiar consolation: *That's the body talking, not the mind.* The sweat cools my forehead and lower back; the racing heart pumps strawberry blood through me. No need to panic or hesitate; I know exactly what needs to be done and in what order. This isn't the first time I've had to leave in a hurry, and each time it happens I assure myself this time will be the last.

My bag is spotted with raindrops as I load up the car. It really starts coming down as I pull out of the driveway. The storm is moving in from the northeast, making for an ominous but beautiful sunset. I catch its best moment as I head up Camus Pass. I look over the burnt remains of the preserve's edges in the last light of day, and blow it a solemn kiss goodbye.

I grip the wheel tightly as I speed around the pass's slicked turns. My heart is still racing, filling my body with energy to push harder, move faster, though my mind considers the coming exhaustion, when the adrenaline subsides.

I consider the options. Paula was the first that came to mind. But I can't picture myself entering her home and disrupting her busy, meaningful life. I know she wouldn't see it that way, and I bet she'd be mad at me for *not* coming. But I can't bring myself to face her, to have to explain to her what's happened and what I have been doing the last six months. I picture her warm face, her beautiful garden, the narrow path that leads through the trees to the raised beds of Tuscan kale stalks, sunburst tomatoes, and little orange squash blossoms. I picture the sunlit kitchen with the splatters of green house plants throughout the shelves and countertops, the cinnamon brown of her two dogs resting in a sunbeam, the smell of incense in the foyer colliding with the smell of peach cobbler in the oven. How could I explain? I feel undeserving of her space, like I would ruin it: an affected bull trampling through the peacefulness she curated. I can't do it. I want out of town.

As I come around a sharp hatchback curve, I swerve to avoid a chunk of rock that has fallen from the cliffside into the road. She's a jagged and sharp mother who birthed little children that scattered across both lanes. It is instant– a harsh popping sound like the first kernel in the microwave; I am lucky not to blow through the rail and fly off the edge. I make it around the bend and nestle my car as close to the crumbly cliffside as I can get.

I sit for a while and stare forward at the darkening empty road ahead. Felicia pounds a single fist against her chest, hard, and I feel it in my own, and she summons my courage. "You know the steps, you are strong, you are capable, you are independent, and you are going to change this tire."

I flip on my hazard lights. The rain is coming down hard. I grab the jack and the lug wrench from the trunk. I successfully loosen the five nuts, working back and forth in a star pattern for balance, just as Cam taught me. I manually jack up the car. I remove the tire. Thunder booms and I hold the damn thing over my head, shaking underneath it, shrieking some kind of pathetic feminist war cry.

But guess what? Trunk's empty. I don't have a spare this time. Cam told me to get one, lectured me and reminded me for months, and I didn't do it.

I toss the tire into the impenetrable orange wall of the cliff; I immediately cower as more rubble tumbles down into the road. I return to the driver's seat to gather my thoughts. The phone rings. My mother.

"Hey Honey, just checkin' on you. It's been a while since we heard from you; did you get the card we sent you for your birthday?"

"I… I did, yeah. Thanks Mom. How's everyone doing over there?"

"Oh we're doing fine, holidays were a bit quiet this year. Diane went on a family cruise and Denise took the opportunity to spend Christmas with Hugh's family out in Indiana. She can't stand those inlaws but now she's crossed it off the list for a couple years. Did you and Tyler have a nice Christmas? Does his family celebrate Christmas?"

Oh right– I haven't told her that he dumped me. Guess it has been a while since we spoke. I exit the car and begin pacing in the rain. Only now have I realized that in my rush to leave, I didn't put on shoes. "Oh yes– Tyler and his family traveled to visit relatives too, but I decided to stay home. I– actually, I volunteered at a soup kitchen. One homeless man brought his old dog, and we made a special bowl for him. A retriever mix, I think. It was really nice."

"A retriever! That's so sweet, you're such a good egg, dear. And how's it going with Tyler? You've been together for such a long time."

"Actually, I think he asked his grandmother for her engagement ring while he was visiting. Should be any day now…"

"You're kidding! Well I'm so glad you called then! We'll have to get ready to celebrate! Oh look– your father just got home. Harry! Come say hi to your daughter."

"Oh, it's alright Mom– I know he–"

"Hey– hey there, Nina." My father's voice sounds weary, strained from a long day at work.

"Hey Dad, how are you?"

"I was just going to ask you the same thing. How's the Golden State?"

"Oh, it's golden alright– I'm actually doing really great." I stand in a bed of gravel on the side of the road. I wiggle my toes and twist my weight back and forth, digging my feet into the ground. I can feel the sting of dirty gravel sink into open flesh; I pull one foot out to see how the color of the blood is mixing with the soup of rainwater and orangey, ferrous rock. The color is pleasing, but is quickly washed away with the pouring rain. I dig my foot back in, pushing deeper, leaning into the sting. "I finally got hired at that place I'd been interning."

"Hired, and paid?"

"Yep, *paid.* I'm an ocean correspondent now. Writing about all kinds of ocean issues. Actually, I'm working on a piece to share the insights of local fishermen to protect the coast's fish stocks. Should be really interesting."

"Wow, sounds like the break you've been waiting for. I'm sure you'll do right by those fishermen, and the fish too. You know I'm proud of you, no matter what you do."

"I know Dad. I– I really miss you."

"Miss you too, kiddo."

PART FOUR

THE SPRING

26
Knoights in Shining Armor

The low rumbling of the engines is soothing. I stare at the little round window, not out at the moving landscape behind it, but at the hundreds of pencil-thin scratches on the clear plastic. *How did they get there? Did a tiny creature try to claw its way out?*

I readjust my focus out the window at the blurring shrubs as we pick up speed. I adore the sensation; I feel it drop from my throat to my stomach, down into my womb, and it arouses me. I think of the similar roar of the Cuda blasting down the highway. As the plane lifts into the air, I inhale deeply and feel sweet relief, the same exhale as submerging beneath the water's surface in my old scuba gear.

The THC lozenge I swallowed at the security gate is kicking in just in time, and I feel entranced by the vibrating rhythms of the plane and the music in my headphones. I am listening to a playlist that I compiled from endless hours of listening to Captain Don's boombox on the *Siren's Revenge*. In his true fashion, the man did not use a smartphone, or even an old-fashioned iPod, and exclusively listened to CDs. I close my eyes and drift off to the tune of "Southern Cross" by Crosby, Stills and Nash, as the journey will be long...

I stir at a large bump of turbulence. I must have been out for a long time; I feel a full night's sleep has passed. The bumps grow deeper; the passengers gasp and remove their headphones. I grip the arm rests and close my eyes…

"I need you to decide for me."

There is a dark brown line below my collar bone, dividing my muddy and bleeding body from my dry shoulders and head. My lower half is soaked to the bone. The tropical cyclone that brought down the plane did not get as far as the porch I stand on. In fact, the house is completely dry, and the sun is out.

Unfazed by my gruesome appearance, he smiles as if he expected me. "Hello, my pretty li'l star." He has the smirk of a general who is about to hear his enemy's surrender speech. "Go 'round back and I'll hose you off."

I stand in John's backyard in a musty gray bathrobe. He lights a cigarette as he cozies himself into his ripped lawn chair. "I have been waiting a very long *toime* for this. I'd hoped it would be before you turned thirty. You're a touch late. Would you care to *siddown*?"

"I'd rather stand."

"So let's hear it, li'l missa," he puffs languidly and glances over his dead lawn and drooping ferns. The sun is warm, blaring. "What am I deciding for you this time?"

I attempt to steady my body as I speak, so as to not collapse under the exhaustion of my journey across the Pacific, and the physical battering of wading through the flood waters, and the sheer weight of my own words. "I have been lying to you, to myself, to everyone, for years. I am lost John, and I am tired– I cannot wander any longer. I am too lost to decide what is best for me, and I need you to do it. I need the heart taken out of the decision, but I am unable to do so. I need sharp, icy truth, but I am too warm.

"I think you know how much I hate you. So much pain and anguish you have put me through– the gutless humiliation, the flippant disrespect, the unearned contempt. The world's widest, deepest ocean and the better part of a decade sits between us. And *still*, you claw your way into my dreams. *Still*, you bludgeon my peace! And I am tired.

"I am tired of pretending not to want you; I'm sick of pretending to be sickened by you– even though I know I should be. I am sickened by my instincts, the instincts that brought me here..."

His smile spreads further across his cheeks.

"I am, I'm sickened by you! I'm sickened by everyone– the whole world. We are so arrogant, thinking we've transcended the brutality of our nature by the might of our intellect and the breadth of our compassion. We dare to think we are ready for other planets? We are *barbarians*!

"And you... you are good at this world. You are a beast among lesser beasts, using not only your brute strength, but your intellect as the sharpest tool of your brutality. I know this, and I despise it with all my being. But it doesn't make me want you any less. My desire for you is a betrayal of myself; it is equal parts visceral and cruel. My blood wants you; my muscle tissues ache for you; but in all my confusion and wandering, my brain and heart are aligned in this one thing: my hatred of you."

John gently nods in approval, leans back and blows a delicate string of smoke into the air. A man has never been so relaxed. The metal frame of the chair cradles his body, creaking as he moves. I close my eyes so I can focus.

"I just want to say it, I just want to say it out loud. I pretend to be brave and strong, but I'm not. I'm afraid. I am scared and I don't know what I'm doing.

"They told us when we were girls that we are *mighty*, that we are the best and the most and we can do *anything* if we want to. *Mighty*. Mighty and beautiful. Mighty and kind. But those things don't go together in this world. How could they possibly? How can we be everything at once? Why *must we* be everything at once?"

John crushes the butt of his cigarette into the parched ground. He sighs and stretches his arms before him, as a man does on a Monday morning before a long day's work. He grabs me with no mercy, throws my body over his shoulder like a sack of grain, and as he ambles into the house, the ferns begin shaking... the ground begins shaking... the whole earth is shaking...

"Nina! Moonie, are you alright? Yuck, you're covered in sweat." Tyler lurches backward as I gasp for air and shoot up as if a rubber band holding me down has snapped.

"The whole earth was shaking…"

"Yeah, there was a little tremble. No big deal, not the big earthquake."

I look around to absorb the reality of where I am, and to shake off the reality my dreaming mind had created. *It felt so real.* It always does.

Tyler coaxes my top half back down onto the bed and strokes my hair. "You were really thrashing that time. Here, have some water. Do you want to talk about it?"

"No, I don't want to dwell on it– and I don't think you'd want to hear it. Can we do something nice this morning? Make strawberry pancakes?"

"You get the pancakes started, I'm going to start packing up. Let's get out of the city today. I just found this hike about an hour from here that ends with a waterfall and a nice swimming hole. Sounds good?"

"But I have–"

"It's Sunday. Give yourself a day of rest before you hit the pavement again tomorrow. You'll find something soon. There is plenty of work around here. And while you get things sorted out, you're welcome to stay as long as you like."

~

June 2020

I come in from watering the plants with a basket full of greens and two little stripes of mud across my cheeks. Playing in the garden makes me feel like a child again in all the best ways. An evening thunderstorm made everything more vivid this morning: the damp smell in the air, the bright green of youthful leaves and shoots against the deep black compost, the earthen scents and textures. I'm in a good mood. To make the most of my dirty smock I decide to do some painting before my night shift.

Tyler has set up a little art station in the corner for me, but lately he's made it his own. He's taking an online botany class to pass the time during the lockdowns, and he's been creating Darwinian sketches of native plants as a tool for memorizing their names and unique features: this one has four leaves, this one has purple blossoms, this one likes sandy soil– you get the idea. He works in the city during the day, and sits in the art corner with his microscope and plant snippings in the evenings. I can tell the nearly empty office is a tough place for him, with its maze of gray cubicles and masked faces breathing filtered air, but he never complains about it. He carries himself with a different air about him these days. It is surprisingly calm, and even has a whiff of confidence in it, despite the anxious circumstances.

I didn't intend to stay. I just kept on driving up Cliffside 84 until I hit the interstate, and once I started seeing exit signs for downtown I realized that I didn't even know where Tyler lived; I had to pull over and call for his new address.

"You live *here?*" I stared at the satellite image of his house, and pinched my fingers over the screen to zoom out over the tight grid of urban sprawl around the little orange pin. "I can't believe you live here. I don't see a patch of green anywhere!"

"Tell me about it," Tyler sighed.

I paused at his front door for a long breath. Before I could knock, he opened it with a tinfoil-wrapped burrito in his hand. "You must be hungry."

I didn't explain where I had been, or why I was in my current state of dried cheek-mascara, stringy hair and bloody bare feet. He was kind enough not to ask. I showed up by instinct and with no plan. Then the world shut down. There are two rumors: either someone eight thousand miles away leaked it from a lab, or ate a bat. Don't ask me which is true; I bet we will never know.

We watch the news constantly, waiting for updates, anxious for answers. It's been a dystopian remake of being a child and watching a blizzard hit town, canceling school and ballet class, making everyone frantically stock up on milk and bread, batteries and toilet paper. Like many things that have happened in the last few years, we were shocked while we first watched it unfold, but not surprised it was happening. "What did people think was gonna happen?" Piper posted a video of herself on the MMED's Instagram. "This is just the beginning. How many ways does Mother Nature need to tell us that we are pushing her too far? When are people gonna wake up? We need you to chip in to our Emergency Climate Awareness Fund–"

I told Tyler I ought to go, but when he questioned me about my destination, he insisted I stay. I am so glad he did. I'm impressed with what he's done with his new place. It's old and drafty, but he has tons of windows and a little patch of yard that he's transforming into an edenic food garden.

I made it two weeks at home. After so many years of hustling multiple jobs, I always dreamed of a time like this– a time to slow down, relax, and finally have the mental space to be creative. But I became an expert at wasting time, somehow unrelaxed but also accomplishing nothing. I couldn't bear to write, and I couldn't sit still. I had to do *something*, but I also felt incapable of real work. I was petrified of putting my resume out there; I'm fairly certain the Earth Defenders have placed me on some journalistic blacklist, if not a warrant for my arrest. It's felt like a steep fall from the top, so I thought perhaps it'd be best to start over from the very bottom.

McDonald's is a place I can go and not have to think. Everything is so automated that working there can feel like entering a video game: light-up buttons, beeping timers, color-coded wrappers and boxes, and hurried, faceless customers. It's a great place to sort out my mind for a healthy thirteen bucks an hour.

Right as I drop the watering can on the back porch, eager to settle into the cozy art corner for an hour or so, I turn abruptly at the sound of the front door closing.

"Nina, *what ah you wearing*? And what's on your face? Were you playing cowboys and Indians?"

John leans back casually against the closed door. I scramble to wipe the dirt off my face. "Don't. Leave it. I *loike* role play. You can be my

Princess Tiger Lily. I guess that makes me Cap'n Hook. I remember you got a thing for boat captains."

Words won't come. The adrenaline pulses and squeezes my jaw. I scan the room for something I can use as a weapon.

"Wow, not even able to *mustah* up some preaching about abbo genocide? I see what you're doing li'l star, and you can chill out. There's really no need to feel *alahmed*. I was just in the neighborhood, an' came here to check on ya."

He moves to the couch and makes himself comfortable. "This is a decent place here, hay. But I know it's not yours. I know you're back with pussy California boy."

"His name—"

"Come now, miss. *Siddown*. Let's catch up. I need to know how you are doing. Things are getting wild in this silly country of yours. Your empire is falling, you know."

I don't move from my place. "Of course I know. It's getting bad, but it will get better, and—"

John throws up his arms and makes his way toward the kitchen. "I'm going to need a drink to get meself through this conversation." He helps himself to the fridge. "*Ya* want anything to whet your whistle before the inevitable kissing begins? I hope your breath is fresher than that outfit."

"I don't think that's funny. And no, I don't want anything. I have to leave for work soon, so please don't make yourself comfortable."

"Well that's great to hear li'l miss. Did you get a job at a local newspaper or magazine?"

"No, I'm—"

"Are you working for one of them annoying animal *roights* groups you love so much?"

"No I'm… working on… a study."

"A study, *hay*? How studious. Tell me about this study."

"Well, it's complex, but— I am studying the dynamics of convenience culture and workforce economics in the food system."

"Oh, that sounds very interesting. And where are you conducting this study? At the local university?"

"No. It's more of an independent study."

"I see. So where will you be headed soon? A laboratory? A library?"

"I'm– it's at…McDonald's."

"MACCAS!" John's body shakes with laughter. He runs his hands over his face and smoothes back his hair. "Fucking *Maccas* Nina! *Ah* you joking?"

"I know it sounds crazy, but I've had a rough few–"

"I don't want to hear it cunt, I really don't. This is perfect actually. I was hoping I wouldn't be taking you away from something important. But here I am straight up *rescuing you*. Workin' at Macca's, living with a pussy. I'm disappointed in you, ay, I really am."

I catch myself about to apologize. *What the hell? Alright, he is good.*

"Wait, what do you mean, 'taking me away'?" It's my turn to laugh at him now. "You've come to kidnap me, have you?" As I say it out loud my own laughter takes off. "What a truly *you* thing to do, John. I believe abduction is your final square on Red Flag bingo." I guess it's the adrenaline. I feel brave. "If you think I'm going anywhere with you willingly, you have lost your mind. I'd rather be at the drive-through window in my 'I'm Lovin' It' hat and a Covid face shield than in a palace with you."

"Obviously you're going to say that. Because every *styupid* movie you've watched has told you to play *hahd* to get. But this really is for your own good. America's broken into riots and is very possibly going to erupt into civil war soon– if not over the *summah*, almost certainly *aftah* the election. I need you to just shut up and trust me this time. You clearly have no safety net. I can't trust the li'l fella who spen's his time doodling flowers to protect ya."

"How is being here alone any less safe than being with you? Besides, it's my civic duty to stay. People need me. The Resistance needs me."

John cracks open a beer and takes a half-can sip. "Oh *yeh*, my brave li'l revolutionary, in your child's art smock. This is a much more important *mattah* than any silly political fantasy you have in your head. I have traveled across the globe with purpose. We are going on our trip."

"Our trip?"

368

"Yes idiot, *our* trip. Jus' like I promised at our waterfall. You think I'd just forget? I've been settin' cash aside for this for years. I'm a man of me word, and here I am, your *knoight* in shining *ahrmah*, ready to slay the tofu-eating pussy dragon and whisk you away to paradise."

He finishes the can with his second sip, and crushes it in his hands while eyeing a painting on the wall. "An' pack *loightly* 'cause I already got a lotta stuff in the car. Oi, you still got that black bikini with the–"

"ARE YOU MAD? *I am not going anywhere with you!* Have you forgotten there is a global pandemic going on? How did you even get here?"

"You know the rules don't apply to me. An' I've thought everythin' out, trust me. Now I suggest you pack before *Mistah* Plants returns home, for his sake."

"Is that a threat?" I edge my way toward the kitchen counter, and as I grab my phone, John snickers.

"Classic white woman, talkin' shit about the cops one minute, ready to cry wolf to 'em the next. Before you dial 911 my little girl, lemme just add a li'l something more to my offer."

John pulls a folded envelope from his pocket and tosses it on the counter before helping himself to another beer. I immediately redden with insult, assuming the envelope holds cash, as if I am available for rental.

But the indignant blush in my cheeks drains to white as I unfold the printout from the *Palmetto Press*, of Cam and I kissing in front of the Cuda at the Palmetto Hills Car Show.

27
Sully's Farm

Christmas Day, 2011

A heavy stream of sweat rolled down the centerline of my spine; I crushed it against the seat before it reached its southern destination. More was coming out of all parts of me. I had forgotten just how hot and humid it would be in Australia's wet, summery Christmas season. In this strange place, north is warm and south is cold, winter is summer, up is down.

I woke up on Christmas morning 38,000 feet in the air, with a festive bag of chocolate-dipped biscuits from the flight crew sitting in my lap. The flight itself was my sole Christmas present, to and from myself– and included my birthday, the rest of the year's holidays, and my graduation present– if I could make it out of college alive. After this long holiday break with John, I had just one semester to go. But things weren't going so hot at home. I secretly resolved to cancel my return flight if the visit went well.

I had royally botched the processing of Don's coral preserve data. No matter how many video tutorials I watched, the data created graphs that made no logical sense, or worse, actively worked against our case. Either something had gone wrong in the way we collected information, or we had chosen the wrong information to collect, or there were variables we did not account for. I couldn't make sense of any of it.

There was only one truly complete dataset that showed a higher concentration of mature parrotfish in certain coral zones. The problem was that the parrotfish seemed to be thriving in older bleached areas that had not recovered but were overgrown with algae, their main food source. I didn't know how to report this information—or lack thereof— back to Captain Don, knowing how important the project was to him, and how hard he was working to protect the reefs and rebuild the fishery community he loved.

One late night while eating cold falafel in the marine science lab it dawned on me that all I needed to do was edit the spreadsheets directly— just a few clicks and taps to add fresh numbers to the rectangular cells— to create the exact graph Don would need. I tinkered and spaced things apart; I included outliers to make it look legit. And as the sun rose over the saltwater tank of dopey hopping tangs, I sent Don a perfectly curated set of data.

The guilt ate me alive— quite literally, as I was regularly vomiting up blood with an uncured ulcer. He gave me a passing grade for the internship and wrote me a glowing review letter, which made me feel even worse. At home I was taking more courses about the demise of other ecosystems, the collapse of other fisheries, and the United Nations' laundry list of urgent global problems, all of which would come to a head between 10 and 30 years from graduation. I was overwhelmed by the bleakness of it, and chose to distract myself with an all-encompassing obsession with the man I both revered and despised.

At the end of that semester at Courtship Hall, when he drove me to the airport and all the social pressure was off us, the animus melted away and we were two lovesick pups clinging to each other desperately, whispering promises of devotion and eternity. After stepping back onto American soil I focused intently on one single task: saving enough cash for a ticket back. I worked any shift I could get my hands on, more than eager to skip classes full of long-winded lectures delivering more bad news. Nighttime sleep was traded for video calls with John and between-shift naps in my car. Meals were traded for granola bars, coffee, beer, and half-eaten scraps swiped from the kitchen at the restaurant. My stomach ulcer raged and further prevented eating and sleeping. Pot was the elixir that glossed over everything and made life tolerable. I reached for the bubbler before breakfast.

"Nu, what the *fahck*? I waited around for you."

"I'm sorry, I picked up a double shift."

"Oi you look *loike* shit. Look'it under *yer* eyes. You're workin' too much."

"You know I've got bills. Aren't you mister rich? Why can't you just buy me a ticket?"

"I will love… I will reimburse ya as soon as you get here. Sully's raisin' me honest. All my wealth is locked into a trust until I'm 25, so I've gotta earn my own way for now. It's better that way anyhow.

"Then in a few years I'll get the seed money for me first business an' it's all uphill from there. China's eatin' up Aussie coal like you wouldn' believe *roight* now. My mates are bringin' in big cash from the mines an' living like kings. I'm gonna open my own camp to start, an' make some good investments, and you'll see. I'm gonna build an empire. An' then I'm gonna treat you like the princess you are."

We spent six excruciating months 10,000 miles apart and managed to speak every day. I'd keep my laptop next to my pillow to call him as soon as I woke up in the morning so I could wish him goodnight. I would stay up past three to chat with him after his economics class. We laughed, discussed, argued, and took off our clothes. We pronounced over and over again what we would do when we finally reunited.

But the moment of reunion outside the tiny rural airport was no slow-motion movie scene. It was more like a scene from a middle school dance: hesitant, sweet, *awkward*.

"*Fahk*, I shoulda brought on flowers, *hay*."

Yes. I thought there would be roses, and music playing, and a big crowd of onlookers– in my mind John was going to scoop me up and kiss me like that poster of the sailor kissing the nurse. But John approached me slowly, and for the first time ever, seemed ever-so-slightly unsure of himself. I was disappointed. But looking back now I can see how much better that was.

He became more himself once we were in his truck, and we fell back into our old dynamic again. "Gonna be a long drive to the *fahm*, so *getchaself* comfortable." He handed me a crooked joint and pulled out a second one for himself. In just a few short miles the human concentration of what John had humorously referred to as a "city" vanished, and we drove across flat, open farmland.

"What's that?" I pointed out my window.

"Sugar cane mostly. Some cottonseed too. Up at Sully's, he grows everything. Mangoes, almonds, avos, capsicum. Fruits n' beans, an' the finest pastured beef in Queensland."

"Mm, that all sounds great. I could go for a good burger. And you said I can ride the horses too, right?"

"Sure thing, if ya want. But don't expect me to get on one of them things with *yah*. I've got a four-wheeler I *roide* 'round the property."

As we drew closer to our destination John gripped the wheel tighter and the creases in his brow deepened. I instinctively stroked his arm. "I can't wait to meet your dad. I have a million questions for him. What have you told him about me?"

"Not much– just that you'll be my *woife*." John's eyes didn't leave the road, but I knew he wasn't really looking at it. "Nu look– you need to understand, Sully is not gonna run up and give you a hug. The man is *hahd* as nails, from the old school. Barely talks. Never stops workin' and doesn't do feelings. So don't expect much."

"Does he run the farm all by himself?"

"*Yeh,* he's got seasonal laborers that come up but mostly he prefers to be up there alone."

"That seems terribly lonely… has he tried to remarry since he split up with your mother?"

John shook off a laugh. "He swore off chooks after Mum 'n I guess I don't blame him. My first memories are of 'em fighting. One *noight* Sul didn't come home after Mum warned him not to stay in town. Sul don't even like the drink or chasing birds. But he won't tolerate bein' told what to do. So he walked through the door the next morning, and Mum was waitin' for him– hit him with a skillet! Had to get his nose stitched up.

"Once after they split Mum dropped us at the farm in a hurry, had to get back to work. Sully wasn't there and the place was all locked up. We stayed in the barn n' drank from the cattle trough. Eventually we got hungry enough, an' my little *brothah* Danny was cryin', so I threw a rock through a window and got us in. Sul showed up just a couple hours *latah* an' beat me with an old washboard. Then I got stitched up too, same hospital. Them nurses knew us after a while, an' always fussed over me. They were drawn to my animal magnetism, even as a lad. Probably why I love that category of porn so much."

John paused for a laugh but looked over to see me in tears. I wanted to turn around and head home, back to campus, back to the safety of his cave in Courtship Hall. I was afraid and John sensed it. He tried to lighten the mood.

"There now, ya soft American! Easy does it, you're *alroight.* That was a long time ago an' I'm grateful for all of it. Sully's parenting made me the indestructible man I am today. Practically immortal, really." He reached out to dry my cheeks with a rough hand. "Tough raisin' makes for a tough man. Sully never hugged us or gave us any breaks. Made us work for every single meal we ate on the *fahm.* Never once told us he loved us. But he showed us how to be men, how to work land and fix what's broken an' prepare meat an–"

"He *never* told you he loved you? Not even when you were small?" My heart was bursting. Truth be told, I had done more crying in the previous few months than the previous twenty years combined. The last year had turned the world into a darker place: the end of coral reefs, the end of a green planet, the end of God.

John exited the truck to unwrap a chain from a rusty gate. The vehicle vibrated as we ran over a series of stock grids. The scent of the eucalyptus trees hung heavy in my nostrils but the air was sharp. The pleasant lushness of our rainforest adventures was blatantly absent. The land looked withdrawn and grayed, as if it had aged. The truck kicked up a cloud of dust around us.

"How cute!" I waved to a small distant herd of cinnamon-colored cows with long droopy ears. John pulled off to the shoulder to allow passage to an incoming truck. He tipped the hat he had just put on and the driver reciprocated. A large metal trailer dotted with black holes clanged behind him. "Wow, I am seeing a whole new side of you, country John." I flicked the brim of his faded and dented leather outback hat.

John's eyes didn't leave the road. "*Yeh*, jus' you wait."

~

The steaks were rare, the bread was moldy and despite Sully's sprawling acreage the green beans came from a can. Sullivan Laidir had barely greeted me but immediately laid into John about a gas cap that was left off a piece of farm equipment. He wore an open plaid shirt– which he didn't button for dinner– and his body glistened with sweat. Dirt and specks of dry leaves were trapped in the matrix of his chest hair. He was slightly shorter than John and didn't have the same intimidating physical presence, but John was clearly different around him: subdued, like a shy pup with his tail tucked cautiously. Over the dinner table they continued their discussion about crop yields, shifting markets and Sully's choice to send two dozen Brahman cattle to the slaughterhouse this afternoon. "They're too lean, we'll get a shit *proice*." He took large bloody forkfuls as he spoke.

"Shit time to sell too."

"I know it. But we haven't had solid precip up here in near a hundred days. Historic floods all over the state this year and we're eatin' dust. I can't afford to feed 'em."

John's spine stiffened at the word *afford*. He had told me that Sully was one of those old-fashioned millionaires, stingy to a fault and still salt-of-the-earth. But as we ate this meal on a cracked 1970s-era vinyl tablecloth, and I glanced around the filthy old shack that the Laidirs called home, I began to wonder.

A reel played in my mind of all John's big talk about being rich, but how he was "grounded" with good work ethic and an old junky car. I remembered the rumors on campus that John's nice watch was stolen from a rich kid named Daffon and the only reason Daff didn't retaliate was because he knew John would steal his girlfriend instead. I remembered John drunk at the pub, gaudily throwing handfuls of two-dollar coins at people; calling them peasants and speaking prophetically about how coins would be meaningless to him when he built his empire.

"Yeh, it's a shame, this drought. Oi, you almost done Nu? Le's get out for a ride on the four-*wheelah* before it gets too *dahk*."

As the scent of the gasoline fumes tickled my nose, I wrapped my arms around John's waist. "Please, *please* don't drive like a maniac," I loudly begged over the engine's rolling thunderous sounds.

"Just hold *on*," John snapped, half-annoyed, half somewhere else. He throttled the engine and we took off down a dirt path, scattering a group of frantic hens and their brown and white feathers into the surrounding fields.

This place was not like the farms we passed on the drive. It was hilly, forested with small groves of spotted gum trees that followed the path of a dehydrated stream. On the hilltops enormous orange and green mangoes hung from tree branches like holiday ornaments. I had almost forgotten that it was Christmas. As I do every Christmas, I thought about my brother George.

George loved Christmas, but not in the way my sisters and I loved it– the coziness and nostalgia, the boisterous singing in the kitchen with the scent of cinnamon and clove in the air. For George and Dad the holiday season was a two-month hustle: a series of engineering challenges to decorate and fix up the house, and an endless quest to bring in extra cash to bankroll the season's festivities. George raked leaves, shoveled snow, ran errands for elderly neighbors, and went with Dad to the shop on weekends to help winterize boats.

They took their Christmas tasks seriously; they strung lights and balsam garland meticulously around every edge, gable, window and doorway until the house looked like it was made of gingerbread. They hung wreaths in the windows with velvet crimson ribbons, and an antique sleigh, built by my father's father, was arranged in the yard, overflowing with wrapped cardboard boxes of green, silver, white and burgundy paper, surrounded by grazing and frolicking wooden reindeer. The scent of the tree filled the house and it was arranged in all its glory at the front window so it could be enjoyed by all. The beautiful ornaments faced the window, and the sentimental ones– the ones made of popsicle sticks, tiny handprints and cotton-ball snowmen– faced the living room. We hung the ornaments while the 1966 *Grinch* played on the TV, and George and Dad worked for days building a tiny, snowy Christmas village around it, complete with an antique Lionel locomotive that circled the tree dutifully.

After George died, Christmas died. We tried to keep it alive for a few years, if only to honor his memory. But my parents' hearts were too broken for any festive spirit to capture them. Cookies turned to ash and the scent of evergreen became sickening. A home filled with laughter and music became silent, and we accepted it for what it was. After Dad sold the shop he started working Christmas Day. The company paid doubletime, and he said he wanted the younger men to be able to stay home with their families. Mom would make a lasagna or casserole in late November and toss it in the freezer so she didn't have to think about cooking.

I mounted the four-wheeler and rested my cheek against John's damp back. I breathed in his scent, mixed with the gasoline fumes, and it smelled like Dad and George. I clung to him tightly as he took us through the groves of trees, across a bumpy makeshift bridge and up a hill to gaze at the setting sun. We came to a sudden stop and I clung for an extra moment. My heart was swollen with love; almost a desperation.

"Oi, let go." He pushed my arms off of him and dismounted. I pushed him up against the ATV and kissed him, imagining our first kiss as husband and wife.

"What a charming place," I said and brushed his hair from his forehead with gentle fingers.

"I knew you'd *loike* it," he grinned and returned my kiss. "Someday it'll be ours."

I gazed out over the sprawling field ahead, the sun preparing for its evening sleep behind the distant treeline. A flock of birds made their hurried way across a citrus sky. I took deep, present breaths. A small group of kangaroos hopped into view from the tall yellowed grasses. By then I had learned not to scare off wildlife with excited squeals, and I silently commended myself for calmly enjoying their presence. Before I could register the familiar clicking sound behind me, the horrific boom sounded and one of the animals went down as the others made a desperate and instant escape. I didn't glance behind; instinct took over and I tore straight through the prickly grass to find the creature with blood rushing from her neck. She twitched and flailed; she was already gone as her body went through its final motions. I shrieked and held her to me like a child clings to a plush toy. Her fur was coarse and hairlike, not as soft as I thought it would be.

John appeared over me, chuckling and shaking his head in satisfied condescension. "Oh boy. This is a pathetic *soight*."

"*Why did you do this?*" I looked up at him with red-faced terror, but he just continued to laugh harder, until he glanced down at the kangaroo and his face suddenly contained a spark of concern.

"Ah, *fahck*, yer not gonna *loike* this. Might wanna look away." John reached down and pulled a pair of squirming pink joeys from the dead mother's pouch. In a swift and jaded motion he decapitated them in the palm of his hand with a pocketknife and tossed them into the grass.

"YOU'RE A MONSTER!" I wailed, charging at him with clenched fists. He threw his head back in laughter as I landed punches to his chest. After giving me a fair moment he grabbed my arms and pinned me down.

"Alright, alright, calm down, jes' *calm down*. I am more than happy to explain what's gone on here. Them steaks at dinner… where'd you think they came from? Ya think they give the cows a li'l surgery and send 'em back out?" My sobs were dense and painful as John forcibly held me tight against him. He tilted my chin up toward a nearby tree. "How do you think that hawk up there feeds 'er chicks? How do you think the bloody world works?" I continued weeping, and his strand of empathy reached its abrupt end. He pushed me off of him.

"You are so oblivious it's disgusting. No awareness *whatsoevah*. Your whole world is fake, you know that? Your aircons and your grassy *pahks* are fake, your food is fake, your clothes and your makeup and your ridiculous movies… you're livin' in fairytale land, you understand? An' you're thrilled to death about it. You're more than happy to take 'n take 'n take, and never question where it comes from and who's *sacrifoicin*' his neck to get it to *yah*. You cunts just roll yourselves in all them bullshit comforts and layers of padding and ask no questions about it. You may forget it behind your *whoite* fuckin' picket fence but around here we look straight down the barrel of *loife* an' we don't fear it; we embrace it an' we deal with it. We ain't separate from this world– your bones 're made of dirt and your food comes from the ground. These grasses are dry 'n nourishment is scarce out here. Roos are a pest competing with the cattle. This is what needs to be done and this is what is done, whether you're here to witness it an' cry about it or not."

I couldn't control my whimpering. He shook his head and patted mine with exasperated condescension. "You're soft, yer just too soft. Most of your whole country– you're a soft people. I'm sorry to be the one to break all this to you but frankly, you needed to see that."

Another lecture from John delivered against my will and through an emotional meltdown. There were many moments when my powerlessness against John's physical force was frustrating, humiliating– and on the opposite pole, intimately satisfying. But in this moment I felt rabid; devastated and outraged to a point of madness. My heart was on fire but my body betrayed me, and held still.

He returned to hold me a moment and stroked my hair while I exhausted myself. When he sensed the time was right and the lesson was over, he released me. I tried to make sense of it, his words and my hysteria. I knew it in my heart that my cause was righteous, that my feelings were valid, and yet I felt foolish. "I just don't understand how you can be so callous about killing. She was a *mother*," I wiped my eyes and nose. "How could you just stand there and laugh?"

"You have to understand that death is not the same thing to you that it is to me." I looked into John's eyes as he spoke. Illuminated by the sunset, their green seemed almost transparent, revealing blue and yellow layers beneath, like Atlantic waves in summer. They were a child's eyes set inside a man; forever marred by the things they had seen, but somehow, their shine untarnished.

"We boys grew up thinkin' about death, immersed in it always. It's how we played, it's how we fed. I shot my first 'roo when I was seven years old. I ran up just *loike* this but with excitement, an' I remember lookin' at that thing in the eyes and watching the life leave 'em. I was solemn then, quiet. I watched it and I understood it. Sul had me *slohtah* my first hog soon *aftah*–said I was ready. An' I was.

"And now, if I need to fight or *hahm* or kill for my territory and my people I'll do it. An' I'll know why an' how and I will know the consequences. That's my place in *loife* and I've accepted it.

"And what about you? What'd you an' your sisters spend your childhood thinkin' about? Complete opposite. Dolls, bottles, babies, nourishin', marryin'. *Loife.* You played in life, we played in death. Watch a few pups playin' tug of war, you're watchin' them get ready to shred a *cahcass.* Play has purpose, you understand? It prepares you for the world and your role in it."

"John, I don't feel so good…"

"Yeh, fair enough. Let's get you a cool drink, *hay.*"

John showed no mercy on the ride back to the farmhouse, speeding aggressively through the dusty twilight.

～

A large spotlight shone from on top of the barn. Under the bright circle of light Sully was working on a large machine with rows of sharp rollers attached to the back of it. John led me into one of the laborer's shacks. It smelled like mildew. "Take a *noice showah,* have a drink. I'm gonna go help the ol' man."

Something was wrong. I was shivering despite the heat. The stale air was stifling inside the shack, which brought me some relief. For the first thirty seconds the water in the shower ran brown. Once it was the color of watery beef broth I climbed in, and cranked the heat way up. I could hear clanking of metal to metal and swears coming from outside. As I toweled myself off in a shaking rush to put on John's flannel shirt and crawl under some blankets, a disturbing sound drew me to the window. The two men were in a physical brawl, and despite John's larger size Sully had the advantage. Blood reddened part of John's face. Eventually his father had pinned him to the ground and a shimmer under the spotlight revealed a knife held to John's throat to immobilize him. My heart gasped and tried to beat its way out of my body. No phone to call the police. John would kill me if I called anyhow. Sully was speaking calmly to John, close to his face. *A lecture.*

John…

～

The vibration of the stock grid stirred me. I was propped up in the seat, wrapped in a nest of ratty blankets that smelled like dirt. "John?"

"Goin' to hospital." His eyes didn't leave the road. One looked almost swollen shut and dirt was caked over the bloody spots on his face and head. The darkness was severe; *must be a new moon*, I thought.

I wanted to ask what had happened, both to him and to me. I was still cold. I chose silence and reached out from the warmth of my cocoon for his swollen hand.

"You are the most precious thing in the world to me. You know that, don't you?"

"Yes John, I know."

If you've ever loved a beast, you know that they exist on a spectrum of extremes. His capacity to break, harm, and destroy forms a perfect symmetry with his capacity for tenderness, fierce loyalty, and soul-penetrating love.

We weren't going to the hospital for him— in fact it took the convincing of several nurses and threats from me to get his wounds examined. He refused to leave my side and insisted they check me thoroughly. He wanted assurance I didn't suffer a concussion from fainting. They said I had gone into minor shock, and that I was otherwise fine. Our bill was only $46.50… I couldn't help but laugh in shock and wonder.

When we returned to the farm, the sun was appearing over the hills and Sully was gone. I didn't ask John where he might have gone, or what they had fought about, or what his father said to him while he was pinned to the ground.

"Is he coming back?"

"Not while we're here, no. We've got to head to Mum's soon anyway, so I can work."

"Did he say anything about what he thought of me?"

John stared at the road and swallowed what looked like a rock in his throat. "Just that you're too good for me."

28
She Belongs to Me

My face is smeared against the passenger side window, contorting my appearance to what I imagine to the outside looks like a bulldog who's had a stroke. I'm not going to defend my current predicament for two reasons: one, when spoken aloud, all John has to say is, "well, at least I don't work at Maccas at thirty," to abruptly end the conversation. Two, you've been along for the ride long enough to agree: what's the harm in one more bad decision? I've made it this far; might as well throw one more wrench into the engine.

Through all the emotional deprivation I've tolerated over the last few months, I've drawn the line at telling Tyler the full truth about it. I'm not certain why I care so much. I walked around hand-in-hand with Cam all over Mount Mirage, and of course, Palmetto Hills. I calculated the risk of associating with a man like Cam and I took it. But to confront my behavior in the form of Tyler's reaction to it is just too much to take right now.

Besides, it does feel like a small relief to leave the United States. There are tanks in the streets. The news is full of images of cities being lit on fire, protesters clashing with small business owners trying to protect their storefronts from bricks and graffiti, and beheaded statues in parks and city squares. I would call it media hype, except that we live in a big city now, and I can hear the sirens every night. It is very real. I am sure there were similarly dark times in our history, but I didn't live through them. This era feels consequential; like an inflection point marking either a serious wakeup call, or the start of a steep decline. There is no speculating how the next six months are going to go, with the pandemic still raging and people splintering ever-further into warring poles: conservative versus progressive, old versus young, rich versus poor, brown versus white, city versus country, women versus men. The election is in November, and everyone's shouting, and organizing, and begging for money– but who will out-mobilize whom is anyone's guess. Both sides genuinely feel the nation is on the line, and somehow, they are both right. It all feels historic, and significant to what path we will take as a human race. But maybe I'm just biased by all Cam's and John's "civil war" talk. Or maybe it's just me being a "self-centered American," as John would say.

"I'll be glad when we've crossed the border, *hay*. I don't get this country." We've pulled off the freeway and are rolling through a town just south of San Diego. It looks like most main drags of suburban American towns: rows of strip malls with the same corporate chain stores, gas stations, fast food places. The occasional square of grass and mulch with a swing set and some benches. The tediousness of the scene is made Californian by rows of palm trees. The streets are quiet, with the exception of joggers and dog walkers, rendered faceless by blue medical masks.

"This really gets me– all these big fat blokes walkin' yappy li'l dogs on a *spahkly* leash. That's the mark of a broken man, *roight* there... bein' pulled down the street by a shitty li'l cunt dog. What have you women done to yer men?" I choose not to respond. "Oi, an' here's what I love too. All these doublewide people waddlin' around in fitness clothes. Ha! Who're these people foolin'? Saw 'em all over the Midwest, too; linin' up at the drive-thru in gigantic cars. How're these people affordin' these cars? Trailers and shacks with brand new *utes* in the parkways."

"Wait, the Midwest? How long have you been here?"

"Coupla' months. Hadn't seen the States since I was a kid, figured I'd see if all the chat I talk about this place is true. It's about as bad as it looks on TV if I'm bein' honest, Nu. Your cities are a disgrace– so dirty, an' so segregated. Did you know that?"

"Oh sure, everyone knows it. Why do you think everyone's rioting? It's about finally bringing an end to racism."

"By burning the poor neighborhoods down? By stokin' more division? That don't make any sense."

"I'm not saying it's working, I'm just saying that's what everyone is so upset about."

"It's not really jus' race though, it's everything." We pull into a gas station. "There's plenny'a poor *whoite* neighborhoods. Shit, you should see *summa* the Rust Belt– what a depressing fuckin' place, *hay*. But it's about the same everywhere: all the healthy-lookin,' put-together people are on one side of town, an' the other side is a straight up dump. It's like *yahs* have a caste system and just won't acknowledge it."

"That's why we need more social programs," I explain, "to create equity across race, gender, et cetera."

"You mean equality?"

"No, equity. It's like, if you had a foot race and you made the track different lengths for each runner, understanding that they each have to start from a different place, and have different hurdles–"

"Oh, *yeh,* great idea. That will make everythin' better," he scoffs and lights a cigarette while I burn a scolding hole through his face with my eyes. "Tell white folks they have one set of standards, and everyone else gets another. What could possibly go wrong with that? Bring on more segregation; treat everyone differently. Create a special li'l calculator for each piece of a person's identity: ten points if you're Mexican, twenty points if yer Black, another ten points if *ya* have a finger or toe missing, and if you're a fruit you get to double your score!" He is cracking himself up; smoke wafts out his nose into the car. "I'd love to see that implemented at a medical school, *hay!*"

"Put that *fucking* cigarette out."

"I believe this is the Land of the Free, is it not?" He flicks ashes onto my leg. "*Let freedom riiing!*"

I jump up and swear, flinging the car door open.

"Give us a nice stretch, Nu, and drain that tiny li'l *bladdah* of yours. This is our last stop for a while."

We both go about the business of road trip rest stopping: he fills the tank, I stretch; he buys snacks, I use the restroom; I check the air pressure in the tires, he pees in a bush.

"Where'd ya learn to do that?" John gives me a condescending grin. "My li'l independent woman." As he goes for the driver's side door, I step in front of him and slam the door shut.

"You know what? I'm driving next."

"Good one. Now step away before you hurt *yahself*."

"I'm serious, John." I straighten my posture, suddenly feeling a rush of confidence that makes both my feet and face feel hot. "Here's the thing, Bear. You have just committed a felony. You're a kidnapper, and a blackmailer. Most people who know me would testify to the fact that I'd never, *ever*, get into a car with you willingly. And here you are fleeing the country. So here are your options.

"If you try to stop me from driving this car, I scream. If you refuse to ride shotgun, I leave you here."

"And if I shove ya aside and get in the seat, I can't be moved. You'll either have to get in or get left. Sun's goin' down soon."

"Then leave. I'll figure something out."

John shoves me aside and slams the driver's side door behind him. With a low grumble to his voice and hunched over the wheel, he does seem very bear-like. Low and slow he says with his eyes locked on my pupils, "Get in the car. *Now*."

I'm nervous but I refuse to show it. *What am I scared of? That he'll hurt me? Humiliate me? He's already done it all. I have nothing to lose.* And so the heat returns to my feet and I call his bluff. I return his tone back to him: low, slow, eyes locked. Alpha to alpha. "Go ahead, Darling. Leave me here." After a pause that feels like an eternity, I turn and start walking away.

"God damnit NINA!" I hear John's fists hit the horn but I keep walking. A painful yank on my forearm turns me to him. His face softens from menacing to coaxing. "You and I both know that it is not safe out here for you." His grip on my arm loosens; I feel blood rushing back through the veins, attempting to make up for lost time. "We're very near the Mexico border, and—"

"What am I not safe from, exactly? The scary *brown* people, is that it?" I shake my head and turn.

"*Men*– men, you idiot! Men who will harm ya, rape ya, even kill ya."

"Men, huh. I see. But not men like you?"

"No li'l star, that is why I'm here and I'll always be here. To protect you." He stood straight, as a militiaman when he hears the national anthem.

"Then I guess there is only one option."

~

My hair is blowing around my face as I roll down my window. I recognize the song on the radio from every kitchen I've ever worked in and I sing along at full blast in my most flamboyant Spanish accent. With a big smile on my face, I smash the gas pedal.

"EASY, cunt– *Jesus!*"

"Sorry, I'm just so full of adrenaline right now! I feel like I am in a movie!"

"Good one or bad one?"

"Mmm…" We share a laugh over the consideration.

"Could go either way I guess, *hay*."

"It's a little troubling, I really can't decide. I guess the distinction between the scary kidnapping and the romantic one is only to be found in the ending."

"Nah, it jus' depends on whether the *kidnappah* is good-looking. So lucky for you–"

"Yeah, yeah, you're *so hot*, I get it. I don't know Bear, the years of steaks and partying have done a number on you." I reach over and pat his belly.

"I'm still out of your league regardless." I shake my head and reach for the knob to turn the radio back up. "You know Nu, that must be the tenth time I've heard you say 'this feels like a movie.' No wonder you get yourself into all this trouble– you seek out the drama."

"*Drama*? I do not–"

"*Yeh*, you do. You make decisions as if *loife* were a movie, as if some director's gonna run out 'n yell *CUT* if things get outta hand."

I picture myself walking into Klipspringer's the first night I met Cam; how smug I was, carrying my little notebook, so ready to find him, so ready to hate him and oppose him, and yet I jumped right in. To use him. For the story. For the drama.

"...Maybe you're right, John," my voice softens as I switch off the radio and glance ahead into the reaches of the desert road. "None of this just falls into my lap. It's me. It's my own fault I'm here right now." The words burn my throat. Giving John the satisfaction of telling him he is right is painful every time, and the last thing I'd ever want to do. But when he's right, I've learned to say it. I didn't used to, until I realized just how many things he'd been right about. When we met, I absolutely was an 'ignorant American with no awareness of the world around me.' I was eating, buying, consuming without a second thought about what I was buying into, or who I was supporting, or who it hurt, including myself. I was a soft and sheltered suburban child who thought she knew a lot more about the world than she actually did.

My first reaction to John's many "life lessons" has been pure unadulterated rage, even fits of shouting or tears. It was a gut reaction, equal and opposite to the harsh brutality of his honesty. I reacted to his criticism the way you would react to someone dumping a bucket of ice water on your head when you've overslept: inevitable shock and outrage, but in the end, you have to admit that you got to work on time because of it. But did it have to be ice water? Wouldn't a firm tap on the shoulder do?

"*Yeh* well look— at least you're takin' some responsibility. Most people can't even do that. You've really grown up, Nina. I'm proud of ya for it."

He takes a bear-sized bite out of a mango, and we pass it back and forth. The car fills with the sweet summery smell of it, and for a moment I wish we were twenty again, buying mangoes from the little farm stand on the side of the Bruce Highway as we head for the rainforest, ready to disappear from the world and disappear into each other.

"We're a generation raised by TVs," he says. "If I didn't grow up on a farm I'd be same as you— just goin' around thinkin' that people should behave the way them characters on shows and films do. None of it's based in reality. An' especially the shows called 'reality'."

"And yet," I muse, "our reality is shaped by it."

"There is no 'our reality,' you see? It's jus' *reality*. It's one thing. How we *perceive* reality is up for interpretation and debate, but to say that you *possess* a reality is nonsense. Didn't they teach you that in uni, my credentialed li'l Macca scientist?"

I swat at him fiercely, but then I digest his words. "With every drive-thru order I fill I further question the value of my very expensive Bachelor's Degree."

"You'll use it someday, you'll use it. You've just gone off track a bit, that's all. You'll find all kinds of opportunities to use what ya learned, in places that will surprise *yah*. You can use the scientific method to determine the best breastfeeding schedule for my sons."

"You know what? You do it too." I spit a chunk of mango skin onto his lap.

"Do what?"

"You have been influenced by media, too. You used to constantly act and speak as if you were the head honcho of some gang. How many times have you said to me, and I quote, 'thugs need love too'? So which identity will you be today, naive country boy, or hardened thug?"

John's belly laugh makes me smile. "Gumma that's not telly! That's music. I guess you've got a point *hay*, I have been influenced by them stories of the streets. But to be fair, with my dashing good looks and my *bouldah*-like shoulders, the thug *loife* was destined to find me."

"I have absolutely no clue what that means. Also you've got a huge hunk of mango between your two front teeth."

"Bitch I like it in there."

The modern world melts away from us as we motor deeper into the desert. We live off of soft fruit, beef jerky, and jars of nuts, and camp under my life's starriest night skies. After I stage a lengthy protest to sharing a tent, we end up laying out on the ground beside a fire, puffs of skunky smoke streaming up from our laughter.

"Do you really want to be a big corporate CEO someday?" My head rests on his chest; it bounces as he chuckles, rises and falls peacefully as he breathes. "It just seems so stuffy for a wild animal like you. Will your neck even fit in a suit?" I laugh at the incongruous image of John stuffed into a suit and tie.

"*Yeh* I reckon I will. I'll be great at it. It's not just about owning and controlling resources, you're leading people– enriching a place, a whole community. The decisions I'll make will affect hundreds, maybe thousands.

"Deciding a man's fate is a great responsibility. An' with that power, if used proper, could lead me other places. Maybe public office. Then I can decide the fate of millions of men."

"*Ahem*– and women. *People.*"

"*Yeh, yeh.* You and your PC bullshit will make you a perfect PM's *woife*. You'll balance me out, get me the bird vote."

"So you've thought this through, huh?"

"Well of course, li'l star. You'll be great. Think of all the good you could do. Hopefully you'll still be fit, or I may have'ta pull a Monica Lewie on ya."

"If you become Prime Minister I'll have all the proof I need that the system is broken. Thugs can't be president!"

"Oh Nu, how can you still be so naive. *Only* thugs can be president."

We sit in silent contemplation of the ugly reality that John continually beats over my head. "Even still. I don't think I would want all that, the power and fame and everything. I think I want a simple life."

"Didn't we just establish how much you love drama? Now shut up and hold me hand. You've got the coldest hands, *ay*."

I reach up to give him my hand, and he raises it to his lips– first to play like he's going to bite off my fingers, then to kiss my palm. I pull away, frightened– not only by his tenderness, but by the warm flush that fills my body.

~

The "front desk" is a porch, topped with a splintered lectern, painted a deep Victorian purple. The lavender house attached to the porch is old and in disrepair, but is charming despite its grittiness. It sits in a small clearing that forms a sandy ring around the house, peppered with patches of tropical grass and palm saplings. There is a faded wooden sign painted white with purple text: *El Cangrejo Mimoso: Casitas, Amigos, Aventuras.*

A path from the purple house to the beach cuts through the jungle like a sand river, and little winding tributaries lead to tiny cottages in various Easter egg colors. The place appears empty– like a well-kept tourism secret that has been forgotten in a global pandemic. The final stretch of the path to the beach is capped by a crude set of planks that look like fallen dominoes in the sand. Past a lineup of twelve rusty frames that used to be lounge chairs sits a tiny tiki bar, turned fisherman's shack. The structure leans toward land, as if the ocean has given it one definitive shove. A litter of teenage cats emerge from it and trot along the planks toward the jungle. Tabby stripes shift along their ribs. The scent of sun-fermenting fruit sits heavily in the humid tropical air.

An old man plays a game of solitaire on the purple porch. His playing cards are yellowed and so are the ridges of his fingernails. His body is identical in form to my own grandfather's: short for a man, deeply tanned and slightly hunched, but solid as an ox. The arms and shoulders have retained their stony muscles and veins from continued daily work, but the legs are thin from not venturing far to do it. His gut is perfectly round, as a pregnant woman's, and his t-shirt gathers in a crease above it before tightly concealing its protrusion from the afternoon sun. He has a plate of squeezed limes and empty mussel shells beside him.

"*Fahcking* oath ol' man. Do you speak English?"

"*Espera.*" I interject before the man can answer. I say in Spanish, "May I speak to you privately first?"

"Of course, little girl. How may I help you?"

I fight an instinctive urge to roll my eyes at little girl, "*Niñita*". Refocusing myself, I continue. "I know this man, but I did not come here with him. Do you know what I mean?... *Él no es mi novio; él es un monstruo.*"

I roll my tongue over the word so John doesn't pick up on the word monster. "What are you sayin' to him? Are you bookin' us a room? Get the *noicest* one. This place is way shittier than I thought it would be."

I smile at John sweetly. "Good idea, Bear." I give his shoulder a little squeeze and continue in the man's tongue. "Sir, it is very important to me, to *us*," I grab John's hand and gesture, "that I am able to separate from him."

"Is he dangerous?" His eyes shift to John, and I quickly realize that this man is fully prepared to defend me, and may or may not be posturing himself to reach for a weapon from under his card table. I feel a kinship to him, like the admiration for a protective father. But I also don't feel entirely certain I want John murdered, for now.

"No— not dangerous, *exactamente*." I glance up at John and give him another reassuring smile. I spot an ornate silver crucifix hanging in the corner behind the podium. "I just need to stay away from him, to... protect *mi virtud*."

"What is *'peligroso,'* Babe?"

"Towels."

"*Pues*," the salty man continues, "You'd like to rent two cottages?"

"I can't afford one, but I can work for you. Help you with room service, washing dishes— anything."

"What is your name?"

"*Me llamo Nina*," and I reach out for John again. "*Esto monstruo es Juan.*" He laughs, I laugh, and John, clueless, laughs too.

"*Me llamo Marcel.* It is just me and my two sons here. We have no guests— no need for a housekeeper—" Suddenly Marcel's eyes light up with an idea. "*Puedes cocinar?*"

"Yes, I'm great at it too. We came in a car. I can shop and cook meals for you and your sons!"

"*¡Ay!* A woman's cooking. You have a deal. Your own place. *¡Berto, Diego!*"

From inside the purple house appear two massive, burly, sweaty young men: Marcel's sons. Berto's square jaw and extended brow make him look tough and goonish, even more so than John. Diego has a much softer look, a little boy's face, offset by his sheer enormity.

"*Dos casitas*," Marcel winks at me. John is finally starting to catch on, and his face reddens. "Who're these fat cunts, the bell boys? Why's this taking so long?"

I turn to John and try to remain calm. I am assured by my new friend and his pair of giant children. I am feeling lucky. I take John's hands in mine and I break the news to him by starting with his favorite words:

"John, darling, you were right. Absolutely right. Life isn't a movie. If it was, I'd fight and protest sharing a room with you, begrudgingly do it anyway, and we would be sleeping together by night three. But this is real life. You showed up uninvited and coerced me to leave the country with you against my will. That is the reality of the situation. We had a fun road trip, but I'm not going to let it end this way, sending you the message that what you did was okay. It isn't. You had no right to break into my life and pretend you know what's best for me." Marcel places two sets of keys on the podium. "Therefore, I will be staying in my own room."

John glances at the men, and back at me again before he erupts with laughter. "You can't be serious." John steps in front of me and leans over the card table. "One room. *Uno.* You understand?"

"*No, you understand.*" Marcel replies with unsteady but legible English. "Two rooms. Or there is trouble for you." He pushes one of the keys across the table and shrugs. "Your choice."

John swipes the key and flips the card table before he storms down the steps. I have never in my life seen or heard of John backing down from any sort of confrontation. I've seen him pick pub fights with men bigger than Berto without blinking an eye. Marcel chuckles to himself, amused as John stomps down the sand path. "He doesn't know which cottage his key goes to. Shall we watch?"

~

I quickly slip into a routine at *El Cangrego Mimoso*, the Cuddly Crab. I am reminded how long it has been since I've been in any sort of routine where the day's duties require me to structure my time from start to finish. I'm a notorious bed-lingerer. I set alarm after alarm, yet I'm still overpowered by my desire to see what happens next in the never-ending drama of my dreams. But here, there is no time for morning dreaming. I rise just before the day's first light and begin preparing breakfast for the boys. The first afternoon, after John sulked to his powder pink cottage and slammed the door behind him, I was relieved to find the keys still in the ignition, and John's stash of cash inside the glove box. I quickly ushered Marcel to the car and we drove the bumpy dirt road into town to shop for groceries. Marcel immediately went for the pyramid of canned sardines. "Marcel, I have a feeling you eat too much salty old fish."

"Are you kidding? I have turned into one!" He holds his belly as he chuckles at himself. "I never thought I'd say it, but I am sick of sardines. *Pescado y huevos, pescado y huevos.* That's all we make at home."

"Not today." My cheeks blushed with excitement. As we toured the store, I picked his brain about what his late wife would cook for the family, and filled our cart with items I could use to make my own version: jackfruits and hearts of palm, peppers, corn and squash, big sacks of dry beans and rice. He explained that there was no need to purchase mangoes, soursop, papaya, various other fruits, and of course, seafood. He said we could collect fruit daily from the dozens of fruit trees surrounding the property. When I reached for a can of coconut he stopped me. "Coconuts are everywhere. I'll show you how to process."

Cooking for 900 pounds of male appetite takes most of the day. I try to prepare extra and get a couple meals ahead, but they always catch up. John refuses to come to the purple house so I bring him his meals. (Since he is bankrolling the operation, I figure it's the least I can do.) He eats like a mad dog on the porch and I sit beside him and watch the spectacle.

"Are you still giving me the silent treatment?" No response, other than the slurping and crunching of devouring his plate. "Come on John, it's been two days of your sooking. You're acting like a— a *woman*." I know it's wrong to say this, but I also know what John will respond to. After a childhood in a coal boom town and half a decade at Saint Yowie Boarding School for troubled Aussie boys, "like a girl" is still the only real insult in his world.

"*Yeh* well you deserve the silent treatment, makin' me feel *loike* some kinda criminal 'r outcast."

Told you it would work.

"This is meant to be our special trip, somethin' we've looked forward to for years– and this is the thanks I get?"

"John, no 'special trip' starts with a blackmail letter."

He cracked a smile. "Hah, I am a lad, *hay*."

"You always say that when you're trying to make light of something bad you've done."

"Maybe if you didn't insist on being so difficult all the time I wouldn't have to resort to drastic measures."

"Would you like to go for a jungle walk when you've finished inhaling your food? I have a long list of fruits I want to glean, and I could use your height."

John and I start spending the afternoons together, gleaning fruit, talking about everything we've missed over the last seven years, and afterward I walk him back to his room. When he tried to enter the tributary that leads to my sleeping place, I beckoned Berto and Diego to me like a threatened hiker calls for the security of two loyal dogs. I am bothered that it takes two whole men to protect me from one. But I am absolutely thrilled it is working. I eat meals with Marcel, sometimes chatting about our plans for the day, or dining in comforting silence. The boys often eat at odd hours as they go off before sunrise on fishing boats or look for work in the nearby town. I make them two plates – that's two plates, *each* – and place them in the icebox for later.

We eat early and the evenings are mine, each one getting a few minutes longer with the blossoming of summer. I walk the beach with a pair of fins and a dive mask in hand. Marcel's friend Pablo hooked me up with a tank, regulator, and a flashlight so I do some diving in the evenings. Safe from the vulnerable exposure of daylight, the reef comes alive with all kinds of creatures at night – ornate crustaceans, octopuses, dense schools of silvery fish. I feel relieved to see that it's all still here. It is hard to imagine that it has been ten years since my time with Captain Don on the Great Barrier Reef. I wonder how those reefs we explored have fared over the last decade. I wonder how Don has fared. I say a little prayer that the world has not broken the spirit of such a man, but then I chide myself for thinking that such a thing is possible.

John gets wind that I am diving alone at night and insists on chaperoning me. "Why not just join me then?"

"*Fahck* no," John unscrews my air and spins me around. "I'm a farm boy, not a sea dog. I don't know her and she *don'no'* me."

"It's never too late to meet someone new," I jest and shuffle my way into the dark sea.

Jungle walks with John become part of the daily routine. After I clean up lunch, I summon John from his porch and we trek around in the bush. By day five, I have to ask: "John, how long do you plan on staying here? You didn't quit your job, did you?"

"Nah. I'm in high demand. Thought we'd travel 'round for a couple of months, but the pandemic is gettin' outta control. I reckon we'll stay another week or two. Depends on how long you take to warm up to me–" I squirm to escape a butt pinch.

"So I guess we'll be staying here forever." I sigh and gesture my hands outward. "This is our home now."

"I'm not so sure about that li'l miss. I think your plan is backfiring."

"Oh?" We walk the path to the pink cottage. "*Yeh*, it's jus' *loike* when we first got talking to each *othah*. There was a slow build, an electric tension that stewed up between us. I knew that you thought I was trouble. And I knew you were somethin' special, something worth waiting for. I knew that you'd resist, that you'd *foight* the urge to be with me, which made you an even tastier *proize*. But after long enough–"

John scoops me up into his arms and devours my mouth with his. It starts strong, passionate and with a bruising pressure, but eases into tender affection as I give into it. His scent overcomes me and all the memories flood back into me; I am powerless against it, like the floodwaters of that dream about him, mere days before he reappeared. Just when he has me where he wants me, he releases my body and beams at me with his cheeky little brat smile. He says matter-of-factly, "Good night my li'l dove. You are the most precious thing in the world to me." My mouth hangs open as he disappears behind the fuschia door.

∾

Marcel and I play cards on the porch. I watch his crusty pointer finger tapping on the edge of his hand of yellowy cards.

"Marcel, how did your wife die?"

"¿*Que*? She didn't die." Marcel places a pair of fours on the table and picks up a third one from the discard pile. "She took my daughter and left."

"Oh– may I ask you why?"

"You just did." Marcel scratches at his round belly and sighs. "This is a small place, a small life. Lita wanted a big life. She was very beautiful– too beautiful for me. My daughter, too– like a clone of her mother. They are glamorous women.

"I was older. She was just nineteen when we married. I was a safe bet for her, for her parents. I was a good fisherman, had a good truck and some land. We'd go into town and sell fish, but *Jesus Christo* how she hated it. The smell, the cold ice, the blood and scales, the bartering. But she loved town, loved the crowds and the tourists. She would go to the general store, order Cokes and watch the TV there. She loved everything the white people on the TV did: their clothes, their words, their music. She was distracted with the kids for a while, but once they could fend for themselves she started to complain again."

Marcel grabs a beer with a green and white label from a small plastic cooler, its white lid also yellowed with age. He holds it out toward me; I shake my head no thanks.

"The nets started getting lighter and lighter, or they'd be filled with bottles, soles of shoes, things like that. Money got tighter and it was barely enough to begin with. Lita was going into town every day to use the internet café. I knew what she might be doing but I didn't have the energy to confront her."

He looked out at the colorful micro-village of cottages. "This place was my last shot to keep her, to bring the white people to her, to bring her the world. And it worked for a while, like a charm it did!" Marcel laughs and takes a swig. "I couldn't believe it. She ran this place like she was born for it. Walked from cottage to cottage with a big bowl of fruit on her head or a basket of fresh pastries, singing, ¡*cantando*! Oh her voice was sweet. She got the place up on the internet and the white people started coming. Young, pretty ones, some Americans but mostly Germans, French. They loved taking pictures with their phones. She loved the French. They became friends and gave us big cash tips. They called us 'Maman' and 'Papa', would extend their stays. Then a few months ago, it was like a candle blown out. *No mas.*"

I looked around at the cottages with fresh eyes. The structures were old, but each one had been fairly recently painted in their pastel colors with bright accents. Flower boxes on the window sills held browned and rotten floral ghosts. Trails of bushes and flowers along the pathways had grown over and conjoined, forming miniature clusters of jungle. "It's amazing how quickly things fall apart," I think aloud as I see nature's rapid takeover of Lita's work, but quickly realize that I've upset Marcel. "Oh Marcel, I didn't mean…I'm so sorry–"

He pulls a crusty bandana from the bib pocket of his overalls and wipes his forehead. He wears the struggles of his life on his face, his life on the ocean, in the dusty marketplace, his broken heart. I wonder now if he's much younger than I first thought. But atop his wrinkled layer, over his scars and his sunspots, something gives him vitality. I think it is acceptance.

"She will not be back, and I can only hope that she will find safety and happiness. There was nothing I could do to give her what she truly wanted; I knew that from day one. But I didn't think I had to. It used to be like that. A basic life was enough. Survival and safety alone, those were valuable. Those were enough to offer a woman. But she just had something different, a new way, that none of the other women here have."

Marcel picks up a card from the pile, and lays down four queens in front of him. "You've got it too, I think. I imagine Kiki, my daughter, will have it too. It's the new way."

"What is? I'm not sure what you mean by this 'new way.'" I reach into the cooler for a bottle of Ting grapefruit soda.

"I guess you could call it *elegir*. Choosing. Choosing to chase happiness. Taking risks when you don't have to. When your needs are already met."

"What?" I laugh, "That's not a new way!"

"It is for most people," he says, seriousness in his face. "It's common now, but for most people, for most time, it is brand new."

~

For the next two days, there are no afternoon jungle walks. There are no night dives on the reef. I hastily cook meals with laser focus and dart back to the safety of the blue cottage. The floorplan is a simple open square with large windows. One of the windows has a crack that runs like a vein from top to bottom. The table and chairs are painted the same robin's egg blue as the porch; the cotton blanket on the bed is faded cornflower. There is a jar of seaglass and shells on the bedside table next to a small lamp. A fan with oar-like blades circles overhead, keeping the temperature barely tolerable. I lie on the bed, little beads of sweat tickling my temples. I pace around; I stack the sea glass; anything I can do to avoid leaving the safety of the sealed blue space. From the moment I sat behind the wheel of that car, I felt in control of the situation, in control of myself. John shattered that against my lips. He knows it, I know it. John's kiss awakened something inside me that I have spent nearly a decade trying to forget. And like every battle we've ever had, he's got the advantage. But I am going down with swinging fists in the air. I refuse to let him win.

You wouldn't know it by looking at me, but I've done some hard things in my life. I've lived a full six days off of leftover taco dip that I stole from a barbecue. I've cleaned a sports bar bathroom on the Monday morning after the Super Bowl, when the home team won. But resisting John is far and away the hardest thing I have ever done in my life. The dream-version of myself that got on that plane to Australia knew something about me that I have refused to acknowledge. It feels like my blood is trying to escape my body and flow under the door in pursuit of him. I try sleeping, overeating, fantasizing about other men I've been with– but then the freckled shoulders appear...

Outside I hear John and Diego laughing, and the sound of a fraternal slap on the back. I crawl along the floor so I can peer out the window without being noticed. The two of them are carrying crates down the path toward the dock. *Getting chummy, I see… you slick bastard.* John's a smart man. He knows how to play people like a fiddle. I've probably got only another day or two before the boys let their guard down and say, "Give him a chance, he's a sweet guy." This thought sends a panic through me – a powerless, cold inevitability that a cow must feel in the loading shoot.

For the first time in weeks, I pull out my notebook, sit at the table, and start to write. I draw a line down the center of the page, and on one side, I list all of my pleasant memories with John: sneaking off campus to swim in those crystalline waterfalls; late nights smoking and driving around aimlessly; laying in his dark cave, taking turns picking out songs on Youtube; eating "Macca's" burgers and fries in his car at 2AM; pretending not to notice each other at pubs and parties, and then sneaking off into a cab, where we shamelessly and feverishly kissed, moaned, and dry-rubbed each other. "They live for that shit," John used to say, assuring me after I'd catch myself feeling self-conscious at the driver's rearview mirror. "A couple of good-lookin' young bodies writhin' around? Best show on God's green earth." The list is long, nostalgic and romanticized in the warm folds of my memories. I've worked myself up even further. *Why didn't I write the bad list first?*

The blue box is hot, absorbing my feverishness and the afternoon heat. The voices outside have faded away. I sneak out the door and tear through the jungle. I *have to* cool off in the ocean before preparing dinner. I half-expect my skin to sizzle as it hits the water.

I throw dinner together early. I ask Berto to drop off John's plate, citing a headache, and I scrub the dishes with haste. I close myself back up into my room like a hermit crab withdrawn safely into its shell. I stare at the empty column on the right side of the page. As I psych myself up to sit down and begin, I freeze at John's knuckles rapping at the door.

~

My back slid down the door and my skirt bunched up, bracing my fall onto the bathroom floor. The tiles were cool against my bare bottom, reminding me of the lacey rose-colored lingerie I wore underneath my outfit. Even as my body vibrated from the violent pounding on the door, I couldn't help but laugh a little at my own foolishness, my sorry naiveté. *Of course he hasn't been at work for three days straight* I thought, shaking my head. I was wearing what my grandmother would call "Sunday Best" – a white blouse with tiny embroidered roses along the neckline and short flutter sleeves. A wrap skirt that matched the little pink roses, a matching headband, and rosy cheeks. I recently purchased the outfit; it was not my color but John said he thought it would look nice on me. I fussed with my hair in the Queensland humidity to set it just right. It was a mess now, all of it a mess now. A full day of work down the drain. I laughed again. I spent the morning cleaning the house– John's mother's house, where we stayed after leaving Sully's farm. I met her only in passing; she was leaving for an extensive vacation with her boyfriend and John helped her load her many bags into a cab. The only thing I remember about her was that she had John's exact eyes, and was decked head to toe in sparkling jewelry.

I dusted, mopped the kitchen tile, hung the laundry on the line, spent the afternoon getting myself ready, shaving my legs and adorning my neck with perfume. I had nothing better to do; I had no car, no money, no courage to leave the house in a town full of burly miners from around the world. I had hoped a warm home greeting could convince John to work less and make the most of my visit. I spent the early evening braising the lamb and vegetables, scraping the fudge brownie batter into the glass baking pan. The pan was shattered now, the tablecloth stained with spilled au jus and candlewax. The dinner was a pile of wet muck in the bottom of the trashcan.

Maybe I shouldn't have done it. It was wasteful and you know me– I'm usually not one to waste. But I couldn't just let him have it after what he'd done. I needed to do *something*, something to punish him for lying, for leaving me alone again, this time for three whole days. For coming back wasted with a ripped shirt and bloodshot eyes.

This time it dawned on me that maybe, perhaps, more than alcohol had been involved in his disappearances. But how could I have known that Australian coal had gone bust– that his friends were losing jobs and spending the last of their money on apocalyptic partying? How could I have known that John had returned to his small hometown for the holidays in the midst of an all-out freefall? Was he doing drugs this whole time, since I left Australia? Or the whole time I'd known him?

He returned home from his "shift" as a delivery driver, looking the most frightening I have ever seen him: red-faced, pinprick pupils, strips of wet hair stuck to his forehead. Veins and tendons popping from his neck as he watched me dump the lamb into the bin. I was in petty-revenge mode; I did not yet realize what exactly I was dealing with, or the impending consequences of what I had done.

"Waste my *fahckin'* money? YOU'RE *DEAD!*" He had lunged at me from across the room and I scurried like a mouse into the bathroom. The rattling of the door became painful and I shot up and jumped into the shower stall just in time. Splintered wood erupted and fell from the door as John's bloody fist thrusted through it. I'll never forget the way his face looked… grinding his teeth, clenching his jaw, he barely looked human to me. I know I have often spoken of him in non-human terms, but this wasn't the same John who playfully ran around on all fours. We had both lost an uncomfortable amount of weight over the recent months of being apart, but in this moment John's remaining muscles swelled over a sickly body; he looked like a hollow, infuriated ghost. I cried like a child, our future suddenly gone, my idyllic image of him forever lost. "Who the fuck do you think you are, trashing my Mum's house, throwing my *hahd-*earned money in the trash?" He shoved me backwards and my lower back hit the toilet seat on the way down. "Get up– when'd ya get so weak? You used to *foight* back. You *use'ta* be a good strong woman. Wrestlin' ain't fun anymore when you sook like this." I sat up, breathing heavily, trying to get my bearings. The room was spinning. Various parts of my body were throbbing, calling out for help. I wanted to speak, but only wailing came out of me.

"*Le's* have'ya clean up ya' mess," he slurred and dragged me by my hair into the living room. The carpet burned my knees. I tried to hold my hair at the base so it wouldn't rip out in John's hand, maybe taking some scalp along with it. I had thrown out the food, but John had completely trashed the place. The garbage bag had been slammed against walls and furniture, expelling its contents everywhere. The left door of the china cabinet, shattered. Standing lamp, shattered. Ceiling fan spinning on a crooked axis, short a couple blades. The splintery remains of one of the dining room chairs hung over the arm of the couch.

He looked down at me. I sobbed on the floor, a pathetic sight curled in the fetal position, rubbing my head. He looked around, his body twitching. He rubbed his hands over his face and head, distraught, and shattered the right side door of the china cabinet with his fist before he stumbled out the door.

I waited a few minutes to get up, listening for signs to be certain he was really gone. I immediately went to the bedroom– but even on a cocktail of God only knows what drugs, John is a smart man. My passport was gone.

John returned the next afternoon, sore and miserable with what he calls "the comedowns." He retired to bed for sports drinks, potato crisps, and video games. I had cleaned the bulk of the mess, hopeful it would patch things enough to get my passport back. That was my biggest mistake– perhaps the biggest I've ever made in my life, cleaning up that mess. Perhaps if he had seen it in a sober state– seen it through my eyes, and cleaned it up himself– things would have been different. But I didn't know the weight of the metaphor. I was too busy feeling sorry for myself, and wanted the reminder out of sight as soon as possible. It was day sixteen of a month-long visit. John apologized for losing my passport on his bender, but insisted he needed the rest of the trip to make it up to me.

"I've been out on the bend for too long, *hay*. It's your turn to be taken care of." Once John recovered, he took me on a trip to what he called a city, but was by an American standard a small town. We dined at an Italian restaurant, we saw a movie, and he bought me a ring with a pink stone. "It matches that beautiful skirt you bought." By day 30, the series of events had blurred into "Nina, I have been working so *hahd* to make sure we have enough money to eat. I have a few drinks with the mates before comin' home, and you throw a tantrum. We both made a mess– but you made the first move, remember that. Completely irrational." Soon we were making jokes about it, and I stopped questioning John's version of the story. I was plenty aware that I wasn't my best, anyhow– deep in the mud of depression, anxious from the past few years of school, work, and constant change. I had a tendency to drift through weeks or even months at a time with no solid memories of my days. I figured there was probably some truth to what he said.

∽

John's knocking at the blue door is gentle, without eagerness or urgency. I press my back against it and close my eyes to focus on the vibration. The memory comes back to me, clear for the first time since it happened. I turn and press my cheek to the door. "Yes, John."

We walk the sandy path to the beach. John carries a handwoven basket filled with an array of pink cashew fruits, starfruit, guava, braided French bread, and a bottle of rum. He's wearing a white Hawaiian-style shirt with red flowers. Per his request, I have freshened up as well. The jungle's palms, ferns, and thick understory open up to the beach and the twelve rusty chair frames are gone.

The fisherman's shack is draped with flowers of crimson, yellow, and white. Several crates and boards are arranged into a makeshift table and chairs, with scattered candles and a sprinkling of fragrant herbs and blossoms. I am stunned that a man as crude as John is capable of such a set up. Certainly the other guys were no help either. *I wonder if he asked Pablo's wife…*

"You are beautiful *tonoight*. Usually I like my girls pale, but the sun looks *roight* on you." John hands me a large plumeria flower from the basket. "For your hair." I tuck the stem behind my ear. "Perfect. Reminds me of our first official public date. Do you remember that?"

"Yes," I giggle, "how could I forget? Your friends lined our walk to the car to ogle and laugh and take photos of us. And you threatened some poor middle-aged man in the restaurant because he 'looked at me too long'..."

"*Yeh* well he did. But looking back it's *hahd* to blame him. That tight little blue dress you wore..." John grabs a handful of my hair, holds it to his face and takes in a deep breath through his nostrils.

"I used to see you from across the dining room, or see you walkin' with yer friends down campus, holding your l'il science books, and you'd just knock me off my feet, *ay*. You jes' took my breath away."

"And now?"

He looks me over. "You haven't aged too bad. Body's still *toight*."

"It's the tropical diet," I smirk, and pat my hips. "Seems like you've shed a few pounds since we've been here."

"*Yeh* I'll admit you've made the most out of the shit food available here. I have been impressed." He leads me to one of the crate seats. "Good cook, soft touch, passionate. Every man dreams of having the *haht* of a good Italian woman." I stare out at the horizon, ignoring John's words. I've heard the 'good Italian woman' speech before, most recently from Cam, and I'm not about to reopen that file in my mind. The sky is just beginning its evening show of colors. A ship glides on the horizon with billowy sails. I recall a romance novel I pulled from Captain Don's library about a woman who slips out of her betrothed's mansion at night, takes to sea and destroys his fleet of cargo ships, convinced he was her enemy from a childhood trauma. No one knew it was her, and the townspeople called the mysterious attacker "the Sea Witch". After sinking her fiancé's ships, she'd grin quietly at the dinner table or in the parlor while he raged at his misfortunes. In the end, of course, she was mistaken, and they end up falling madly in love. *Ugh, she should have just sailed off while she had the chance.* My Caribbean fantasy is cut off by the touch of John's rough hands over mine.

"Are you ready to be my *woife* now, my li'l star?"

I cover my mouth so he doesn't see my incredulous smile. "John... is that– is that really what you thought? I need to know. Did you really think the outcome of this whole thing was for me to *marry you*?"

"Yes idiot, of course I did. Isn't that what I've been saying? I've only been talking about it for ten years. I even gave you your dream trip, and your bloody movie, happy ending an' all." He gestures at the tropical scene around us, which I admit is picturesquely romantic, and a perfect setting for an engagement.

"Yes, but I always thought you were joking, or just messing with me– that you were just saying that stuff to get me to tell you I love you. You've always done that John, and I get it. It comforts you, to know that you can affect me, *still*, 10 years later, 10,000 miles away."

"*Oi* I'm not going to deny any of it. But to me you've been mine this whole *toime*, since the moment we met. I've just been waitin' for you to come back around." I shuffle uncomfortably on the crate, get up and sit on the sand. John sits next to me. "An' look, I know there was bad times. I don' remember a lot of it but honestly I can't believe you fell for me when you did. I thought I was a man at 21, but I wasn't. I was a loser and I didn't even know it." John delicately lifts my chin to raise my eyes to his. "But I'm a man now, Nina." The green eyes glow, and he looks through me. "I'm on the rise. I'm powerful, got the career. Money is comin' in an' it's gonna keep comin'. I know who I am and I know what I want. An' you're it. My first love–"

"Oh John, I–" He cuts me off before I can speak with his kiss, and my body becomes a bowl of butter.

"More than anything, more than all the money in the world, maybe even more than power– I want a happy, stable family. I never got that. You did. You don't know what it's *loike*–" He runs his thumb along my chin, and wipes a tear across the ridge of my cheekbone. "Jus' imagine it, imagine all that we could do, all that we could have *togethah*. I want to come home at the end of the day to the *laughtah* and cheers of my sons, poundin' down the hall to gimme a big hug or to tell me about some trouble they've gotten into. I want to see you in the background shakin' your head, settin' the table, or swinging to a little music while you add some lovin' touches to our home. Is that so terrible? Is it so much to ask out of *loife*?" I lean onto John's shoulder for a moment and try to imagine myself in his fantasy. I register the truth, that his fantasy has been my own. At my worst and most lonesome moments over the last ten years, I have retreated into the exact same vision– a billowy, fluffy fantasy; an impossibility, a utopia that will never be, not because we don't want it, but because of who we are, down to our very bones.

"It's not too much to ask, but I don't know if we are capable of that kind of peace. Have you asked yourself that? I mean really, to your core, asked yourself if you are even capable of that kind of life? Stability, devotion…sobriety? After all those years of partying and adrenaline, and God only knows what else you've gotten into over the years, do you really think you could be that man who settles down, who dutifully provides for his family and sets an example for his children, and is faithful to his wife?"

"It's because I've had so many experiences that I know I'm ready. I've seen it all an' so I'm ready to settle down."

"I want you to have those things if you desire them, John. I love you and I would love nothing more than to see you happy– it's already been a dream come true to see you healthy again. I am stunned at how you have turned your life around, and I'm so proud of you. I sincerely thought you weren't going to make it–" I swallow a sob in my throat. "Fatherhood could be the very thing that transforms you into the man I have always seen inside you. Real responsibility just may be the only thing that will tame the beasts in you… But it might not. And I can't wage that bet."

"So you don't believe in me?"

"It's different now, now that we're older. I would have gladly jumped into the fire with you when I was 20. But now I am able to comprehend the weight of the real thing, being bound together forever, and raising children. I want to believe you've changed, but what if you haven't? What if it's not that you've tamed your demons, but simply put them to sleep, and they could be woken up suddenly?

"What would I do if I had borne your children? I know what you would do to keep them in your life. If I needed to get away from you, to protect them or myself...I couldn't."

"I wouldn't let that happen– I would never let you leave me. I refuse to give a kid a broken home–"

407

"So you see? Whether you really have changed or not, I would be stuck. I'd be a prisoner to you. A prisoner to a man who has spent his life living recklessly, making enemies, disrespecting women—and disrespecting himself. Why would I ever put myself— but more importantly, my children—in that position?"

"But if you gave me a child you would be my whole world, Nu. A family of me own's all I ever wanted. It's why I've learned to clean up my act. If you give me my legacy I will give you everything and more. I would love you so good bub, with everything in me. You're the only woman I've ever loved." John kisses the smooth skin on the back of my hand.

I reach out for John's hand. "The life you describe is beautiful, and it's something I want now more than ever. It's something I have put out of my mind for years, maybe because it has seemed so out of reach. But you know I can't trust you at your word, John. You know that. You showed off your bag of tricks and then you tried to dazzle me with magic. I know too much about you to believe you, even if I wanted to."

"Is this about the other girls, about sex? Or this about the drugs? 'Cause I'm clean now, I promise. I'm—"

"I think you're an addict, John. Do you know what it's like to love an addict? Chasing highs from girls and porn, highs from drugs or the drink, highs from fighting. It doesn't matter which poison you choose. One will replace another, and the cycle goes around forever. I bet it's work now, isn't it? I bet you work compulsively and that's why you're doing so well. It's been torturing you, being here without some rush to pursue, hasn't it? …I guess your current pursuit has been me."

"Exac'ly, so what? So isn't it good that I've got drive, that I'm ambitious? That I've channeled it into working *hahd*, and building a good *loife* for us? I'm keeping my promise."

"Maybe you're right— maybe there is some healthy way to use it. But I still feel like you're building a castle out of sand. Until you confront those beasts in you *for real*, head-on— until you truly understand what created them, and what they feed on— I don't know. I just know that during those bad times, the rollercoaster of it exhausted every part of me. It was a new heartbreak every week, and a relentless powerlessness that brought me down with you. I hated you, I pitied you, I hated myself for enabling you, and from across the ocean there was nothing I could do about any of it. You were reckless with my love, John. You were reckless with your own life."

"Well, you left. It was a *hahd* time. I thought I'd never see you again. My life wasn't in my control back then."

"That's what was so hard for me to understand. I always saw you as you described yourself: authoritative, proud; a fearless leader. A man in control of himself and obsessed with controlling his own universe and conquering the world. I took you at your word, I worshipped your mind; I worshiped this image of you that you had created. But you were just a boy, a boy still at the mercy of his own impulses. And as I watched you spiral out of control, my image of you fizzled out into a delusion. I am afraid I have fallen in love with a person who doesn't exist."

John adjusts his posture in the sand, and turns his head away. It is almost as though I can feel the same pain he is feeling: that rigid tightening of every core muscle in the body to prevent a tear from falling. I place his hand against my cheek so he can feel the moisture of my own tears. He yanks his hand away, and his body heaves a single involuntary sob; I cower, thinking he might swing back and hit me. He tries to get up to leave; I quickly climb into his lap and wrap my legs around his waist, holding him tightly to me.

"Please John, it's okay. Please. It's okay. *Please*." I run my hands over his hair as his body heaves up and down; it is like being on the *Siren's Revenge* in a squall. I cling tight and coo into his ear as my teardrops illuminate the freckles on his shoulder. The sounds that come from his body are like the roars of a bear who has stepped in a trap but refuses to die. His grip leaves bruises on the flesh around my ribs.

AN ETHOLOGIST'S NOTE ABOUT WORKING WITH WILD ANIMALS

If you read the journals of any of the great wildlife biologists who took their places in the field beside their subjects– the Jane Goodalls, the Dian Fosseys, the Timothy Treadwells– they always say some version of, "I acknowledged the risk, and I took it."

We mustn't forget that we choose to study the wild things in the world because we admire them, or at the very least because we are fascinated by them; because they possess things that we don't. We have to accept that where there is strength, there is both danger and potential. Where there is unknown, there is both danger and potential. If the unknown holds potential evil, there is potential for good in equal measure– for the best things we can imagine. So we acknowledge the risk, and we take it.

No matter how close we get, or how much time we spend, or how much we project our romantic, anthropomorphic images upon them, they will always be *wild*. There will always be danger. There will always be teeth, muscle, venom or claws. There will always be instincts that cannot be fully subdued or overridden.

There are laws beyond ours; laws that are greater, more powerful than all the combined millennia of human civilization. We are just children. Nature is our mother. God is our father.

The greats knew this; they acknowledged this truth and pressed on anyway. They chose to commit their lives and risk their flesh for a connection to something that we have lost; a transcendence beyond the lines of genetics, species, and ancestry. Were they brave, or insane? Were they altruistic, or were they narcissistic? Where does the desire to understand for the other's sake end, and the desire to understand for one's personal sake begin? Were they imposing intruders, or foreign friends?

We see ourselves so arrogantly separate from our wild counterparts. We are civilized, we say; we are self-tamed. But anyone who has lived in the wild amongst our distant relatives understands that the barricade between us is flimsy at best, illusory at worst.

29
Leave Lady Leave

"Did you see him before he left?"

"Sí– he lectured us for nearly an hour on how we have to protect you, and take care of you, and make sure you are safe–" Diego passes me the pot of coffee. "I don't know what happened, but he sure loves you, *Niñita*."

"I know he does." I pour the steaming, thick coffee over a cup full of ice. I haven't slept and my heart is heavy, but in a small way, I am relieved. I used to have this gripping fear that I'd never see John again– that on some idle afternoon I'd get the call from one of his friends– that he'd overdosed, or crashed his car, or got his skull smashed open in a fight over a lewd comment made about the bouncer's girlfriend. Or if not that, I feared that on the night before my wedding I'd have the Daisy Buchanon panic shoot through me– I'd have the vision of those sleepy green eyes and those freckled shoulders, and I'd have to call the whole thing off. But now I have answers. I have closure. I have a fresh understanding of what cosmic, visceral thing exists between John and me– something as clear and unyielding, inexorable and unfathomable, dangerous and beautiful as nature itself. I have to accept that I'll never stop loving John Laidir as long as I live. But now I know.

I fall in love with my simple life at the Cuddly Crab. I dive the reefs every day. Berto teaches me how to spearfish, after much protest. "*Dime* a more direct way to get your food."

"It's not that, it's just that, they're my… *friends*. When I'm down there, I feel like I'm one of them."

"*El pez se come al pez, ¿no?*"

Soon enough I become addicted to the adrenaline of the hunt, and the boys dine with big grateful smiles on their faces.

I score some watercolors from town and I paint rainbow parrotfish, sea fans, eagle rays and flamingo tongues. I fill my notebooks, writing about Cam, John, and everything that has happened. When a notebook is full, I build a bonfire on the sand by the ocean, and toss it into the flames. I dance around it, chanting, singing and wild-eyed, like one of the kids from *Lord of the Flies*.

I help Marcel and the boys with projects to restore the touches that Lita had left behind. "The pandemic won't last forever," I assure them, "and people are itching to get out of their homes. With freestanding cottages like this, and all the fresh air, it will be a perfect place. They just need to know we exist."

I take them, after insisting and begging and chocolate cake bribery, to the internet café in town. Diego is a natural with computers; Berto crosses his arms in disgust until he discovers La Perla's online lingerie catalog. Marcel is interested but believes himself to be too old to learn. "Bullshit, old man. If I can learn how to filet a red snapper and butcher a coconut, you can learn to write an email."

I hang a chalkboard to-do list for the inn's reopening:

Establish Covid safety and cleaning protocols.
Set up wireless network.
Create Facebook page.
Take photos of rooms, property, amenities.
Repair Buy new lounge chairs.
Convert fish shack back into tiki bar.

With the brunt of hurricane season rolls in a feeling of apprehension in town. People move about their business quickly and the restaurant and general store are quiet.

"Everyone is saving up for plywood and gasoline, just in case."

"People are saying it is getting worse every year," Diego frets over his fishing pole.

"I heard this peninsula won't even be here in fifty years."

"I heard twenty-five. People say–"

"'¿*La gente?*'" Marcel casts his line. "*La gente dice, la gente dice.* They have been saying things like that since I was born, and look who is still here. They will always say that. Especially if they have nothing else to worry about."

I sit with my feet dangling off the dock and I sketch them.

The evenings set in more hurriedly now, and I prepare dinner early. "Let's take a walk," Marcel touches my shoulder after dropping some plates next to the sink. I look down at the pile hesitantly, uncomfortable to leave it to crust up. "Leave them," he says. "Run a little water over first." We've made it to that comforting place where we can see full sentences in each other's faces. We walk the path with flashlights in tow as dusk darkens the jungle. I carry my fins and mask for a little night dip. "You can't get enough, can you?"

"Being down there– it's just its own world, you know? I feel like I'm exiting everything I know and experiencing a whole new existence, as an outsider."

"Isn't that what you're doing here?" I pause and look up into Marcel's tired, reddened eyes. I'm a little hurt to be called an outsider, even though he is clearly correct. "Well, I hate to pull you from your ocean tonight, but we are staying under tree cover. I want you to meet some *amigos* of mine." We cut out of the main path and walk parallel to the shore before cutting back into the thick understory of ferns, enormous tree trunks and flowering bushes. I have never noticed this narrow path before, though John and I have explored these trails many times now.

Marcel takes my hand to guide me over a fallen tree and through thick brush. As darkness falls on us the jungle gets louder, crowded with birds, frogs, and insects calling out for each other with repetitious chants of desire and desperation. A family of howler monkeys rustle the branches above us, startling me and making Marcel chuckle at my jump. He settles himself into a tiny clearing just large enough to fit his sitting position. Our flashlights illuminate the dome of bright young leaves above us; it looks like a place fairies would gather for a town hall. Marcel opens a little waxed cloth sack and pulls out some diced mango and a few hard boiled eggs. He makes a high whistling call that cuts through the other jungle messages, and all at once I hear them: claws scurrying along bark and rustling leaves, closer and closer. The sound raises the hair on my arms and my heartbeat quickens. It sounds like the rats in my walls in the Mirage foothills; I feel as though I'm about to be covered in unknown crawly things and I shudder at images of lizards, scorpions, spiders and rats. Finally they begin to reveal themselves in the periphery of the glowy dome of light, first as a terrifying display of large round eyes shining in the dark. They enter the light, but I still can't comprehend what they are. They look like teddy bears with monkey tails. Several of them gather on Marcel's shoulders and lap. One curious juvenile shuffles out onto a drooping branch and hovers before my face. Marcel passes me a few pieces of mango. I cautiously hold one out for her; a protuberant pink tongue grabs the piece and she opts to sit on my shoulder to eat it. Her fur is soft and she smells like a graham cracker.

"What on earth are these things?" She lets me scratch behind her ears as her tail curls around my neck like a scarf.

"*Son kinkajus, o, osos de miel*– honey bears. Not bears exactly, as you can see. Daniél here has been my friend for ten years." Curled in Marcel's lap, content as a housecat, sits a ragged old honey bear. I hand him a piece of egg and sit beside Marcel.

"So, *Niñita*. We all want to know. What are you doing here?"

"You brought me here…"

"No, no, *mija*. What are you *doing* here?"

"I don't know– waiting out the pandemic of the century? Catching up on my long-lost hobbies? Helping you and the boys get the inn back up and running? I guess more than doing, I'm *being*. Being here with you. Existing, on Earth. Swimming, fishing, cooking, eating. Just being a person. It's really kind of wonderful."

"And when is the last time you've called home? Do your parents even know where you are?"

A jolt of angst punches my gut. I haven't checked my email in months. Haven't called home. Haven't checked to see if my student loan bills are still on hold from the pandemic.

"Nina, *otra vez*– ¿*Qué estás haciendo aquí?*"

I get angry. "I'm fucking *happy*, alright? Is that so terrible? I am happy here with you. I'm not like Lita. I like this little life."

"You like it now, but you aren't happy, Nina. *Te estas deslizando*. You are coasting. You can enjoy it here all you want, and say you're content, but you cannot help your own design. You are from the new way, *mija*. It is how you managed to send a financially successful and physically powerful man who is deeply in love with you stomping into the jungle. That's not for you, he's not for you, and here is not for you. It would be easier if it was, for both of us. I don't want to lose you– we all love having you here. You brought life back to this place, to our bellies. I am so grateful to you for that."

"See? I can't leave you here–"

"*Equivocado*, Nina. Wrong. We love you here, but we do not *need* you here. You are not our savior; just a visiting angel." Marcel reaches out and just barely touches my cheek; I am moved by the tenderness of such a salty old man. It makes me feel like a little girl again, being carried to bed in my father's arms. The little girl who didn't think about the future, or hurricanes, or dying corals; the little girl who had the freedom to dream of fairy domes in the jungle filled with mysterious creatures, because she was safe.

"There is a part of me that wishes I could just forget," I muse aloud. "Forget about all the problems of the world, of people and nature. Just call it none of my business. It would be so freeing, to just– be. Things are only going to get worse…"

For the first time since arriving here, I think of Tyler.

Later, back in my blue box, the first place that has felt like home to me in many years, I pull open the dresser drawers and set the few items on the bed. I reach under the bed for the one bag I brought, and open it up for the first time since arriving. I start dropping in my clothes and books. I unzip a hidden side pocket and remove a folded, wrinkled letter. I read it aloud:

12/24/2019

Tyler,

I've spent the past weeks battling with myself to avoid calling you, so I am going to write these words instead. I need the outlet; I've wanted to speak to you desperately. I did not realize how lonely I was until our last conversation, and the realization has made me quite angry, because I wanted so badly to do better alone.

It is a dream I have long envisioned for myself: living alone in a space procured solely for my purposes and for my taste; succeeding alone, free to pursue whatever I want or need in whatever moment I desire to do so; being alone, unbound from distractions or obligations to anyone but myself. It is a fantasy rooted in reaction, passed down to me from a long line of dissatisfied and burdened women, bound to husbands they resented and children they did not plan for— staring out of kitchen windows and smoking cigarettes on porches, locked into lives that were in many ways handed to them, players in a game that they did not sign up for and obeying rules that were never going to be in their favor.

But even as I reread my own words, my own perception of the women in my life, I am led to question the lens by which I have seen them. Did I always view them this way? Did they always seem to be helpless victims of circumstance, of an age-old system of oppression and disparity? Am I giving them no credit for their own agency, their choices, their shortcomings and incredible strength?

I've gratuitously succeeded in being unlike them, but without much thought to what the alternative would or should be. There are many possible outcomes to rejecting the nuclear, the "normal", the expectations of life as a woman: marriage, motherhood, nurturing and domesticism, pink-collar work that is just an extension of the former; the succession of titles, of maiden, bride, wife, mother, grandmother. But how many of the alternatives lead to a misery of their own kind? Surely the woman who builds a family out of cats or dogs is neither free nor happy. The cost of litter and vet bills alone is cumbersome. The woman who over-educates herself so deeply into resentment at an unjust world becomes imprisoned by her own ideals, alienated inside walls of anger. The woman who imitates the man and achieves external achievements like wealth and success in business also achieves the emptiness that comes at the end of a man's life, an empire built on nothing but an addiction to building it. What lonely throne then, do I choose to sit on?

Lonely, lonely, lonely. That's the word that continues to plague me— that I can't supersede my social apeness, and I am doomed to desire to belong to something bigger than myself.

I am furious at you Tyler, because the awakening of your voice, that forsaken sense of home found in another, has shattered my fantasy, and left me to confront the fact that even though I may not need a man to protect me, to provide for me, or to complete me, I still desire one— and even worse, perhaps I do need those provisions in a world still ruled by weak men and prowled by broken ones.

I become more hateful toward you with every word I write, because admitting my desire is admitting an excruciating sort of defeat. Anything you allow yourself to desire has power over you. This is my greatest fear: a relenting of my freedom, an admittance of dependence on anything or anyone but myself.

Three simple words from you, "Are you okay?," have opened a wound that I worked tirelessly to suture; your concern ran down my chest, split me open, and pried out the question that I am now forced to ask myself: If I am to admit that I desire a man, I must choose one, and what kind of man should that be? By which instincts do I make this decision?

There is the rational, pragmatic approach that many women strive for: to choose a man with the most wealth, regardless of attraction or treatment, for the sake of security. But this security is a fallacy. Nothing can make a woman feel more desperate than a cavernous wing with high walls, cold marble floors, and a man she hates waiting at the other end. I've seen this, and the thought of it sends a deadening chill down my spine.

There is a more primitive form of security, the physical kind, which means choosing a large, strong, fearsome kind of man. This sort offers the most intimate of safeties, visceral safety, and perhaps a special sort of intimacy, which is all very alluring to a delicate or sensitive woman who sees the world through fearful eyes. The decision takes for granted that this man's strength and dominance will without fail be pointed outward at the world, and ignores the reality that at any moment that force could be turned inwardly at you.

There is a third kind of safety, emotional safety, found in a sensitive and caring man. A man who is faithful and agreeable, and unlikely to cause emotional pain, but may not offer physical protection, financial security, or the excitement of polarity and discord. This type runs the risk of becoming overly agreeable, the pushover, the "whipped" or "neutered" man, who forces a woman into becoming the proverbial male in their dynamic: domineering, aggressive, in control. This dynamic brings out the worst in both parties, because an imbalance of power between lovers will always create fissures of resentment and suffering, no matter which sex assumes the higher seat. Perhaps it is not the novelty of this role reversal that has inspired such a societal outrage and fear of this increasingly common power dynamic, but more that it is a reversal of nature itself. I never thought I would speak this way; never in a thousand years.

Could a world exist in which the dynamic of power is gone? Could man and woman walk together as co-supporters, as partners... dare I say... as equals? We will always bring different gifts and weaknesses to the table. That would be true for any two individuals, regardless of sex, wouldn't it? But over the course of history and billions of people, we do have proclivities. How much is it in our nature, and how much of it is nurture? Can we nurture our way out? Or is our attempt at such engineering what's making everything so confusing?

How do I join the world? What purpose do I have, if I serve only myself– or serve only the world as a whole– a thing to which I have no connection whatsoever?

I am tired of trying to excavate my true nature from a lifetime of nurture, but I have no choice. I must walk on, steadily but slowly; lost, but comfortably so; not panicking at the setting sun nor the holes in the map I hold.

PART FIVE

THE SUMMER

30
Pink Tax

2018

"Almost ready!"

That was a lie. One of my most badly worn out lies. I was *not* almost ready. Not even close.

I tried so hard to be waiting and ready at the door in time for Tyler's arrival, but you can't magically find something in your closet that doesn't exist. I got rid of most of my winter clothes upon moving to California, naively thinking the whole state had the climate of San Diego. I took only what would fit into my car when I left Dean, and sacrifices had to be made.

I had nothing relevant for a camping trip: no warm jacket, no sleeping bag, not even a flashlight. When I hesitated to agree to this trip, Tyler assured me he'd bring everything we would need. "Just bring lots of layers, a good backpack, and a swimsuit. We can grocery shop on the way."

I didn't realize how long it had been since I had gone camping, hiking, or canoeing. Had I ever canoed? My family isn't exactly outdoorsy. In the summer my mother would place cinnamon Eggo waffles and orange juice on the picnic table in the yard and lock us outside until lunch, but we never left the neighborhood, which had been recently built and only had a few newly planted young trees. When we did venture out as a family, we went to the shore. We ate porkroll-egg-and-cheese bagels in the sand, walked the boardwalk with giant soft serve ice cream cones, had hush puppies and coconut shrimp with cherry pineapple sauce at the Shrimp Shack. Food was the focus, and the ocean provided a nice backdrop. Speaking of which– *what kind of food do you eat while camping? Beans? What about clean water? Do you have to bring it?*

As I stood there brooding with eight pairs of bundled socks in my arms, it dawned on me that I had never *actually been* camping before. I had attended barbecues and picnics at campsites, or sang campfire songs at Disney's Fort Wilderness with Chip and Dale– but we always returned indoors and slept in beds. *Oh sweet Jesus…*

"…Everything okay?"

I jumped at the sound of Tyler's voice, horrified that he was suddenly behind me, standing in my room for the very first time. "How did you get in here!" I started frantically pushing him toward the door.

"The old lady let me in– whoa, take it easy!"

I had vowed to *never* let any new people I met into my house, especially not a date, until I could afford to move to less embarrassing accommodations. My first place in Mount Mirage was filthy, old, and creepy. I had seven housemates, ranging from a seventeen-year-old boy who had been kicked out of his parents' home to a sixty-eight-year-old social worker who screamed in her sleep. I shared the downstairs bathroom with four of them– three men and the screaming lady. I had an air mattress on the floor, clothes in a couple of duffel bags, and a collage of boxes and shopping bags all over the room that held the rest of my earthly possessions. It smelled like the previous tenant was a heavy smoker and a night-sweater. I shoved and prodded Tyler out into the hallway. "Ten more minutes, please. And forget everything you just saw."

Tyler's car was packed haphazardly with supplies for the long weekend; I shoved my bags into any soft-looking gaps and we drove due north to leave town. "I'm so glad you could get the time off work."

"Thank you so much for planning this," I rolled down my window and exhaled. "I can't wait to see some *treeeees!*" I reached over and tickled Tyler's rib, which momentarily sent the car darting toward the other lane.

"*Nina!*"

Something about those rare outings with Tyler made me feel freer–free to be sillier, and a little careless. He had all the knowledge and gear, and did all the planning. For once I got to simply be a passenger.

The walls of my bedroom were filled with charts: planning charts, budgeting charts, sticky notes with ideas and goals and inspirational quotes. Before the idea for *Gasoline* colonized my psyche, I was gunning for a paid job with the Earth Defenders, but more than that, I wanted to start my own business. I had the perfect idea: a zero-waste store in the heart of downtown. It would have bins of bulk dry goods like beans, pasta, tea, flour, snacks, spices, and a selection of local farmers' produce. A household section with bulk soap, shampoo and all-purpose cleaner; canvas bags, metal straws, bamboo toothbrushes, the whole enchilada. I figured I could get buy-in from the local environmental groups and use the space to fundraise for them too. It could be a community meeting space, where we could screen documentaries, host discussions and town halls– I had a whole vision for it. It was inspired by this empty storefront in town. I looked inside the empty space and I could just see it, clear as day, exactly what it would look like. *Could* look like. I called the phone number on the "commercial space for rent" sign and everything. When she stated the rent so plainly I burst with incredulous laughter. "Yes, yes that makes sense," I chuckled, and told her to have a nice day. It's no wonder a quarter of the storefronts in downtown Mirage are vacant.

Eventually the walls of my bedroom were taken over by the vision of my movie, plastered over with notes about villains, MMED slogans about intersectional climate justice, and charts describing structures of power in the world. At that time, I wasn't sick of looking at it yet. The vision was still so clear; it was still fresh in my mind, a ripe idea, juicily beckoning to be picked and cashed in.

Tyler has no lists, no sticky notes– only maps and field guides. He has spent most of his life's free hours in the remotest parts of Mirage backcountry, and I've accompanied him to places I would never have had the wherewithal to find on my own. But this day we were driving up to Tyler's family cabin.

"The land has been in my family for generations, since they settled out here during the Gold Rush." Tyler talked often of his travels, but the cabin was the setting for most of the stories that lit up his face.

We crossed the second mountain pass and began the descent into a valley. From above, a thin yellowy film obscured our view of the little town below, surrounded by sprawling citrus groves and cattle feedlots. "The worst part of getting there," Tyler sighed as we curled around the descending switchbacks. "At least we get it over with early. I'd roll your windows up."

It was a sobering sight; a peek into the real California, where the coast's gas and groceries are made. Underneath the smoggy layer now, the sky was a sickly washed-out blue, and the ground was hard and yellow. The trees were geometric and perfectly aligned in multi-mile long grids, which were traced by black irrigation hoses. Red signs every fifty yards warned visitors that the fruit was private property, and touching, picking or tasting was a felony. But at least the green leaves and the imperfect patterns of bright orange and lemon yellow ornaments broke up the frightening uniformity of the landscape; on the feedlots we passed, not a speck of color was to be found. The animals, doomed from birth with their numbered slaughter tags pierced into their ears, stood lifelessly in a foot-thick soup of their own excrement and mud, packed together under shaded overhangs, or in front of a few large fans blowing ninety-degree air. I could see the thick swirling clouds of flies from the car... I could almost hear the relentless buzzing assaulting their ears and causing their back muscles to twitch incessantly.

Tyler pulled into a gas station. "I am going to buy some propane and use the bathroom– do you need anything?"

"I don't think so."

"Great, can you fill us up and put air in the tires?" I looked at him as though he just asked me to rebuild the car's engine. "The machine's right over there. Quarters are in the center console. Thanks."

He ambled off and I gasped with disbelief and disgust.

"Unbelievable!" Debbie protested. "It's the *may-an's* job to do car stuff on road trips! The *nerve!*" I shared her sense of indignant revulsion. She continued, "and *ah* we supposed to be PAYIN' for this gas, too?"

Felicia wasn't having it. "Don't make her think she's helpless! Are you saying that we *can't* put stupid air in a stupid tire? If a *man* can do it–"

"Alright alright," I shook them off and begrudgingly set to my tasks, both irritated and a touch anxious to figure it out before Tyler returned so he wouldn't witness my cluelessness.

He returned after a suspiciously long time– as if he saw me struggling with the air-hose-thing and decided to hide in the store until I was done and had calmed down. As we continued the drive in casual silence I was glowing inside from my little self-sufficiency victory. The landscape continued its monotony for hours, and a similar debate between Debbie and Felicia ensued once Tyler asked me to take a turn at the wheel. Ultimately I agreed, but regretted my decision as we began a winding ascent.

"Pull off to the right in about a quarter mile," Tyler noted while his finger traced a white line on a paper map.

"*Tsss– paper* map," I scoffed to myself. It seemed ridiculous and garishly antiquated, like a hipster riding a unicycle through the park in a porkpie hat. But I had failed to notice that we had been out of cell phone service for over an hour.

"Here!" I barely made the turn– jerking the car back into our lane on the narrow road to the campground.

The sun was just tucking itself under the ridge, coating vertical strips of the enormous sequoia trees in golden syrup. As we carried our belongings down the short trail to our campsite, the bright gold stung my eyes, and I stopped midway to rifle through my bags for a pair of sunglasses. Tyler, always prepared, kept to his task, and had lapped me with a second load of things by the time I reached the campsite. There wasn't much to it– a rusty fire ring, a splintery picnic table, and a flat patch of earth behind it in a grove of ponderosa pines. The only sounds were a few bird calls and the subtle babble of a distant creek.

We both paused for a moment to enjoy the stillness after a long day of motion. "Let's get the tent set up before dark, then we can relax by the fire. I brought my guitar." He pointed to the compact tent bag. "Can you get it started? I still need to grab the firewood."

Debbie looked up from buffing her nails. "What did he just say to us?"

"I can't," I called to him as he walked away. "I don't know how."

"It's a really easy one— I'm sure you can figure it out. It's color-coded." And he continued on the trail.

I didn't try to calm Debbie's rage as I emptied the contents of the tent bag onto the flat spot. I let her rant about how ladies should be treated, how chivalry is dead and how its murderer is the so-called culture of the West Coast. As I stared at the jumble of metal sticks and synthetic fabric on the ground, I noticed a diagram on the side of the bag. The tent sits on a simple X-shaped frame; the sticks all fit into each other and the ones with the red stickers are the ends. The orange metal stakes go through the orange rings at the tent's base and hold it to the ground. One by one, I snapped together the sticks until I had two poles. I laid the tarp down and arranged the flat tent over it. As I started feeding the first pole through the blue loops, Tyler reappeared with an impressively-arranged bouquet of wildflowers, tied together with the red twine from the firewood bundles. "Nice work! Here, let me help you." He began feeding the other pole through the opposite side, and soon enough we had a tiny little home in this wilderness. I stared at it for a moment with my hands on my hips as if I had just felled a bunch of trees and built a cabin from scratch.

"I have a surprise for you." Tyler placed the bouquet in my hands and walked me past the tent to a tiny footpath in the forest. Between two trees hung a hammock and a lantern. In the hammock I found my jacket, hat and writing bag. "I am handling dinner tonight," he said, and turned me around for a kiss. "You can write, or read— or just listen to the sounds of the forest. Just relax, and enjoy."

I tried to read, but there were too many distractions: birds flitting through the trees, squirrels chasing each other among higher and higher branches, as if in a contest. The frogs singing from the creek's edge. The weird mixture of guilt, pride, and shame I felt about my behavior and thoughts throughout the day made my stomach uneasy. I picked at the wildflowers while I tried to make sense of it. Was Tyler inconsiderate, or incredibly considerate? Was Debbie throwing a fit for no reason? Why did I think I was incapable of something as simple as setting up a two-person tent, or putting air in a car tire? Did he actually wait in the gas station on purpose to let me figure it out on my own, and if he did, isn't that condescending? Or empowering and good-intentioned? I came to zero conclusions before Tyler called me over for dinner. I made a silent resolution to myself to not complain for the remainder of the trip.

"It's hot– let's get the campfire going before we feast."

"Can I help?"

Tyler smiled. "Was hoping you would."

I was *hungry.* We had bowls of brown rice, spicy black beans with roasted corn, tomatillo salsa and avocados. We passed a bag of tortilla chips back and forth and enjoyed our meal in silent satisfaction. I sighed deeply upon my final bite. "Wow, that was good. This whole scene– it's what I didn't know I needed. Thank you." I squeezed his hand. "This is the first weekend in months I won't be working on the campaign."

"Is it just writing the newsletters still?"

"I wish," I sighed again– but a different kind. "First it was the newsletters. Then it was designing flyers and posters, and morning door-knocking. Now they want to 'promote' me to set up and manage a social media campaign for them."

"Well that's great! Right?"

"It would be if I were getting paid. But between Vero's and Earth Defenders I'm working over 60 hours a week to barely cover my bills at the end of the month. Some of their interns have been there for *years.* I just wish I could do something to help the environment without having to serve martinis to rich people. It's degrading."

"I recently became a monthly donor– maybe I should just write you checks instead!"

"Maybe you should." My words came out a touch more severe than I would have liked. I stared at him stone-faced and he turned his sights to the flames.

"So…vegan s'mores?"

Tyler laid his open sleeping bag on the dirt and pine needles. We stared at the ring of starry sky revealed by the clearing of our sleeping place.

"I like it here. It's so quiet. I can hear my own thoughts. It's like I can almost hear the synapses firing in my brain… little lightning bolts. *Zap, zap…*"

"And what are you thinking about?"

"I don't want to say." It was money. I was thinking about money. I was doing some mental math– an estimate of how much I could save on groceries if I packed up more client food from the Vero's kitchen and brought it home. I know it sounds gross, but you can cut around the one bite they took out of it, and then you have a $44 dinner for free-ninety-nine. "What are you thinking about?"

"I'm thinking I'd like to stay here. For a week. A month maybe."

"But I thought you were excited to show me your family cabin?"

"Eh, yeah. I am more excited about a special surprise pitstop on the ride up tomorrow. Unless you'd like to stay here…"

"You just said 'special surprise', so any chance of staying here is now gone. Sorry."

My no-complaints resolution was a struggle. When we crawled into our tent for the night, I felt dirty and cold. The ground wasn't so flat now that we were laying on it. I had drank too much water before bed, and had to exit the tent twice in the night. The first time I scrambled my way to the camp pit toilet, and nearly dropped my flashlight into it. The second time I gave up and squatted by a bush near our sleeping quarters. I jumped when his head suddenly popped out of the tent and I shouted, much too loudly, *"Don't look at me!"* He laughed and held out a wad of tissues.

"Just thought you might want some of this. Do you realize you are directly uphill from the tent?"

Tyler woke me gently– and too early– the next morning so we could hit the road and reach the cabin before dark. I surprised myself when I asked to drive first. The morning was crisp and gorgeous, and something about the forest air had put me in a good mood. Or perhaps it was the strong instant coffee hitting me. I otherwise struggled to feel light-hearted with dirty hair and body odor. "I love the way you look right now," Tyler kissed me as I rolled my eyes in vain disbelief. "I like when you look a little wild." Perhaps I was on a high from disassembling the tent by myself while Tyler boiled water and packed the car. Either way, and despite all smells to the contrary, I felt ready for a fresh start. The cabin was guaranteed to have a shower, after all, so my self-consciousness had a clearly-defined endpoint. No need to complain or question– *just relax*, I thought, *and enjoy this*.

The landscape was pleasantly wilder on this leg of the trip. We'd be in a dense tunnel of trees, little flickers of penetrating sunlight bouncing off the windshield like sparks, and then for a brief few moments there would be a break in the ranks of trees, and an alpine vista would appear. I was on the hunt for bears, desperate to see one in the wild for the first time– so desperate that I nearly ran us off the road, mistaking a charred stump to be a snoozing black bear. Tyler took the wheel so I could focus, but I soon fell asleep. When I woke, our dreamy surroundings had turned nightmarish. The hillsides in the distance looked like an old man's buzzed head. The forests had been fully scooped-out of all hues of green, replaced with browns, black, and the burnt orange of dead pine needles. It was Honalee from the childhood cartoon of *Puff the Magic Dragon:* stripped of rainbows and smiling bouncing bushes, replaced with eerie nothingness.

"It's pretty fresh," Tyler explained, sensing my horror. "The ecosystem was already weakened by an invasion of bark beetles. Many of the trees were already dead or struggling."

"Does that mean it won't come back?" I gasped at the idea, reliving my days of mourning the Great Barrier Reef.

"I don't know exactly. It certainly won't be the same, but something always comes back. That's what brings me comfort; the resilience of life. When some creature can no longer survive new conditions, something else that can will come along and take its place. No matter what we do to this place– how much we wreck it for our own survival or greed, it will be paradise for something else– like the bark beetle," he forced a chuckle. "But no, it won't be what it was. These old growth forests have trees that are hundreds of years old– even some millennials, I think."

"It's such a shame…"

"It's our own fault, bad karma. We should have listened to the Native Americans," he said.

"What do you mean?"

"Their idea of conservation was to do what was best for the land first. They used to regularly burn the forests when the underbrush would get too thick. The forests need it; it's cleansing. The sequoias require the dry heat of fire to open their cones and spread their seeds. But when we came over here and took the land, we thought coddling the forest was how to take care of it. Every time a fire would start, we'd rush to extinguish it. Centuries of that behavior and we've turned the West into a tinder box. Add in the drought and increasing temperatures from climate change, and well…" He motioned to the overcooked landscape around us. We were descending down a hill and the remnants of a small town began to appear.

"Tyler, you keep saying 'we', but– I mean– you're *Asian*," I uttered cautiously. "I don't think you have a share in the guilt here. It's us white people who are the ones who wrecked everything, not you. You don't need to take that upon yourself."

"Isn't your family Italian? When did they get here?"

"My grandpa on one side, my great grandma on the other."

"So you're not really the 'we' either, just because you're white. My family was here like a century before yours."

"Yes but Columbus was–"

"Well, he sailed under Spain."

"Yeah but, you're not–"

"Not what?"

I wanted nothing more than to stop talking about this. Tyler was looking carefully ahead, searching for something. All that was left of the tiny old town around us was a series of burnt-out car frames and sporadic rows of semi-crumbled chimneys poking out of rubble. Few sights are more haunting than this. All I could see was Santa Claus, coming to deliver presents, still having the chimneys active on his software, and encountering this charred warzone: the battle of feeble humanity and Mother Nature. I couldn't help but think of it in a selfish way: *Will my home burn down because of climate change someday? Or will it flood? Which is worse? Is there any place that is safe to live anymore? I'll probably never afford to have a house anyway.* It's a conversation Tyler and I have had many times: where should we settle down to play the best odds of avoiding natural disaster. Climate change was ubiquitous and creative; there is nowhere to hide.

Tyler turned down a dirt road. We breathed a simultaneous sigh of relief; the charred areas were becoming more patchy. Some trees had blackened trunks and a ring of deadened orange needles, but their living green tops were beacons of resilient, heartening life. We stopped in front of a large NO TRESPASSING sign suspended on a rusty chain across the path. "We can walk from here."

"No, we can't." I didn't leave my seat. "Do you not see the sign? We're in the middle of burnt nowhere– I am not getting murdered, even for a surprise."

"*Murdered?* Nina, there is no one here. Come on, don't worry." He opened my door and extended his hand.

"Oh, so now suddenly you're chivalrous?" I grumbled and joined him on the private side of the sign. After about ten minutes of walking I broke my private resolution and asked, "How much further? Where are we even going? I don't like this."

"You'll see, soon," Tyler said. The patchy area that had seemed to be improving along our walk suddenly came to a severe halt, and Tyler with it. "No…"

He began running and crossed the black line into a patch of decimated forest. I followed him, suddenly panicked, as if our own home may be reduced to a chimney in these woods. After catching up I found him stopped at a small pile of rubble and the ghost of a modest square foundation. The only recognizable item was the rusted, cracked, fragmented remnants of what I guessed was a wood-burning stove. Tyler's eyes were glazed and red. "The best moments of my childhood, they were here... it's been my favorite place... since 1849..."

"*1849?* Are you a ghost?" I quickly threw my arm around him. "That was insensitive... sorry." I stroked his back as his sobs dissipated to a few silent tears on his cheeks.

"I just can't believe it's gone. Obviously driving up here I knew it would be a possibility, I just– I couldn't even picture it being gone."

He said he would explain on the walk back, once we crossed over the black line.

"Running through all this ash is not good for us– I just wasn't thinking."

We felt tremendous relief to cross back from completely-scorched to partially-scorched land. In comparison the semi-charred forest now seemed sluggishly alive, like a bear waking up from hibernation. I noticed tiny green growths sprouting from the ground; a few rustlings in the green part of the trees. And I felt grateful for her resilience; this Mother we've abused so diligently in our pursuit of success. At this point I was dying to know what structure had sat in that patch of clearing.

"It was my great-great-great-great grandfather's," he explained. "Very few Japanese people were in America before the Gold Rush. He was among the first. Yūto Shisōka was his name. He signed on to be a merchant sailor at thirteen, and after four years at sea, he decided to stay in California. He pretended to be Chinese, hoping to find community– the Europeans didn't know the difference– but the Chinese of course did. So he was kind of a loner. He built a small cabin in the wilderness with a friend, and they tried their hand at trapping. Once word got out about gold being found up and down the state, they had heated debates about whether or not they should go prospecting. Yūto didn't believe there was as much gold as the rumors claimed, and he let his friend go. He turned the cabin into a supply store for the prospectors. He sold picks, pans, camp supplies, dry goods. He buried his money in the woods and lived like a poor man, selling his supplies for cheaper than his competitors. He brought over family, and wrote love letters to his childhood neighbor, eventually convincing her to come here and marry him. He made a small fortune; they used it to buy parcels of land

and they farmed. A lot of the land is still in my family today. He died old, surrounded by family, happy. And it all started in that little shack…" Tyler and I climbed into the car, covered knee-down in ash and soot.

"That is a crazy story… is it true?"

"As far as I know, yes. It's been the pride of my family forever; this notion that we are a clever people who make the best of our circumstances, and that we are a part of this area's history. We would always stop here on the way to the cabin to pay our respects and the old people would tell old family stories. It was my favorite place to play. I'd pretend I was him and try panning for gold in the creek."

"Whatever happened to the friend? Did he strike it rich?"

"Doubtful– most people didn't. The rush ruined a lot of lives. It was like the X-games of gambling. There was a rumor that he returned to Yūto's farm years later and begged for a labor job– but I don't know if that's true."

"I'm so sorry it's gone– but maybe you could put a plaque out there or something. I bet there is a historical group who would love to hear that story."

"Eh– it's always kind of been our secret," he said, "and my dad definitely wouldn't want some group or government entity involved. He's kind of alternative." It dawned on me that after dating Tyler for almost a year, I had not met his father, or heard him mentioned. I sort of assumed he was dead.

We drove back through the haunted rows of chimneys and returned to our route to the Shisōka family cabin. I could tell Tyler was in his head, probably replaying childhood moments. I tried to distract him for a while with light conversation and music, but realized it was best to leave him to his thoughts.

Tyler's bright blue Subaru meandered through a patchwork of crumbly switchbacks, hollow forest and tiny gold rush towns. I wrestled with my curiosity, hesitating to ask him to pull over so we could explore the ghostly little main streets. While his inner child was grieving, mine wanted to play cowboys and Ind– prospectors.

435

Around dinnertime we pulled into a town that stood generations apart from the others. If you looked closely you could see the bones of an old main street fitted with modern flesh, all with a cohesive ski-lodge architectural style: Verizon store, macaroon and boba shop, high end outdoor clothing and gear stores. It was inherently "normal"– the typical logos, typical people– but after the day's drive, it all seemed so excessive; so unfittingly modern against the natural surroundings. "It's pretty close to the National Park," Tyler read my mind, "and no one really cared about it until they built a luxury ski resort." He shook his head. "It's been blowing up since I was a teenager. But don't worry, the cabin's far enough away from this madness." We pulled into a grocery store to stock up for the week. The weather was chilly and overcast so I went for comfort foods: soy sausages, butternut squash ravioli, frozen tater tots, brussel sprouts, lima beans, ingredients for biscuits, chili, and cornbread. "I think this is enough– we have zero-chance of getting snowed in, just so you know."

"Can't a girl dream?"

At checkout I unloaded the cart and Tyler bagged. "So since I eat more than you I was thinking we split this 60/40. So that means you owe…$88.20."

Debbie attempted a lunge with her sharpened fingernails out like a feline, but Felicia stuck out her muscular arm and clotheslined her.

"…That makes sense," I said, and reached for my credit card.

After one final turn at the wheel I leaned against my window and drifted into a deep sleep. I dreamt of strolling through a garden of coral, schools of tiny fish circling, rays soaring above my head– but the corals, like a tiny rainbow forest, were on fire: plumes of black smoke filtered and swirled their way up the indigo water column. I stood there on the ocean floor, staring helplessly. *How does one extinguish a fire sixty feet under the sea?*

"Wake up, mermaid," Tyler gently squeezed my shoulder. "We're here."

He gestured to leave our bags so we could take a tour first. I stood beside the car for a moment. There was an unsettling incongruence to this place. Surrounding the front door was a small, rustic rectangular structure that looked like one of my childhood Lincoln Log projects come to life. Lichens and moss grew between the logs, seeming to seal them together. It looked historic; quintessentially American– as if Teddy Roosevelt escaped here for long weekends to gather his thoughts and hunt big game. But this old rectangle was encapsulated by another larger, more modern building– so blatantly encompassed that it seemed as though the monstrous building had swallowed the cabin whole, and it sat there unchewed, but slightly digested, in its belly.

The larger building looked like the fancy ski-chalet-themed strip malls we had passed earlier. It had large geometric tinted windows, exposed river rock, a burgundy standing seam roof and several balconies. I was so taken by it that I didn't notice Tyler walking up the driveway and disappearing around the side of the place. I ran over to catch up with him.

Again I was dumbfounded upon reaching the monster's backside: it sat on the bank of a sparkling alpine lake. The surrounding hills were covered in pines and yellowing tamaracks; distant mountains were dusted with what my mind perceived as powdered sugar.

I grew up near tall buildings– some tall trees, sure. When I first came west, Mount Mirage's foothills blew my mind. But *this? These? People actually get to live near these?*

I couldn't contain my awed joy. "Oh Tyler, it is…spectacular!"

"Can you help me lift this?" Instead of unpacking and settling in, cooking dinner, and taking a hot shower, which I was looking forward to most, Tyler was standing next to a rack of kayaks and canoes. I stared hesitantly. Debbie heaved a passive-aggressive "I give up" sigh.

As I grabbed the large green canoe and gained a sense of its weight, I asked, "What about the groceries?"

"It's cold out here– they'll be fine for an hour. I think we'll feel better if we move around a bit– and sunset on the lake is worth it, trust me."

It did feel good to work my arms, pushing the canoe along, breaking the crystalline surface of the water. The amphitheater of mountains were going through their evening color cycle as the sun's last rays approached them: the stone became purple, then darker; the snowy tops were arranged with hues of orange and then a rosy pink. A bright light snatched my eyes from the beautiful display, and back across the lake. It was the cabin– if you could even call it a cabin– the monster, instantly all lit up like one of those bioluminescent killer fish. There were many other cabins tucked in the woods surrounding the lake, but they were constructed to be harmonious with the landscape, earthy and unassuming. Tyler's "cabin" looked like advanced creatures from outer space had demolished a chunk of forest and set up an outpost: a landing pad in the form of a lakeside tennis court, a ceremonial patio and dining area, and a bathhouse with a diving board and spa mere yards from a perfectly good body of water.

"The automatic lights– I should have turned them off. Sorry." He grimaced toward shore, even more uncomfortable with it than I was. "It wasn't always like this. When I was a kid, it was just the little cabin in the front. It didn't even fit us all; we kids would camp out in the yard. My great-grandpa died when I was 13, and my grandparents began construction almost immediately. At first it was kind of exciting; no kid can resist a diving board and an entertainment room with video games and an air hockey table. But I eventually realized that the woods we played in were gone; the little redwood I planted on my fifth birthday, gone. And one day, my mom and I canoed out here for sunset, and those lights came on, and I just felt– *sick*.

"I've heard other people talking about it– some are envious, some wonder if a celebrity or a mysterious billionaire bought the property. I've heard a rumor that it's Jackie Chan's vacation home. Kind of insulting, kind of funny– whatever. But most people are disgusted, and worried. A precedent has been set now. No one has sold yet, but there are worries that another bad inheritance or two could turn this place into something it was never intended to be. Anyway, if you get a dirty look from anyone, that is why. Nina? Uh, are you okay?"

There was just enough light left in the day for Tyler to see my reddened face and bulging eyeballs. As soon as those lights came on, I stopped hearing his words. One thing had become abundantly clear, and that slow simmer of the last two days was pushed to a furious boil.

"$88.20? $88-*FUCKING-20?*"

"What?"

"You're having me pay for groceries and gas? Paying my own way on dates? You're *fucking RICH! LAKESIDE TENNIS COURT RICH! ONE-PERCENT RICH!*"

My voice echoed across the lake, and it was embarrassing, but for the first time maybe ever, Debbie and Felicia were in agreement on something, and I felt them shaking my braids like they were horse reins. "All I do is fret about money, and rent, and you always tell me how I work too much. And all this time, you've just let me suffer, acting like you're some broke grad student in a faded t-shirt. I bet you don't even pay for your education. I bet you don't even pay your rent! Do you? *DO YOU?*"

It had become dark enough, but Tyler's face was glowing white. He looked genuinely afraid, like I may tip this thing and hold him down. "Look– I'm sorry– I– I thought I was doing the right thing. I thought you wanted to pay…"

"*Wanted* to pay? Are you out of your–"

"Wait, please listen, Nina, you have to understand I would never purposely try to hurt or upset you… I just thought, well, she's taking out her wallet and if I don't let her pay, maybe it would be patronizing, or disrespectful, in like, a feminist way. I wanted to treat you as an equal– I thought that is what you wanted?"

"But we *AREN'T* equal!" This admission stunned me. I walked it back, "…at least not in a social or economic sense. By calling yourself a feminist you are acknowledging that!"

From here, truthfully, things began to go a bit off the rails. It was like every silent speech I made in my head or in the shower, combined with every *#smashthepatriarchy* meme I had ever read online, all spewed out of my mouth simultaneously. I wandered from the unspoken etiquette of taking out your wallet purely as a gesture to the pink tax on women's razors and lotion and the cost of tampons and the relative composition of women in Congress compared to the national population. Tyler listened dutifully, though his face hinted uncertainty about where this runaway train of grievances would end. "And on top of all that, do you know how much time, money, and energy it takes just to be 'socially presentable' as a woman? The shaving, plucking, seruming, the makeup and the haircare… all for you guys just to take it for granted, or mess it up!"

Tyler seemed to find a safe place to enter. "You really don't need to do all of that…" but he immediately realized he had stepped on a landmine.

"Oh really? REALLY? Do you even want to know what kind of *swamp creature* you'd be dating if I didn't do that stuff? And besides, it's not just for you. It's… it's–"

An unwelcomed guest forcefully appeared in my brain, shoved both Debbie and Felicia aside, and grabbed the mic.

"Well well well, li'l star… looks *loike* you've learned absolutely nothing. Irrational, simply irrational. You had *stahted* with a fair point– this bloke is clearly not takin' proper care of you like a man should. But you've managed to spiral completely outta control, victimized *yahself* in about ten different ways and blamin' him personally for what sounds *loike your* problems. You've completely invalidated yourself." I cringed at John's stupid accent finding its way into my thoughts, especially because that is truly what he would have said in this situation, and he would have been right. *Ocker bastard.*

I looked at Tyler helplessly, too far gone, and honored a gut impulse to remove myself from the situation as quickly as possible. Unfortunately this meant jumping into a lake on a chilly evening about a quarter mile from shore. "'Bout four-hundred meters, you mean," John's disembodied voice chuckled as I breathlessly treaded toward the brightly-lit mini-resort in my heavy clothes.

≈

I had once again placed Tyler between a rock and a hard place: paddle after her and help her, or let her go and retain some dignity? He chose the balanced option of paddling quietly behind me and treating me for early-stage hypothermia.

He removed my clothes and wrapped me in a fluffy bathrobe with bears baking pies on it. "Here, lay on the couch– I'm going to cover you in blankets and get you some tea." I was cold to my bones, and quite embarrassed. *This guy must think I am absolutely nuts.* But the icy water was sobering, and perhaps what I had deserved. I couldn't even remember how the conversation started, or what grand point I was trying to make. He's got rich asshole grandparents, so what? What does that really have to do with how he treats me, or who he is? He hasn't even known me that long. Why have I spent so much energy resenting him for not solving my own problems? I knew enough about him to believe in his sincerity; he really did perceive his actions as respectful, or at the very least, cautious.

"You know, if you are bothered by something, we can always talk about it. I would like us to be able to talk about it." Tyler placed a mug on the coffee table and sat across from me with his own mug in hand. Slowly the feeling was returning to my lips but my words came out wobbly and slow through chattering teeth.

"Ty, I feel like an ass. I'm really sorry, I don't even know what I was talking about."

He laughed quietly to himself, as if at a fond distant memory. "It's okay– I think you just had too many thoughts all trying to escape from you at once. And I understand about this place– it often inspires strong reactions. It's not who I am. ...I hate it." He shifted uncomfortably in the leather recliner. "And I'm sorry too– about the groceries and the gas. I really thought I was doing the respectful thing. It's so hard to know what is the right thing to do. There's no manual for being both chivalrous and feminist."

"Maybe this makes me a hypocrite, or a bad feminist… but I do want to feel taken care of by someone. Not contained, or kept– just– supported. And I want to give that in return, too– to count on someone, and to be someone counted on. If I can't count on my partner in life, then who else is there?" This spoken thought shocked me. It countered everything I thought I believed and spoke about for years. Independence, self-sufficiency. Being whole, complete, alone, without a man. I had prided myself on that; built my identity around it. "...Forget I said that. I don't think it's relevant. I–"

"No, it's okay. It's a reasonable thing to desire. I think on some level, almost everyone does. That feeling of finding a sense of home in someone else– to feel fully understood. I've never felt that way with someone... but I imagine it takes a lot of time." He knelt next to me; I felt like a human burrito under all those blankets. He kissed my cold lips with warm gentle ones.

"Tyler, did you purposely wait in the convenience store so I would put air in the tires on my own?" He hesitated, uncertain of whether his answer would complete a moment of tenderness or spark a new fight. But he chose honesty.

"Yes. I just see you limiting yourself all the time, assuming you can't do things– and it's like, have you looked at your life and all the things you've been through and done? You're the most tenacious person I know. You're capable of anything."

"Thank you," I smiled. A warmth came up from deep inside and began to thaw my bones. But the smile quickly vanished and my eyes bugged out so wide it frightened Tyler.

"What is it?"

"I left my makeup bag at the gas station."

We spent ten blissful days at the Shisōka cabin "and Bot Resort" as we playfully called the sprawling extension. We used the word "bot" to tease the modern, basic people– the people who prefer shopping to exploring, pools to lakes, and screens to maps. We rose early, packed snacks and spent our days hiking through the mountains or taking the canoe to tiny hidden beaches around the lake. On day six came the first snow of the season, and we bundled up and sat in rocking chairs on the back porch to watch it come down. It dusted the hundreds of pines on the hills in powdery, sugary snow. The snow didn't slow us down; it only made our hikes more interesting, and our returns to the cabin more cozy and satisfying. We cooked hearty meals, drank cocoa and played board games. We talked about going to the nearby lodge for a drink but we were too contented to bother.

Tyler insisted we sleep in the old cabin, which had a damp earthen smell and was a bit dark, but only added authenticity to the experience. I read books from the family's collection about the Gold Rush, the Native tribes of the West, and the first Japanese settlers in California. I read insatiably; more than I'd read in years. I tried to grasp the relatively recent yet primitive existence of people back in Yūto's days– what it must have been like to see this place undeveloped, still purely under Nature's rule. We mostly ignored the newer part of the house, and I quickly learned to ignore the mirror. Twelve days with nothing but basic dental hygiene, bar soap and a bottle of oatmeal lotion that Tyler brought. By day three I started to feel good in my skin. By day six I stopped even thinking about it.

We made love often, and in the golden syrupy light of late afternoons I let him explore my body without my usual sense of self-conscious shame, which heightened the pleasure for both of us.

31
A Barn of One's Own

"Life is bristling with thorns, and I know no other
remedy than to cultivate one's garden."
-Voltaire

2021

My mother gave my sisters and me a lot of one-off tips growing up– tips to help us become strong women, to advance in our careers, to achieve financial independence so we were never in a vulnerable position with a man. She was very open with us; we'd all lay in her bed with a big bowl of popcorn and talk, and no topic was off-limits. We were encouraged to ask questions about anything we heard in school, or weird things going on in our pubescent bodies, or what to expect in our budding romantic lives. She gave it to us straight; we giggled, buried our heads in the blankets, and gasped in horror.

Mom was born in 1959; she watched her older sisters disappear into the Summer of Love and came of age in the social upheaval of the '70s. Then she went to secretarial school and became a bookkeeper in the '80s. She wore blazers with shoulder pads and big hoop earrings, pants with stirrups and little black pumps that clicked through the kitchen. Sometimes Grandma would watch us while she was at work and in the evening they'd sit at the kitchen table, smoking cigarettes and playing cards, arguing about what should and should not be explained to us. Grandma's advice clashed severely with Mom's: Grandma gave us tips on how to be a lady and how to make "ladylike" choices, how to practice good manners, keep a home and cook well, and find a good husband. Some were guidelines, and many were hardline rules.

"Even when you're just running to the bank or grocery, look your best. People treat a pretty lady with more conscientiousness and respect."

"Indecisiveness is irritating to others and shows weakness of conviction. Know your values and act on them with every decision you make."

"Throwing out that food is throwing your father's money into the trash. Food is a gift from God, every single meal– that's why we pray at the table, isn't it? If you're not going to eat it, at least give it to the dog."

"Never, *ever* pass gas around a man. *Ever*. Friend, boyfriend, husband– *never*. When a man sees that part of you, you diminish a certain *mystery* about you, and it's never the same."

"But Gramma, what about George?"

"Yes, I suppose around your brother is fine."

To this day I am still trying to decipher which of these tips are useful, which should be taken with a grain of salt, and which are absurd. Over the years I absorbed bits and pieces of both Grandma's and Mom's advice, adhering to one version of moral code one day, and the other the next– until I have woven together the colorful quilt of philosophical contradiction by which I live my life.

But there is one bit of advice in particular that has stuck with me, and though the modern housing market has not exactly allowed me to do it, it has been a rule I've kept in my back pocket as a form of inspiration: "It is important for you girls, even mandatory, for you to have your own space for *at least* a year before you marry. It is so important to have that time, and that special space for yourself, before you commit your life to caring for your family."

Mom closed her eyes and took a deep breath. "*At least a year*. I'll never forget my little place in Vongola Beach, just a minute's bike ride to the boardwalk." It was a story we had heard before. Diane and Denise's attention wandered elsewhere, but I always liked this story. "It was a little dump, honestly– with cracked tiles, stained shag carpet. My air conditioner was louder than the train! I worked three jobs to keep that place..."

I liked picturing my mother as she described herself in her twenties– working hard, scrappy, fit, tanned skin. Riding her bike down the shore boardwalk in crisp white shorts with an ice cream cone. Petite and polite, but tough as nails... didn't take shit from the businessmen whom she waited on at the diner, didn't take shit from her boss or the other waitresses, from anybody. She had a giant Dobermann pinscher named Ajax, who she took to the Burger King drive-thru for cheeseburgers and spooned at night. "I was close; I had that place for eleven months and twenty-two days. And then on day twenty-three, I was pregnant with George." A little smile curled across Mom's lips. "Your father was so good; he sprung right into action, didn't even hesitate. We were married four months later– moved into the house after our little honeymoon in Sand Dollar, and he carried me over the threshold. Another blink of an eye and I was pregnant with twins..." Diane and Denise snapped back to attention at their mention. What a little miracle you all were..." Her voice petered off with her words, and she stroked Denise's head as she looked off into her memories.

I have had various versions of my "own space," from my sweaty bunk on the *Siren's Revenge*, to my closet-sized bedroom in the Mount Mirage foothills, and even the blue cottage at *el Congrego Mimoso*. But truly having "my own place" has been a desire never quite realized.

Living at Paula's may be the closest I get. A barn behind her property has been sectioned off into a workshop and my current living quarters. Its beauty lies in its simplicity: all the necessities have a place, and the only excesses to be found are potted houseplants and herbs, which Paula would call necessities. Lines of wire zig-zag against the lengths of the interior walls, and a large jar of wooden clothespins sits on the counter. "For your use," she says. "Hang your notes, your art, clippings of things you like, quotes and photos of people you admire and respect. Surround yourself in what inspires you– except in your sleeping space. Keep the walls quiet so you may quiet your thoughts before bed."

The north side of the barn has been gutted of its stalls and the exterior wall has been replaced almost entirely with windows. The space holds a basic kitchen in one corner, across from two horse stalls converted into a bedroom and bathroom, respectively. The other half of the barn is a workshop space, with everything from power tools to paints and canvas, a sewing machine, and a huge wooden work table.

The wall of windows looks out to the property's edge: a treeline that leads to a swimming hole that is mostly dry. From the east I hear the bellowing of two donkeys named Cacamabo and Reverend Casey, and the occasional clucking of a small flock of turkeys who follow the donkeys around their paddock, using their bodies for shade and comfort. On the south side, a native plant nursery and garden separate my humble lodgings from the main house. I enjoy the privacy, the nature, and the access to a creative space. My body is still adjusting to the labor and lifestyle.

Paula welcomed me to live in the barn on a few conditions. "If you stay here, you will be living on my schedule," she said. "On this property we operate under what I call 'the ritual of the Sacred Four: physical work, creative work, nourishment, rest. All four should regularly include learning, expanding horizons, or pushing limits– and all four must be practiced daily."

I was immediately turned off. "Sacred Four" sounded like some weird religious or hippie thing. I'm not into routines; I like to keep it loose. "That seems like a lot to pack into every day … I don't know if I'm even capable of that kind of discipline," I admitted.

"You'd be surprised." I followed Paula around the garden as she pruned a row of hummingbird sage. "One branch of the Sacred Four feeds the others. Tell me this, Nina. What gives you the ability to be creative? To focus on your work?"

I considered her question. The idea for *Gasoline* came to me more than two years ago. How much time had I spent *actually writing* it? All the year's distractions flooded through my head, most of them thanks to men, of all things. I blushed in embarrassment. I reached for my old default answer. "Money," I grumbled, "I think it comes down to that. Creativity is a luxury. If you're too worried about your basic needs, like I've been all this time, you don't have the mental space to create. You don't have clarity."

"Sure," she said, "but that's what the Sacred Four are really about: basic needs. You can't have clarity without rest, and you can't rest unless you're tired. You need physical work– to use your body to clean something, or fix something, or build something. That work can be paid, sometimes. In your case, farm work is how you'll be earning your room and board here. Work earns you nourishment. And you can't use your body well unless you nourish it– nourish it properly, with care, with real food. The ritual of good nourishment feeds the body, soul, and mind. Then, with a contented body and nourished mind, you can access your creativity. And creativity gives purpose, which feeds the spirit, and motivates the desire to work and nourish." She draws a circle in the air with her finger.

"When you put it like that, it makes sense. But I'm still not sure I–"

"Not a question," Paula anticipated my doubt and snipped it the same way she was snipping weeds and dead branches. "This is the formula for how you will live while you're here. Now, whether or not you live here is fully your choice. I know you think you don't have a lot of choices right now, but what you really have is a lack of *good* choices. But it's a big world and there are a million places you could be. Your choice to be here will lead to a giving up of certain choices: ones that don't serve you. Sleeping too many hours. Wasting hours on your phone as you transition your mind between tasks. Contemplating, *what should I do next?* instead of knowing by instinct or routine what you should do or must do. Free will is a beautiful thing, but *choosing* structure with that free will is how people really bloom, really *flourish*. And what is more freeing than flourishing?"

"What do you mean by flourishing? I am picturing a garden, all grown in and green, but that just may be because of where we're standing." I gestured to our lush surroundings. Paula has done a beautiful job with it. The green rows of food are dotted with fruits and flowers of red, yellow, orange, and green. Butterflies and hummingbirds zoom around the flowers. It feels and smells *alive*. "But in the human sense, what does flourishing actually mean? Is it to be happy, or successful?"

"Not quite. 'Happy' is an emotion, a temporary state of being. You're 'happy' when you eat a chocolate bar, or play with a dog, or have an orgasm. Experiences of satisfaction and pleasure are fleeting. Some serve your greater self, some don't. But to flourish is to self-actualize."

"Like, to know yourself?"

"To recognize and embrace your authentic self, and to live in harmony with that person. To do what you were made for. Flourishing is thriving on a physical, emotional, and spiritual level. To meet your potential."

Reverend Casey brayed behind us. "That's right, Baby," Paula nodded in agreement.

Potential... I can't get away from that fucking word. At least she's sharing how to get there, instead of berating me for wasting it.

"You won't be happy all the time– but you're not supposed to be. A self-actualized person can see beyond that. Instead of choosing to chase expedient and fleeting pleasure, she will choose to hold a mindset that is humble, grateful; *hopeful* during the tough times. Aware that bad times are temporary, as are the good times."

"That sounds really hard to do– almost imp–"

She nipped that right in the bud and talked right over me, "It's exceedingly rare, sure. Perhaps only impossible for those who live under oppressive cultures or societies. It's what makes a free society like this one– at least in theory– so desirable. To provide people their best chance possible to climb that ladder and self-actualize makes all the other flaws of a free society worth it. Creating that chance includes giving people space, yes, but it also includes giving them structure. Balance my dear, balance, is how we climb that ladder."

"You keep talking in all these vague terms... I don't follow it. I want to self-actualize, it sounds great. But the *how* is not so clear. What am I supposed to be climbing on, exactly?"

I followed her toward a shed next to the animal paddocks, and without a shred of irony Paula opened a stepladder and set it down. With ever-so-slight condescension she said, "I can show you, *like, literally.*"

She disappeared into the shed. I could hear the clanking sounds of her tinkering around, and she reappeared with her arms full. "Open your hand, Nina." She placed tiny specks in my open palm, light as air. Tomato seeds. "That's us," she said. She plucked a ruby red tomato from a nearby plant and placed it on the top rung of the ladder. "How do you go from here," she pointed at my palm, "to way up there?"

"Water and sunshine?"

She placed a watering can on the bottom rung. "As basic as it gets. These seeds will stay seeds without water and food; in their case food is sunlight." She yanked a lemon off of a nearby tree. "Pretend that's a sun." On the next rung she placed a small clay pot and a handful of soil. "Soil is home; soil holds water and nutrients, and provides safety from the harsh sun– too much of a good thing, you know." She winked at the lemon. "The pot is the same– keeps the predators away from the roots."

On the third rung, she placed a tray of tiny seedlings. "Did you know that plants communicate with each other and exchange nutrients through networks of roots and the mycelium of fungi? The science is relatively young on this, but apparently there is a whole other internet going on beneath the ground."

"What does that have to do with anything?" I suddenly caught myself sounding rude, impatient to move in already. *She's offering me a pretty great deal– I should at least listen to what this crazy old bird has to say.*

"One little seedling in an open field alone– what chance do you think it has of becoming that?" She points up to the tomato.

"Almost zero?"

"Exactly. I know you've been on your own for a long time. But from what you've told me, it sounds like you also seek that out. It's doing you no good." Before I could respond– "Like it or not, we need community, connection to something; a sense of belonging. When's the last time you felt that?"

I thought of sitting around the dinner table with Marcel and the boys. "Cuddly Crab…"

"What?"

"You're right," I admitted. "But this feels like a hard time and place to meet new people…"

"Time, yes, with the pandemic. But that is temporary. Place, no. I host dinners, open mic nights, fruit gleans. And you're going to participate. Seedlings who stick together take root." She pointed up again.

"Okay, what's next?" I was starting to like this metaphor now; I felt compelled to reach tomato status. She grinned at my responsiveness and set her pruning shears on the rung below the tomato. She grabbed a handful of trimmings off the ground and placed them next to the shears.

"You'll notice this one is a little messy. It comes back to what started this whole conversation– choosing structure. Sure, you can let a tomato plant grow out of control. If it's got plenty of food and water, it will explode with growth. A number of things could happen at that point, but it will most likely outgrow its available resources. The outer branches will start yellowing, and the new growths won't have the energy to survive. The little green tomatoes won't ripen, but slowly grow rotten. Suddenly the plant has all this heavy dead stuff weighing it down. But –" she gave the shears a loud *snip snip*, "if the plant is given a little structure, it will flourish." Paula grabbed the tomato and bit it like an apple. She passed it to me and I sunk my teeth into its juicy red guts.

∾

So I bought into the "Sacred Four" thing, telling myself I could easily fake it after I had settled in. I was wrong. The first few weeks felt like boot camp, with Paula waking me up early, prodding me along to do farm work, cook meals, keep the barn tidy. She insisted I keep my phone in a drawer for most of the day. "Fine, *fine*, no one is calling me anyway."

"Gee, with that attitude I can't imagine why. It would be better if you were actually talking to people you cared about on the phone instead of just scrolling through apps and feeds. Our brains are not designed to absorb so much compressed stimulation like that." She's right, annoyingly. She's been right about many things.

I feel like a child under Paula's strict routine, but like a child who is growing up. The truth is, I've never felt this good, except maybe my last few weeks with Marcel– but it's a different kind. I am energized and focused; present and calm. The days have never held so much potential and so many hours. Each day is like an orange that I am squeezing for every last sweet drop, and drying the rinds to make candies or kitchen cleaner, because nothing goes to waste at Paula's. I spend my creative time writing stories, painting watercolor sketches of the animals and the garden, practicing techniques for making semolina bread, mending and tailoring the clothes I bought from the thrift store. I've been here for about eight weeks and I sort of feel like a different person. I wake up without an alarm now. My body is strong. I rarely look in the mirror, and without Instagram constantly reminding me of the faults in my appearance it's never felt so good to be in my skin. I read 30 to 50 pages each day: a little at breakfast, a little after lunch, a little before bed.

I spend a couple hours writing each morning after farm chores– sometimes for *Gasoline*, but mostly journaling and "thinking through the pen," as Paula says. She gave me a list of important questions to ask myself. "The thirties are great, an important time– especially getting them kicked off. In your twenties you're an explorer, out in the field forging pathways, getting lost, collecting information. You spend your early thirties as a scientist: organizing and analyzing the data, drawing maps of where you've been and where you want to go. You present your findings to yourself around the mid-thirties. And then in your forties you get to use it all."

The questions seem simple, she says, but she advised me to keep 10 pages between them in my notebook so I can consider them fully:

Who am I? What do I love? What am I good at? How do I learn? What do I value? What/who is important to me? What am I afraid of? What am I proud of? What am I ashamed of? What does ~~flourishing~~ "tomatoing" look like to me? What prevents me from getting there?

As part of my rest time on the Sacred Four, Paula has insisted that I pray. "But I... I don't know how I feel about God at this point, at least not in the 'praying' sense."

"It's not about God– not about some man in the clouds, or a woman with six arms. Pray to be peaceful. Pray for the strength to face your challenges and pursue what you want. Pray to express gratitude, for the trees that feed your lungs and the fields that feed your body. Pray for forgiveness. Pray for hope. Pray for the ones you love– and for the ones you hate."

Once again I begrudgingly take her advice. I kneel beside my bed as I did every night of my childhood. "Dear white guy in the sky who watches me sleep and pee and bake apple cake: please divert resources from the ill and wartorn and starving to hear my prayer in regards to an ingrown hair on my thigh. I know you have a Divine Plan, oh compassionate God, but I'd like to cash in my free will to ask you to change your plans for me, as I am certain I deserve to win the Pick Six lotto this Thursday." I scoff and look to my sides like a middle school bully looking for reassurance from her stooges. But it's just me in my horse stall bedroom, and I feel like an ass. "Sorry... I had to get that out of my system. Okay..."

I play the original rhyme in my head. "Now I lay me down to sleep, I pray to... the Lord... my soul to keep. Watch me safely through the night, and wake me by the morning light, Amen. Please bless..."

This is the part where I used to list off everyone I wanted God to bless– everyone I cared about. I remember listing everyone by name, quickly at first, as the obvious ones rolled off the mind's tongue, and then slowing down as I got to various Disney characters, stuffed animals in my room, and random people from the neighborhood or Sunday school. The gaps of silence between names would get longer and longer, and then as if counting sheep, I would fall asleep. In those evening prayers I rarely got to the phase of asking for what I wanted. Those prayers usually happened in the moment of the desire, like "Please let me be her one day!" while admiring a dolphin trainer at a show, or "Please God, *no! Why now?!*" while holding in a gas bubble while being spooned by my high school boyfriend. I didn't pray for big things, not for any specific destiny or ability. Except to breathe underwater maybe. Or to raise a bear cub.

"Please bless... my parents, the twins and their families, George's memory. Marcel, the boys, Pablo and Maria, the kinkajous. John... whatever might've happened to him. Tyler..." I am surprised to see his name appear, but I suppose he was my inspiration for coming here in the first place.

ETHOLOGICAL STUDY OF THE GREAT WHITE
GORILLA: RESULTS AND CONCULSION

The majority of scientific studies conclude by not concluding at all, with a flaccid intellectual shrug, saying "further research is needed."

Before taking on the tedious, slow, and complex process of an authentic scientific pursuit, the author of this study would have called that statement a simplistic copout. She has been humbled.

Perhaps the humility of "further research is needed" is precisely the attitude that our scientific zeitgeist is losing. As society leans further into the ice-cold, secular pragmatism of what we call "The Science", we seem to become ever more arrogant– despite the bulk of our pursuits and studies ending in the same elegy:

> *The data is inconclusive.*
> *Additional variables were discovered that were not accounted for.*
> *The models we have available are flawed.*
> *A larger sample size is necessary.*
> *Further research is needed.*

Needed– not desired. Needed.

If science, in its most pure and noble form, is the earnest pursuit of truth, how do we account for science being practiced by flawed, corruptible human beings? How can we protect the nobility of science itself from losing its credibility from the malpractice of bad actors with political or ideological aims?

Knowing what you know about the modern world, who would you trust with the sanctity of the scientific method: the man working alone for decades in an old woodshed, who nearly starves in his refusal to cooperate with large institutions? Or the large institutions themselves, with state-of-the-art machinery and computer models, state-of-the-art minds produced by other large institutions, and a state-of-the-art office facility that hosts a media relations team?

The great white gorilla, the dominant adult male individuals of the white Western gorilla, *Gorilla-industria violentus*, was my chosen topic of study– chosen for its malignant global significance to the scientific community. A species considered invasive almost everywhere– a blight on the world, with its mighty fists gripping ever-tighter on the Earth, compressing it like a stress ball.

I invited this creature into my life; I welcomed it into my thoughts, learned about its hopes and fears. I imitated it and attracted it to myself. I let it speak, and listened: I asked it questions, asked it anything, asked it what it is and why. I made it feel at home with me. I let it into my arms and heart; I laughed at its jokes and heard its stories, pressed it against me and warmed it with the heat of my body. I made it laugh, gave it a meal and observed how it eats. I lived amongst it, watched it groom, rest, play, mourn, enjoy; I observed how it comforts itself, how it cares for itself, how it hurts; what it desires and what it is willing to do to get it.

The data is inconclusive.

Additional variables were discovered that were not accounted for.

The models we have available are flawed.

A larger sample size is necessary.

Further research is needed.

32
Press Tour

"*UGH*– Did you hear me? I was so… cheesy. I feel gross. Call her and tell her to smash the tape before it airs." I pull on my hair.

"I don't think they use tapes anymore… but I thought you did great. You spoke from the heart. I was a nervous wreck inside but I think my part went well too."

"I hate the idea of being on TV. I don't ever want to do that again."

"Oh come on, it wasn't so bad. I kind of liked it."

Tyler and I walk through the orchard, picking up items that were staged for the press tour: a ladder, shears, a basket full of peaches. We drop them at the tool shed, and take the peaches inside. "What do you think, cobbler or pie?"

"Hm… pie."

"Now I kind of want cobbler."

"Whatever, if you're makin' it, I'm eating it."

I turn on the light in the farmhouse kitchen, and I stop and stare at it a moment. It's the most beautiful place in the world, laid out to my specifications, decorated to my taste and fitted with the equipment I chose. This kitchen is a living place: sourdough starter bubbling, kombucha and beer brewing, food scraps waiting for their trip outside to the compost to begin the process of renewed life. A row of little herb pots stretch across the window pane for a taste of sunshine. This is my office, my home, my laboratory. And it's mine. *Mine.* I share it with Tyler, I share it with the kids we bring in for field trips, and the couples who come for cooking classes, but *I* am the captain of this ship. I even had a little plaque made to hang over the sink– in old-timey calligraphy it names the place *The Siren's Redemption.* I pull out a bowl, cutting board, and knife to get started on the peaches. Tyler bursts back in.

"She just sent a link! Do you want to watch it?"

"Absolutely not."

"Oh come on, like you can resist. Maybe if you see how it went, you'll feel better." We gather around the phone and he presses play. The woman in a blazer with a ton of cleavage and a nasally voice begins:

"A simple plot of depleted old farmland, and a dream of living a simpler life: that's what this couple began with when they set out on the journey to build Full Moon Farms. They use their own home and kitchen to educate young and old alike about gardening, cooking, and the lost art of home economics. Today they celebrate the grand opening of the Moonbeam Cafe, a barn converted to a market and eatery where patrons can enjoy the fruits of the land in a picturesque rural setting.

'It's about bringing back the skills and appreciation that have been lost,' says Co-Founder and Education Director Nina Distrella."

"Look at you! You look great!"

"*Shhh!* I want to hear what I said– I blacked out when that blinding camera light was on me."

"'Generations before us passed along knowledge that was built from thousands of years of trial and error: how to make the most of what you have, how to cook and eat real foods, how to be healthy and grateful and happy. But as we've allowed modern conveniences into our lives, we've lost a lot of that knowledge– and it hasn't done us any favors.

Here at this place, we attempt to return to the basics. And it just so happens that simpler living can save us money, is much better for the environment, and makes us more productive and content people, too.'

"Miss Distrella is leading the charge in the domestic space: how to make foods and other household items from scratch, how to prevent waste, and how to organize your household to make time for all these activities. Her Co-Founder counterpart and Conservation Director, Tyler Shisōka, leads the outdoor space: he has spent the last four years restoring the property and has managed to bring fertility and life back to this plot of land.

'It has taken a lot of work, but I knew that it had potential, if only it was put back into its natural balance.'"

"Oooh, look at you, stud! You were made for the screen!"
"Shh!"

'We have been able to turn this land into a productive ecosystem again, but there's always more to do. We go beyond teaching gardening, into the principles of ecosystem management— because that's what this all is. Even a city is an ecosystem, with its predators, scavengers, recyclers, and thousands of niches. It's about letting all the elements of a place serve their purpose, and doing so in balance of each other. If you pay attention to what the land needs, it will tell you.'

"The couple has received backlash on social media about their unspoken promotion of traditional gender roles—"

"Wait, pause it— backlash on social media? Did you know about that?"

"Nope, she didn't mention it. I don't remember reading any comments on our page about that."

"Is she just making that up? What the hell?"

"Unpause it, let's see what she says."

"—but they are committed to being a partnership of equals.

'We both do a bit of everything, but we tend to gravitate toward what we like. There's always a give and take; lots of work to be done around here.'"

"That's fucking slimy," I growl. "Promotion of gender roles… she totally made that up."

"They have to add some element of controversy to it, what can you expect?"

"The last journalist that came here didn't do that."

"Yeah but he said my laugh sounded 'donkey-like'. I did not appreciate that."

"HAH, your laugh does have a little bit of donkeyness to it."

"Nina!"

"Oh don't get upset, I like it. Can you finish peeling these for me, and I'll take it from there? I want to go walk Hank."

"Sure, go ahead. I'm going to respond to her and tell her we look forward to the story airing."

It's the best time of day, when the sun is hidden under the hills but it's still light out, and the air is cooling. The more fearful hens are heading into the coop in anticipation of sunset. I take my time walking to the barn, swinging a bag of dented apples for my boy.

"What's good, Chinaski?" I scratch his silver neck. Hank is my gorgeous blue roan horse, my middle-school-dream-come-true, my pride and joy. I hold out apple after apple, listening to the pleasing sounds of his happy crunching. "Shall we go for an evening stroll?"

I walk him past the house and the garden, and turn us around to look back at the place. Every day I think the same thing: *I can't believe we've done it, I can't believe this is ours.* We built something. It's probably aged me ten years, but we did it. Every day I come out here with Hank and look back at it; my amazement has not faded one drop. All the self-inflicted suffering in the last few years, and the pondering, the dreaming and planning and digging myself into holes; bashing my head against the wall, searching for something, searching for purpose, for dignity, for a good story, and saying yes to anything and everything stupid, cynically hopeful to be proven wrong– and here I am, in defiance of all odds, whole.

The golden stillness is broken by the powdery sound of wheels on the dirt road below. Hank's ears pin behind him and he starts to shuffle his feet. I glance around and squint down below. A 1971 Plymouth Hemi 'Cuda convertible, black as night, one of only four of its kind in the world, speeds around the curves of the hills toward the driveway, kicking up a trail of pale dust in its wake.

THE END

EPILOGUE

By Tyler

Months went by unannounced. Seasons changed, friends came and left town, holidays passed. I didn't notice any of it. I tried not to take her disappearance to heart; I knew that I had to leave her to do what she needed to do alone and unseen. I knew she was out there, scraping herself against the concrete, opening up the skin one more time to let the poison bleed out of her, so she could scab over and finally heal.

The more I've learned about Nina, the more her behavior has made sense to me. She was an animal caught in a trap: the more she snarled and snapped at my reaching fingers, the more she was hurting. Each time she pushed away my affection, she saw potential bullets bouncing off her shell, and it was a victory.

I tried not to think about her after she vanished– tried to focus on my life in the city and finding little ways not to hate it. On the train and walking down the street I tried to observe people the way Nina did, making up little stories about where they may be going or why they look so tired. I worked miserable hours of overtime and looked into taking a second job. I put the money aside in case she ever returned. I would ask her to marry me.

Some time after she left, I guess it was around the end of 2020, I received notice that my paternal grandfather had died. I didn't cry or make any phone calls. It was no more than an announcement, like the man on TV describing a storm in Chicago or the lives lost in a foreign war; an inevitability, never top of mind, but acknowledged as a sad thing when it happens.

My grandfather raised me, in some sense. My mom left my dad during the early stages of her pregnancy, certain that following around various psychedelic rock bands was not the best environment to become a parent. When my grandparents learned of the situation she was welcomed to move into their estate on the Mirage Hills Golf Course, and I spent the first twelve years of my life there. Grandpa Samui was the patriarch of the family but felt more like a menacing phantom: rarely seen, but always heard in the deep recesses of the house, thundering at colleagues over the phone, slamming doors and throwing books onto his desk, cursing whatever project he was working on in the garage. I was terrified to approach him and defaulted to my grandmother for assistance and company, as my mother was always working, eager to afford her own space and own life. Grandpa Samui was often described to me by my dad as everything that's wrong with this country: a bitter miser, a wine-snob workaholic who never spared his wife or children his time or affection. To his credit, he was only fifteen when his family was forced into the Japanese-American "relocation program" in 1942. That'd make anyone a bit of a villain. The Shisōka family wealth and deep community roots prevented them from the worst of the camp conditions and scrutiny, but his inheritance of our family's enormous estate of farmland was greatly diminished. He wielded what was left to buy up all the coastal land he could find, put up walls and fences, paid his workers brutal wages and bribed authorities to squelch any whispers of labor organizing. Dad showed me scathing editorials he had saved about him in the local papers. He grinned as he looked over them, as if poring over fond memories in a scrapbook.

I never told Nina about him; he was the quintessential landowner in her precious *Grapes of Wrath*, and when her eyes welled up at the tales of abused farmers, I felt a sickness of inherited shame in my stomach. But the chain broke at my dad. He moved into a van at nineteen and refused to take part in the family business— or any business for that matter. Grandpa openly resented and disparaged him of course, as entitled, irresponsible, and lazy. "He refuses to participate in real life but has no problem cashing checks when he needs something."

Grandpa sold the bulk of our apricot orchards years ago to a developer, and a luxury gated community took their place. My grandparents gathered the family for a formal dinner at their country club to announce the sale and celebrate the fortune they planned to spend in their old age. I pictured the groves of trees, endless rows of green that I chased my dog through as a kid, being bulldozed and replaced with astroturf and infinity pools. I bit my lip until it bled.

As it would turn out, his choice to liquefy his assets in his final years added a twist to my own destiny. Inside the smeared-ink letter from my grandmother announcing the news of her husband's death was a check with a stomach-churning number of zeros. In the memo my *sobo* had scribbled: "For your dreams."

I didn't need to brainstorm or daydream. I spent the next three weeks poring over topographic maps, farmer's almanacs, and land grant data, and purchased a desolate scrap of land a few hours northwest of the city. I gathered every document I could find about the place, spending late nights in the library and flirting with the elderly women in the public records offices of the nearby town. The group of plots were ironically named "The Timbers"; it had been a lush temperate forest before settlers cleared it in the late nineteenth century. Native plants were replaced with tall yellow European grasses that would feed grazing livestock. Over a few generations a primitive family settlement became an established network of hog farms.

I found receipts, deeds, records, letters between three brothers who owned the largest plots. The letters turned from boasts about yields and family gossip to arguments and trembly frets: the scarcity brought by the World Wars drove up the pressure to squeeze more and more animals per acre, and farm labor disappeared into soldiers' barracks and factories. They pooled their money and invested in mechanized slaughterhouse equipment, built with the latest industrial technology of the era. They scaled up their operations dramatically to meet the demand of a post-World War II boom, and the Timbers soon became a micro-model of industrial farming. The three families who owned the Timbers later sold out to a major pork producer with dreams of moving to Los Angeles. In a final letter from the youngest brother:

We live in Tomorrowland brothers, an era of progress, and who are we to miss the best of its offerings? It's time we trade our work boots for bare feet and our swimming holes for swimming pools!

I looked the family up online, which became a juicy rabbithole of research that consumed me for weeks. Two of the brothers moved to LA and became men of great political and corporate influence, embroiled in crass scandals and frequently featured in the local tabloids. One was ultimately murdered by a pair of his mistresses. The other ran a successful campaign for mayor. I couldn't find anything about the middle brother.

The corporation that bought the land did not anticipate the lack of forethought taken by its previous tenants. The aquifer was sucked dry by thirsty mouths and irrigation equipment; the soil was eroded and compacted by trampling hooves and overgrazing. Native animals were hunted out decades prior. The land was considered useless and the machinery outdated. In 2001, the corporation cut their losses, shut down the farm and liquidated the herd to slaughter. The property was deserted.

My mother got wind of what I was doing and begged me to reconsider. "Tyler, this is money you will need for your wedding, your first home, to start your family." She knew I had no interest in those things, but mothers hope. "Even if you aren't ready right now– this inheritance is meant to help you build your future."

"But that is what I am doing. If we don't restore what has been lost, there is no future. There is only this plot of dirt. And in ten years, you're not going to recognize it. I know what I'm doing, I promise. I'm doing this for our family, for our name."

It eventually became clear to me that I viewed this project as an act of restitution, a corrective measure for the sins of my forefathers. Though they were regarded as great men in our family tales, I have spent many sleepless nights considering the fact that they were villains in the modern perspective. They colonized and privatized Indigenous land– mostly to grow food, but at the expense of the natural environment and for a profit. They gave their family a good life, but they garnered wealth, and took more than they needed. They created me, a child of privilege, who has benefited from the exploitation of others, and now has to live with the guilt of possessing a life unearned. I know Nina was always repulsed by that, sometimes only subconsciously, sometimes openly. Or perhaps all of this was really about one man, the one I needed to absolve myself from, the man who destroyed the family cabin and turned tamaracks into tennis courts. It didn't matter. It would be done.

At first I drove up on the weekends. I strapped one of my mountain bikes to my car so I could ride around and survey the land. It was barren and dusty. I could barely get my tent's stakes into the crusty earth. There were remains of shacks and barns scattered throughout the acreage, and two slaughterhouse structures were still standing. After a week of avoiding them, I finally ventured inside. I chose a sunny and pleasant morning; I knew it was going to bring to life all the horrifying nightmare stories that Nina had shared with me, and I was not excited to experience the live version. Even though I had become vegetarian before I met her for my own environmental reasons, she had scolded me for never doing the research about factory farming on my own. "It's not enough just to stop eating them," she said. "To truly understand the level of cruelty, one must see it." I couldn't bring myself to do it. My insides squirm at the sight of blood. If half of what she said was true, it would be traumatic just to read about it, let alone to watch it on video.

The slaughterhouse had been out of use for a generation but there still lingered the ghost of a smell I can only relate to death. The place felt haunted. Black and rust-colored stains covered the walls, floors, gathered around drains and old machines. Around some of the hooks and chains were scattered bones. I shuddered and hurried out.

I started to compile a list of everything that needed to be done: wells and irrigation, tilling, aerating and regenerating soil, planting trees, procuring equipment, building structures… I broke out into a cold sweat when the list reached a third page. I planned to build a barn, a greenhouse, and three dwellings– one for Nina and I, and two cabins for guests and potential staff. I reached out to a friend from college, Erin, who agreed to help me design them. She and I met during a permaculture internship in college. She was an architecture major, but wanted to learn about growing food. "Homes of the future will have foodscapes, not landscapes," she said. Erin went on to open her own net-zero firm, which builds homes that generate their own energy needs and are designed to use as little resources as possible. Some of her designs look like the 1950's imagery of the future, like a country getaway for the Jetsons. Others look like the perfect home for a pair of hobbits to start their family, built into hillsides and covered in grasses and moss. She was happy to hear from me about the project. "I will have some preliminary plans for you in a month, pro bono. I can help you find the right contractors, too– I've got some people that focus almost solely on my designs. But I want it to be exemplary and I want lots and lots of press."

"I don't like the idea of press, but if it's your face in the paper and not mine, then I'm in."

The labor was hard. I brought friends up to help me get started. They were thrilled at first– it's a rare opportunity to work with your hands on something tangible for coders, UX designers, and SEO strategists– and they jumped on the romantic notion of it. But one by one they stopped answering the Thursday evening messages. My friend Matt was the only one who stuck around. He had spent his whole life in the heart of downtown, trapped behind the steaming grill of his father's Wendy's franchise, until he got into a Forestry master's program in Tacoma. But he ended up back in the city during the pandemic. He said he wanted nothing more than to breathe fresh air, no matter what the circumstances.

We worked all day and walked to the river to wash up before sunset. We built a little shack to warm up at night and dry our clothes, modeled after Great-Grandfather Yūto's, the one that had burned down. We spent evenings sitting around a fire and cooked cans of beans and those vegan sausages that crisp up on the outside and bleed on the inside like animal meat. I stared across the campfire and could see Nina sitting there, chewing merrily and talking with her mouth full. "They're made of coconuts and peas. Peas! Little green creeps. I've always hated them, and look at us now, getting along just fine. What a time to be alive!"

Matt and I passed a bottle of bourbon back and forth and talked about our childhoods, about women we loved, about our fathers, about our fear of a looming draft when World War III pops off.

"It sure'd be a shame to leave after all this work," Matt chuckled and pulled a cigarette from his shirt pocket. "But I'm not the man who is going to take the life of another poor man for a rich man's whims. I don't have it in me."

"I don't either. Do you think that makes us lesser men?"

Matt took a heavy swig from the bottle and looked into the fire. His gold chain hung outward as he leaned over; he rubbed the dangling gold cross between his fingers.

"They'll call it a lot of things: treason, weakness. They'll say we aren't 'real men,' whatever that means. They'll call us what they need to to stop other men from doing the same, because there's nothing more sacred to take from a man than his manhood. But what makes a man? Is it his ability to follow orders, to kill, destroy? Or is it his ability to reason, to choose for himself, to solve problems for the people who count on him?" He lit the cigarette and watched the smoke travel upward and disappear into the empty sky. "I think the only force that can stop humanity from continuing this endless cycle of war lies in the hands of men like us: for men to refuse to submit to the will of lesser yet more powerful men. It's those in power who are weak, who avoid conflict by sending others in their place, the aching shoulders of the men we all sit on. I wouldn't refuse to serve just for my own sake. I want us all to stay home."

He passed me the bottle. "I wonder if we will ever make it to that place. Or if we will destroy each other entirely before then."

"In our lifetime, no— we have to accept where we are. Been to a movie lately? Our society still worships violence. It used to be the strong prey on the weak, but now it almost seems flipped. There will be more war. But the blood won't be on my hands. If it comes down to it, I'm down to leave if you are. Our girls will understand." I wondered if Nina would understand. We shook on it.

I became stir-crazy at work. I begged my boss to let me work remotely so I could be closer to the Timbers. I subletted my room in the city and rented a room from an elderly couple in the nearby rural town. The man, who I started calling Pop, was vocal in his disapproval of what I was doing. He said I was blowing my chance of ever being with Nina again. "I get what you're trying to do, and it's noble and all, but you've got to understand: a woman wants security. You are only showing her that you're willing to blow a perfectly good nest egg on a selfish fantasy."

"You're probably right about women– I've never really understood them. And you do have a few more years under your belt. But if I know this woman like I think I do, this could be what finally wins her over. And if she never returns, I'll have something meaningful to show for my life."

His wife, who I started calling Big Mama (because she's four foot ten and ninety-eight pounds), disagreed with her husband, but only in private. "You're exactly what the world needs, my dear. I do hope she comes back. But I need you to stop being a goddamned millenial and please eat some of this stew."

"I'm sorry Mama. I'll make dinner for all of us tomorrow. Did you know they make sausages out of peas now?"

One week I headed back to the city for a series of annual meetings at my job. I had dwindled down to part-time hours and wanted to show my face so they'd have a harder time firing me. I stopped by my old apartment to browse through the months of unopened mail. Mid-stack I found a letter with no return address. The envelope had a bear paw drawn in the right hand corner where the stamp should go.

Dear Tyler,

It's me. I am alright. I think you'll understand that details aren't necessary for now. But I need to see you, when you are ready. Call for me and I will come to you.

There was no date. I was curious how long it had been sitting in there. She could have just texted, but I was sure she enjoyed the romance of the gesture.

She wanted to meet in a public place, at a restaurant or café. I picked a place I thought would be quiet. It wasn't, but I found a table tucked away by the window.

I stared at the door and tried to control my heartbeat. When she first walked in, I looked right past her. I wouldn't have recognized her if I didn't suddenly feel her giant eyes lock onto me. Her hair was parted harshly to the side, slicked back into a bun behind her head. She wore glasses with square black frames, a white blouse buttoned almost to her chin, and a charcoal pencil skirt. Her scuffed black pumps clicked as she marched toward me. Long charcoal gloves concealed fingers wrapped around the handles of a tattered briefcase. I knew seeing her would be a little jarring at first, and I prepared myself for that. But her costume nonplussed me. I could tell I was wearing the confusion on my face, because her face held a great sense of joy layered under serene confidence. Out of some impulsive, involuntary instinct to be formal I rose and stood next to my chair with my hat in my hands.

"Hello Tyler." She reached out a gloved hand; I shook it. She squeezed hard. "Shall we begin?"

"Begin what, a job interview? Why are you dressed like that?"

"I am here on business, Tyler. I had hoped that you would dress appropriately for the occasion, but I suppose I was a bit vague. Please sit down. I'm going to go order something to drink. Would you like anything?"

"I can get it. I–"

"Please, sit."

I did what I was told. It was too much– seeing her, seeing her like that. I was relieved to have a minute to collect myself, and for my confused erection to subside. *I should have expected this,* I thought.

She returned minutes later followed by a man in his early twenties holding a tea tray. "Eighteen dollars for two teas and a vegetarian sandwich, Tyler. *Before* tip. Can you believe that?" Without looking away from her I removed a twenty from my pants pocket and placed it on the table.

"Twenty dollars for bread and hot water. Two thousand bucks for a locker to hold your books and your bed for a month. What are we doing in these silly cities, anyhow? How much are they paying you, sir?"

The waiter went from disassociated to indignant. "Twelve an hour," he scoffed.

"Twelve an hour, ninety-six for a full day's work...half the money for a bed and the other half for hot water and bread." Nina patted his shoulder and took the twenty off the table. "Keep this, but work extra hard today. And make sure your boss sees you do it." His face lit up and he jetted off. I was pissed.

"That was for the check."

"Yes but obviously I had already paid. Consider it your first downpayment."

"Alright, that's enough of the games. Please just sit down and tell me what the hell is going on."

She smiled and rolled her eyes playfully as she plopped herself down into her chair. "Fine fine, you're right. Consider the meeting commenced. First order of business: you look good Tyler. You have gained weight."

I sat up straighter in my chair. "I've been.. doing some yard work to stay busy."

"Yes, I can see the color in your skin too. It looks great on you. I'm very happy to hear that Tyler. Very happy to hear that. Perhaps more than anyone I've ever met, you belong in the outdoors. You are a wild creature."

"Yes, I've realized that more than ever after being in this city for so long."

"And wouldn't it be lovely if your job was to be outside, to garden and plant and tend, and to teach others how to do the same, and to respect the land?"

"Well sure, of course, and that's why I–"

The gloved hand went up. "Sorry Tyler, it was a rhetorical question. I am leading up to a point. And the point is that I have a business proposition for you."

Nina opened the antiquey briefcase. The stale smell of an attic emanated from it. She removed two cardboard folders, with the same crescent moon from her letter etched on both their covers. She handed me one of them.

"Tyler, it has taken me so long to get to this place. But I finally know what I want now. It's as clear as the Milky Way on a desert evening. It is truly remarkable how obvious the solution to a puzzle can seem to a person once it is solved. Suddenly the long, frustrating hours of pondering and puzzling seem absurdly unnecessary. But it is only through the untying of the knot that we reach the simple straight line. My struggle was necessary and I chose it. With fresh eyes I can see it all clearly for exactly what it is." She closed her eyes and inhaled deeply. I could see a little thought cloud appearing above her head.

"I attended a rally called 'Go-America-Go' my senior year of high school. A speech about freedom ended with a passionate crowd chanting, '*We owe nothing! We owe nothing!*' The man with the microphone said that the world owes us nothing, our country owes us nothing, and we owe nothing to the world. He said, 'The only thing a man can count on is his own resolve, his own back, and his own salt. A man chooses what he gives to the world, and he is free to choose to give nothing at all. And that's what America is about.' The crowd went wild; you should have felt the energy. One thousand people who had enough cash for a $75 amusement park admission ticket, giving up their cares to a world that they believe has given them nothing. Little teenaged me felt that energy and began chanting with them.

"Ten years later I'm standing at an Earth Defenders rally, co-hosted by Mirage Socialists for America, and listening to a speech about how clean air and water aren't the only human rights: food, education, and housing are owed to us too. *But from whom?* I wondered. I could hear an old friend in my head, a rancher's son, reminding me that *someone* has to grow the food. *Someone* has to build the house, and fix the plumbing. *Someone* has to pay for all of this stuff. They began chanting 'United struggle, united fight! Open borders, climate strike!' The energy was the same— indignant, fervent, angry. And lost, single, broke me felt that energy, and I chanted with them.

"I can now say that I have tried giving nothing, and I have tried giving everything. Both are death sentences for the human spirit. The only alternative then, is to seek balance. Laughably simple, isn't it?"

"I feel like I've told y–" The hand went up again.

"Independence is freedom, and feeds the mind. Community is connection, and feeds the soul. Without one, a part of the spirit starves. This is the balance that has been chipped away from our society, stripping us of our ability to fight the greedy and powerful few, and keeping us in a state of scarcity– preventing us from shielding one another with love and compassion.

"How does one possibly achieve this balance alone, if the world around them is spiraling into warring poles? You and I have fantasized about departing from society, exiting the turmoil, and taking from the world only what we need. Departure would satisfy one part of us, but we must admit to ourselves that the spirit would carry with it a sort of guilt for abandoning the whole." Nina opened her folder, and waited for me to do the same.

"You must leave the city, Tyler. For our sanity's sake, for our safety, we must. But we have an obligation to learn, and to teach the ones we leave behind what we know."

The first page said in big bold print *FULL MOON FARMS*. There was a sketch of a cabin sitting on a hill under a big blue moon. "We both have beautiful and rare gifts: intelligence, creativity, and most of all, adaptability. Let us take these and bring them exactly where we want to go, and lead by the example of our lives. I want to learn how to run a household like people used to, with pride, frugality, self-sufficiency, and sound economics. I want to make soup stock out of vegetable scraps, mend a ripped pair of pants, preserve fresh fruit for the winter. I want you to show me how to grow food, and to teach other people to do it– in their backyards, on their rooftops, or on their kitchen counters. I want to show them that we can keep the benefits of modernity but create a new path, to restore our relationship with the natural world, to live *with* it rather than in opposition to it or removal from it.

"I want us to show people that we don't need to buy all the garbage they're selling us, that it's what's breaking us down and making us sick; that if we could just unravel the useless layers that have been keeping us apart that we can do this; we can save it all."

I flipped through the pages and was not surprised; it was as thorough and elegant as anything I've ever seen her do. It held a meticulously researched business plan, sample budgets, fundraising prospects, drawings, curriculum ideas.

"I've got the business end figured out. It would be a home that functions as an education center, with tours, workshops, and community events. It would be open to everyone, and everyone is free to learn the skills that interest them, regardless of their age or skill level. But there's something more. It can't just be done anywhere. I want the entire place to be a symbol of the transformation that is possible within all of us. And this is where I need you."

She went to reach out and touch my hand, but swiftly stopped herself, like an invisible hand reached out and slapped hers back to its place. She leaned back and settled back into her businesswoman character. "I want to restore a place. Find some crappy piece of land somewhere, maybe outside of a small town, maybe near a university. We'll regenerate the soil and grow food around the house, and re-wild the surrounding parts. I want to build a home that serves as a model of homes of the future: natural materials, energy efficient, solar-powered, self-sustaining, practical, and most of all, modest. I want to build it together."

She reached inside her briefcase again, and handed me a battered envelope dated "XMAS EVE 2019".

She looked down at my folder and then back up at me. The eyes never seemed bigger, more glowing, more terrifyingly beautiful than in that moment– swollen with her vision for the future, and for the first time since I'd met her, swollen with hope.

And in that moment I finally understood; I got to feel it, finally, for the first and maybe the only time. It was warm and sensational, like a sip of whiskey in the snow. I finally understood why she constantly sought it: the feeling of knowing something that the other didn't.

I placed my hand over my mouth and started laughing, a subdued, humming chuckle at first. But as I pictured all the work I had already done, my own vision and my own hope that had been unearthed and aerated like that impenetrable old dirt, the feeling coursed through me and I threw my head back, the veins tensed in my neck and on my temples. Tears ran down my face. I laughed for every moment that she orchestrated between us, every test and every game, every opportunity to measure me and calculate if she would allow herself to love me, to choose me. I laughed like the mad man on his way to a straightjacket, like I won some twisted battle with her, to wrestle her heart out from her own suffocating claws. I laughed with my whole body, letting it go until the pain in my chest brought me back to catch my breath. I looked across the table at her and the eyes looked like they might cry. I dove across the table and grabbed her hands to lift her from her chair, scooped her up by her waist and lifted her up; held her over me in the air and spun her around. Her heel got caught in a mug handle and flung coffee and porcelain across the room. She gasped in delight at the crashing sound and began laughing with a shared intensity. Our twirling circle expanded into the middle of the crowded place, knocking over chairs and forcing confused customers to dive out of the way. She opened up her arms and threw her head back in pure exaltation.

ABOUT THE AUTHOR

Lilian Fish does not like to talk about herself.

She prefers to be outside, near a campfire or a body of water, with a good book to read or a blank notebook to fill.

She finds the modern world both fascinating and irritating; so deeply incongruent with our nature as human beings and yet so full of novelties, pleasures and privileges, that she can't help but write about it.

WHAT'S NEXT?

Want to stay tuned for the sequel to *Great White Gorilla*? Want to learn more about the characters, the story, the author?

Scan this QR code to learn more.

www.ingramcontent.com/pod-product-compliance
Lightning Source LLC
Chambersburg PA
CBHW030847030726
47495CB00005B/1405